A
SHADOW
AT THE
DOOR

JO DIXON

FICTION

First Published 2024
First Australian Paperback Edition 2024
ISBN 9781867250326

Published by
HQ Fiction
An imprint of Harlequin Enterprises (Australia) Pty Limited (ABN 47 001 180 918),
a subsidiary of HarperCollins Publishers Australia Pty Limited (ABN 36 009 913 517)
Level 19, 201 Elizabeth St
SYDNEY NSW 2000
AUSTRALIA

A catalogue record for this book is available from the National Library of Australia
www.librariesaustralia.nla.gov.au

Printed and bound in Australia by McPherson's Printing Group

ABOUT THE AUTHOR

Jo lives in rural Tasmania, where she wrangles an ever-growing collection of animals and is kept busy transforming blackberry-infested paddocks into beautiful gardens. She has been a dental assistant, an event coordinator, and a sales rep in the travel industry. Now she writes full-time, creating twisty, suspenseful stories that feature flawed characters who've made mistakes, but who turn out to be stronger than they think.

Jo's debut novel *The House of Now and Then* was released in 2023. This is her second book.

You can find Jo on Instagram at @jo.dixon.writes; on Facebook at Jo Dixon, Writer; or on her website jo-dixon.com.

For Mum and Dad, who have always, always been there for me.

PART ONE

INTRUDERS

CHAPTER ONE

Monday, 10 July 2023

Remi flinched when the knock finally came.
Smack.

Smack.

Yep. That had to be Simon. Only her ex-husband could rap an elegant brass knocker and make it sound both smug and demanding. She took a slow, deliberate sip of tea, set down her mug and vigorously extended both middle fingers in his direction. The act of defiance was satisfying, and completely pointless. Today she could not be fierce, today she would be sweet. Beg, if necessary, and persuade him to be reasonable. She stood, tugged at her jumper and walked up the hallway, rearranging her face into what she hoped was an expression of nostalgic joy with a hint of excitement at seeing him after all this time.

'Simon, thank you for coming,' she said, after opening the door, cold air sliding into the house. She put a tone of delight in her voice.

He looked good. Slim dark jeans and a tailored, hip-length wool jacket. His thick hair longer, a little grey, swept back in that way some men did when they aged, proudly lauding it over their balding mates: *No shaved head here, you poor suckers*. He was handsome, sharply expensive and more than a bit overdone.

'Hello, Remi.' He beamed, his arms open, inviting her in for a hug, waiting for her to cover the distance between them. A charismatic leader expecting the adulation of an awe-stuck follower.

The last time she'd seen Simon, they'd been on opposite sides of a gleaming conference table, lawyer on his side, none on hers. Eighteen months had passed since she'd left him and he'd still been touting his version of the truth: the divorce was her fault. Her desperate insecurities and her need for drama were to blame. He wouldn't have strayed if she'd been a better wife. He held no grudge. The settlement offered was the best possible. They didn't have the assets and cash she seemed to think. But he was a good guy, a decent guy. He wanted to help her. He was sympathetic. Here was an agreement that would let her keep the house. The Hobart house, of course, not the Sydney apartment. That was mortgaged to the hilt. And because Simon was such a great guy, he'd not only let her buy him out, but he'd accept her money in instalments. With a reasonable interest rate, only slightly higher than the bank. Plus, here was a nice lump-sum settlement. If only he could do more, but this was his best offer. Remi, don't fight this. Don't make things worse. Don't drag it out. Let us both move on. Sign here.

There had been only the one call since that day, on December thirty-first, 2020. The first New Year's Eve after they had finalised the divorce and settlement. Boastful as always,

Simon had wanted her to know that, despite the intrusion of a pandemic, he still got to be on a boat on Sydney Harbour with expensive champagne and awesome food. His life was amazing, he said, but he still thought of her, and didn't she regret leaving him and giving all this away? Then Kayla could be heard in the background, wanting to know who he was talking to, and he'd hung up. Remi had laughed, then cried a little, drunk her cheap bubbles and continued scribbling down her goals. She was alone in her old house with barely enough superficial interaction to keep her from becoming a shuffling, mumbling hermit. It wasn't social or glamorous, but it was the life she had chosen. And still wanted.

Which meant hugging the bastard.

She let wistful longing flit across her face—enough to stroke his ego—and stepped into his embrace. He squeezed her too tight for too long, his aftershave an unfamiliar spicy fog she'd have to wash out of her shirt and off her skin. When he finally let go, she let him inside and followed him through to the kitchen.

'Babe, the place is looking great.'

Babe? Seriously? That had been tolerable when they were married; completely infuriating now they weren't. 'Thank you.'

'I mean, look what you've done here.' Simon turned to inspect the large open-plan space at the back of the house, his gaze passing over the dark cabinetry, feature light fittings, top-range appliances and sleek wood heater. He slid a hand over the white marble of the benchtops. 'You extended.'

'Yes.'

'Good job.'

'It's been a long, hard slog. But worth it.' If Remi could make him understand what the house meant to her, he surely wouldn't kick her out. This was her home, her joy—and her obsession for the last four years. Through months and months of stress, hard work, sleepless nights, council negotiations and unexpected disasters, she had brought out the best in the old girl. 'You remember the original kitchen, that funny little red-brick lean-to? It was obviously way too small. The only way to get the space was to push outwards. The council allowed the alterations. Eventually. When they saw the facade and main floorplan would stay and I wasn't destroying the heritage value of the property, they recognised I was preserving and improving the building. These extruded steel window and door frames and the black zinc external cladding give a clear distinction between the heritage sandstone and the modern addition. The council liked that.'

'Hmm.' He walked to the sink and flicked the tap on and off, as if he were checking the water pressure, then turned to face her. 'I can see where all my money has been spent. I think you might have been a bit loose with the budget.' He rested against the edge of the bench, arms folded. 'A few emotional decisions here, I reckon.'

And there it was. Build her up in one breath, knock her down in the next.

'It wasn't your money,' she said evenly.

'Really? That fat lump sum that poured into your account came from some other magic money fairy, did it?' His wide smile was meant to make it a joke, a bit of banter, but she knew the snide intent was real.

She bit back a terse reply, tried to keep her voice neutral. 'It was the agreed settlement. It wasn't over the top.' She hadn't fought his offer, not wanting a drawn-out, point-scoring squabbling match.

Simon shook his head slowly and huffed an exaggerated sigh, as though being forced to explain a simple concept to a dim-witted customer. 'A very generous payout. I've always looked after you, Remi. You know that half-mill was money I'd earned. It came from me.'

Sure. At the time of the divorce he had been earning a hefty salary, paid by his old man from a family company valued in the billions. For a job he had been crap at, in a position he hadn't worked for. He'd liked having Remi by his side, seeing her as a vital part of a social package. Funny thing though, before they'd got married, before his family finally allowed him into the business—before Remi's career imploded—she'd been the main earner. For the three years she'd been on TV, she'd been earning way more than him. Back then, she'd been the one paying all the bills and taking them on holidays. She'd saved, too. But after she quit, her stash had evaporated. Simon considered those years irrelevant. There had been no point in trying to get him to acknowledge her role, or her value, in their relationship.

'So, let's see where that money's gone, shall we? Are you going to give me a tour?'

She didn't move. 'You can find your way around. The layout hasn't changed significantly.'

Pushing away from the bench, he gave her a condescending pat on the arm as he stepped past her. 'Fix me a drink, babe.' He threw the order over his shoulder as he left the kitchen, his heavy footfall on the stairs both familiar and disconcerting.

After five minutes, he returned. 'Gotta say, Remi, you've surprised me. Done a half-decent job.' He took the glass she'd poured. 'Overcapitalised in places, of course, but that's your inexperience showing. And some things still aren't finished,

but you've improved the place. Still a slob, though, aren't you?'
He chuckled as though only teasing. 'Piles of crap everywhere.
Don't you have a cleaner?'

No, she did not. These days she didn't have the same pressure to keep her home immaculate. It was a work in progress,
she lived alone, no one visited, and if there were teetering
stacks of magazines, jackets over chairs and piles of random
stuff, well, her mess affected only her.

He sat across from her at the island bench and took a large
mouthful of the chardonnay, screwing up his face as he drank.
It might have been the cheap wine, the distaste of offering her
a smidgen of praise or judgement of her slack housekeeping.

'Kayla and I got married last October.' As he changed the
subject Simon glanced at her, looking for a reaction. The
look on his face almost conciliatory, as though expecting his
announcement to be an emotional blow.

Not even close to the truth.

'Yes. I heard that. Congratulations.' She'd heard the news
months ago. A few minutes of digging through social media and
the *Daily Mail* had told her the story. The photos of the wedding were impressive—if ostentatious styling and over-the-top
self-promotion were your thing. According to the likes, shares,
mentions, followers and comments, the whole event was utterly
fabulous. What a story! The gorgeous influencer and her new
husband, the dashing heir to the Hanland retail empire. An
exclusive island setting, with several changes of dress over the
course of the wedding and reception. The whole event extend-
ing over four days. A cash-splash no one could ignore. The
cohort of young—and not exactly young but good at faking
it—wealthy elites was highly photogenic. All with that illusive

social cachet: a combination of their family pedigree and the allure of their own social media enterprises.

'Yeah,' he continued. 'Amazing wedding. Huge. Quite an affair. But there's a positive flow-on effect for the business. I know, I know. Sounds a bit mercenary, but Kayla is right onboard with controlling our image and brand. You know I've established a luxury goods empire, right? Watches, jewellery, high-end products. Much more my thing. Kayla is our principal creative advisor. Anyway, Dad's business wasn't the right fit. Learned a lot from the old man but building up a mid-range homewares chain isn't me.' He beamed, inviting her to agree. 'So, Hanland Luxury is now coming up to the end of its second year and it's been massive. So much exposure. We've opened four shops. All very, very glam. Four more planned. Really high margins. Huge demand, and we're not talking the stuff that any old suburbanite or upper-middle can afford. We are looking after a first class, niche market. We have an enormous turnover. Doing really, really well.'

Simon finally stopped talking. He shifted his expression to appear humble, pretending to be amazed at what he had achieved, waiting for Remi's praise and adulation. He leaned back in his chair and rubbed a hand up and down his chest. If he'd made a fist and thumped his pecs she wouldn't have been surprised.

'That must be satisfying.' Remi knew she should make more effort. She wanted him in a benevolent mood. 'It sounds like you've created a successful business. I'm happy that you've found your passion.'

'Yep. It sure feels good, and we're only going to keep hitting those goals.'

'That's great.' She rested her hands on the benchtop, softly stroking the marble. 'I know how it feels to find your passion. That's what this renovation has been to me.'

Simon took another gulp of wine, swallowed hard. 'Have to admit, I thought you were a bit nuts when you set your heart on buying this place. I mean, bloody hell, nobody was buying in Hobart back then. What did we want with some old slum? At least we got it cheap.'

Once a grand home, the splendour of the building's sandstone facade had been hidden behind a tacked-on wooden verandah and a pair of ancient, dehydrated pencil pines. The front garden had been filled with grubby, once-white pebbles, broken pots with dead plants and a disintegrating foam sofa. Inside the scene had been worse. Years as cheap share accommodation had left squalor and dank mould. But Remi had seen beauty. Wide floorboards beneath stinking carpet. A magnificent banister on the staircase. Plus an inner-city position, off-street parking and a small garden within the rear walls.

Since then, the building had been transformed. Like a woman shedding her rags and dowdy image, the house had been pampered and preened, tucked and lifted. Now she was beautiful and glamorous, and Remi recognised the lust in his eyes. Simon wanted to get his hands on her.

'Though what does one girl, all on her own, need all this space for? This is a family home. You'd be happier in a cute little apartment.'

'How do you know I don't have plans to fill it?'

'Ha! Do you?'

She wasn't about to discuss the state of her life. 'Besides, I love this house.'

'So, you're still ruled by emotion then?' He smirked. 'I always adored your enthusiasm. You creative types are so, well, dramatic. Aren't you? But not the best heads for business.'

Patronising arsehole. She hid her irritation with a shrug that meant nothing.

'Anyway,' he continued, 'you will make a nice little profit out of this. And you can clear your debt.'

Like hell. She fixed her gaze on a point somewhere over his left shoulder. 'That's what I wanted to discuss. I'm not selling.'

He shook his head. 'You don't really have an option. Did you read my email?'

'Yes, but—'

'And did you read over the contract? The contract that you signed?'

'Yes, but—'

'Then you obviously grasp what's going on. You're not stupid, Remi. You know you've got yourself in a mess. The terms are quite clear. If you default on repayments, as your mortgagee, I have the right to sell the house.'

'But—'

'Which is exactly what has happened. Isn't it?' He shifted to put himself in her line of sight, forcing her to look at him. 'Remi. Your payments have been over a month late on several occasions.'

'Twice.'

'Sure. Twice. And you're only days away from making it three times. You know what that means, don't you? Remi? That's too many. Do you have the money today?'

'No, but—'

'This time next week you will have officially been in significant arrears three times and I will be putting the house on the market. I know it's not quite how a bank would do it, but then no bank would've lent you the money, would they? I want to call in my loan and the only way to achieve that is to sell. Which is why I've spoken to an agent. One of the best in town, a guy who deals only with the premium end of the market. Which, of course, is peanuts compared to the Sydney high end. Still, he drives a Maserati, so sales must be doing okay. Anyway, he's coming later this week. He was super keen to get through the door.'

'You're getting way ahead of yourself.'

'Am I? I don't think so. Let's find out what the place is worth. What we'd get—'

'No.' She spoke loud enough to finally cut him off. 'No. I told you, I'm not selling.' Her intention to be sweet and persuasive now getting lost in a furious panic. 'I know I'm behind on this month's payment. I will get the money to you tomorrow. But can't we restructure the agreement? I mean, it's only paperwork between you and me, it wouldn't be hard.'

'Except, sweetheart'—Simon's tone was one of endless patience and righteous calm—'I don't want to. Selling makes sense. When you hear what it's worth, you will feel differently about off-loading it. Hmm? Trust me, you'll come out of this in a good position. You can move forward.'

'No. Just no.'

'Remi.' He was treating her like a petulant child. 'Don't be silly. I can take care of it.'

'Please stop.'

'I would've thought you'd like to show the place off to a professional. He really was interested in seeing what you'd achieved. Seemed confident you'd added significant value. You should be proud.'

Of course Remi was proud. Shaping the house into this gorgeous home had given her a sense of worth. Had made her feel capable. This had been her greatest achievement—better than being an actor and definitely better than being a smile-on-demand trophy wife. Her beautiful home was also her sanctuary. She wasn't leaving. Here, she'd finally felt safe and at peace.

'Why are you doing this?'

'Sweetheart. Aren't you listening? You know why. Don't make me play the bad guy. The sale will be triggered by the terms of the agreement.'

'I'll make the payment,' she said through gritted teeth.

Simon laughed. 'Can you really afford to keep the place?'

Her throat tightened, but she refused to break down in front of him. 'If, and only if, I fail to make the payment deadline can you bring an agent through. Right now, this is my home. And you do not have my permission to bring anyone into it. Or, for that matter, to enter uninvited yourself.'

'Remi.' Now he sounded exasperated.

'Do you still have a key?'

He huffed. 'I'm pretty sure that's a new front door, with a new lock. Now, stop being so bloody ridiculous. It's time to be realistic.'

She turned away, staring out the kitchen windows to the small courtyard garden. She took a long, slow breath. 'I will get the payments up to date.' She couldn't bring herself to look at him. 'Would you really force me out?'

He hitched his shoulders, refusing to comment.

She grabbed the wine she'd been ignoring and drank, then raised her chin. 'Think of what this means to me.'

'Babe, I *am* thinking of you. I'm not a bad person.'

'Fine. Let's go with that. You're a good guy—a great guy. Therefore, you'll be happy for me when I say there is absolutely no way I'm selling. I will be in this house till I've paid you out. Till I own it outright. And for many, many years after that.'

'Really?' His sanctimonious smile made her want to scream. 'Is that why you asked me here? To tell me that?'

'Yes.' She set down her glass. 'That's exactly what I wanted to say. And now that it's said, it's probably time for you to go. I have things to do.' She'd hoped for an amicable discussion, been prepared to lay out her case and convince him to rewrite the agreement. Now she saw there was no point trying. When Simon made up his mind, when he had righteous conviction, there was no moving him. She should've known better, shouldn't have allowed herself hope.

As soon as she had closed the door behind him, Remi returned to the kitchen, took a seat at the table and opened her laptop. A week ago, she'd had the idea to take in a couple of tenants, which had seemed like an uncomfortable but viable solution to her struggling cashflow. She'd seen three applicants and it had been jaw-clenchingly horrible every time she'd let another random person into her home. Living with any of them was unthinkable. When Simon had let her know he would be in town, she'd taken down the listing and put her hopes on a negotiation.

What a waste of time.

She'd move on to Plan C. Her bank account held a smidge over eight grand but given the rather tragic state of her finances, she had been holding off paying Simon, waiting for the payment from her last narration job to come through. She couldn't wait any longer. She'd pay Simon, force him to back off, and make do until her last invoice had been settled.

She logged into her account. Her heart slammed upwards, a choking thud high in her chest, as the totals for her debit card and savings account appeared on the screen. She refreshed the page, read the numbers over and over. Checked each account. Stared at a long list of transactions that made absolutely no sense.

Her money was gone.

CHAPTER TWO

'Digital gift cards?' Remi hunched forward in her chair, her phone on speaker clutched in front of her face. 'Why would I buy eight thousand dollars' worth of gift cards? My account has obviously been hacked. Those are fraudulent transactions.'

'I see you transferred the eight thousand from your savings to your debit card last night.' The person on the other end spoke patiently. 'A few minutes before the first purchase.'

'No. I didn't. I didn't do that.'

'Okay. Because that can only be done by logging onto either our online banking site or the mobile app.'

'Yes. I know that.'

'Does anyone else have access to your account? Have you shared your log-in details, including your passcode, with anyone?'

'No! Of course not.'

'Do you have your log-in details written down somewhere that could easily be found?'

Well, yes, she did. But that was beside the point. 'I live alone.
And I haven't had anyone here.' Other than Simon and a few
potential tenants. But none of the applicants had been out of
her sight, and Simon had only been here today. Apparently
her account had been compromised last night. At two thirty-
six am, according to the statement on her laptop screen. In
the middle of the night, someone, somewhere, had logged into
her account, moved money from her savings account and then
gone crazy on a digital gift card site. Where had those cards
been sent? The bank couldn't tell her, she'd have to contact the
gift card company. And even then, what chance did she have?
She had no record of the orders, no idea to whom they'd been
emailed. Even if they could somehow track them down, the
money would have been spent, the email addresses would be
anonymous and impossible to trace, and it would all lead to
nothing.

'Has someone approached you and asked you to send payment with gift cards?' the bank person was now asking. 'It is
quite a common scam.'

Remi clenched her free hand. 'No. I'm not that stupid. As
I have said, I did *not* buy those cards. I did *not* transfer the
money out of my savings account. I did *not* give access to my
account to anyone.' She stood and moved to the long sideboard
against the wall, pulling open one of the drawers and rummaging through the mess. She was only half listening as the
person on the other end explained what the bank could do in
this situation—which amounted to not much. Her money was
gone and Remi should contact the police.

She ended the call and continued her search. The small red
spiral-bound book was still there, and on the third page were
all the details a clever little thief would need: her account

number, the passcode for the bank's app, the log-in password for the online site.

But that would mean someone had been in her home.

There had been plenty of tradespeople over the last few years. None recently, of course, since the renovation had mostly been completed, and she couldn't afford to pay anyone. But one of them could have taken a record of those numbers, filing them away until now. Which didn't really add up, because if the thief had any brain cells whatsoever, they would've pulled this stunt months earlier, when she'd had more than eight grand to her name. Why wait until now?

Had someone else been here? Had she been broken in to, and not realised?

No. That was ridiculous. There would have been damage to a door or window. Other things would've been taken. Someone with a key, then. Which was even more crazy. The only other person to have a key these days was Luke, her oldest and most trusted friend. And he lived in Sydney.

Maybe she had left the door unlocked. Maybe someone hacked into her computer. Maybe some anonymous little creep had accessed data online. Maybe her details had been picked up in one of those data hacks. She'd never know.

Remi swore loudly, strode to the island bench where the bottle of cheap chardonnay still sat and poured a large glass, ignoring the fact it was no longer chilled. The wine was a sour acid in her throat, but she didn't care. There was absolutely no point contacting Simon to ask for an extension. She could beg and plead, and explain what had happened, but he wouldn't change his mind. The man was intent on forcing the sale of her house and she had no doubt he would be thrilled that her situation had become so dire.

'I'm not giving up,' she muttered into the glass. 'He is not going to do this to me.'

Sitting around wailing about the situation would achieve nothing. In six days, she would officially be in breach of their repayment contract and then it would be all over red rover.

She topped up her glass and returned to her laptop. There was no choice. Between a forced sale of her home and sharing her space with strangers, she was choosing the latter, and it had to happen immediately. There must be a couple of people she could tolerate for six months.

She opened the house-share site, shut down her revulsion and got on with fixing the problem.

***

By the following afternoon, Remi was tentatively hopeful.

'Cup of tea, Josephine?' she asked the woman standing in her kitchen. Already dark at five thirty, with rain hitting the windows, the room felt especially welcoming. The fire flickered and the soft scent of honey and wild flowers drifted from one of her artisan candles. Josephine had commented on how charming she found the house and had seemed impressed when Remi described how much the building had changed. As she'd given Josephine a tour, their conversation had been easy and Remi's relief had been immense.

'Thank you, that would be lovely.' Josephine draped her long camel-coloured coat over one of the stools and took a seat at the island bench. 'Black is fine.'

Remi filled the kettle and switched it on. 'You've been travelling?' she prompted, wanting to dig a little more into why this woman—who must've been in her early fifties—was looking for share accommodation. 'Why Hobart? It's the middle of winter—wouldn't you rather be somewhere warmer?'

'I'm quite enjoying this proper cold weather. In Brisbane we simply complain and suffer through the six or so weeks of our subtropical non-summer. Down here there are fires and heaters and people layer up with coats and scarves. It's great. Much more comfortable.' She accepted the mug Remi passed her then lifted the teabag to give it a jiggle before squeezing against the teaspoon. 'And yes, I've been travelling around Australia for about four months. I retired earlier this year and thought it was a good time to have a bit of a solo adventure.'

'And now?'

'Now? Now I feel the need to stay somewhere for longer than a couple of weeks.' She took a sip. 'I've been in Tasmania for a while and this seems a good place to settle for a time.'

'How long, do you think?'

'Maybe until the new year.' She looked at Remi. 'Does that fit in with what you're looking for?'

Yes, it did. This could work. This calm, well-presented, obviously intelligent woman surely couldn't be too difficult to live with? She had quickly assessed Josephine's practical but good-quality black pants and jumper and the diamond studs in her ears and had been reassured. 'Yes, I think it would.'

The clack of the knocker at the front door startled them both.

'Excuse me, won't be a second.' Remi set down her mug. If this was Simon, she would not be allowing him into her house. Not now. Not ever. She marched up the hall and yanked open the door.

The wind pushed through, bringing with it a spray of cold rain. It wasn't her ex-husband on the doorstep.

'Hello. God, I'm so, so sorry I'm late. Hobart traffic is way more stressful than I thought it would be.' The girl stuck out her hand, water dripping off the edge of her umbrella onto the sleeve of her magenta and orange jacket. 'I'm Emerson.'

Remi hesitated for a second, then took her hand. 'I'm Remi.' She stood back and held the door wide. This potential tenant had been due at four, nearly two hours ago. 'I didn't think you were coming.' She considered telling her it was too late. But she'd done the sums and two paying tenants was better than one.

'Sorry. I couldn't get to my phone. I ended up doing the whole length of the street and had to come back around. Several times, if I'm being honest. Which is way harder than it sounds. But obviously, I mean, you'd know that, right? I could've walked. I'm staying at the Grand Chancellor. Probably would've been quicker. Except for the rain. And me not knowing where I'm going.'

Emerson collapsed her umbrella as she stepped inside. Remi took it from her and hung it on the coat rack as she shut the door. The noise of the busy road immediately muted.

'Look, I do have someone else here. Another applicant. I didn't expect there to be an overlap,' Remi said politely.

'Oh. Gosh. Okay.' Emerson glanced down the wide hallway towards the kitchen. Remi sensed the girl deflate. She looked close to tears. 'Sorry. Okay, I understand. Would you like me to come back another time? I can come back whenever it suits. Really. I could wait in my car, if you like. Or come back tomorrow morning. Whatever works for you.'

Remi didn't have the heart to push her back out into the rain. There was nothing to be lost by showing her around. 'That's fine. You're here now, and you look like you need to dry out. Hang up your coat and, I don't usually ask this, but could you take your shoes off.' They were purple with white daisies and looked particularly sad and soggy.

Remi gave her the condensed version of the tour, showing her the front bedroom on the left, with its gorgeous bed, and the lounge room on the opposite side of the hall. She waved a hand in the general direction of the staircase. 'That door under the stairs goes down to the basement where I work. My room is upstairs, I have an ensuite, and there is the main bathroom and the third bedroom. There's more of a view from up there.'

'Of the street?' the girl asked.

Remi almost laughed. 'Yes. And of kunanyi.'

Emerson's face remained blank.

'Mount Wellington,' Remi added for extra clarification, realising this applicant must be another recent arrival to Tasmania.

'Oh, yes, of course.' She nodded vigorously and Remi had the distinct impression she had no idea a mountain loomed over the city. Which, to be fair, might be easy to miss in this weather. When the clouds came in low, the mountain did completely disappear, and it had been like this for a few days.

They reached the kitchen at the back of the house and Remi introduced her two candidates. 'Emerson, this is Josephine, who is very likely going to be living here soon.'

Josephine stepped forward, shook the girl's hand and said hello.

Emerson talked quickly. 'Hello. Hi. Nice to meet you. What an amazing house. Totally gorgeous. Not like some of the places I've looked at. And it's warm. What an incredible fireplace. Are you going to live here, do you think?'

Josephine raised her eyebrows and smiled. 'Yes, I think so.'

'Tea or coffee, Emerson?' Remi didn't want to encourage the girl to stay, but not offering would have been rude. 'Take a seat.'

'Do you mind if I stand near the fire? I'm a bit wet. And a bit cold. This is a perfect spot for a dog to curl up, don't you think? Do you have a dog? Or a cat?'

Did she always talk like this? Remi suspected Emerson would be exhausting, that she would crave interaction and company. Would she want to fill the house with a passing parade of other like-minded take-on-the-world gen Zs? The thought made Remi wince, but she hid her reaction.

'No pets. I did have a dog, but she passed away recently. But, yes, she loved to sleep there.' Now was not the right time to dwell on the absence of Mavis.

'Oh, okay. That's good.' Emerson looked anxious as the words kept tumbling out of her. 'I mean that's not good. Obviously. Sorry, that didn't come out right. That must be very sad for you. I'm allergic to dogs, so I probably couldn't have lived here, if there was a dog. I'm not so bad with cats.'

Seriously? 'Why don't I run through a few basics with you while you warm up? Then we can have a think about whether this is the right place for you.'

Remi knew she would not be offering Emerson a room.

CHAPTER THREE

Thursday, 13 July 2023

Remi curled onto her side, pulling the doona tight around her shoulders. She missed Mavis's warm body and the slurpy morning kisses the dog used to deliver the minute Remi opened her eyes. She missed their routine too. Regardless of the weather they'd done a thirty-minute walk before coffee and breakfast, then another walk around six in the evening. Now, Remi couldn't bring herself to do the walk alone.

It had been over a month, but the absence of her dopey, furry friend was an ache that continued to press against her heart. Sometimes the grief caught her by surprise, smacking into her with such ferocity that she'd find herself sobbing till her stomach hurt. She liked living alone, and Mavis had provided all the affection and companionship she needed. Without her, there was a hollowness to Remi's days. A vague sense of restlessness and longing that had left her wandering through her home at odd times, as though looking for something she couldn't identify.

It wasn't loneliness, she told herself. She revelled in not having to accommodate the needs, wants or demands of others. Liked being free to inhabit her emotions fully—sitting on the kitchen floor crying for Mavis, shouting angry obscenities when her ex-husband sent her passive-aggressive emails or dancing and singing with abandon when things went well. She didn't want to contain herself or to consider others; she'd spent way too many years doing that. She'd become selfish and entirely self-reliant in this phase of her messy life and that was fine. Having full control was worth the odd night or two of feeling isolated.

There'd been a week when her parents had flown down and stayed, which had been bearable because she could count down the days until they left. But having two strangers living here, day in and day out, well, that would be a whole other story.

Her sweet, satisfying solitude was about to be sacrificed. *Think of the money.*

She wriggled and twisted until she had flipped onto her other side, reached for her phone and tapped into her bank account, fumbling the new passcode twice before successfully logging in. Josephine was as efficient as she had appeared. One month's rent had already been transferred, even though she wouldn't be moving in until Saturday. And amazingly, the invoice for Remi's last narration job had finally been paid. From zero to a bit over four thousand overnight. Enough to send to Simon, with a few dollars left over. That should shut the smug prick up for a while. Her repayments were due on the twenty-sixth of each month, so she had less than two weeks till he held out his hand again. No need to panic. By then, she'd have a second tenant and maybe her last two auditions would land her some narration work. She could live frugally and five years from now, the house would be completely hers and her finances would be easier. Hopefully she would be back to living alone before then.

So, toughen up princess, she told herself. The pity party was over. No more complaints. No more whining. There were things to do.

***

An hour later, Remi sat at the kitchen table, laptop open, trying to gather the last flakes of toast crumbs from her plate. Unfortunately, two applicants had sent messages, saying they had found places elsewhere. Now she was back to reading the profiles of other potential tenants. She was eliminating all the uni students from her search when the loud, repeated clunk of the knocker echoed through the house.

Now what? She wasn't expecting anyone. She had no real friends down here and there were no tradies booked. Maybe the girl from the other night had decided to come back. Emerson appeared to have the confidence to drop in unannounced and Remi had sensed that she had been both surprised and disappointed when she'd let her out the front door, saying only she would be in touch.

Josephine, with her air of efficiency and quiet reserve, had immediately fitted Remi's hope of continuing privacy and calm. Emerson, on the other hand, was young and a little too vibrant. She seemed eager and vivid and loud. If Josephine's colour was black and Remi's were bland and beige, Emerson was clashing shades of magenta, red and yellow; a young woman happy to be noticed. Although her face alone would draw attention—dark skin with darker freckles over her nose and cheeks, enviously thick perfect brows and large red-framed glasses that accentuated light-brown eyes like amber lit from within. She was startlingly attractive and, next to her, Remi had felt like a washed-out, featureless blob of epic dullness. None of which had been the problem.

Emerson's energy had been Remi's concern. Even though Josephine had suggested quietly that she would be more than happy to have Emerson in the house, Remi's instincts were it would be too much. If she was on the doorstep, Remi would have to be firm in her rejection.

She pulled back the door. Simon stood two steps down, hands on hip, looking back towards the mountain. He looked over his shoulder at her, baring his teeth in a smile intended to dazzle. 'Hello.'

He sprang up the steps, full of overdone enthusiasm as though needing to proclaim his vigour. He clapped his hands, rubbing his palms together like the charming dastardly villain of every pantomime she'd ever seen. 'How are you? So glad you're home. I'd meant to call.'

'What are you doing here?'

He stepped forward. She didn't move.

'Let me in, it's freezing out here.'

She kept one hand on the door, blocking his entry to her home. 'I paid you. Money should be in your account tomorrow.'

'Oh. Okay. Thanks.' When she didn't relent, he sighed. 'Come on, Remi. Look, there's no need to be obstinate.' He shook his head, gave her a look of amusement. 'I forgot how damn stubborn you can be.'

Stubborn? When they'd been together, she'd been an expert at giving in to his ideas and plans. Only after leaving him had she become more obstinate and determined.

'I will get the next repayment in on time too. And the one after that.'

'Excellent, excellent.' He reached out, rested his palm on the door. Didn't push, but made it clear he could. 'Babe. Can I please come in? Have a coffee? Warm up a bit.'

'Why?'

'Well, we've got a few things to talk over.'

'No, we don't. And, *babe*'—the word heavy with the sarcasm—'there's a coffee shop just up the road. That way.' She pointed towards South Hobart.

'Oh, come on.' His frustration was showing. 'Seriously? Why can't we sit down like two civil people and talk?'

'Because there is nothing to say' She was trying very, very hard to stay even-tempered.

'Remi.' His exaggerated calm made her want to push him down the stairs. 'Stop being unreasonable. Look, you always do this. Make a big deal out of things that don't matter. You know that, don't you?'

Only in the aftermath of their separation did Remi come to realise how patronising and manipulative Simon could be. If at any time she became angry or upset, especially over something he had done, he would be composed. It almost didn't matter what he said, because her rising emotions would make her seem the crazy one. In the end, she'd be in tears, he'd be expressing his hurt, and she'd be trying to figure out how to make him happy. These days she could recognise what was happening.

'Goodbye, Simon. We'll speak again in five years, when the mortgage you have over this house is finalised. Actually, we probably won't even need to talk then. We can stick with emails. Good luck with your business. And your new wife.

Hope you have a good trip back to Sydney.' Not wanting to hear anything more, she stepped back and began shutting the door.

This time he did push, his arm rigid against the wood.

'Don't you dare. Don't you dare. I have rights. When did you get so stupid?' Two deep creases were carved between his eyes, his ever-smiling mouth now clamped tight. He shoved with increasing force against her resistance. 'For fuck's sake, Remi. Let me in.'

Shock made her stop.

His strength won and he barged past her into the hall. 'Shut the door.'

He was breathing heavily, one hand repeatedly pushing through his hair. He glared at her with such venom she took a step backwards. He marched towards the kitchen, doubled back just as quickly. Jabbed a finger in her direction.

'What is your problem? Why are you making things so bloody difficult? Why don't you try being reasonable? Try seeing things from someone else's perspective? Stop being so fucking selfish.'

He strode away, leaving Remi wilting under his attack, her heart racing. She closed the door and leaned against it. What the hell just happened? Simon rarely lost his cool, or dropped his facade. Right now he was being vicious. Aggressive. And he was in the house. Shit. The only other time he'd lost it had been the day she'd left him.

'I feel sorry for you,' he had sneered, holding his ground in the middle of their rented Sandy Bay apartment. 'You'll regret this. Being married to me was the only thing going for you. You're a has-been with no talent and your looks are gone. Nobody will want you. You will be stuck down here in this shitty little city with no hope of ever being anything. You will see me living the good life, I'll be a huge success, people in awe of me, and you will wish so hard that you hadn't been so stupid. You'll always be thinking, "If I had tried harder that life could've been mine."'

She'd left and checked in to a hotel, where she'd locked herself away and cried for twenty-four hours. Her husband was a lying cheat, but he was right. She was a has-been. Her chance of success had come and gone. She would never achieve anything. She was alone.

On the second day she'd come to this old house—her newly acquired passion project—picked up a crowbar and ripped out the cheap, plywood built-in wardrobe in the third bedroom. Sweaty and filthy, she'd begun to find her peace. She'd cleared a room, bought a mattress and set up camp, putting behind her the life of luxury and ease.

Now Simon was here, once again behaving horribly. She could see the commonalities: Remi standing her ground and denying him what he wanted. The day she left him, she'd walked away from his temper tantrum. Today she couldn't. She wiped her hands down her thighs as she went to the kitchen.

He stood at the sink, an empty glass in one hand. He held it under the tap then sculled the water. He set the glass carefully on the bench as though forcing his hand to move with care. Finally he turned and his gaze slid over her, settling on some point to her right.

'An agent will be here in'—he jerked his wrist out and up to reveal a heavy gold watch—'ten minutes to do a valuation. It is within my rights as mortgage holder of this property to gather that information.' He appeared calmer, but she sensed he was struggling. 'I don't need you here, so it's up to you whether you stay. And I'm sure you really don't want to be acting like a crazy woman when he arrives.'

An agent? A valuation? What the hell? Remi stood in the doorway, unsure what to do. She doubted Simon would listen to anything she said. He certainly wasn't going to leave.

'Why are you bringing an agent here?' she asked, managing to keep her voice calm. 'I told you my repayments are now up to date.'

He folded his arms and stood with his feet apart, legs braced. An unmovable rock of arrogant entitlement. 'Let's face it. The chances of you keeping up with payments are slim to none. We both know you're crap with money.'

'I won't be late again.' Not for the first time, she mentally kicked herself for not picking up on this ridiculous clause in their agreement.

'I don't share your confidence.'

'There have been extenuating circumstances. Last month I had to take my dog to be treated at the after-hours emergency vet. The bill was horrendous and unexpected.'

Simon looked around. 'You don't have a dog.'

Remi took a deep, steadying breath, pushing down the surge of pain. 'She couldn't be saved.' The vet had tried and Mavis had hung on for twenty-four hours. But the damage from whatever poison she had eaten had proven too much. 'And this week someone hacked my bank account and emptied it.'

'Hacked it?' He scoffed. 'Really?'

'Yes, really.'

'Right. Well, that's not my problem. The fact you don't have the savings or even the credit to cover emergency situations doesn't bode well, does it?' He shook his head. 'I really thought I was doing the right thing by agreeing to the buyout arrangement, especially at that ridiculously low valuation. But being your mortgagee has put me at a considerable disadvantage. Hasn't it?' When she didn't agree, he repeated himself. 'Hasn't it, Remi? I looked after you, even though you were the one ending the marriage. Even though I was the one who had to move, make a fresh start. I don't think you've ever really acknowledged how decent I was to you. You got exactly what you wanted, didn't you?'

'I was—and am—very grateful you allowed me to buy your half. And no, I could not have kept this house if you hadn't provided vendor finance. Thank you.' Of course she had been grateful. By the time their divorce had been finalised and the settlement signed, she had been well into the plans for the renovations, fully in love with this building and committed to finishing the job.

'Well, you're not showing me respect, are you? I can't financially carry you anymore. When you miss payments, that's more money you're taking from me. I doubt very much that you ever think of things from my point of view. Do you?'

'No.' Was he an actual, fully-fledged narcissist now? Did the money she put in his account make such a significant difference to him?

'I'm protecting my asset. I absolutely expect you to fail in your payments. You're barely getting by as it is. Call me a fool, but I'm optimistic you'll eventually stop being so pig-headed, that you'll sit down and realise you can't afford this place, and you'll move ahead with a sale. And when that happens, I want to move quickly to recoup my losses.'

'Losses?' She shook her head. 'You're kidding. The buyout figure you set was hundreds of thousands more than what we bought it for!' By the time they'd progressed to finalising their financial agreement, Hobart house prices had risen steeply and she had already significantly improved the house. Even having the plans and development approval for the renovations had added value. 'By the time I've paid you out, you will have made a decent profit. And you're charging me interest.'

'Of course I'm bloody charging interest! Money isn't free, Remi. And the rate is only a fraction above bank rates. And don't ever forget, it was my money that paid for this place. This was an investment. Making a profit is generally why people invest, right? And while I continue to hold the mortgage over this place, then I have a stake in what happens. Right? Remi?' He wanted her to say it, to agree with him. 'Isn't that right?'

'Sure.' She bit down on the words she really wanted to say.

'Great. Glad you understand. So, don't be a drama queen. Don't make a scene when this guy gets here. Let him do his job. And when we're done, I can leave you to whatever it is you do.'

Someone knocked at the door and Simon lurched into action. He shook out his arms, stretched his neck, tugged his jacket into place and twisted his mouth into a garish showman's grin. As he headed towards the front door, he stopped to rest a hand on Remi's shoulder while he delivered more unwanted words of wisdom.

'And, babe, you might feel differently when you hear how much you'll get. Everything always looks different when you see the price tag. Money changes opinions. Trust me, it's a fact of life I get to see every day.'

***

Remi retreated to the basement. For twenty minutes she sat in the cold at her desk, outrage throbbing through her body.

Simon was an entitled, smug, cheating arsehole. It wasn't easy to remember why she'd once adored him. Of course, their time together hadn't been all bad. There were plenty of good memories. The surprise trip to Morocco. Or weekends when he'd organise a lavish picnic. The time they'd both got the giggles at an oh-so-serious health retreat, the two of them escaping in the middle of the night. Exuberant sex, with a good dose of laughter. Sometimes she thought of those times without remembering the crap that came later, but not today. Now he wanted to take what mattered to her most: her home.

She opened her laptop, hoping there would be more responses to her housemate listing, but nothing had come through. Neither were there any responses from the audiobook producers. She opened her rudimentary budget spreadsheet. If she rented out both bedrooms, if she completed at least one decent job each month, if she cut spending, then she could keep up with the payments to Simon. Might even be able to get ahead and clear the debt a few months early, which would be amazing. On the other hand, income could be fickle. She'd have to work hard, complete her commissions quickly and take on more work.

She was rereading Emerson's profile when the door at the top of the stairs opened.

Simon called down. 'Hello, love, just wanted to show Jonathon what you've got down here.'

He didn't wait for a reply and walked down the stairs ahead of a tall man wearing an immaculate suit and tie, his black and grey hair clipped short. Lean and suave, with an air of money-eyed professionalism, the sort who could both earn Simon's respect and subtly boost his ego. Remi had no doubt this man was well experienced in keeping wealthy clients happy, even if he had to negotiate his way around irrational demands and unrealistic expectations.

The agent stepped forward, held out his hand. She shook but remained sitting. 'Amazing job you've done here. I drive past nearly every day and have watched the transformation. The house is looking incredible. It's a really top-notch job. You must be happy with how it's all come together.'

'Yes. Very happy. Thank you.'

'This is a handy space,' he said, looking around the large, unadorned room. 'Quite unusual to have one of these half-sunk basements in Hobart.' He indicated the high windows in the front wall, which looked out at street level. 'Reminds me of the Victorian terrace houses in London with those windows. A bit *Upstairs, Downstairs,* isn't it.'

'Yes, probably.'

'Do you see it being finished before you put it on the market?' He assessed the unpainted walls and the lack of refinements.

'Oh, yes. Well before it ever goes on the market,' she said. *Twenty years from now.*

'What's down there?' He indicated the two doors at the other end of the room.

'I have a small recording studio set up.'

'You're a musician?'

'No.' This whole conversation was an effort. 'I narrate audiobooks.'

'Remi used to be an actress,' Simon added. 'A long time ago. Not much money in this book thing, is there?'

Prick.

'Well, you timed the market perfectly.' The agent must've sensed the tension. 'Bought before Hobart took off, before the rush. If I remember rightly, you would've got this place for, what, a few hundred thousand?' He shifted the question from Remi to Simon.

'Four-oh-five, and that was overpriced,' Simon said with a laugh. 'The place was a feral dump. Absolutely stank. Couldn't believe people were living here. But we could see the potential and I had a feeling Hobart was on the brink of a turn around. I could feel the energy in the town starting to build. Turned out to be an opportune investment.'

'Absolutely.' The agent nodded, focused on the bullshit coming out of Simon's mouth.

Remi had no patience for this farce. She switched off the computer as she stood. 'I'll leave you to it. I'm going for a walk.'

She climbed the stairs quickly and headed out the front door, making sure she had her keys in her pocket. The day shone clear, but the air had bite and she hadn't bothered to grab her jacket. Hopefully a vigorous walk would warm her up.

Two blocks down the road, she slipped her phone out of her back pocket. Emerson wasn't what she'd had in mind for a housemate. Remi wasn't even convinced that a freelance illustrator would be able to keep up with the rent, but she didn't have the luxury of waiting for another applicant.

'Hello, is that Emerson? This is Remi.'

She listened as the girl bubbled out an enthusiastic reply. There was no doubt she would bring brightness and vivacity to the house. Remi tried to convince herself that wasn't such a bad thing.

'I'm hoping you're still interested in moving in.'

'Yes. Absolutely. I'd really love to. Your house is so gorgeous! I think it would really suit me. When could I move in? It's just that, if I hurry, I can check out of the hotel now and I might not be charged for another night. Which, I have to say, would be a really good thing. Money, and all that. Would today be too soon for you?'

Remi pressed her hand to her cold cheek. Sharing wouldn't be so bad, would it? She could do this. She could.

What choice did she have?

'Sure. Why not.'

CHAPTER FOUR

Saturday, 15 July 2023

R emi wrestled her legs into woollen leggings then pulled her oldest jeans over them—the ones with the baggy arse and the stains down the legs. She layered a faded sweatshirt over a long-sleeve tee and pulled thick socks onto her feet. She'd woken early, hunkering down in the isolation and warmth of her bed, until thoughts of her sneaky, entitled ex had slithered right back into her head. The bastard was not going to win.

Her solitary life had been decimated before she even had a chance to adjust to the idea of sharing, her finances were still far from stable and yesterday Simon had sent a perky email with the agent's valuation and a proposal for listing the house. Yes, the numbers had given her a moment of pride. No, she was not going to sell. And for now, there was nothing more he could do.

She was tempted to wallow in her self-pity for a while longer, but that would get her nowhere. There were still jobs that needed doing and she would not let Simon's threats put her off finishing this enormous project. Starting with the tedious job of painting the basement.

She crept down to the kitchen, the closed door of the lower bedroom an unavoidable reminder she was not alone. After coaxing the embers in the wood heater back to flames, she grabbed a mug and considered the coffee machine. Firing up the beast might have to wait. Emerson had been in the house for two nights and yesterday had not emerged from her room before ten. Chances were she'd probably sleep through a minute of coffee extraction, but Remi didn't want to be inconsiderate. Damn, was this how life was going to be? She took her coat and a beanie from the hook near the back door, slid some coins into her pocket and stepped outside. Hunched tight against the cold, she marched up the street, telling herself a brisk walk was always an invigorating way to start the day. Or would be, if the frigid air wasn't making her face sting and tears leak from the corner of her eyes. This was ridiculous and fiscally irresponsible. Her coffee machine was amazing. Her kitchen was warm. Yet here she was on the street at dawn, walking for ten minutes to get something she could make at home. In theory, she'd understood compromise was always going to be a part of sharing her space, but maybe this was going too far. From tomorrow she'd be making her own coffee, to hell with the noise.

***

Two hours later she was bent over at the waist, letting her head and arms hang towards the floor, trying to stretch out the kinks. Painting the ceiling, even with an extended roller, was literally a pain in the neck. From her upside-down position, she saw Emerson enter the basement. Today she was wearing an apple-green woollen pinafore over a pink turtleneck and black-and-white chequered tights. It was a combination that screamed, 'Look at me, I'm creative and carefree.' Which was probably a bit harsh. Honestly, it would be great to have the confidence and flair to wear something other than boring, go-with-anything neutrals.

'Good morning.' Emerson didn't sound quite awake.

'Morning.' Remi curled upwards, rolled her neck and shoulders and put on a small smile.

'Are you doing yoga?' Emerson lifted her mug and blew on it before taking a tiny sip. A pale green teabag tag dangled over the side. Herbal, Remi guessed.

'I'm painting the ceiling.' She pointed. 'I'm trying to unknot the knots.'

Emerson sipped again, turning to take in the space. 'It would be a good room for doing yoga, though.'

Remi looked around. The basement would have originally been the working area of the house. Partially below ground, the ceiling was low and underneath the drop cloths were large, uneven flagstones. The wall at one end was dominated by a stone mantel around a cavernous fireplace. A century ago, laundry and drying would've been done down here. At the other end thick brick walls divided two smaller rooms. So far, the windows had been repaired, the floors and fireplace cleaned. Plasterboard had gone up and been sanded months ago, after Remi and her builder had decided the stone walls were too rough and unattractive to leave exposed. The original builders hadn't bothered with well-cut sandstone blocks in this utilitarian section of the house. The overhead lights and heat panels were yet to be installed, but there were power points. In other words, the space was usable but needed work.

'I think the floor might be a bit hard and cold for that,' Remi said.

Emerson wandered over to the fireplace and squatted down so she could peer up the chimney. 'Does this work?'

'It doesn't. The chimney is a bit of a fire hazard. Probably burn the place down if I lit that.' She picked up the roller, ran it through the paint tray and lifted it to the ceiling.

'So, what are you going to do with all this space?'

'Well.' Remi smothered a sigh. 'At the moment it's sort of my study. And the recording studio for my narration work is down here. Other than that, I'm not too sure.' Maybe, if she didn't land some work soon, she'd have to turn it into another bedroom—or even a suite of rooms—to take in more strangers. Turn her lovely home into some sort of lodging house. With her as landlady in an apron, duster and mop in hand, pottering around, cleaning up after the boarders. Huddling in her room at night.

'Media room?' Emerson suggested, now investigating the smaller rooms. 'You know, recliner leather seats, big screen, black walls, those teeny twinkling lights that look like stars in the ceiling.'

'God, no.'

'You should put racks in here and turn one of these into a wine cellar.'

'That's how they would've been used originally. Unfortunately, I can barely keep a bottle in the fridge.'

'What about a pool table? You could definitely fit one. That would be super cool.'

Remi dipped the roller again but stopped to think. 'I used to love playing pool.' She looked around, imagining how that would look, then gave a short laugh. 'Great idea. But one small problem.'

'Let me guess: those stairs are the only way in.'

'Yep. There's no way a pool table is going to squeeze down those.'

'Bummer.'

Remi went back to rolling on paint. Emerson stood at a window, watching the traffic, her eyeline almost level with the tyres. 'It's a strange view of the world from down here.'

'I like it. It feels kind of secretive.'

Emerson turned. 'Absolutely.' Her face lit up. The tea must've kicked her into gear. 'You're so right. Kids would love it. Little kids could go nuts and teenagers could get up to their own kind of mischief. If I'd grown up in a house like this, I would've claimed this for my space. Big enough for a bed and sofa and a big screen. A huge work table.' She pointed to where she would fit everything. 'This would be a divine space for a teenager. They'd never leave home. You don't have kids, do you?'

Remi ran the roller back and forth. 'No. No kids.'

'Did you want them?' Emerson asked. 'Sorry, I probably shouldn't ask that, should I? In case you wanted them and couldn't have them. Or something happened. Or you had them and they don't live with you anymore. I always forget it's a tricky question. I shouldn't have asked.'

'It's fine.' Dip, lift, roll. Walking back, Remi kept her focus upwards. She didn't know this girl and was not about to share such personal information. Not that she really thought Emerson was going to blab details to the wider world. For a start, the wider world had no real interest in an ex-actress, ex-society wife. Her days of social currency were long gone. But she wasn't about to shed her hard-won privacy. 'It was one of those things that didn't fall into place.'

After the attack that ended her career, she had taken a year or two to heal physically and emotionally. She'd married Simon and tried to disappear into her new role as wife. In the beginning they hadn't even talked about children. When she finally brought it up, he'd been surprised.

'Sweetheart, are you really the maternal kind? I couldn't have a more beautiful, classy wife. But I've never imagined you as someone who wants to push out a few sprogs.'

'Don't you want to be a father?' she'd asked him.

'Not particularly.' He'd cited a long list of the things they loved to do, the things they'd lose if they had a baby: the travel, the holidays, dining out, sex in the kitchen. He needed the freedom to concentrate on his career and the business, to reach his full potential, to be someone important. 'Look, we're selfish people, babe. That sounds bad, but it isn't. What would be bad would be bringing a child into this world for no other reason than it's the expected thing and then being a bit resentful.'

Since she had experienced no strong yearnings, since she was committed to being the best wife she could be—to keeping Simon happy—she hadn't asked again. Occasionally she'd let the thought flutter into her mind. She'd give it space to settle, turn it over, picture herself with a baby, tested herself to see if, deep down, she did want to be a mother. But the pull was never strong enough. Not even to discuss the idea with Simon. Now she was glad there had only ever been the two of them. Being tied to Simon by children would've been horrendous.

Emerson continued. 'I can understand the whole not-wanting-kids thing. I'm not sure if I want to be a mum. I mean, I might, I guess, one day. But it's hard to imagine. Although there are some really cool mums around, who keep travelling and doing creative stuff and starting businesses and have amazing inner-city places. Life doesn't have to change because you have a baby, does it? Plenty of women even do it on their own. My last boyfriend wanted to be a dad. I said he was way too young to be planning something that big, but maybe he was right. Being a young parent would be kinda awesome. Yeah? My baby would have the coolest clothes, I'd make funky little outfits for her. Or him ...'

Her chatter didn't stop. A torrent of mindlessness that could barely be described as a conversation. Did she not have an off button? Emerson managed to blab about babies, boyfriends, homemade soap and her appreciation of male facial hair, tequila, vintage caravans and empanadas before suddenly asking if it was okay if she used the kitchen to, like, cook up some lunch.

'Of course.' *Quick, be gone you chattering, lurid parrot.* 'Make yourself at home. Use whatever you want.' In her eagerness for quiet, Remi was being unintentionally generous.

By the time the undercoat was finished, Remi was hungry and aching, and aware there were other tasks urgently needing her attention. Despite the rent money putting a band-aid on her immediate financial problems, she really needed the money from the audiobooks as well. She would follow up on her auditions that afternoon, maybe do some prep work for any new projects that would suit her voice. But first, she needed food.

With plans to defrost a tub of leftover curry and spend an hour or so turning the pages of a design and interiors magazine, she climbed the stairs. But thoughts of peaceful downtime were snuffed out as she entered a scene of mess and disruption. What the hell?

Around the sink sat a toppling stack of mixing bowls and chopping boards, and scraps of vegetables and eggshells littered the bench. A loaf of fresh bread had been hacked into thick slabs and piled next to the toaster amid a drift of crumbs. Emerson was at the island holding a cast-iron pan Remi had never used. And on the original-condition antique wooden bread board was a perfect golden circle of fluffy frittata, resplendent with chunks of mushroom and zucchini and slivers of red onion. Emerson set the pan on the stove top and scooped up a handful of chopped parsley from a bowl, sprinkling it on both her creation and the floor.

'Yay. Perfect timing.' Emerson wiped her hands on the pink gingham apron she was wearing. 'Hungry?'

Remi was. But seeing her kitchen brought to life through someone else's efforts was confronting. Like lending a dress to a friend and knowing they wore it so much better. Annoyance rippled through Remi and she tried to shut it down.

'Did you make this?' she asked stiffly. It was a redundant question. Emerson had quite obviously whipped up a lunch worthy of a decent cafe.

Emerson pulled a knife from the block and cut the frittata into quarters. 'Thought you might like something to eat. You've been down there for hours. Besides, my god, this kitchen. It's a love affair, I tell you. I couldn't resist any longer, I had to take advantage of this luscious room.'

'Thank you.' She had to stop being so critical. This was a lovely, generous gesture. Right? 'That looks amazing.'

Remi sat on one side of the counter, Emerson on the other, their plates piled not only with a generous serve of fluffy egginess but a side of rocket salad as well. At least there was blissful silence as they ate.

'Wow, this is so good. Is there feta in it?' Remi didn't have to fake her appreciation.

'Sure is.'

'But I didn't have any feta in the fridge.' Or leeks or fresh parsley.

'I went to the shops.' Emerson said lightly. 'This is such an excellent spot. I mean, you're on a main road and all. But inside you hardly notice the noise. And everything is so close. I don't even need my car. There's a supermarket-deli kinda place one street over, with everything you need.'

Remi had feared she'd have to label her food and hide the chocolate. Had wondered how the three of them would juggle their forays to the kitchen. Communal meals and equal contributions hadn't featured in her vision of a bleak share-house existence. This was not how sharing had been when she was a desperate fledging actor and full-time hospitality worker.

'I'll give you some money towards the ingredients,' she offered.

Emerson flicked her hand. 'Nah, that's okay. It wasn't much and I wanted to say thank you for letting me stay here.'

'Are you sure?' Remi had gotten the impression Emerson was not exactly cashed-up.

She waved away Remi's concern. 'It's all good. And don't worry about the mess. I'll clean up.'

Was Emerson going out of her way to make a good impression? Probably. Remi felt a flash of guilt for her grudging response to Emerson's efforts. 'I'll help,' she said as she stacked their plates.

'Seriously, it's fine,' said Emerson. 'You've been working all morning. I really don't mind doing this.'

Yep. Definitely trying to impress. Which was sweet, wasn't it?

Remi hadn't stopped to consider it, but living with two older women might be a strange arrangement for Emerson too. It probably wasn't the usual setup for someone in their mid-twenties.

As Remi retreated to her room, the question bounced around in her head. Why *had* Emerson chosen to live here and not with people her own age? Remi had been in such a hurry to find housemates she hadn't asked many questions. She should have been a little more inquisitive because, really, she knew nothing about this young woman.

CHAPTER FIVE

They were clearing the kitchen when Josephine arrived, Emerson skipping to the door with the uncoordinated exuberance of a puppy.

'Is that it?' Emerson insisted on carrying Josephine's possessions up the stairs. 'One suitcase and these?' She wiggled the two carrier bags in her hands. 'That doesn't seem much.'

Remi had to agree.

'Well, there's a bed arriving this afternoon,' Josephine answered as the three of them stepped into the bedroom. Remi had offered Josephine the choice of bedrooms and she had chosen the room upstairs, which had yet to be furnished.

'But what about clothes and, you know, other stuff?' Emerson settled the bags on the floor and wedged her hands in the front pockets of her dress.

Josephine gave a quiet laugh. 'I used to have stuff. Lots of stuff. Then I got rid of it all. Since then, I've been travelling light.'

'Wow. And I thought my life was compact. You mean you actually, really got rid of everything?' Emerson seemed fascinated with how Josephine could exist with so little. 'Like, all your home stuff? Cushions. Pots. Cookbooks. Towels? Pictures and art. What about the art?'

'I do have a towel.' Josephine set her suitcase in one corner of the empty room. 'And I was never big on cookbooks. But, yes, I gave away some paintings.'

'But what about the sentimental stuff?' Emerson frowned. 'Or the things that are too gorgeous to live without? I mean, I don't have much. Everything I own was squeezed into my car when I came down here. I did sell some furniture. Let me tell you, it's hard to find a buyer for badly assembled flat-pack furniture. Some of it I left on the side of the road for someone to claim. But everything that meant anything came with me.'

Josephine nodded as though she understood. 'Sometimes there are things I miss, and I have a small storage unit in Brisbane, but mostly the feeling of being light and free more than compensates.'

'But why? Why would you do that? What would make you offload everything? I mean, decluttering is all the rage, I get that, but this is a bit extreme. Did you have some sort of epiphany about consumerism? Or did you want to initiate a big life change? Did something happen to force you to do this?'

Remi flinched at Emerson's tactless questions. But Josephine simply tilted her head, giving the question thought. She appeared unconcerned, even amused.

'Not forced. No. There was, perhaps, a catalyst.'

'What happened? Did you go broke?'

Seriously, it was one thing to be curious and interested in people, but this unfiltered inquisition was too much. Once again, Remi sensed she had stuffed up. She shouldn't have rushed. Shouldn't have given Emerson the room. The dynamic was awful and there was going to be tension between the three of them. She would have to slink around her house, avoiding interaction.

Josephine's laugh was unexpected. 'No.' She was shaking her head but smiling. 'Although, I guess I am now unemployed. It wasn't about money. My son left. I was on my own. So, yes, I saw the opportunity for change.'

'Sure. Okay. But still. I mean, when I moved out of home, my mum had a clear out, but only of my old room. And only so she could turn it into a craft room. The last time I visited, the place was overflowing with glue and paper and stamps and sparkly glitter stuff. Won't your son come home? What happens then? Won't he want to stay or at least visit?'

'It might be a while till he gets back. And he knows there's been some changes. Although, I think he was a bit upset about me clearing out his old Pokémon card collection. Apparently, some of those cards might have been worth something.'

'Oh my god. Yes! Did you sort through them first? If there were cards from the base set or secret rares they'd be worth something for sure.'

Somehow Josephine managed to direct Emerson out of the room and they made their way back to the kitchen, all the while receiving an unasked-for education in Pokémon cards.

When the bed was delivered, Josephine and Emerson assembled it together. Then, with the construction out of the way, Emerson offered to make dinner. Remi attempted to deflect this suggestion, but Emerson seemed oblivious to her efforts. Nothing fancy, she had said, before disappearing on another trip to the shops.

By seven they were all sitting around the table with bowls of pumpkin soup topped with crumbled chorizo. Remi had considered opting out of this group meal, but acquiesced in the end, realising how churlish she would seem. It was disconcerting how quickly the routine of her life had been disrupted. The control she'd had over her environment and how she lived was being diluted by the enthusiasm and obliviousness of Emerson. The soup, though, was delicious.

Josephine raised her glass, the light red of the pinot noir she'd supplied catching the light. 'Here's to new chapters,' she said. 'And to living in harmony.'

Remi hesitated then lifted her drink. Anyone looking in from the garden would see a perfect, convivial moment. But Remi's cynicism was like constrictive shapewear under a glittering dress: the outside appearance was beautiful, but in reality she was uncomfortable, could barely breathe and couldn't wait to be free of the restriction.

Luckily, conversation was flowing between Josephine and Emerson as they found out a little more about each other. Before she had thrown her old life aside, Josephine had run a small retail business. Lately she'd been travelling around Australia. Emerson talked about her work as an illustrator and graphic artist and brought out some of her work, gorgeous pieces with quirky illustrations and free-flowing script. She'd shared her enthusiastic, highly optimistic, plans to conquer the world from this hip little city.

Finally, their attention had turned to Remi. As though unable to hold back a question she'd been longing to ask, Emerson leaned forward on her arms and mock-whispered, 'You were on that show, weren't you?'

'"That show"?' Remi frowned. By this stage, three glasses of wine had eased some of her reticence. 'Oh, you mean *Our Street*? That tale of two families and the highs and lows they shared.' She spoke in her best TV commercial voice. 'Is that the show you mean?'

'Yes! That's it. That was you, wasn't it? Katie? Karen? I can't remember the character's name.'

'Caitlyn.' Josephine supplied the answer.

'That's it. She was the best thing on there, apart from the guy who played her boyfriend. He was sexy. But you were awesome.'

Remi sat back in her chair. 'Yes. I was on TV a really long time ago. I'm surprised you even know the show.' *Our Street* had run for two more seasons after Remi left. When she heard of people downloading and streaming such an old piece of television she was always surprised. Especially when there was so much excellent content these days.

'Classic piece of early noughties nostalgia,' Josephine said. 'You were very good, Remi.'

'Oh, no. Not you too.' A smile tugged at Remi's mouth.

'Absolutely. I watched every week, after I put Sam—my son—to bed.'

Emerson had tucked her feet up to sit cross-legged in her seat. 'I only discovered it recently, like about three years ago, I guess. I watched it on catch-up. I can't believe I'm sitting here with you now. Who'd have thought?' Her eyes were wide at this amazing twist of fate. 'And you haven't been on anything else?'

'Nope. I gave that game away.' If these women remembered her from TV, there was a chance they could also recall the dramatic plot points of her early life. She was absolutely not going to delve into that story. 'These days my only gigs are narrating audiobooks.'

'That sounds interesting,' Josephine said. 'I've listened to a few books lately. There's so much more to the process than just reading out loud, isn't there? I imagine acting skills are vital.'

'I think they are.'

Remi gave a quick rundown of her path from TV to audio work, without mentioning the ugliest bits. She skipped the attack, the months of healing and the hollow, aching year that had followed quitting the show, and picked up the story a few years after her marriage to Simon, recounting how bored she'd been, how she'd taken a little voice-over work, something to fill her days, rather than a clearly envisioned career path. That she had enjoyed the work had been a surprise. Then the gorgeous wife of one of Simon's friends had published a book on finding your own style and living fully in your fabulous self, and Remi had recorded the narration. She knew she had only been hired to please Simon, by those who wanted to be in his favour. No one had thought Simon's decorative wife—the ex-actress with a shadow of gossip still hanging around her—would be better than competent. For Remi, satisfaction had come in doing the work well, seeing the client's surprise and in getting paid. They hadn't needed the extra income. But for her sense of self-worth, it had been invaluable.

'Anyway, these days I'm proud of the work I do. I set up a home studio downstairs and can do the recording, editing and file conversion from here. I don't have the super, super high-end equipment, but I've got a small soundproof room, a good mic and decent recording software on my computer.'

'Do you only do Australian books?' Josephine asked.

'Yes, I'm limited to the local market. But I've worked with some great writers, a mix of traditional and indie published books. The authors I've worked with have been very happy. And the work fits nicely around managing this project.' She opened her arms to encompass the house. 'I'll have to show you some photos of how this place looked when I began. You'll be shocked.'

Emerson had her phone out, her finger flicking over the screen. 'Where would I hear a sample?' she asked.

'Try the Audible site, you can search by narrator there.'

'I imagine it's not as simple as picking up the book and reading out loud.' Josephine was genuinely interested.

'There's quite a bit of preparation. It varies but generally there's about three hours' work for every hour of actual recorded narration. I read the book, then mark up the text with things like colour codes for when the different characters speak, plus emphasis and pacing, and phonetic spellings for tricky words. Then there's the actual narration, checking the recording, making corrections and editing.'

'How do you get paid?'

'There's an hourly rate, calculated on the length of the finished book. Let's just say, it's not a high-paying job. Still, I enjoy the process and the income helps pay the bills.'

'Did you find some of Remi's books?' Josephine asked Emerson, who had her phone in one hand. The other hand was lifted to her mouth as she nibbled the corner of her thumbnail. She glanced up at Remi, pushed her glasses up her nose, then looked back at her screen.

'Something gone wrong in the world?' asked Josephine.

Emerson kept tapping, paused to read, tapped and swiped again.

'What is it?' prodded Remi.

Emerson put the phone down on the table and looked up at Remi. 'Um, do you keep an eye on your reviews, you know, what readers or listeners or whatever say about your narration?'

'I don't read them regularly but, yeah, I know they're there. Nothing but nice words so far. Five-star reviews. Why?'

'Right. Well, I think you may have pissed someone off.'

'What? Why do you say that?'

'When I look you up, I can see the reviews for the audio-books you've done, and there's a score for the story itself and a score for the performance, and at a guess, I'd say someone has dumped a shitload of one-star ratings on you. Then there are quite a few where they've left reviews. They're not nice. You might want to have check them out, because it looks like someone is determined to mess with your business.'

CHAPTER SIX

Sunday, 16 July 2023

I couldn't get into this book. The story seemed okay, but the narrator was dreadful. She read the book in the voice of a bored, whingeing kid. Just couldn't stand listening. Pity, because I was looking forward to this book.

Oh my god. The voice drove me nuts. So overdone and pathetically dramatic.

Good story completely ruined by narrator. Heads up to the author, find someone else for your next book or I won't be buying.

Usually I have no trouble staying connected to my audiobooks, but with this narrator I kept drifting off into my own thoughts. She was so boring. Could not engage at all. Really awful.

This book was completely spoiled by the narrator. Can't believe she used to be an actress. No talent at all. None! Returned the book for a refund.

Remi put her palms on the edge of her desk and pushed her chair back. Carefully, she reached down, stretching to pull the small bin closer, fumbling as she wedged it between her feet. Bent forward, arms around her stomach, she let her head hang, sucking in deep, shuddery breaths.

Don't vomit.

Last night, this poison had torn apart the evening. She'd left the kitchen and locked herself in her room, unable to stand the pity on their faces. She was not going to be a victim, not again, and the thought of these two women feeling sorry for her or worse, thinking the nastiness was somehow deserved, was horrific. She'd barely slept and had come to the studio this morning, to read and reread the reviews and comments. Refreshing the pages. Scrolling. Selecting the worst to read again and again.

A sip of water might help, but she couldn't move. Getting up from her chair and walking up the stairs to the kitchen felt dangerous. She had to stay immobile, wait for the nausea to pass. She was aware of footsteps, a gentle voice.

'Remi?'

Shit, she didn't want to be seen like this. She smelled the tang of peppermint and opened her eyes enough to see a mug of tea being set on the desk. 'Thanks.' Her throat was tight with the effort to keep her stomach contents from heaving upwards.

For a minute nothing more was said, then Josephine squatted down beside her. 'This can be dealt with. You will get past this.' Her tone was confident, as though she had dealt with worse dramas and survived. But Remi didn't need platitudes or an observer.

'Sure.'

'There's a process. It requires patience. And persistence. These monolithic tech giants don't work quickly. Quite frankly, they couldn't care less when their systems are used to harm.'

Remi lifted herself a little so she could turn her head. 'I won't survive. No author or publisher will hire me.' She didn't bother to keep the bitterness from her voice.

'Only if you hide in shame and wait for it to go away.'

Easy for Josephine to say, she wasn't the one whose professional reputation had just been demolished.

Remi pushed herself upright and leaned back in the chair. The nausea was still there, but the sense of imminent explosion had eased. As she picked up the mug, the sharp scent rose into her face and she breathed deeply.

Josephine pulled a chair around the desk and sat beside Remi, apparently in no hurry to leave. 'Do you have any idea who would do this?' When Remi shook her head, she said, 'There are two possibilities. Firstly, it's a competitor attempting to undermine your business for their own advantage. Does that sound likely?'

Remi sighed. 'I don't know. Australian publishing is not exactly a huge market by world standards. There are only so many books recorded each year. The competition for the jobs is a bit tough.'

'Is the market growing or shrinking?'

'Growing. Audiobooks are taking off.'

Josephine nodded thoughtfully, looking towards the computer screen and the swarm of revolting words.

'What's the second option?' Remi couldn't help asking.

Josephine crossed her legs, hooking her clasped hands around her knee. 'This might not be about your work, as such. It could be more personal than that. To use a line from every crime show ever on TV, do you have any enemies, is there anyone who would want to hurt you?'

'No, of course not.' Remi was absolutely not going to get into this with a woman who was little more than a complete stranger.

She sipped the tea until, under Josephine's silence, she felt the need to say something. 'My ex-husband isn't happy with me at the moment. And his new wife, well, I haven't had anything to do with her for a couple of years, but she was—is—a bit nasty. But I don't see what she'd have to gain from this.'

Josephine thought this over before answering. 'Some people do things, cruel things, for no other reason than because they can. Acid can be thrown from a distance, without splashback. The internet is the perfect tool. For some, there's satisfaction in seeing, or even just believing, they have affected their victim or taken them down.'

'I'm not a victim!' Remi was more terse than she'd intended, but she despised that label. Once again, she was being defined by the actions of others. She was intimately acquainted with people who took their hate and bitterness and envy and lashed out. And while vicious comments were nowhere near as damaging as, say, a steel fence picket repeatedly connecting with her body, her mind had clearly sensed danger and was choosing to freeze over flight or fight. She had to get a grip.

'Pity they chose to attack my business.'

'It's the easiest option, your point of greatest exposure. You're not in the public eye anymore, so they can't go after your reputation in the wider arena. The most damage they can do, without resorting to physical acts, is to use the scattergun approach. Shoot rapid and wide and presume something will cause hurt and injury.'

Remi shut her laptop. There was no point staring at those comments. 'Not the greatest of circumstances to be dumped in, on your first day,' she said, loathing herself for sharing this ugliness. 'You don't know me—all this could be true. Maybe I am, in fact, utterly crap at my job.'

'Well, in that case you went from great to dreadful very suddenly. All your older reviews are unanimously positive. Obviously your performance and acting skills have carried into book narration.'

Remi had, until now, believed this to be true. She'd prided herself on building tension with only her voice and the control of her breath. Had thought she understood mood and pacing and characterisation. Maybe she had an over-inflated opinion of herself.

'I was never really that good,' she said. It wasn't false modesty; she was being realistic about her short career. 'I knew how to find my mark, not look in the camera, remember lines and convey some emotions on my face. Really, I was given the role because I had the right look. I fitted the part and could play a few years under my actual age. Sweet, quirky young girl, about to go through love, loss and triumph on the screen. Viewers responded to the character as she was written. It wasn't so much about my acting ability.'

'That sounds cynical.'

Remi gave a snort of agreement.

'Is that why you gave it away? You didn't believe in what you were doing?'

Remi closed her eyes. Opened them to look directly at Josephine. She'd quit acting because she was gutless. Because she lacked tenacity. She'd walked away because being in the industry got too hard, and she was mentally and physically broken. None of which she felt inclined to discuss.

Silence stretched out for several minutes.

'I quit the show because of a smear campaign. Because I couldn't handle the lies and gossip that were printed. Or the sneaky photos that were misconstrued. Or the way the public turned on me.' She shut her mouth. What was she doing? That was more than enough sharing.

'I imagine that would've been distressing.'

Remi nodded and set down the tea. Surprised herself when the words continued to flow. 'And then, partly because I was scared. Another actress …' She raised a hand and rubbed her face. She hated talking about this. Yet she couldn't seem to stop. 'Another actress believed those lies and decided to teach me a lesson, take me out of contention.'

'How did she do that?'

Did Josephine not know this story? The whole thing had been spread across the papers and magazines for weeks, the public salivating over the gruesome details. Remi shut her eyes and tipped her head back. 'Physically and effectively.'

She waited for more questions, but Josephine was silent. When she opened her eyes, she saw the slow lift of Josephine's chin, a squaring of her shoulders. Was that disgust or anger on her face?

'Anyway,' Remi continued, 'the studio gave me time off to recuperate, rewrote the script to accommodate my absence. Not that they had much of a choice. I never went back.' She picked up the mug, set it down, ran her hands through her hair to pull the knotty, unwashed mess off her face. 'That was a long time ago. And has nothing to do with this.'

Josephine gave a noncommittal nod of her head. 'Maybe not. But I imagine this feels somewhat similar. Not physically brutal, but this would seem to be an unjustified personal attack. What I suggest you do is go upstairs and have a long, hot shower.'

Remi bristled at the impertinence of being told what to do. She was not some poor wee thing who needed to be looked after. Although, she had to admit, a shower would be great.

Josephine stood. 'Emerson has been busy in the kitchen again. I think you're going to be presented with muffins. She's been rushing to and from the shops, talking about what a glorious kitchen you have but pointing out the appalling lack of baking utensils.'

Remi's laugh was small and tight. 'I don't do a lot of cooking.'

'Neither do I, much. My son, Sam, was better in the kitchen than I was. He was good with pasta. Maybe it's a thing with this younger generation.'

Remi stood to follow Josephine up the stairs. 'I'm sorry you have to witness this drama,' she said. It was all so humiliating and pathetic.

Josephine considered her for a moment, then looked away. 'Don't worry about me, I can handle a little drama.'

CHAPTER SEVEN

It was only eight, but Remi was already in bed, the ends of her hair damp, her skin pink from too long in a hot bath. There was a pressing ache behind her eyes and a band of tension circled her skull from her forehead to the back of her neck, the two Panadol she'd taken doing nothing to ease the pain. She rearranged the pillows and tugged and smoothed the doona as she wriggled down, but couldn't get comfortable.

Slivers of light moved across the ceiling, the headlights of passing cars finding gaps in the drawn curtains. The muted woosh of the traffic a familiar background. She closed her eyes and concentrated on her breath, trying for a slow, deep rhythm. Rolled onto her side. Hugged a pillow. Tugged at the t-shirt she wore to bed, where it had wound tight around her waist. Waited for the pull of sleep.

Nothing.

Unbelievable. How could she still be awake? She'd only managed two or three broken hours of sleep last night, her brain spinning in a relentless, feverish loop. She flopped onto her back. Listened to the strange noises in her house. A door closing, footsteps on the stairs, the shower running then shutting off, the soft murmur of the TV in the lounge below. A burst of laughter came from the main bathroom at the back of the house, then the quiet voices of her tenants.

What were they talking about? Emerson and Josephine were so different yet had immediately connected. She'd seen them in the kitchen, their heads together, whispering, their conversation hushed when they noticed Remi. What did they possibly have to discuss? To laugh about? Was Remi the joke? Were they having a giggle over those dirty, ugly comments about her work? Or her little meltdown? Underneath their supportive words there were probably some unvoiced judgements. Maybe they thought she had somehow brought the reviews on herself, or that she deserved them, or that she was being ridiculously over the top in her reaction.

This was exactly what she had dreaded, this sense of being exposed and vulnerable, of being both observed and judged.

But then Josephine had been kind. This morning, after a shower and with food and coffee in their systems, Josephine had returned with Remi to the basement, where they'd begun the frustrating task of reporting the fake reviews. Having Josephine by her side had been helpful. She was focused and determined, drafting emails and investigating strategies. In fact, Josephine had been more than capable, her fingers tapping in rapid bursts, whizzing from page to page on Remi's computer, attacking the task with confidence and skill. It had been hard to keep up with what she was doing. Josephine was obviously someone who knew her way around technology and online business. Remi had been more pessimistic, researching how others had dealt with such attacks. What she'd read hadn't been encouraging.

Now her mind was racing again: *I'll never have another client. My business will completely fail. I will lose my house. Someone hates me. Someone hates me. Someone hates me. Again.*

A nasty anxiety wormed up from her stomach to settle in her chest as a new thought appeared. Mavis dying, the stolen money and the destruction of her reputation as a narrator. Could they be related? Did someone hate her enough to do all of that?

She shoved the doona away. Pressed the heel of her hands into her eyes. 'Shut up, shut up,' she muttered.

She was being paranoid. The vet had said there had been a few cases of dog-baiting around Hobart. The hacking was probably some cyber-crime gang. The reviews could be from a deranged keyboard troll. She should be happy that her tenants were getting along.

Rolling over, she padded her hand around the bedside table till she found her phone. She held it above her face, tapping the glowing screen till she found Luke's number.

Everyone should have at least one friend they could call at any time. Someone to talk to when things go very wrong in the middle of the night. Luke had been her emergency contact back in 2009, when she'd woken in the back of an ambulance with blood in her mouth, one eye swollen shut, pain and panic slamming through her body. They hadn't always kept in close contact. The years after she'd married Simon had been quieter between them, but since the divorce they'd spoken and seen more of each other. Remi had never doubted she could turn to Luke when she needed to vent—such as when the renovation went off schedule and way off budget or she had to find solutions to problems the builders and tradesmen hadn't foreseen. Or when Mavis died.

She was also a little in awe of her friend. There was something about him. How, with intense, unwavering focus, he'd pursued then surpassed all the goals he'd ever set. He began his career by working through the trainee program in record time, then being promoted continuously until he became manager of the Worthington Hotel. Two years after that, he was co-owner of a boutique hotel in Sydney. Then outright owner. She had no idea how he'd found the money. Then there'd been another hotel. And another, until he'd built Strike Hotels into a small chain. Then one more in Hobart, bringing the total to four. All of them gorgeous, all of them blending old-world class with modern edginess, all of them on the must-stay lists of the travel magazines and praised by the well-to-do, the media, movie and fashion darlings, and even the footballers and their wives. Everyone wanted to share the Strike experience. Which made the hotels highly profitable. Not bad for a boy from Cairns.

Luke's personal life was a different story. He was a serial dater. He flitted from one woman to another, never letting a relationship extend too long or take the shape of a serious commitment. She frequently teased him about his bachelor ways.

He answered as she was about to hang up. 'Hello, I wasn't expecting to hear from you again so soon.' She'd rung him a few days before, ranting after Simon's first visit. Luke had, of course, been furious, the animosity he had always felt for Simon on full display. 'How is everything? Did you go ahead with the housemate plan?'

She gave him a quick rundown of Emerson's buoyant arrival and her talents in the kitchen. 'Josephine arrived last night,' she continued. 'We had a dinner together, but everything went a bit south.'

'A generational clash of personalities?'

'No, nothing like that.' She hesitated, pulled herself up to sitting, a pillow in her lap. 'We were talking about ourselves and Emerson was looking up the books I'd narrated. Turns out there's been some review activity around my work. Some awful comments have been posted.'

'What do you mean?'

'There's a stack of one- star reviews. The actual books are rated well, but the comments about my narration are vicious. Josephine and I have reported them, sent emails, that kind of thing. It's revolting and no one will ever want to hire me.'

She could hear the clicking of his keyboard, then silence as he read. 'This is serious.'

'Yeah, it is. Looks like someone has a vendetta or is on a mission or something.'

'Any idea who?'

'That's the million-dollar question, isn't it?'

'Simon?'

Remi hugged one arm tight around the pillow, like a child with a teddy bear. 'I don't know. I don't think so. He was angry with me. He really didn't like me saying no to selling the house. For some reason he really wants that mortgage cleared now, not later. But what does ruining my career achieve? It's so vindictive.'

'You said his aggressive reaction the other day was also out of character.'

'Sure, but he only puts effort into things that benefit him.'

Luke was still tapping keys. 'Maybe he thinks trashing your reputation *will* benefit him. If you lose jobs because of these comments, it will damage your cashflow.'

Which was, of course, her biggest worry. Still, it all felt too underhand and cruel to have been Simon's doing. Even if the outcome could end up being what he wanted.

'Why is he so determined to sell this place from under me? He doesn't need the money.' Simon had never needed money, the family wealth had always padded his life. And now he had his own business. She'd seen pictures of his most recent store opening. Kayla posing for the cameras, an elaborate gold necklace around her exposed neck, a matching cuff on one wrist. Her dress a knee-length, strapless, pale pink number. The expensive, heavy fabric tailored to fit all her curves. Simon's second wife was sexy in a plush, preened kind of way, and with her puffy mouth toned down with a subtle lipstick, she was almost classy.

Then there were the photos of dinners and lunches, trips to the races and a polo event. Perfectly staged pictures of Kayla in designer clothes, shiny trinkets and branded accessories from the store all tagged and highlighted. Money did not appear to be an issue. Sure, Simon's love of spending appeared to have escalated, but he had learned his business acumen from his father. Remi's ex-father-in-law was an intimidating self-made man and no fool. Nor would he accept foolish behaviour in his only son, even if that son was forty-three years old.

'Understanding Simon is quite beyond me. I have no idea how his logic works,' Luke said with clear dislike before his tone softened. 'But more importantly, how are you coping with all this? Are you okay?'

His gentle words were almost her undoing. She struggled, and failed, to stop the tears, swallowing hard and breathing slowly to keep her crying silent. Her nose began to drip and she sniffed loudly. Shit, she hated being weak.

'Oh, Remi. Do you want to come up here for a few days to have a break?'

'No, that's fine. I need to stay here and sort this mess out.'

'Hold on.' He clicked and tapped. 'Right. I need to come down to Tassie for a quick check of operations there. I'll bring forward my travel by a few days and we can at least go and have lunch somewhere nice.'

'Don't do that.' She gave another shuddering sniff.

'I have to be there anyway, I want to touch base with our new GM in Hobart and I'd like to see you.'

'Honestly, don't rush down. There's nothing that can be done. And I'm a big girl. I just needed to vent.'

He waited a beat before he spoke. 'Okay. But I really do need to visit. I'll be in Hobart in the next week or so.'

'Will Genevieve be joining you?'

There was the slightest pause. 'We're not together anymore.' She wasn't surprised, even though his latest girlfriend had out-lasted the others by at least six months.

'I'm sorry to hear that. She sounded lovely.'

'She is. We wanted different things.' Which Remi took to mean Genevieve had wanted commitment and Luke hadn't been inclined to settle down. 'Get some sleep,' he said. 'Try not to dwell on all this too much.'

'It's knowing that someone has deliberately done this that's so awful. It's so personal.' She hadn't even told him about the disappearing bank account or the revolting idea that wouldn't go away: that these things might be connected.

'Remi, think of something nice. You have no need to worry. I promise you, there will always be options for you.'

'Goodnight, thank you for listening.'

'I'll see you soon. And remember, you are magnificent.'

She set the phone down and moved deeper into the bed. She was lucky to have him as a friend.

As sleep finally wrapped around her, Luke's last words echoed in her head. To him, she was magnificent. She didn't agree with his assessment, but it had always been a beautiful thing to hear.

She wondered how different her life would have been if she'd paid more attention the first time he made that declaration.

CHAPTER EIGHT

January 2005

You are magnificent.

Those words probably weren't the first thing Luke ever said to Remi, but they were the ones she remembered.

The staff of the Worthington Hotel held their Christmas party during the second week of January, well after the craziness of December and New Year's Eve. Remi had been excited about her first big social event with her workmates. In the six months she'd been at the hotel there'd been plenty of after-work gatherings. As with most hospitality staff, the end of a night shift often wrapped up with a few drinks in a nearby pub. Buzzing after the craziness of another large function, they would need to unwind, get out of their stiff-collared shirts, knotted ties and long black aprons, literally let their hair down and have some fun for themselves. But the Christmas party was bigger, more organised. The upstairs space at the pub was booked, the Christmas Party Fund drained to pay for the drinks and huge trays of dim sims and chicken tenders. Hardly fancy, but they didn't need gourmet.

'What does everybody wear?' Remi had asked Brittney.

Brittney had given the question serious thought before answering. 'Well, you need to look hotter than you ever look at work. Definitely use a touch of glamour. You know, like wow, who is that girl and why haven't I ever noticed her? But this thing is not the Brownlows or Logies, so do not go for over the top. Make it fresh and sexy and special. But not try-hard. Nothing worse than someone who goes just that bit too far.'

Remi had laughed. 'Right. That helps.'

She had met Brittney at a film audition, Remi immediately in awe of the confidence the dark-eyed, dark-haired girl possessed. They swapped numbers when their paths crossed again at an open call for a stage production. By the time they both got call-backs for a fast-food commercial, they were friends. Brittney had been the one to suggest Remi apply for a job at the Worthington. Now they worked side by side in the function rooms, both holding on to the dream of being a professional actor. They each had tiny successes. Brittney landed a non-speaking walk-on spot on *Home and Away*. Remi smiled and said two lines for a car insurance ad. Brittney scored five lines on an ABC miniseries. They competed against one another without animosity. They were both twenty-one, and convinced success was right around the corner. Each was pleased for the other when the small wins came their way, even if there was a smidge of envy.

In the end, Remi wore a soft, short dress in burgundy that looked like it cost more than it had. The halter-neck design left her shoulders and back bare. With her hair out and a pair of dangling silver earrings, she'd felt pretty. Then she saw Brittney and immediately felt like a teenager trying and failing to dress like a woman. Dressed in skin-skimming red, her friend looked exotic and powerful. With her hair wound high on her head, her eyes dramatic with winged eyeliner and long lashes, and luscious red lips, she was fiercely gorgeous.

Brittney insisted they couldn't arrive any earlier than an hour after kick-off, instead preparing them with a drink at her apartment. By the time the taxi let them out near the pub, Remi was fizzing with anticipation and half a bottle of cheap bubbles. The night opened before her, full of possibilities. Maybe she would kiss someone. Actually, she was sure she would. Quite determined. After all, she did work with some cute boys. And it wasn't like there hadn't been some flirting both at work and at pub drinks. Remi knew she didn't have the presence or impact of Brittney, nor the sort of confidence that drew people close, but there'd be someone for her. Even Brittney couldn't keep them all busy.

The heady atmosphere washed through Remi as soon as they climbed the stairs to the party. Music loud enough to vibrate under her skin, but not so deafening as to rule out conversation. The large room was filled with people eager to make the night memorable. She had a vodka and soda in her hand within minutes. Guys who looked fine in their uniform and normal in their after-work clothes seemed to have morphed into handsome men now they were wearing decent shirts.

Brittney found space for them in a crowded corner, squeezing onto a sofa between two guys. Remi smiled at the young man beside her, their thighs pressed firmly against each other. She'd seen him on the function floor only a few times, usually when others had called in sick or the event warranted extra waitstaff.

'I'm Simon.' He shook her hand.

'Remi.'

'I like your dress.'

'I like your smile.' The words slipped out before she could think to stop them. His grin widened. It really was a spectacular smile. Especially when one eyebrow hitched ever so slightly, as though he was amused or asking a question or even flirting.

'I like your hair,' he said. He was squashed into the corner, one arm lying along the back of the sofa. He wrapped a strand of her hair around his finger and gave a gentle tug.

She lifted her glass to her mouth. Stopped smiling long enough to take a sip. This was going to be a great night.

The first two hours sped past in a happy blur of loud, silly conversation and icy vodkas. Once or twice Brittney dragged her up to the pokey dancefloor, where they shimmied to popular party tracks. Then they'd work their way back to the sofa, Simon making room for her every time.

Brittney suddenly stood up and raised her arms, demanding attention. 'Let's play a game,' she called out. 'A new game I've come up with.'

She was met with a loud, somewhat raucous response, as people gathered closer.

'Strip poker.'

'Hide the sausage.'

'Wet t-shirt competition.'

'Games are for kids' parties.'

She shook her head, held her hands up for silence, then pointed a finger at the guy who'd dared suggest games were beneath them. 'Mike, you obviously haven't learned to play with the grown-ups. There are games and there are *games*.' This was met with whistles and hoots of laughter. 'Pay attention, everyone. This game is easy. And fun. And a little bit naughty. It's called Guess the Kiss. Or Kiss and Guess. Something like that, I haven't decided. I need a lucky volunteer to demonstrate. Make room everyone. How about you, Mike?'

Mike groaned but let himself be pushed and hauled into the centre of the group.

'Okay, make room everyone. Give our victim some space.' The crowd formed a loose circle around them, while those on the chairs and sofa stayed sitting. 'Now I need a blindfold. Anyone? Anyone?' She looked around, spotted one of the guys who was wearing a tie and vest. 'Gavin, quick, pass over your tie.'

In seconds she was knotting a blindfold around Mike's head. He was looked a little nervous.

'Don't worry, sweet cheeks,' Brittney said, patting his face. 'You're going to enjoy this. It's easy. Here's what's going to happen. You're going to be kissed twice. Good, proper snogs, okay. No tight-lipped pecks.' She directed this to the expectant crowd. 'And you, my lucky victim, firstly say which kiss was the best, and then guess who it was. If you get it right, you get a prize. Got it?'

'Alright. Bring it on.' Mike waggled his hands in front of him. Brittney firmly pulled them behind his back.

'No cheating, no groping. You receive your kisses like a gentleman. Now, who wants to be our first contestant?'

For a moment, no one responded. People looked around, waiting for someone else to put their hand up or step forward.

'No takers, Mike. Mate, no one wants you,' one of Mike's friends called out.

Brittney put her hands on her hips, rolled her eyes in great exaggeration, then stepped in front of her victim. She reached one hand behind his head and leaned in to plant her lips on his, as everyone else whooped and clapped.

After that, everyone wanted to play. The first three rounds
of the game had the crowd in stitches, even if only one girl cor-
rectly guessed who had delivered her favoured kiss.

Then Remi found herself being dragged up by Brittney.
Not that she minded. The alcohol had given her a lush, warm
awareness of her body. She was sexy. She was fun. She was
going to enjoy every minute. The atmosphere was exciting, the
game raunchy but not intimidating.

When Brittney knotted the blindfold, she felt a ripple of disquiet run through her. Being blind in a revved-up crowd made
her feel vulnerable.

Brittney rubbed her arm, leaned in close. 'You can thank me
later.'

Remi relaxed at the sound of her friend's delight.

She could sense someone standing in front of her. Then a
hand on her jaw, tilting her mouth up. The kiss was decent
and tasted of bourbon. Firm lips, perhaps a little too much
pressure, their mouths opening together. She could hear the
appreciation of those watching, felt suddenly self-conscious
and pulled back a little. The kisser didn't stop, reluctant to end
their party pash. Then he got the hint. As he moved away, she
lifted a hand to her mouth, dragging her thumb over her lips.
Knew there would be stubble-rash on her chin.

Remi waited. There were whispers, a hushed discussion, a
murmur of interest from the audience. She turned her head,
trying to follow what was happening. Caught a whiff of aftershave or cologne, something deep and warm. She lifted her
nose, trying to follow the scent. Had an urge to nuzzle into
that body.

He was behind her. His hands resting on her shoulders. The
slight movement of a finger on her skin. Awareness of someone's

head bending close to hers. Warm breath on her ear. Then she was being carefully turned. She raised her face in anticipation.

The kiss, when it came, was tender. A brush of their lips. A questioning pause. Then growing ever so slightly more intense till there was real pressure, the tips of their tongues touching. Sensual. Intoxicating. When he pulled away, she wanted more. The smell of him sending all the right messages through her body. Except now there was space between them, even if his hands still rested on her shoulders.

A deep-voiced whisper in her ear, 'You are magnificent.' Then she was standing alone.

Was that Simon? No. He'd been close to her for most of the night and he had not smelled as divine as this man.

'Okay, girlfriend, blindfold off. Time for your verdict.' Brittney was by her side as Remi pushed the tie off her face.

At least twenty of her workmates were watching her, a tight circle of people sitting and standing, bodies leaning one against another, arms across shoulders or around waists, some girls sitting on the laps of others. Most everyone had a drink in hand, faces flushed with alcohol, heat and the fun of the game. Many she knew, some she didn't. Some were vaguely familiar. But who had she kissed?

'Come on, first question is easy. Which kiss rated highest? Which thrilled your socks off? Which pash was perfect? Would you want more of number one or number two?'

Simon was on the sofa, his body relaxed and taking up space. The look on his face was suggestive, a single finger in front of his mouth, as though urging her to shush. Or giving her a hint.

The first kiss was not the best. But she liked Simon. Really liked him. He was good looking, had a decent body, was funny and obviously popular. He'd given her special attention all night. She liked that he was a bit older and spoke about goals and five-year plans and investment strategies and buying an apartment and travel. She'd been wanting to kiss him all night and would be happy to kiss him again. Wanted to do more than kiss. He gave her the giddy anticipation that came when you hoped someone might be more than a one-nighter.

And this was only a game. It didn't matter which kiss was better.

She glanced around quickly.

Brett. Michael. Kurt. Noah. Guys she worked with regularly. They were all watching her, whooping and urging her to hurry up. Behind them someone she knew only in passing. One of the management trainees, for whom hospitality was more than a part-time gig. These members of staff dipped their hand into every department of the hotel, learning all aspects of the business from housekeeping to functions to staff management. She remembered his hair: dark brown and thick, neatly swept back from his face. He was tall, his stance steady and upright. A pale-blue collared shirt, open at the neck. Angular face, cheekbones and high-bridged nose. An intelligent face. His eyes held hers. A small upwards pull to his mouth as she considered him. Not smug or teasing. Simply acknowledging their connection and what had passed between them. Then one of the rowdier boys gave his shoulder a nudge, confirming what Remi had guessed. This guy was her number two.

She chose number one.

As she walked back to Simon he raised his hand, flipping the bird, his gaze not on her, but someone on the other side of the room. She glanced over her shoulder. Number two was glaring at Simon, hands deep in his pockets, a look of complete disdain on his face.

For a moment she was confused, had an uncomfortable sensation of being irrelevant to what had just happened. Then, as she turned back to Simon, he pushed up from the sofa and stepped forward, drawing her into his arms and kissing her with a possessiveness that sent their workmates into whoops and cheers.

She was the prize, and she didn't care.

CHAPTER NINE

Monday, 24 July 2023

'But I'm always so careful.' Remi sat forward and gripped the edge of the mechanic's wide, tidy desk. 'I can't believe I'd do that. I mean, I always read the label on the bowser thingy. Check every time.' Obviously, not *every* time. She'd made a stupid, stupid mistake. How much would this cost her?

'Don't beat yourself up. It happens all too often. People in a rush or have their mind on other things. And the unleaded petrol nozzle fits the diesel fuel tank, so, bingo. Wrong fuel.'

'How bad is it?'

'It's not good.' He scuffed his knuckles across his cheek. 'What happens is the petrol mixes with the diesel and creates a solvent. When the engine starts, it goes through the entire fuel system. Makes a mess of the filters, fuel pump, injectors, the fuel tank. I'll draw up a full quote for you.'

Remi covered her mouth with her fingertips. 'Ballpark?' she whispered.

'I'd rather wait till the lads have done a full assessment.'

'Are you talking hundreds?'

She watched him shake his head.

'Thousands?' Her throat tightened.

'I'm afraid so. But I should be able to give you an exact figure later today.'

How could she have done something so idiotic? Sure, she'd been distracted; being on a financial edge had that effect. But making such a mistake was not like her. She hadn't fallen that far apart. Yet. Okay, it had been well over a week since she'd read the poisonous reviews and there had been no new work. There'd been one query—a referral from a self-published client—which had resulted in a big fat zero. She'd been upfront with the author, explained the rather nasty campaign being waged against her and given her a list of other clients happy to vouch for her work. But the author had gone elsewhere. Remi didn't blame her. Whether people believed the reviews or not, no one wanted to take the risk or get involved with something so nasty.

For now, her only income came from Josephine's and Emerson's rent. Josephine was paid up until the middle of August, but Emerson was paying by the fortnight and was due to make a payment before the twenty-seventh. Not that she had a job, which was another worry at the back of Remi's mind.

Remi stood, thanking the mechanic as he walked her out.

'How far did you drive?' he asked. 'After you put in the petrol, how far did you go?'

'It's hard to say. I didn't drive much today. From Macquarie Street out to Woolies at Kingston. How far is that?'

'Ten k's.'

'Okay, and what's today? Monday?' Without work deadlines, keeping track of the days had become difficult. 'I didn't drive at all yesterday. On Saturday afternoon I did a quick trip to the paint shop. On Friday I drove out to Cambridge and back, then around the city. I filled up, I think, on the Monday afternoon before that. So, a week ago.' After Josephine and Emerson had moved in.

He folded his arms, rocked back on his heels. A man digesting a problem. 'You're saying you filled up a week ago before all that driving, and there's been no sign of trouble until today?'

'Yes. Getting to the supermarket was fine. Then it started making god-awful noises as I left to come home. Thick smoke from the exhaust and everything went kaput right before I got on the Outlet to come back into town.'

He gave a slow shake of his head, seeming unhappy with her answers. 'I'd have expected the engine to cook itself a little sooner. That's a fair bit of time, a fair few k's, to have petrol sloshing around a diesel fuel system.'

'I'm positive there's been no sign of anything wrong, not until today.'

'When you filled up, can you remember how much you put in? Did you top up or did you put in a full tank?'

She thought back. She remembered noticing the fuel gauge. She'd stopped at the first service station she'd found. 'Half a tank. It was nearly on empty, but I only filled it to half.'

'Right, so, if that was when the unleaded went in, it would've been almost ninety percent petrol in the mix. And you filled it yourself?'

'Yes.'

He dropped his hands to his hips, studied the floor for a moment before raising his eyes. A paternal worry was written across his face. 'Look. Don't take this the wrong way, but it all seems a bit odd. You don't have anyone who would want to, you know, do the wrong thing by you, do you?'

Not that question again. 'What do you mean?' Was he suggesting her car had been sabotaged? 'I thought you said the
wrong fuel caused the problem? Are you saying something else
happened? Something deliberate?'

'It's definitely the fuel. We tested the mix in the tank. But
if you're sure you filled the car a week ago and you've been
driving since then, it doesn't add up. I do know of an occasion
where the wrong fuel was added deliberately. A nasty situation
where a woman put petrol in her ex-husband's diesel Triton.
He loved that truck, and she set out to make a mess of it. It
worked too.'

'But how? Wouldn't he have noticed if she'd taken it?'

'Jerry can. Brought the petrol with her and did the deed at
night. The truck was unlocked, or she had a key. Can't remember. Anyway, she just opened the driver's door, flicked the lever
for the fuel cap and bingo.'

Something tight and sharp gripped Remi's throat. Despite
living in the inner city, she rarely remembered to lock the car
when she arrived home. She always parked behind the house,
out of sight of the main road, and her Subaru wasn't exactly a
bright shiny new vehicle. Even Emerson's little red car, which
was now parked next to hers, was newer—and better looked
after. Yesterday morning she'd seen Josephine and Emerson
out there, checking the oil, or washer fluid, or something under
the bonnet.

She put her hand on her stomach as nausea churned. This
couldn't be happening.

The mechanic registered her distress. 'It might not have been
a deliberate thing. Every situation of misfuelling is different.
Your Subaru might be tougher than most.'

'The woman who did that to her ex, how did they know she'd done it?'

He grimaced. 'Would you believe, she boasted about it to friends on Facebook.'

Her laugh was small and forced. 'Well, I can't see my ex-husband creeping about with a can of petrol. He wouldn't want to get his hands dirty. It would ruin his manicure. And we're on good terms.' Which was more than a slight stretch of the truth. But this couldn't have been Simon. His last visit had been nearly two weeks ago and she doubted he would still be in Hobart.

'Yeah, it's probably just one of those things then.'

Maybe it was. Ill-timed coincidence could make a person paranoid.

***

The rain held off, but the wind rushed down the side of the snow-topped mountain and sliced an icy path through the city streets. Remi hunched into her coat, hands fisted in her pockets, wishing she'd left the house with gloves and a hat. She would have to walk across the city, couldn't afford to flag a taxi or summon an Uber. The grid of one-way streets was compact, the central shopping and office area tightly circled by car yards and light industry, by larger furniture display stores and the city library. Buildings were mostly no higher than a few floors, heritage facades next to uninspired utilitarian commercial spaces. The central zone at least offered more charm, showing signs of Hobart's confidence with a shiny Myer, glossy chain stores glowing with light and tiny coffee boltholes jammed into unlikely places. Those dispensers of caffeinated joy lured her closer. But stopping was out of the question, despite the pinpricks of cold in her fingers. She couldn't afford the splurge.

When—if—Emerson paid her rent on Thursday, she'd be able to pay Simon. But there would be nothing left for the car. Pride had stopped Remi from asking, but she wondered what happened when she couldn't pay for the repairs. There would, at the very least, be the charge for towing the car back to her place. Her RACT membership had covered the cost of getting her to the mechanic, but she was sure that was as far as they went.

As she turned into the lower end of Macquarie Street the wind became more vicious. Paper wrappers and brittle leaves sped across the road and footpaths, a torn cardboard box whacking against her leg, then spinning away.

The day was foul. Exacerbating her misery. The more despondent she became, the more the idea of deliberate sabotage took hold. Did she have a stalker? Had she pissed off someone? Was this all a consequence of something from her past? Or was it about the present—somehow connected to letting strangers into her home? Was this about revenge or obsession or something else? What had she done for someone to justify such behaviour? She knew all too well there were people out there who saw the world through a dark lens and wanted to lash out.

Like Brittney.

When Remi landed the role on *Our Street*, Brittney had been thrilled. They'd thrown a party in their tiny apartment and drunk several bottles of cheap sparkling wine. Then Remi had moved to Sydney and been caught up in the frenzy of scripts and costumes, long days filming, events and socialising, and had little time for phone calls or emails or messages. But their friendship had held and after a year, Brittney had arrived, keen to try her luck in a different city. For six months they laughed, played and commiserated together, even if the dynamic had shifted. Now Remi was the one giving advice on what to wear to parties and events. She introduced Brittney to people in the industry and worked with her on preparing for the few auditions she landed. Then Simon had joined the exodus to Sydney and reclaimed Remi's attention. Her time spent with Brittney became less and they'd drifted apart again. It was Remi's fault, she should have been a better friend—a more considerate friend. Even now she was ashamed of how she'd let Brittney down. In all the years since, she'd never had anyone like Brittney in her life, had never again had the sweetness and solidarity of true female friendship.

Two years after she arrived, Brittney had still been trying to get established. She'd done some stage performances, had a few small parts and a year of drama study on her resume. Exhausted and despondent after repeated rejections, she had auditioned for a lead role in Connor Mallick's new limited series. She'd received two call-backs and was waiting with increasing optimism that *this* would be her big break. Afterwards—long after Remi had healed—she'd heard from Brittney's flatmate that Brittney hadn't slept more than seven hours in three days when she'd seen the pictures of Remi and Connor. The rumour about them had begun a couple of weeks earlier, but here was so-called evidence. The accompanying lines of text reported that an 'anonymous hotel staff member' had seen the two of them getting intimate before heading up to Connor's room. The dark, blurry pictures of them saying goodbye outside the hotel had sent Brittney into a fury.

That night Brittney had followed Remi as she walked home from the gym and had shoved the offensive magazine in her face, spitting out a barrage of condemnations: this was *her* role and no trashy TV whore was going to fuck her way into the job. Their friendship was dead, she'd screamed, accusing Remi of using people and then dumping them. Remi had tried to reason with her, to explain there was nothing going on with Connor, the rumours weren't true, were lies that had already brought her relationship with Simon to an end. He had believed the gossip too. Remi had tried to leave, walking away in the hope Brittney would give up.

Which was when the steel picket came into play. Remi had no idea where the weapon had come from—perhaps yanked from a nearby garden—but that detail was irrelevant. The first strike knocked her to the ground, surprise countering any fear for the first few seconds. Until the second blow, and then Brittney was crouching down to hiss at her, 'You can't play dirty and not get taken down.' Remi didn't keep count of the number of times she was hit. She did remember when it stopped, remembered hearing Brittney crying and swearing, then calling the ambulance. 'I'm sorry, I'm sorry, I'm sorry,' she'd sobbed in the moment before she ran.

Some people did things for reasons that made sense only to them, which made those people unpredictable, illogical and dangerous. Was what happened all those years ago somehow connected to what was happening now? She couldn't see how. What had followed for Brittney had been terrible and Remi had never seen her again.

As she waited to cross at the lights, a new fear slid into Remi's mind: *What next?*

By the time she reached the house, every step required effort. The mountain loomed in the distance, blurred by low, dark cloud. An ominous hulk pressing down on the city, squeezing any joy from the streets. Her home, at least, looked welcoming. The windows of the ground floor shining a soft gold against the dead grey of the day, promising warmth and comfort. Inside a bath and a hot meal awaited. A glass of wine. Or the whole bottle. She stepped through the gate, stopping as she reached the front door, preparing herself to enter. She was filled with weariness at the thought of listening to Emerson's prattle or pretending everything was okay under Josephine's perceptive gaze. She didn't want to be with these people—these strangers. She wanted to be alone, wanted to give in to the weight of her fears, to cry and wallow, and drown her misery in a steady procession of strong drinks. Conversation was beyond her and she didn't have the strength to be anything other than miserable. She wanted her home to herself goddammit. Not filled with these women who, let's face it, could be complicit in the damage being inflicted on her. It was a scenario she couldn't rule out.

She fumbled through her bag for her key, remembering, after a minute, that the house key lived with her car keys. Which were with the mechanic.

For fuck's sake, she couldn't even get into her own home. She banged the knocker.

Josephine opened the door, dressed in her new uniform of hiking pants and polar fleece, thick socks on her feet. Her smile was warm. 'Did you forget your key?'

Remi scowled. 'It's on the keyring with my car keys, which are in the hands of a mechanic.' She stepped inside and stopped to struggle out of her shoes.

'Car trouble?'

'Broke down on the way back from Woolies. Had to be towed.' She intended to keep the story to the bare basics.

Josephine walked ahead of her through to the kitchen. 'You poor thing. How inconvenient. Had you done a shop? What did you do with the bags?'

Remi stopped, her hard-edged laugh making Josephine turn to look.

'I forgot them. I forgot the groceries. They are still in the back of the car.' Two hundred dollars' worth of shopping. Meat. Milk. That extra special little tub of Maggie Beer ice cream she'd allowed herself. Which would by now be a soggy puddle of burnt fig and honeycomb. What a stupid, stupid waste. Money thrown away. And she couldn't afford a taxi to go back.

'Where's the mechanic?' Josephine switched on the coffee machine and expertly packed the grounds. 'Latte?'

'Sure.' Remi considered heading straight to her room but sank onto a stool. 'Patrick Street.'

'That's right in town?'

Remi managed to nod as the machine rumbled into life. One noisy minute later a tall, milky coffee was slid in front of Remi. She wrapped her hands around the cup, the warmth thawing her aching hands, giving some small comfort.

'Back in a minute,' said Josephine, heading down to the basement.

Emerson had come home the day before, struggling with a cheap trestle table and two desk lights, raving about the amazing world of hardware stores, entranced by the fact she could buy furniture and lights and trees and rugs. 'They have everything. Not just, you know, hammers and stuff. They've got all the basics covered.'

Remi, who was on intimate terms with hardware stores (and paint shops and plumbing suppliers and flooring showrooms) had held back a sarcastic remark. 'Wait till you actually need hammers and nails and drill sets, then you'll get really excited,' she'd said with a forced smile.

When Remi saw Emerson setting up the table in her bedroom, she'd suggested she use the basement. Her own desk didn't take up much space and she wasn't doing any recording any time soon.

'Really? Are you sure?' Emerson had asked.

'Well, there are no overhead light fixtures yet, and no heating. No window treatments.'

'But I can plug in a desk light?'

'Sure, but you'll find it a bit cold.'

'What about a portable heater? Would that be alright? If I bought what I needed, could I set up down there?'

Remi was already regretting the offer. More of her house was about to be taken over. Already the kitchen had changed, her fridge full of food that wasn't hers. Coconut yoghurt and kombucha for Emerson and half-empty takeaway tubs from Josephine. A large glass jar of homemade biscuits sat on the counter, a note taped to the side giving details of the latest creation and saying, *Please eat!* Sure it was a lovely touch, but it contributed to the changed feel of Remi's space. Her piles of magazines and notes, which had once dominated the kitchen table, now took up space on the narrow side table against the wall, making room for a large, lush houseplant. The green of living foliage repeated with little pots on the island bench and the windowsill. They looked good. But that wasn't the point. She would've added these touches herself. Eventually. That one of her housemates introduced them so quickly felt like a subtle critique of what the home lacked.

Sketch pads and pens were also on the table alongside a neat stack of Kathmandu catalogues, laminated fold-out maps and books on Tasmania's walks. There was a new pair of fancy-looking hiking boots at the back door and coats on the rack. The house smelled different. Unfamiliar cooking and baking, scented steam from the bathroom, the waft of perfume and hair product and deodorant. Every day there was noise: conversations and laughter between the other women, music, doors opening and closing, footsteps on the stairs and bangs in the kitchen. Nothing too loud, but still present. The alliance between Josephine and Emerson didn't include Remi, a situation which was adding to her wariness. None of these things on their own was enough to warrant the itch of unease, but together they made the change to her life—to her day-to-day living—more profound.

Now, at her own suggestion, this loss of her space would continue.

She was being ridiculous, she knew. The basement was barely being used. What the hell did it matter if Emerson wanted to brave the chill down there and set up a table?

'Go for it,' she'd said, hiding her disquiet. 'But please make sure you turn the heaters off when you leave.'

Emerson had attacked this project with her usual exuberance, a state of excitement and energy Remi had come to realise was her default position.

Josephine came back into the kitchen, headed to the side table and retrieved a set of keys from the large ceramic bowl which held everything from rubber bands to receipts.

'I'm taking Em's car. If you phone the mechanic and let them know I'll be calling in, I'll collect your shopping.'

Remi stared at her. 'You don't have to do that.'

Josephine was already pulling on her black puffer jacket. 'It's fine. I'm not doing anything. And you've had a rubbish day. You look like you need warming up and a rest.'

It had not occurred to Remi to ask for help. Yet here was Josephine to the rescue again. Which made her feel both guilty for her negativity, and humiliated that she needed this support. 'Thank you.' She stood up. 'I can come with you.'

'I'm right. You get warm and put on your comfiest trackie daks.' Josephine stepped out the back door, then stuck her head back in. 'Don't forget to call them. I don't want to be nabbed for trying to steal your cornflakes.'

Remi watched as the car headed down the driveway, Josephine was being kind, she told herself, she should be grateful. Instead she felt useless and indebted and suspicious.

CHAPTER TEN

Tuesday, 25 July 2023

It was eleven in the morning and there was no point in getting out of bed. Remi pulled the doona higher and curled herself around a squishy pillow. There were no client deadlines. No manuscripts to read and mark up. No jobs to do on the house that didn't require spending money.

Josephine was probably out. She'd taken to marching up the mountain on the days the weather allowed and wandering the streets on others.

Emerson, in the meantime, would be busy in her space down below. Yes, her space. The basement was well and truly an Emerson zone now, the blank canvas of the huge room transformed by all the extra details flamboyant people seemed to need. Two cheap, brightly coloured rugs on the stone floor. A small, frayed armchair she'd found at the tip shop, draped with textured throw rugs and cushions. More pot plants. Several large pinboards leaning against a wall, bright pins holding sketches, paintings, pages ripped from magazines, artsy postcards and prints of Hobart scenes. Two desk lights on her table, a multitude of jars filled with specialised pens and pencils, and a stack of large sketch pads. Even an expensive-looking drawing tablet. There were piles of trendy magazines on an upturned milk crate and a small speaker to stream her music. Over the back of her work chair, a hot-pink fluffy blanket for when the heaters struggled to warm the room.

Remi rolled over, unfurled her legs, pulled them back, rearranged the pillow under her head. She wanted to sleep, if only to reduce the length of her day. Because she had only one task on her to-do list. One she didn't want to face.

Late yesterday afternoon, her car had been returned. When the mechanic told her how many thousands it would cost to fix, she'd organised a tow truck. Repairs were an impossibility. Even transporting her car back to the house took a huge chunk of the money earmarked for Simon. Now she didn't have enough. Again.

She had no real choice, either beg or borrow: beg Simon to take what she had and let her make up the difference later or choke down her dented pride to ask for a loan. She knew her parents wouldn't help. To ask them for money would be to ask for a terse lecture on giving up, failing and her general lack of resilience. Sins made worse because of *the great and costly sacrifices we made to support your acting dreams*. Jane Lucans was a bitterly disappointed stage mother, who had parked her hopes and aspirations on her daughter's wagon and did not forgive the crashing of those dreams. The marriage into money had gone some way to healing the rift. Unfortunately, Remi had thrown that away, too.

Which left Luke who, she knew, would say yes. But Remi despised herself for having to ask. One of the best things about leaving Simon had been rediscovering her independence. Before that, the last time she'd been in full control of her life had been her first year in Sydney: 2006. The year before Simon reappeared and insinuated himself back into her heart and before the trauma of the attack had rendered her so desperate and broken. Achieving what she had with this house had been exhilarating and her confidence had been boosted. Being back in a position of need was demoralising and humiliating.

It was close to twelve by the time Remi dragged herself to the shower. Another thirty minutes before she shuffled into the blissfully empty kitchen. There were dirty dishes in the sink and the faint sound of music drifted up from the basement. Josephine's hiking boots weren't in their place by the door and Emerson's car was missing. The two women seemed to have come to an arrangement, Emerson lending her wheels to Josephine when she didn't need them. Another sign of their growing bond.

Remi should be glad. She *was* glad. Better than having housemates who irritated or disrespected each other. But their friendliness irked. She felt excluded. Which was stupid. Nobody was cutting her out. Josephine had been a lifesaver yesterday and even the ice cream had survived. On her first day in the house, as Remi fell apart, Josephine had been calm and clever. Emerson baked. Josephine cleaned. They both talked to her but had the manners not to intrude when she retreated to her room—which was often. The only person excluding Remi was, well, Remi.

Which was pathetic. But people—and friendships—were so damn hard, and her growing paranoia wasn't helping.

Remi yanked opened the fridge door then stood for two full minutes, unable to decide. She was hungry and a little seedy.

Last night she'd washed away the mental grime of the day with a bottle of wine. The whole bottle—about three glasses more than she'd normally consume.

She shut the fridge with enough force to make the bottles and jars rattle. She needed hot, greasy, salty food. She grabbed her bag and coat, making sure the key was in her pocket as she pulled the door behind her. She was going to treat herself to a decent lunch. Guilt and self-recrimination could wait until she felt human.

***

Hobart was showing off with one of its perfect winter days as though making up for the miserable weather of yesterday. Huge blue sky, a nearly warm sun and the smallest of nippy breezes. The exertion of walking down to the waterfront helped lift Remi's mood, not to the point of optimism, but at least to a quiet resignation for today's task. There was no avoiding it. If she didn't pay Simon on time, he would sell the house.

She'd gird herself with starchy carbs, then ring Luke.

She wandered into Fish Frenzy and ordered, taking a seat at the window. Yachts floated in neat rows on the black water. Clusters of seagulls watched proceedings from atop light poles and bench seats. Rugged-up tourists drifted along the docks, stepping on and off the red double-decker sightseeing bus or boarding the MONA Roma, the catamaran ferry that ran up the river to the Museum of Old and New Art. The air was biting fresh, the sounds of the city muted down here, near the water.

The large paper cone of crumbed fish and fat chips arrived promptly at her table, delivering the warm, deep-fried food hug she needed. She ate without hurry, washing her meal down with a tangy ginger beer. When she'd finished, she wiped the salt and grease from her fingers and walked back out onto the dock. She found a quiet, isolated bench near the edge, away from people. Phone in hand, she prepared words in her head, trying to phrase her request in a way that didn't make her sound presumptuous or demanding. Or like she was pleading for a handout. Which she was. Maybe not a handout, but a loan. Which she would pay back. Somehow, one day.

'Remi?'

She lifted her head, looked around, disorientated by the unexpected interruption. Fuck. An impeccable figure strode towards her. Layers of cashmere over skin-tight black pants, heeled boots, the strap of a red leather bag across her body and a swathe of saccharine blonde hair falling over her shoulders, held back by large sunglasses pushed up to the top of her head. A look of forced friendliness on her face.

'Kayla. Hello.' Remi stood, aware of being shapeless and shabby, her parka jacket practical and unflattering, her runners adorned with paint and dust. She wore no make-up and hadn't brushed her hair. Knew her face would show the puffy, grimy signs of a boozy night and bad sleep. None of which should matter, except it absolutely did. Being confronted by her ex-husband's new wife was horrendous enough but the disparity in their appearances made Remi want to run away. Why today of all days? She wasn't hung up on her looks, hadn't put much effort into her appearance for years, but standing next to this polished, preened woman left her feeling inadequate.

'I thought that was you.' Kayla stopped, a flick of her eyes assessing Remi. 'I didn't want to be rude and not say hello.'

Remi could count on one hand the number of past inter-
actions between them, none of which had held any ease or
warmth. Simon had always been present and had done the
talking. Once the two women had crossed paths in the toilets
of the solicitor's office. Remi, taking the high road, had com-
plimented Kayla's shoes. Kayla had made a few snide comments on the generosity of the settlement.

If Kayla had ignored Remi and kept walking today, the rude-
ness would've been welcomed.

'What are you doing here? Is Simon with you?' If he was
planning another unannounced visit to her door, Remi wanted
to know.

'I'm here on my own, on business. I'm still considering our
options for opening a shop down here.'

'Okay.'

There was an uncomfortable pause before Kayla continued.
'Simon says you haven't been taking his calls.'

She hadn't. Being lectured on her financial circumstances,
life choices and the benefits of selling was a long, long way
down her list of desired conversations. 'Well, that's between
me and Simon.' Although she had no doubt Kayla knew all the
details. 'There's nothing to discuss. He's already made himself
clear.'

'Hmm.' Kayla placed a hand over her flat stomach. 'He
also wanted to let you know. We're having a baby.' She smiled
benignly as though she was the clever, yet humble, winner of
a glorious prize.

The news hit Remi with a smack. 'Oh.' What the hell? A
baby? Simon didn't want children. Together they'd agreed par-
enthood wasn't for them.

'I'm sure this is a shock. Or not. You must've known how desperately Simon wanted to be a father.'

'No. He was always adamant he didn't want kids.'

'Really? That's not how he's been with me. Maybe he told you that because he knew you lacked a maternal streak.'

Remi tried to remember the conversations they'd had. What had been said, and by whom. Tried to grasp what her feelings were before Simon had declared his opposition to being a parent. Because he'd said it first. Of that, she was sure.

'Well, congratulations.' The words were hollow.

'Thank you.'

Normally a cascade of questions would follow such an announcement. When are you due? How are you feeling? Morning sickness? Boy or girl? But it wasn't a conversation she could be bothered faking. Instead, she gathered up her bag and made to leave. 'I hope it all goes well for you.'

Kayla blocked her escape. 'Did you read Simon's email? With the valuation for the house?'

'I read it.' Two point three. Million. More than enough to pay out Simon and buy herself a compact, generic apartment.

'I don't think you understand how difficult this situation is for us.' Kayla's big eyes fixed on her with a troubled look, a tiny pucker fluttering between her handcrafted eyebrows. 'We are, in effect, carrying your debt. Selling the house would finally release Simon from supporting you.'

'Supporting me?' Was that how Simon saw it? 'He's not supporting me. We have a loan arrangement. I am repaying that loan.'

'I told him,' Kayla continued, not paying any attention to Remi's response, 'when the settlement and agreements were being drawn up, that he was being too generous. That offering to finance your debt would only result in you maintaining a dependent relationship with him. And it has, hasn't it? You have only been able to continue with your obsession with renovating that house—a process you can't afford by the way—because of Simon's support. Don't you think that's just a bit unfair?'

What the hell? Seriously? *Unfair?* There was nothing unfair about the arrangement. At the time of settlement, they'd held significant assets. The house in Macquarie Street, of course. Plus the apartment in Sydney, a shares portfolio, two cars—her Subaru and his Porsche Cayenne. The split had not been fifty-fifty. Not even seventy-thirty. She hadn't asked for nor wanted more. All she'd wanted was to keep the house she loved and a chance to see her vision come to life. Simon wasn't completely stupid—not when it came to his own interests. Recognising her emotional attachment, he'd made a low-ball settlement offer: five hundred thousand and her old car. Not a pittance, but a long way from generous. In exchange for accepting the offer without fuss, he *let* her buy out his half of the house, providing her with an arrangement to do so.

'I will not discuss this with you,' Remi said. Her heart rate had kicked up a notch as her anger unfurled. Was this woman wanting to make her feel guilty over a financial arrangement? Where did she get off lecturing Remi?

'Why not? I'm Simon's wife. His business is my business. We're a fully united team.'

'Good for you.' What a self-righteous bitch. 'Then I'm sure he told you what I've already said. I am not selling the house. And I'm tired of repeating myself. He will get his money as per the terms of the agreement.'

'Really? How's that going for you? Isn't a payment due, um, *tomorrow*?' Kayla's eyebrows rose, punctuating the sarcasm in her voice. 'Because you're one default away from a forced sale. And I don't see you pulling in much of an income.' She looked Remi over, from her grubby hair to her battered sneakers.

'I'm doing fine.'

Kayla's eyes widened, the tilt of her head expressing her snarky disbelief.

'Not that it's any of your business. But the house is paying for itself,' Remi said, needing to defend her position. 'And I have my work. Despite someone's best efforts to undermine me, I will still get jobs.'

'Undermine you? Why would anyone do that? Who on earth would care about taking down someone who records herself reading books?'

'Well, someone has. I was targeted by someone who wants me to fail.'

'Wow. I mean, just, wow.' Kayla slowly shook her head. 'You might want to dial back on the paranoia. Do you really think there is anyone who cares enough to want you to fail?'

'Thanks, Kayla. This has been lovely.'

She turned to leave, but Kayla kept talking. 'You're, what, almost forty? And you're living in a share house.' Her laugh was short and nasty. 'Hardly screams personal success or a financially stable future, does it?'

'I don't give a shit what you think of me.' She didn't. Even though the words stung.

'Yes, you do. I'm younger. I've got Simon. I'm pregnant. I'm successful.' She raised her left hand and pushed back a strand of hair, her spectacular engagement ring sparkling in the weak sunlight. Remi had once worn a ring like that, one that flashed and glittered and had made her self-conscious.

'You post pictures of yourself on Instagram,' Remi interrupted, snapping out her words with all the scorn she felt.

'Oh, you poor old thing.' Kayla was unflappable. 'Don't you know that's where the power is these days? Social media is marketing. It's a part of business. Social media creates businesses. Of course, you must have an eye for style and styling. For curating the images. For colour palette and story. For creating a brand. You need to have a life worth showing, an understanding of what others desire. Before they even know themselves.' She lifted her hand, flipped it from one side to the other, her tone and gesture full of self-importance and superiority, as though giving a dumbed-down explanation to someone inferior.

Enough. Remi couldn't listen to another word. 'You can let Simon know his payment will be through by the end of the week.'

'Why do you put yourself through this?'

'Through what?'

'The struggle. Take my advice. Sell the house and you'll have a nice little sum to sort yourself out. No more struggling. Wouldn't that be lovely? You've achieved what you wanted. The house is finished. More or less. Through sheer luck you'll have made a decent profit. Move on to something else.'

Remi leaned forward, putting her face close to the tight, smooth skin of her ex's wife. 'Take your advice and shove it.' She pulled back. 'Why do you even care about this? You've got your new empire. Go and worry about that.'

A flicker crossed Kayla's face. A flinch. But the moment passed too quickly for Remi to read her.

'Here's the thing, Remi.' Kayla spoke with emphasis. 'I don't care what you do. But we won't continue to carry you. Stop leaning on Simon. Get the hell out of his life. Completely and for good.' She turned then, satisfied with having the last word, and sashayed down the docks as though she were a celebrity parading through an awestruck crowd.

Remi could only watch her leave, a roar of retaliation trapped in her head. The woman was a fake-faced, delusional, egotistical, evil bitch. Remi was not leaning on Simon. She wasn't in his life and didn't want to be. It wasn't like that. Their only interaction was financial. That was all.

She sank onto the bench, letting her head rest on the back of the seat. Despair dampened her anger as quickly as it had risen. Kayla was right. Oh god, even thinking it hurt. To admit that, yes, she was struggling. And worse, others could see how useless and pitiful she'd become. She didn't envy Kayla her life, or her manufactured gloss and glamour, or even the glittering rock on her finger. She'd once had all of that—in fact, she still had her ring in a box at the back of a drawer somewhere.

What she wanted was to be seen differently. For people to be impressed by what she achieved. To be recognised as resilient. To be judged as talented and tenacious. To have something to be proud of. But all she had was a whole lot of *almost* and a whole lot of *fail*. Her acting career had almost been great. Three years on the show before the incident, before she ran away like a frightened kid. She'd applied herself to learning how to do voice over and narration, recording and editing, and she was more than competent, almost good. Now that had failed. Her marriage had failed. She'd kept the house but failed to manage her money. She'd almost finished the renovation but she'd failed to complete the work. She was one of those people: full of big ideas, but lacking what it took to really achieve anything.

Self-loathing poured through Remi like lead, heavy and dull. Her whole body pulled towards the ground. She longed to lie down right here on this bench and shut out the world. Getting up and walking home was too hard.

She didn't want to end her life, she just wanted to get away from herself for a time.

When she felt her phone vibrate, she didn't respond, too sluggish to answer. When it rang twice more, she pulled it from her pocket. Luke. She hesitated before putting the screen face down on her thigh, too exhausted to speak to even him.

She pushed herself to standing and began to walk.

CHAPTER ELEVEN

It took Remi twice as long to walk home as it had to reach the docks. The slight incline had somehow become a massive hill, and full-body weariness was making every step hard work. She trudged along Macquarie Street without any sense of delight at coming home, wanting only to sink further into her self-pity and resentment for the rest of the day.

She let herself into the house quietly, listening for the presence of the other women. From the kitchen she could hear someone talking softly, the lack of response indicating they were on the phone. They didn't seem to have heard her, so Remi scurried up the stairs to avoid any sort of interaction. She slipped into her room and closed the door, shucking off her shoes, pants and jacket. Wearing knickers and t-shirt, she climbed into bed, then changed her mind, realising she should at least wee and wash off some of the grime before she slept.

In the ensuite she used the toilet, then filled the sink with warm water and scrubbed her face. She was drying herself when she noticed the candle. It was one of her favourites. Sitting on the bench next to her hairbrush. But what was it doing here? She never put candles in her ensuite. Sometimes she'd have one in the main bathroom if she was having a bath, but never in here. She picked it up. Hadn't this been in the kitchen? She'd left it on the sideboard, she was sure of it.

Had someone moved it? Had one of her housemates been in her room?

She'd never specified her room was off limits, but surely that was a given? She certainly hadn't been into the other bedrooms since the tenants had arrived. Why would Josephine or Emerson move a candle to her bathroom? What had they been doing in here?

She walked back into the bedroom, setting the candle on the bedside table. Was there anything else out of place? The pile of not-quite-clean, not-quite-dirty clothes was still draped over the armchair in the corner. The doors to the built-in wardrobe were half-open, but that was normal. She moved around the room, trying to determine if anything else was out of place. There was nothing obvious, and after a few minutes she sat on the edge of her bed, staring at the candle. Had she brought it up here? She was distracted, stressed and tired. She could've been distracted, mindless in her actions.

Groaning, she flopped back into the pillows and lay staring at the ceiling, waiting for answers to magically appear. Nothing. She pulled her legs up and pushed them under the covers, then wormed her way deeper into her bed. She needed to rest, to clear her churning mind. Everything else could wait.

Sleep pulled her under, a thought flickering at the edges of her mind in the moments before it went quiet. A picture of Kayla's hand raised, ring glittering. Remi's engagement ring had also been worth thousands. Why hadn't she sold it yet?

By the time she woke, the light had drained from the day. The long nap had left her befuddled and disorientated. She stayed in bed, waiting for her body to come to life, for the fogginess in her brain to clear. By the time she hauled herself upright, her stomach was loudly demanding food.

As soon as Remi opened her bedroom door, the sounds of her housemates drifted up from the kitchen. For a moment she thought about retreating. The longer she locked herself away, the harder it was to emerge. But she couldn't avoid interaction forever. For a start, whatever they were making smelled amazing—she was practically drooling. She hitched up her pants. She was now wearing her favourite comfort wear, an oversized sweatshirt and baggy tracksuit bottoms. They weren't cute casual, she looked like a potato—one that had been left at the back of the pantry for far too long. Her bed socks made her feet scuff along the floor and her hair still needed a wash. She looked exactly how she felt: lumpy and faded.

Whatever. She wasn't a TV star or the wife of an affluent man. She was a nothing. And, yes, she knew that was a self-defeating label. Too bad. She'd work on her attitude another day. Today, she was a grumpy, scruffy recluse.

'Hello,' Emerson said the minute Remi entered the kitchen, immediately ending the quiet conversation she'd been having with Josephine. She was like a bright blinding light after living in the dark. Too much. 'I've made a vegetarian lasagne. And herby, cheesy garlic bread. It's almost ready. Are you hungry?'

Josephine turned and gave Remi a smile. She was perched on a stool, her hair wet from a shower, a glass of red in hand. 'And I bought some wine.' She made a tiny *oof* sound as she stood. 'You look like you could use a glass.' She took one from the cupboard and filled it.

Remi nodded. The warmth of the room and the scene of comfort and camaraderie had her wanting to both escape back to her room and to shuffle into the fray. She couldn't decide. 'Um, yes, thanks,' she finally said, the need for food winning out. 'Yes to both.' She took the wine from Josephine, hesitating for a moment before following her to the island bench. For a second she considered asking about the candle in her room, but she didn't have the energy for that conversation. She would wait and ask the women separately.

The guitar playlist in the background was gentle and joyful. Emerson opened the oven, plucked out two silver-wrapped lengths of bread, dropped them on the bench, then lifted out a large baking dish, the top of the lasagne brown and bubbly. She set it down on a wooden board in front of Josephine and Remi.

'Well, it looks good,' she said. 'Let's see how it tastes.'

'It looks and smells amazing,' said Josephine. 'And, I have to say, it's rather splendid being looked after like this.'

Emerson laughed. 'Josephine took herself to the top of the mountain today,' she explained to Remi. 'From bottom to top and back again.'

'Firstly.' Josephine held up a hand. 'I didn't set out from the bottom. I walked from the Springs. Secondly, I took the easiest route.'

'Details.' Emerson waved her away. 'Thing is, you spent five hours getting to the top and coming back down. That is an impressive effort. I couldn't do it. Have you done it?' she asked Remi.

'No. I haven't.' Why hadn't she? The mountain was right there and she used to like walking. 'I don't do anything remotely adventurous.' Which was true. She barely left Hobart and had seen little of the island, despite vague ideas of visiting the Tarkine or Bicheno or Maria Island. 'Since I've been in

Tassie, the most physical thing I've done is ripping the guts out of this place.'

'With a sledgehammer?' Emerson looked excited.

'Sometimes.' Despite herself, Remi felt herself responding to Emerson's interest and enthusiasm. 'And a regular hammer. And a crowbar. And my hands.'

Emerson passed out plates laden with gooey pasta and chunks of steaming bread. 'You know, when I've watched those renovation reality shows, I've always thought the demolition looked like the best fun. Did you wear a sexy hard hat?'

Remi bit into her garlic bread, crisp flakes falling to the bench. She shook her head. 'No hat. But I have a tool belt.' She got the words out before she took another bite. 'This is so good.' She made involuntary noises of contentment as she chewed. 'How are your legs?' she asked Josephine, pushing herself to make more of an effort.

'Well, I'm stiff and shaky all at the same time, if that's possible. And sore. The muscles of my bum hurt. My thighs won't stop trembling. And getting up and down is a slow, uncomfortable process. I think I'll sleep well tonight.'

'Cheers to you,' Emerson said, holding up her glass. 'Here's to Josephine tackling the mountain and winning.'

Remi raised her glass, then took a long sip. 'Have you hiked much before?'

'Nope. Not at all. Not until two weeks ago.'

'You just saw that mountain and something compelled you to tackle it?' Emerson asked.

Josephine set down her fork and rested her elbows on the table, her chin on her clasped hands. 'I had to do something big. It was that or go a little crazy.'

'Why? Are you okay?' Remi asked, conscious of how little effort she'd made getting to know her housemates.

There was a long pause before Josephine answered. 'My son Sam is travelling. He was in London, today he lands in Thailand. I worry about him. A lot. Obsessively, even. I can't seem to relax.'

'His girlfriend is with him. She's new on the scene.' Emerson filled in some details, obviously having already heard this story. She had different glasses on tonight, the large white frames making her eyes even more dramatic.

'What do you worry about exactly?' Remi asked. Focusing on someone else was actually a good distraction.

Josephine sipped her wine. Picked up her fork, set it down again. 'I worry about him making bad choices. About the consequences of those choices,' she said, sounding weary.

'Has he made some bad calls in the past?' asked Emerson. 'I mean, how old is he?'

'Nineteen.'

'Right, so he's a fully-fledged adult. Is there a reason to worry about what he might do?' There was no judgement, only curiosity. Emerson would see the situation through a different lens, thought Remi. Only a few years older than Josephine's son, she'd be wondering what there was to fret over.

Josephine gave a light laugh, seeming to recognise her unnecessary protectiveness. 'He's a great kid. A few experimental missteps, but mostly on the straight and narrow. He's happy to stick his hand up to be designated driver. Always has his phone charged and a spare fifty tucked away in case his debit card doesn't work. He told me smoking pot was nice, but he didn't like being sleepy and boring.'

'Sounds like he's very sensible and careful,' said Emerson.

'After the lectures he got from me, he could've gone either two ways: take it all on board or rebel like crazy. Luckily, he wasn't particularly rebellious. And he's not new to travelling. He flew on his own for the first time when he was sixteen. To London. That's where his father lives.'

'So you trust him,' Emerson said with emphasis. 'He sounds like a good guy. Why the worry?'

Josephine huffed out a sigh. 'Because of coward punches. And spiked drinks. And because good people end up in the wrong place at the wrong time. Because there are plenty of dickheads out there who aren't smart. And because even the most sensible people can make the wrong choice, with disastrous consequences.' She said the last bit with a sad intensity.

'You sound like you know about wrong choices,' Remi commented without thinking, realising, as she spoke, she might be wading into a sensitive part of Josephine's life. Did she really want to delve any deeper? This was how friends talked. Or how friendships were made. By sharing the past, digging in beneath superficial pleasantries. She didn't want or need to go there. Polite, superficial conversation was one thing; deep and meaningful and personal was something else. She didn't have the emotional space to take on other people's angst. 'Sorry. That's personal. You don't have to explain.' Remi tried to pull the conversation back. 'This lasagne is delicious.'

A knock at the front door interrupted any more revelations. Before Remi could even lay down her fork, Emerson had jumped up. 'I'll get it,' she said as she trotted down the hall.

Remi ducked her head, an irrational fury at this takeover of such a simple task making her mouth tighten again. This was *her* home!

'Hi. Hello.' Emerson's greeting was enthusiastic. Followed by a deeper, distinctly male voice in response.

'Luke!' Remi looked up as her friend stepped into the kitchen. She stood and moved into his embrace. He squeezed her hard, then kissed her on the cheek. 'What are you doing here?'

'I told you I had to come down.' His presence warmed her and she didn't even care she was a shabby, unshowered mess.

'Hi, I'm Emerson.' Before Remi could make introductions, Emerson was shaking Luke's hand.

'Luke Darlby. That smells good.'

'And this is Josephine,' Remi said as Josephine stood.

'Hello,' they said as they shook.

'Are you the Luke Darlby from Strike Hotels?' Josephine asked.

'Actually, yes.' Luke didn't mind being recognised. 'Have you stayed with us?'

'Twice. And I saw you speak at an Australian Entrepreneurs event two years ago.'

'The one in Brisbane? Hopefully I said something of some worth.'

'You did. I remember you being adamant that business expansion should only be built on a solid foundation.'

'Indeed. A mistake too many make.'

Josephine gave a polite smile, nodding in agreement. 'It was a good talk. Not applicable to me at that point, but worth listening to.'

'Glad to hear it. And there's nothing wrong with maintaining a solid small business. Expanding isn't the right path for everyone. Nor the best measure of success.'

Josephine raised her eyebrows, a twitch of bemusement on her face. Remi had the distinct impression Josephine was refraining from further comment.

Remi offered Luke a glass of wine and he joined them at the table, turning down the offer of the last piece of lasagne. There had been people in Remi's kitchen before, but a morning tea with biscuits from a packet for the tradies was different from this. Was this what the house had been craving? Movement and babble and energy? No. An evening of interaction was fine, but she longed for the return of her solitude. It would be better if these women weren't here.

Within minutes the conversation was flowing. Emerson asked Luke about his hotels, saying that while she had yet to stay at any of them, she did love exquisite destinations and luxury resorts. Remi cringed when the younger woman began enthusiastically describing other hotels, but Luke appeared fully engaged, asking for her opinion on facilities, décor, and ambience. After a discussion about the merits of in-house spa treatments, Luke shifted the focus to Remi's flatmates. When he asked Emerson about her graphic design she lit up.

'May I see some of your work?' Luke asked Emerson after the table had been cleared and they'd all had another glass of wine.

'Absolutely. Hold on.' Emerson dashed off to her room, returning with her large black folio and a flipbook. She slipped out some sheets of thick paper, spreading the artworks on the table. 'I like to try different styles, but generally there's a whimsical, loose but edgy feel to what I do. And you can see I do a lot of free-form font work.' She opened the flipbook, turning the pages. 'Here's some of the stuff that's been used. This was a campaign for a folk festival. This was an invitation to a launch for a new organic food line. These are some of the pages from *Wisdom*, the magazine I worked with.'

Even though the women had seen some of Emerson's work, they all gathered around.

Josephine picked up one of the pages, admiring the stylised flowers and leaves that wove together, a woman centred among the riot of foliage. 'I really like this.'

'Thanks. I've always drawn. Art was about the only subject I did well in at school. Well, that and drama. But art was the bigger passion. I did a course at a private college, which helped me figure out my personal style. Then I got lucky. Word of mouth. And social media, of course. But things can change.' Emerson sank into her chair. 'Like *Wisdom* wrapping up.'

'It was a good magazine,' Luke said. 'They featured our Melbourne hotel when it first opened and we advertised with them regularly. I was sorry to see the run end.'

'Not more than me.' Emerson rested her chin on her hand. 'It's put a serious hole in my finances.'

'I'm sure you'll find some work,' Remi said. If Emerson was as cash poor as she said, she might not be able to afford rent. She also shouldn't be stocking the kitchen with baking tins and ingredients and whipping up extravagant cakes.

Luke was quiet, flicking through the pages, considering each piece of work. When he'd finished, he closed the book and sat, legs crossed, wine in hand. 'Are you free the day after tomorrow?' he asked Emerson.

'Um, yes. Besides updating Insta and doing some spec drawing, I had nothing planned.' She looked puzzled and eager at the same time. 'Why?'

'Why don't you come to the hotel on Thursday morning? We could have a chat about a project I've got coming up. My original idea was more conventional than this.' He put his hand on the book. 'But you've given me something to think about. A different direction.'

'You mean a commission?' Emerson sat up straight, a smile stretching across her face. 'Really?'

'Maybe. Wouldn't hurt to run through the job details with you, see what ideas you might have. What do you think?'

'Best offer I've had in absolutely ages.' She was bouncing in her seat.

Luke met Remi's eye, amusement in his tamped-down grin. And a hint of something else. Bragging? As though he was showing off, proclaiming his generosity and ability to save the day.

CHAPTER TWELVE

Wednesday, 26 July 2023

'Let's not talk about it anymore.' Remi looked out the window as Luke drove, desperate to clear her mind of the nastiness of the day before. Luke was now interrogating her about the conversation with Kayla, having already asked her about the reviews. She hadn't brought up the situation with her car, knowing there would be another flurry of questions that she had no energy to answer—or even answers to give.

'If that's what you want.'

'Any plans for a new hotel? You must be restless. It's been a few years since you had a new baby to fawn over.'

'There might be something.' There was amusement playing across his mouth.

'I knew it. Where's this one? You've got Hobart, Sydney, Melbourne and Brisbane.' She ticked them off on her fingers. 'Let me guess, Perth next? Or Adelaide?'

He gave away nothing.

'Is it even a hotel?'

'Maybe. Though there are more important things than beds and bars and occupancy rates.'

'What? Who are you and what have you done with Luke?'

He glanced at her with obvious amusement.

'Not even a teeny clue? I promise not to divulge any information to any of your competitors. Wait … is there a new woman who's won your heart?'

'Let's just say'—he kept his focus on the road—'it's something with a personal interest for me. Something I've wanted to do for a long time.'

Remi sighed like a diva denied her demands. 'Will I find out eventually? Hopefully sooner rather than later. I am, after all, your most passionate admirer. Remember.' She laid a hand on his arm. 'I believed in you when others thought you were a lowly trainee with big ideas.'

'I never forget that. And, yes, you will find out. And I'm expecting it to be sooner, not later.'

Remi watched out the window as he handled the car around the bends and down into Kettering. Years ago, when she was new to Tasmania, she'd travelled through here with Simon on a daytrip to Bruny Island. Today, though, Luke drove past the turn-off to the ferry.

'Where are we going?'

'Not far now.'

The views became more spectacular as they drove along the edge of a small bay, then climbed back through pastures, emerging high on a headland with wide panoramas up and down the D'Entrecasteaux Channel and across to the low hills of Bruny.

'I really don't get out of town enough,' she said. 'I'm so focused on work and the house I forget to go out and enjoy this amazing place.'

'You need to give yourself breaks. Get away. Remind yourself about the rest of the world. When was the last time you went to Melbourne?'

'What?' she scoffed. 'Go to the mainland? Get off-island? Impossible.'

'Why stay locked away down here?'

She didn't answer straight away. There were a lot of reasons, none of which she wanted to talk about.

They headed down a twisty section of road into a green gully, emerging out the other side at the outskirts of a village.

'I don't think of it as being locked away,' she said at last. 'This is home, and I feel ...' Safe? Anonymous? In control? What was she trying to say? 'I feel at home here. But, yes, a trip across to Melbourne might be nice. For a weekend. Or a few days. One day when I can afford it.'

'If you come to Melbourne and don't stay at Strike I'll be seriously offended. You know I'll always look after you. And if you don't want to be in a hotel, you can stay with me at the apartment.'

The view of the water opened ahead of them, the road taking a sharp turn to the right, while a thin strip of bitumen peeled off to the left, hugging the small knob of land as it led the way down to a tidy little jetty. Rising out of the bend, Luke swung left into a carpark. A modern building sat unobtrusively on the far side, a sharp ridge running in an uninterrupted line from the ground to a high point above the doors.

'Peppermint Bay,' Remi read from the sign. 'I haven't been here yet. Heard of it, but never could find the energy to get down this way.'

He shook his head as he parked the car. 'You've got to make time for yourself.'

'I do make time for myself.'

'Really? And what do you get up to in your moments of self-indulgence?'

Remi shut the door behind her and came around to his side of the car. 'Actually, I've started going to the movies. On my own. And, before you say anything, I make it special. Last time I went to the State Cinema on a Friday afternoon. You can buy wine at the bar and they let you take it in with you, and the cinema was underground with old sandstone walls. The theatre was tiny and cosy and felt rather special.'

He put his arm around her shoulders, pulled her close and kissed her on the forehead. 'It doesn't take much to impress you, does it? And tell me, how often do you take yourself off for afternoon sessions of movie luxury?'

'Well, okay, so I've only been once. But the experience was so nice I'm planning to go again.' When she had spare cash. The weight of her situation settled back around her. She couldn't even afford to go to the movies.

Luke squeezed her then stepped back, letting her enter the building first through the sliding door. The interior was sleek and dark. A bar ran the length of the room, tables and several counters with high stools filling the compact space. There was a fire at one end and they passed the mounted head of a magnificent white mountain goat, its amber-coloured horns curling upwards. She couldn't tell if it was real or fake. But the most striking feature was the glass wall and the view across the channel. Outside there were large wooden tables and benches, umbrellas folded tight. In summer, this would be a spectacular spot.

They sat shoulder to shoulder at the counter in front of the window, Luke heading to the bar to order two glasses of chardonnay before they made their choices from the menu.

'I'm going to say something. It might surprise you a little, but I'd like for you to hear me out,' he said.

'Uh-oh. Thanks, but no thanks. With a warning like that, I'm going to opt out of this conversation.' She put her hand on the beard he'd grown, aiming to distract. 'I like this new look. I never thought beards would make a comeback, but they've grown on me. Or rather, they've grown on you. They don't suit everyone, but luckily you look rather scrumptious with facial hair.'

He ducked his head briefly as she pulled her hand back, then shifted in his seat to face her. He wasn't going to be deflected. 'You know my opinion of Simon. The man is an arrogant wanker. And I would be delighted to see him fail completely. I also wonder about his personal motive for wanting to sell, but I think he may have a point—'

She held up a hand, cutting him off. 'Please don't say it.'

He shook his head. 'The fact you even know what I'm about to say makes me wonder if you don't, to some degree, accept the reasoning behind it.'

'No. I don't accept it,' she said. How dare Luke take Simon's side in this. Did he honestly not know what the house meant to her? 'I mean, I get it.' She forced herself to sound calm, not wanting to fight. 'I can see why, if you look at the numbers and the market and my situation, why selling might seem like a sensible idea. If you strip every ounce of emotion from the analysis, then sure, it sort of makes sense.'

She stared out the window. A small boat with two fishermen puttered away from the jetty and seagulls hovered on the wind, snatches of cloud skidding across the washed-out blue of the sky. Accepting there was logic in selling was a betrayal of her beautiful home. Even being in this position was a failure, and she couldn't let herself be defeated any further. She'd chosen the house, had seen beneath the grime to what it could be, what it needed. Had put everything into giving it a new life. She hadn't been proud of herself for a long time, but she was intensely proud of what she had achieved with that old girl.

'Walking away is not an option,' she said. 'Failure is not an option. And that's what selling would be. It would be admitting I took on something I couldn't handle. That I wasn't good enough. And I *can* do it. I just have to fight harder. Because I love that house, and I want to live there for a very long time.' She drank some wine then folded her arms. 'Surely you of all people must understand how that feels? To love something you have created?'

Luke laid a hand on her back. 'It's not about your ability,' he said. 'What you've achieved is amazing. I couldn't have done a better job. But I'm worried about you.'

'Well, don't,' she snapped. 'There's financial pressure at the moment. But I'll sort it out. Can we drop it, please?'

The waiter appeared with their meals, the interruption breaking some of the tension. They both ate, commenting on the quality of the food, the view up the channel, how spectacular Tasmania was even during winter. Remi asked about the Hobart hotel, how well it was doing, the reviews they were receiving. Luke told stories about guests and staff, making her laugh.

The hotel had been operating for four years and Remi hadn't been back since the night of the opening party—the last night of her marriage. Their social calendar had been devoid of such events since she and Simon had moved to Hobart. Remi hadn't minded at all, she'd become obsessed with the old house they'd bought, but Simon had returned to Sydney frequently for occasions he 'just couldn't miss'. For Luke, though, she'd been happy to pull a frock from the back of the wardrobe and buckle on some torturous heels.

At one point during the night, Remi had slipped away, finding a dark, quiet spot on the terrace. Leaving her shoes to the side, she had walked to the edge, the ridges of the paving soothing under her bare feet. Finally, she was able to really enjoy her champagne. From up here she could still see the rigid canvas of the marquee and the blur of colour where guests gyrated and lights shimmered. She could make out the long tables made lush with floral artistry, and the band on the low stage. And in the darkness right below her, tucked in behind a verdant curved garden bed, she could see a couple entwined. Away from the lights and throng of the party, the pair had mistakenly thought that corner of the garden offered them privacy. Oops. Not quite as private as they had hoped.

The couple had shifted, moving out of the shadows. Soft light from the rooms above reflected off the woman's silver dress. Fell on Simon's face.

Simon. His hand pushing through his hair, clutching his crotch, rearranging pants that were suddenly too tight.

Her husband.

With this woman.

There was a beat as Remi's mind tried to make sense of the scene. Then a frantic, flapping nausea rushed from stomach to throat.

Over the eight years of their marriage, she'd had suspicions, but he'd convinced her she was paranoid. Eventually, she'd stopped believing he would do this. Had stopped waiting to find evidence of a cold, slimy truth.

But here he was.

His focus was on the woman's body. Her floor-length dress had been cut to reveal her back from the neck to the top of her buttocks, and the plump, apple-round side of her breast was exposed every time she moved an arm. Everything sleek, with the sheen of expensive attention: skin, hair, flesh.

He lifted his hand to twist the woman's long ponytail around his fist, his grip tight. He pulled, playfully possessing, the woman's head tilting back. Then he let go, the swag of hair flipping free as his palm now slid down her skin, stopping at the curve of her lower back. His head dipped towards her ear, a smile on his face.

Remi's chest tightened, a squeeze of breath escaping her lips. She knew that smile. He'd used it too many times, over too many years. Delight and mischievous intent expressed in the lopsided curve of his lips and the hitch of one brow. To be honest, it was a practised smile better suited to a younger man. On Simon it was beginning to resemble a leer, not a flirty suggestion. Despite his best efforts—and his efforts were considerable—he had aged. Sure, better than most, but he wasn't free of sag or crease. Or pathetic self-denial. In his own words, he was not going to be a sad, try-hard tosser, living out the banalities of middle-age. Yet here he was, a tawdry cliché of a man, fondling another woman.

This was too much.

Her hand trembled as she drained the champagne from her glass. A drip ran down her chin and she wiped the back of her hand across her mouth, smearing her lipstick. She didn't care. Her looks were obviously not enough. *She* was obviously not enough. A mostly good marriage was obviously not enough. She clutched the glass to her chest, strangling the urge to lash out.

Simon's hand delved deeper, edging beneath the low-cut folds of fabric. His hand flexed as he cupped then clenched the woman's round arse. The confident gesture of a man familiar with his lover's body. The woman remained impassive, only the shift of her hip and the slight turn of her head towards him suggesting she liked his attention.

I wasn't wrong, Remi wanted to scream. All those times she'd asked questions, all those times he'd calmly told her to stop being an insecure, paranoid woman. Despite the pain there was a flicker of relief in knowing she wasn't delusional. Anger, too. Not only at this sordid spectacle, but at his ability to deny, to always make it about her flaws, not his.

Simon's hand wriggled free, skimming up the woman's back, then he stepped away to return to the crowd. The woman waited, reaching up to clutch her hair, dragging the length through her hand, a satisfied cat preening. She smoothed her hands from her waist to her thighs, brought them back to rest on the curve of her hips. Elbows out, head up, chest forward. Satisfied. She slowly tucked her chin to her shoulder and half turned, looking up and back. Straight at Remi. Wide eyes fringed with ridiculous lashes. Glossy lips pulling into a smug smile.

Remi had gasped, feeling an irrational guilt at being caught watching. Her arms dropped to her sides and she stepped back, her foot catching the hem of her dress. She lurched, the champagne flute smashing on the slate paving. The woman laughed as she raised her hand and fluttered her fingers before touching them to her mouth and blowing a fuck-you-I-win kiss.

Kayla had never been afraid of confrontation.

CHAPTER THIRTEEN

Saturday, 29 July 2023

Remi was half awake when she remembered she had yet to
send this month's payment to Simon. 'Shit!' After lunch
with Luke she'd managed to put aside her pride and ask for
a loan, which he had immediately sent through. Relieved to
know she'd be able to make the payment, she'd then promptly
forgot to do the transfer. She really had to get her act together.

She scrabbled in the dark for her phone, squinting at the
harsh glow of the screen. Two thirty-eight, Saturday morning.
There was no point moving the money now. 'Voice memo,'
she mumbled to her phone. 'Don't forget to pay the bastard
his money.' She dropped the phone back on the side table and
rolled over.

It was fine. She was only a couple of days behind. No need
to panic. Emerson had paid two weeks' rent and Remi could
scrape together enough money to cover the payment. She had
been putting it off, but she was also going to sell her engagement ring. What she'd get would only be a fraction of the

purchase price, but that would be something. Even thirty per cent of a twenty-five thousand dollar ring would be useful, and she didn't need to keep the flashy piece.

She leaned over and pulled open the drawer of the bedside table, lifting out her jewellery box. She didn't wear any bling these days. No rings, no necklace, no bracelets, she even left her ears unadorned most of the time. But she did have a few pieces from her previous life. Apart from the engagement ring, there were other high-value pieces—like the diamond pendant Simon had given her on their fifth wedding anniversary. Maybe she could sell all these useless trinkets. The idea was so obvious, why hadn't she thought of this sooner?

She ran her fingers through the small collection, searching for her engagement ring or the pendant. Then she sat up, turned on the bedside light, and tipped the contents onto the bed. Separated each piece. Stared at what was laid out. Her Hardy Brothers white gold one carat diamond ring was missing. So was the quarter carat marquise cut pendant. She clearly remembered putting them in this box the day she'd left Simon. She also knew the only time she'd looked at them was that first New Year's Eve in the house, when Simon had rung from the boat. For a moment she'd let herself admire the sparkling evidence of her life with him. She hadn't looked at them since, intent on firmly closing the door on that life.

'What the fuck?' she whispered. Had they been stolen? When? How?

She thought of the tradesmen who'd been through the house. People coming and going, everyone busy, her stuff being moved from room to room as the work progressed. How accustomed she had become to the presence of those busy men and women.

The jewellery could have been taken at any time over the last three years.

Then she thought of the women now living here. One of them had brought the candle into her room, she was almost certain of that. Was Josephine or Emerson light-fingered? Or was this connected to the hacking of her bank account? Was this more evidence that someone had accessed her home?

She couldn't take any more of this bullshit.

Somewhere in the house a door opened. The basement door, she thought. It always stuck a little when it was opened fully. A floorboard creaked. Silence again, then the soft thunk of the front door closing. One of them was up late.

She returned the small pile of worthless jewellery to the box, and was setting it back in the drawer when a thought speared into her mind.

Emerson wasn't here. She was at Luke's hotel for the night. Josephine wasn't here either. She had left on Thursday for a three-night guided walking tour of Maria Island.

Remi had been blissfully alone since mid-afternoon, revelling in the emptiness of her space. What had she just heard? Who was here? Her heart raced hard and fast. She'd never been afraid in this house. Not even in the early days when it was still rotten and dark. Mavis had arrived the week after she'd moved in, and the dog had always been alert to the comings and goings of others. Was that why her dog had been targeted?

She couldn't move, sitting in the soft light staring towards her half-open bedroom door. She could hear nothing; even the street outside was hushed. No rain or wind or traffic. The silence had weight, the heft and solidity of the building pressing down around her.

There. The faintest whine of a metal hinge then the clink of the front gate clicking shut. The noise released Remi from the grip of inertia and she rushed to the window. The muted yellow glow from the streetlights did little to cut through the soft mist of the night. She could make out movement: an indistinguishable figure striding away towards the centre of town. Moving quickly. Black puffer, black beanie, black pants. She couldn't even say if it was a man or woman.

A flicker caught her eye. A shift of light on the ground below. She craned forward trying to decipher what she was seeing. A fluttering glimmer coming from the basement. Orange and amber, becoming brighter.

Then a noise inside. The sound muffled by stone and wood. Something had fallen and shattered.

She grabbed yesterday's trackpants from the floor and was hauling them on when the ear-splitting shriek of the smoke alarm reverberated through the house.

For two long seconds, she froze. Then a tsunami of adrenaline flooded her body and panic took over. Fuck! She grabbed her phone and ran from her room to the stairs, the alarm piercing her skull, throbbing in her head. Was this a false alarm? Could she smell smoke?

She looked to the floor below. Could see the door to the basement was wide open, the shifting light visible. Fire!

She had seconds.

She rushed forward, leaping to the ground floor before she'd reached the last step. Her knees and hands hit the floorboards, phone skittering out of her grip. She pushed to her feet and ran to the back of the house. At the basement door, she hesitated. A shadow was rolling upwards, backlit by the pulsing glow. The acrid smoke immediately burning her lungs, rough coughs ripping through her chest and stomach. She couldn't go down there and if she couldn't douse the flames, then she needed to slow the spread and contain the smoke. She slammed the door shut, then found the light switch. Nothing. The power was out. Stumbling back to the foot of the stairs, she dropped to the floor, sweeping her arms wide till her right hand connected with her phone. Hands shaking, she fumbled as she swiped, trying to access the keypad. She managed to tap in 000, as she stumbled to the kitchen.

'Fire!' she yelled over the scream of the alarm when the operator answered.

She kept a fire extinguisher under the sink. Except it wasn't there. She flung aside the bottles of dishwashing liquid and the packs of sponges, as the operator efficiently asked their questions.

'Yes! Macquarie Street. Yes. In the basement. I've closed it off. I can't find my extinguisher. I can't leave yet. No! It'll get into the rest of the house. Yes, there's smoke. Please hurry. Yes. Yes! Okay, fine. I'm going.'

She wrenched opened the kitchen door and escaped into the courtyard, sucking in the biting cold air, the cobblestones icy beneath her bare feet. This couldn't be happening. Not this. Not now.

Sirens carried through the night. Lights appearing in the buildings behind the stone walls of her courtyard. The neighbourhood being woken.

The front door! They'll need to come through the front door. She started down the driveway, realised she didn't have the keys, and turned around. She had to go back through the house. The smoke was thicker, seeping through the space beneath the basement door, spilling into the ground floor and beginning to rise. Her eyes stung and her breathing faltered as she sprinted down the dark hall. She fumbled the lock, then threw open the door, the circling red lights of the engine lighting up the street, the firefighters already moving into action. Hoses unfurling. Shouts and commands bouncing off the buildings. Efficient people in protective gear moving past her in a controlled rush. Someone leading her out of the way, asking if there was anyone still in the house.

'No,' she gasped, trying to suck in air between coughs. 'No. There is no one else here. I'm alone.'

PART TWO

SUSPICION

CHAPTER FOURTEEN

EMERSON
Thursday, 27 July 2023

Emerson parked in the Strike Hotel carpark, immensely pleased with herself for being early. Really early. Like, a full thirty minutes before her meeting with Luke. Which was a much better situation than the night she'd arrived on Remi's doorstep. That had been completely humiliating.

She'd been in Hobart a week by then, her plan for a fresh start teetering like a stack of Jenga blocks being pulled apart by day-drinkers who'd been on the wine for six hours. Except drunk Jenga was a laugh. This move was not. The first shock had been the lack of affordable rentals. She'd soon realised her vision of an inner-city warehouse apartment was totally unrealistic. Discovering that even a decrepit, manky, hideous box of a space was beyond her budget was completely demoralising. Not to be defeated, she'd adjusted her expectations and searched for a decent share house. Sharing was great if you got the right people, and was also the only way to afford to live in inner-city Melbourne. Or, as it turned out, in inner-city Hobart.

After three days of inspections, panic was kicking in. One place had delivered a reality which was nothing like the pictures used in the listing: the bathroom was crowded with empty shampoo bottles and dirty mugs filled with floating cigarette butts, there was a hairball the size of a rat in the shower and the toilet had never been cleaned. One place had been home to a truly weird girl who stood too close, didn't blink and had an obsession with incense. One place had been clean, comfortable and came with the parting comment, *Sorry, nothing personal, I don't think you're the right fit.*

Initially she'd passed over the listing for Remi's house. Nothing in the description had the right vibe. But her funds were evaporating rapidly and only one of her three cards had any available credit. Payments were overdue on all of them and she was being chased by the banks. Her envelope of cash was getting thinner by the day and her savings account held exactly one hundred and thirty-six dollars. She was getting desperate.

When she'd arrived at that shiny black door she'd been impressed. The house was completely gorgeous! Remi herself had been another surprise. She was ordinary but also had 'it' without even trying. She'd been dressed in worn jeans, a white t-shirt and a long, out-of-shape beige cardigan. Light brown, shoulder-length hair pulled back from a beautiful face. High on her cheek, under her left eye, was a constellation of three small moles. It had taken a while to figure out why she looked familiar.

Josephine, however, had seemed more intimidating. Her eyes were direct and intelligent and a luminous, clear blue that seemed to assess and read Emerson thoroughly. Standing in that glorious kitchen, Emerson had felt like a kid pretending to be a grown-up. The two women looked way too together for a share house. And Josephine, how old was she? She was in reasonable shape. But still, probably north of fifty? By that age, a woman should have a family. A house of her own. Be financially independent. Not that Emerson had meant to be judgey. Josephine was, quite likely, a very nice lady. But she couldn't imagine them sharing Thai takeaway and cheap wine at midnight during a binge-watching marathon. Or moaning about failed love affairs, disappointing sex, what a mess the planet was in, or how Boomers didn't understand how tough life had got. They wouldn't be chucking around ideas and inspirations for cool new start-ups. They'd have nothing in common, in attitude or experience. What if she was a conservative? And how awkward would it be if Emerson brought someone home? Would *she* be judged?

Remi, at least, was younger. Mid-thirties at a guess. And an actress, which made her a fellow creative. A year or so ago, Emerson had shared with an actor for a few months. Had even read lines with him, for the fringe festival indie thing he was putting together, which had been fun.

While Remi had made her a cup of tea, Emerson had considered doing a cut and run. Surely there would be other places she could check out tomorrow? She wouldn't find another house this spectacular, but she might get a better fit of personalities. More her people, young, motivated, arty, risk-takers, taking on the world. People she understood and could relate to.

Or maybe there'd be no other options and she'd waste even more money on hotel rooms until she was forced to downgrade to a backpackers. Till she had nothing left and she was living in her tiny car. It was all so grim.

Maybe she *could* live in this warm, classy, adult space and she'd find her people elsewhere. This arrangement wouldn't be forever, just till she got herself sorted and back on track.

She'd made a good choice. Two weeks later and things were happening. She had somewhere to live, Josephine was actually really interesting and was an excellent listener. Remi was a bit of a mystery and had a few personal dramas, but seemed nice—although a bit spiky. Still, Remi didn't give her any grief and had let her set up a work table in the super cool basement. More importantly, her new home had led to this, her first potential commission since she'd left Melbourne.

She got out of her car and gave her tights a hoist to stop the crotch from sagging towards her knees. Confident they were in place, Emerson grabbed her portfolio and tote bag from the back seat and headed for the entrance. After Luke had left last night, she'd done a quick spot of research. Obviously, she'd heard of the hotels, but she wanted to be fully informed. This one, for example, had once been a stately home, then a school, then a boarding house. Built in 1864, Luke had bought it four or five years ago. A bucketload of money had been spent on the refurbishment, including adding bathrooms and all the mod cons to every room. Plus they'd stretched the floor plan with a glass-and-timber extension. He had transformed a tired old building into a divine boutique hotel, with restaurant and bar, crisp sheets, stunning furniture, funky wallpaper, local art and impeccably cool staff in smart, trendy uniforms. Like the graceful girl behind the desk; with her tight bun and elegant neck, she looked like she ought to be in a tutu doing pirouettes and bendy things, not attending to guests.

'Hello,' said Emerson. 'I'm here for a meeting with Luke Darlby. I'm early.'

'Certainly,' said ballet girl. 'I'll let him know.' She picked up the phone, announced Emerson's arrival, made a few *yes, Luke* replies then hung up. Smiling, she passed on the message. 'Mr Darlby asks if you wouldn't mind waiting in the restaurant. He suggested you order tea or coffee and some cake, if you would like. He said morning tea is on him and he'll be with you shortly.'

'Lovely. Thanks.'

Ballerina gave her directions to the restaurant ('Down the hallway, second door on the right, before you reach the terrace') and Emerson set off, delighted to have a few minutes to soak up the luxurious yet quirky surrounds.

The restaurant was classy but relaxed. Not too big. Cosy, but without tables being jammed up against each other. A few people were seated. The quiet clink of cup on saucer and fork on plate, the murmur of voices. The waiter was dressed in a white shirt and floral waistcoat and had a black apron tied around his waist. When he asked if she needed a table for one, Emerson got a small kick out of saying Luke would join her shortly, and could she possibly have a larger table, as she would probably need to spread out her work. The waiter obligingly cleared two places away from a table for four and brought her a pot of tea and a raspberry mousse slice. After two mouthfuls of gooey decadence, she relaxed, deciding not only was the food delicious but the waiter was too. The delighted look he kept giving her was more than polite.

She was about to introduce herself when Luke arrived. He wore a two-button slate-grey suit, no tie, his pristine pale shirt open at the neck. He owned the room. Well, duh, he owned the whole goddam hotel. And a few others. No wonder he carried himself with such commanding ease.

Emerson stood to shake his hand, surprised when he also bent to kiss her on the cheek.

'Sorry to keep you waiting. Does our cake live up to your excellent standards?' He sat as the waiter hovered at his side. 'Hello, Kristof, I'll have an espresso, thanks.'

Kristof. Yummy waiter now had a name. She'd file that away for later. For now, she had to concentrate. Listen to the brief and convince Luke she could do the work. Because she could. Emerson doubted many things about herself—her looks, her money sense, her *common* sense—but she never doubted her ability to create art.

As she finished her tea, he explained the project. Luke wanted to improve the guest compendiums in the rooms. At present they were far too generic and he wanted to imbue them with a greater sense of style. Turn an item common to every hotel into something more specific to Strike Hobart. If that worked well, he would probably extend the idea to the other hotels in his collection. She asked him how far he wanted to take the design elements. Did he want a few creative touches such as titles in free-form writing, or a more extensive theme with illustrations? Maybe details to reflect Tasmania? They could be simple black and white sketches or full-coloured pictures. She showed him examples as she talked, flipping this way and that though her portfolio. He stopped her at some menus she had done for a Melbourne cafe.

'I like these,' he said, looking closer. 'Perhaps we should discuss an upgrade to our menus.'

'Well.' She felt torn between not wanting to sound pushy and needing to make suggestions. 'I think, and this is just an idea, that while I work on the preliminary concepts for the compendiums, we should keep in mind styles and images that can be repeated across a range of items in the hotel.' Then her excitement for the potential of the job took over. 'You know, you could have a collection of work across the whole Strike chain. There are four hotels, right?'

'Yes.'

'Right. So, each hotel in each location could have compendiums, menus, room notices—like, you know, those notes about leaving towels on the floor if you want them replaced, that sort of thing—oh, and door hangers. The Do Not Disturb sign. Each hotel would have unique illustrations and details, but with a common style and look. That would be amazing.'

'It would.' He gave her a generous smile. 'Let's start with initial concepts for this hotel and we can take things from there. Invoice me for a mock-up of your ideas.'

'Of course.' She laughed, self-conscious at getting carried away. Better to focus on the first job and impress the socks off Luke. Then he'd be so excited at her vision he'd want to extend the project. 'I should be able to have something for you within the week, if that sounds okay with you.'

'It does.' He finished his coffee, giving a nod of thanks as Kristof cleared the table. 'So, tell me, how are you finding the house? Remi's house? Have you settled in all right?'

Emerson had closed her work and readied herself to leave so was surprised when Luke made no move to stand. She settled back in her chair, mirroring his relaxed pose. 'It's great. I hadn't planned on doing the share house thing. I might have been a little delusional when I left Melbourne. I presumed Hobart would be, well, cheap. Or at least way cheaper than a proper city. Not that Hobart isn't a proper city. Obviously, it is. It's just so much smaller. Anyway, I got a shock when I couldn't find somewhere to rent.'

He nodded. 'Like everywhere, there's been a rental squeeze down here.'

'So I discovered. Probably should've done some research before driving my car onto that ferry. I was in way too much of a hurry.'

'Why was that?'

'Oh, you know.' She waved a hand. 'Keen to make a new start.' She didn't need to elaborate, some things were better not talked about. 'Anyway, I hadn't imagined myself sharing with older women. It was weird at first. I've shared with heaps of people, but they've all been like me. Or not like me, but around my age. I always thought someone Josephine's, or even Remi's, age would have their shi—' Oops. She had to watch her language. This was a client. Potential client. 'Would have their life together and wouldn't need to bunk in with other people.'

Amusement snuck across his face. 'Sometimes people find themselves in unexpected circumstances.' He tapped his hand on the table. 'Remi can be stubborn, too. I wish she were less so. She has an unnecessary need to prove herself.'

Emerson settled back in her chair. 'You've known her a long time, then?'

'Yes. Since we were your age. She is a dear friend and a remarkable woman. I adore her.' He gazed at a point in the distance. When his attention returned to Emerson, he gave his head a slow shake, as though unable to understand the situation. Unrequited love, thought Emerson. There was something so attractive about a gorgeous man pining for the woman he wanted.

He walked her through reception, stopping as they passed the entrance. 'How would you like to stay here a night, get a feel for the hotel? I'm heading back to Sydney later today, but

I'll leave the details with reception. Say, tomorrow night? Give you an insight into our style and vision. No charge, of course. What do you think?'

'That would be most beneficial.' Her professional tone lasted less than five seconds. 'That would be absolutely freakin' amazing and very, very helpful. Gosh, how lovely and generous of you to offer. Thank you so much.'

His gaze shifted to something behind her, a frown appearing then disappearing just as quickly. He said goodbye and Emerson turned to walk to her car. A woman passed her on the path. Sleek and perfectly groomed, blonde hair swinging, outrage evident in the jut of her chin and the tight line of her glossy mouth. Her coat and bag were expensive. Her language and attitude screamed of entitlement. Oblivious to her surroundings, she was entirely focused on her phone and her loud conversation. Emerson stepped off the path as she strode past.

'Make it happen, *babe*! You have rights to the place. For fuck's sake, get a goddamn lawyer. How hard can it be to get her out?'

Charming.

Emerson glanced back as she climbed into her car. Luke had intercepted the woman and didn't look impressed. Their body language was giving off every indication they were arguing. He must know her, Emerson thought as she started the car. Before she drove away, she connected her phone to the Bluetooth and flicked through Spotify till she found the right playlist. Then, singing 'Born to Be Alive' at the top of her voice, she began the short trip back to the house. Things were definitely turning around. Maybe not fast enough to fix all her money problems straight away, but working for Luke was a good start.

CHAPTER FIFTEEN

EMERSON
Saturday, 29 July 2023

'Hello again.' Kristof, the yummy waiter, gave her a grin with a dash of both recognition and interest. 'Are you joining us for breakfast?'

Last night, after she'd spent several hours enjoying the hotel, Emerson had been thoroughly disappointed when Kristof hadn't been on dinner service. This morning, despite the cosiness of the bed, she'd gotten up earlier than usual, hopeful he'd be rostered on for breakfast. And here he was, in all his blond-haired, blue-eyed fabulousness. Even his earrings were cute. Better still, the restaurant was not even half full and he didn't appear too busy.

'Yes, please. Just for one. It's just me.'

'Are you charging back to your room?'

She held his gaze. 'Room two-oh-two.' She watched him enter the details into his tablet. 'Emerson Blake,' she said, even though he hadn't asked.

He reached for a menu. 'And did you have a good night, Emerson?'

'I did, thank you. Everything about the hotel is gorgeous.'

'Glad to hear that.'

They grinned at each other as though they were play-acting the roles of guest and server.

'Come on through.' He led her to a table overlooking the terrace, beyond which lay the gardens and the water.

'Stunning view,' she said. 'It can't be too bad working here with a view like that.'

'Yeah, it's not bad. Are you visiting Hobart?'

'No. I'm a local. Well, sort of a local. I moved here from Melbourne three weeks ago.'

'Three weeks? You're a very fresh arrival. And how are you finding it?'

She began to explain the horror of her first week and the serendipity of finding a share house that led to a job offer but stopped talking when a guest stopped at the restaurant's front desk. She was the woman from the other day, the one she'd seen talking to Luke. 'Maybe I can tell you about it later. I think you're needed.' She gave a small nod towards the woman.

'Thanks. I'll be back to take your order.'

She read the menu, casting sneaky glances across the room. The woman wasn't snarling today, but neither was she giving off warm and friendly vibes. Not even lukewarm. She barely acknowledged Kristof as he seated her, took her order and returned with a coffee, her focus entirely on her phone. She looked vaguely familiar, and not just from two days ago. Emerson was sure she'd seen her before. Or at least a picture of her.

The vibration of her smart watch interrupted her thoughts, and she glanced at the alert. An incoming call. From Giselle. She flipped over her silenced phone, where the image of Giselle and Emerson, cheeks pressed together, cocktail glasses raised in salute, lit up the screen.

An icky twisting sense of shame strangled Emerson's mood. She couldn't put this off forever. Well, she could, but that would make her a really, really bad person. But neither was this the right time to take the call. She gently set the phone back on the table. Face down.

It was one thing to dodge calls from the banks, it was altogether something else to avoid talking to her friend. Probably ex-friend. Emerson had absolutely done the wrong thing by her ex-flatmates. But she would fix it. The second she had money coming in, she would pay the girls back, clear what she owed them and repair the friendship. Which, fingers crossed, could be very, very soon. Although, she might have to pay her phone bill first. There was no way she would let her phone be cut off. And she had to make a bit of a dent in the overdue repayments on her cards. And pay Remi her rent, she couldn't risk being kicked out of her new home. But then she'd absolutely pay them what she owed.

Kristof strolled back to her table. 'Sorry to keep you waiting. Have you decided what you'd like to order?'

'Eggs Benedict and a pot of tea, please,' she said. Might as well enjoy all the benefits of her everything-included visit. 'Hey, can I ask,' she said quietly before he left. 'That woman who came in, do you know who she is? She seems familiar.'

He didn't turn to look. 'Kayla somebody.'

'Is she an actress or something like that?'

He gave the smallest snort of derision. 'Influencer,' he said, heavy on the sarcasm. 'And she's married to some rich guy.'

'Does she stay here often?'

He angled his head. 'No. I don't think so. I used to work at Strike Sydney and she was a bit of a regular there, though.'

'Okay, thanks.' Emerson didn't want to ask if there was a connection between her and Luke. That might be a little inappropriate. 'So, you're a new arrival too then?'

'Grew up in Tassie, then headed to the mainland straight after school. But I've been back for eighteen months,' he said. 'I got a job on a film crew and sort of stayed. It's nice being back, and there's a few more options here now. I could give you some recommendations for excellent venues and bars and the like.'

'Could you? That would be awesome. My current housemates are older than me, and I haven't found anyone yet to get out and about with.'

House, job and a new friend. Moving here had been the right thing to do. Soon her life would be back to fabulous.

***

With a full stomach, Kristof's number in her phone and ideas for the Strike project bouncing in her head, Emerson returned to her room, excited to get back to the house. She needed to get seriously stuck into her process. A message from Remi arrived as she was slipping the complimentary toiletries into her bag.

Did you come back to the house last night?

Strange question.

No. Spent the whole night here. At Strike. Why?

She waited but there was no reply, and no indication Remi was typing an answer.

Everything OK? Emerson asked.

Still nothing. She continued packing, figuring she'd find out what was happening soon enough.

The room phone on the desk rang as she was about to leave. 'Hello?'

'Good morning, this is Emily from reception. Mr Darlby has asked me to pass on a message for you.'

'Okay.' Unexpected, but maybe he wanted to say something about her time here.

'He's asked that you remain at the hotel for another night.'

'Oh. That's lovely, thank you, but I really need to get home.' As nice as the offer was, she didn't need more inspiration. She was itching to start sketching out her ideas.

'Actually, he also said to advise you that Ms Remi Lucans and Ms Josephine Jordan will be joining you at the hotel after lunch and will also be staying the night.'

'What? Why?'

'I'm sorry, I don't have any further details. But if there's anything you need, please let me know.'

What the hell? Emerson set down the receiver and walked to the window as though peering into the garden and watching the rain would give her answers. This was seriously weird. Did Josephine know about this? She wasn't due to be dropped back from her little hiking trip until late afternoon. Did she have phone reception on Maria Island? Had she even taken her phone?

Emerson checked for more messages from Remi. Nothing. She tapped into her contacts and rang her instead, but she didn't answer.

Right, that was annoying. Something was obviously going on, but nobody was giving her details. She wasn't going to sit in this room—lovely as it was—until she knew why she was there. Leaving her overnight bag on the bed, she headed for her car. She'd make a quick visit home and see if she could find out what this was all about. At the very least, she would collect some art equipment.

Passing through the foyer, she saw the Kayla woman at reception, looking even more displeased. Emerson waited until she wheeled her suitcase towards the doors, phone at her ear. She stopped outside the entrance in the shelter of the portico and Emerson hung back, pretending to be engrossed with something on her own screen. It wasn't like she was actively eavesdropping. She was simply close enough to hear the woman's raised voice and to catch the odd word.

'Stop worrying. I'm leaving … calm down … for fuck's sake … Not. My. Problem.' Plus, a whole lot of fierce talking at a lower volume. Then, as a dark SUV pulled up, she ended the call with, 'You know what? Nobody died, so get over it.'

Emerson knew she'd be googling Kayla the influencer at some point. She was curious to know who she was and what was the goss. The rich and entitled were fascinating, and this little vignette was like watching *The Real Housewives of Somewhere* in real time.

***

Arriving home, Emerson was surprised to find there was no room to park her car at the back of the house. Remi's sad Subaru was there, where it had been for the whole week, plus two others. She reversed carefully back into the flow of traffic, thankful when someone took pity and stopped to let her out. She took ten minutes to go around the block the first time, then she went around again trying to find a parking spot. Which was made trickier because she didn't want to do a reverse park in the heavy flow of cars. Relieved to find a double space she could ease in to, she then had to wait for the traffic to stop before she could wriggle out into the rain. She darted around and onto the footpath, then yanked her bag and umbrella from the front passenger seat, pulling loose one of her notebooks, which landed in the flowing gutter. Shit!

With all the cryptic messages that morning, the extra cars at the house and not being able to get hold of Remi, Emerson was distinctly uneasy. Was any of this about her? No. It couldn't be. She was in a bit of financial hole and people were chasing her for money, but it hadn't got to the stage of being hunted down. Had it? Guilt was making her nervous.

Crossing the street at the lights, she walked back to the house. She was nearly at the front gate before she noticed the mess. The narrow width between the front fence and the house was decimated, the rows of dormant lavender bushes trampled and broken. The basement windows were smashed and the lower section of the honey-coloured sandstone facade was filthy with something dark and ugly. Soot? Oh fuck, had there been a fire?

Emerson stopped, wary suddenly of going through the front door. She backtracked and went up the driveway at the side, coming around the back to the parking area and the walled garden. At the kitchen door she hesitated for a moment before gently turning the handle. The lights were off, the fireplace devoid of flame, the room cold and unwelcoming but appeared undamaged. An unpleasant smell of burnt plastic and pungent smoke hung in the air, catching in the back of her nostrils and throat, coating her tongue so she could taste it.

Voices came from further in the house and, as she crossed the kitchen, she saw torchlight moving on the basement stairs.

Remi emerged first, followed by a man and a woman.

'What's happened?' Emerson blurted in a loud, wavering voice.

Remi spun around. 'Bloody hell, Emerson. You scared the shit out of me.' She sounded pissed off. 'What are you doing here?'

'I didn't know what was happening. There was your question about being here last night. Then Luke sent a message—through reception—about staying at the hotel and telling me that you and Josephine were coming to stay too. I couldn't get hold of you, but it was obvious something was going on. And I wanted to work on the Strike project, I needed my stuff ...' She trailed away into silence.

In the gloom of the unlit hallway, she could see Remi close her eyes and raise a hand to rub her forehead. She looked exhausted.

'There was a fire in the basement last night.' Her speech was clipped, as though she had zero interest in explaining anything to her tenant. 'These are the inspectors from the fire service and the insurance company, checking for the cause and assessing the damage.'

The basement. Where Emerson had set up her things, where she worked, where she used an electric heater and plug-in fairy lights. Her stomach flipped horribly. 'What time? How did it start?' She choked out the questions. 'Did I do this?'

She couldn't have. She always checked and double-checked that the heaters were unplugged before she packed up. She was sure she hadn't left anything turned on when she left yesterday. Or had she? She couldn't remember. Had she been too excited about going to the hotel? Too busy packing a bag and dreaming of luxury?

'Two am.' Remi said with restrained anger.

The woman behind Remi stepped forward. In sturdy boots, practical work clothes and a high-vis jacket, she looked like someone who knew lots of important stuff and could solve problems. 'It looks like the fire was ignited by a number of unattended candles,' she said evenly. 'There was also a significant amount of combustible material. Plenty of paper, books, synthetic fabrics, the tables themselves.'

Was she being blamed? 'But I've never lit a candle down there.' Emerson looked at Remi. 'I promise. I've never used a candle in the basement. I mean I had some on the table, because they smell nice, even if they're not lit. But that's it, I swear.'

'Fine,' Remi said wearily.

'Oh no.' Emerson suddenly grasped the reality of what this meant. 'All my drawings and sketchpads and pens. My drawing tablet. Is everything gone?'

'Yes.' She didn't elaborate or offer sympathy.

Emerson took a step towards the basement door.

The other inspector, an older man with heavy glasses, shook his head. 'It's a mess down there with water and smoke damage. There's nothing to be saved.'

'Oh.' Emerson stopped, swallowed hard against tears. This couldn't be real. All her beautiful things, gone. 'Okay. Can I get things from my room?'

'Yes, that's fine,' he said. 'There's no real damage up here.'

'Other than water and the stink of smoke.' Remi reached out and dragged her hand over the wood of the banister. 'And this.' She stared at her blackened hand with a fierce expression.

'If you hadn't acted so quickly and shut that door, the outcome would've been significantly worse,' the woman said. 'I've got a few more things to check. But I'm fairly confident you can come back in a few days. We'll confirm after the wiring and electrics are assessed. I should have someone here for that this afternoon or tomorrow morning. In the meantime, you'll need to get the basement windows boarded up for your own security ...'

Emerson stopped listening. Leaving Remi to deal with the inspectors, she walked to her room. The floor of the hallway was wet and filthy, a slurry of dissipated foam and black water. They must've dragged the hoses through the front door. She imagined the smoke alarms going off, Remi finding the fire. The panic and trying to call triple zero. It would've been terrifying. Now Remi's beautiful house was a mess. The only relief was in knowing the outcome could've been much worse.

Emerson went to her clothes rack, grabbed two handfuls of fabric and pushed her face into them, sniffing deeply. Not smoky.

How had this happened? If it wasn't Emerson's carelessness, and Josephine hadn't been here, that left Remi. But Remi wouldn't have been sitting in the basement at two am on a cold night with candles. She'd have been in the kitchen or lounge. Wouldn't she?

She wished Josephine was here. They needed to talk. They'd both agreed to keep quiet about the awful emails they'd received, deciding that Remi was stressed enough with all the other crap happening—she didn't need another thing to worry about. They'd thought the sender was probably a vindictive troll. Someone who wanted to make things messy by insisting it wasn't safe to live with Remi Lucans.

Maybe they should've taken the messages seriously.

CHAPTER SIXTEEN

REMI

Remi couldn't stop crying. Sobs tore at her raw throat as she sat at the bottom of the shower, scrubbing herself with a facecloth and soap. The stench of smouldering plastic, wood and paint lingered in her skin and hair, and no amount of luxury hotel body wash was going to erase it. The stink of destruction. Of panic and fear, and of attack.

She covered her face with the cloth to muffle her angry scream.

This was too much. Her resilience was depleted, her defiance gone, shattered by this act of sabotage. Any doubts that her run of bad luck was actually a deliberate campaign had been obliterated in the fire. This series of calculated, cruel events was intended to destroy her life. To destroy her.

None of these things could be coincidence. The hacking of her bank account, the bad reviews, her car, the fire. Maybe even her missing jewellery. And what about Mavis? Had this all begun with the death of her dog?

Why? Why would someone do this? What had Remi supposedly done to elicit such an extreme level of vindictiveness?
When would these attacks stop? And who was responsible?

It had to be someone with a key. That list was short: Luke,
Josephine, Emerson. Simon had said he didn't have one. No,
what he'd said was the door and lock were new. He hadn't said
he didn't have a key. Had Remi ever given him one? She didn't
think so. And there was a different key for the back door—
maybe he had one of those. She'd given her builder a back-door
key when he'd been here full time, but he'd returned it. Maybe
someone had made a copy of her key. Or someone had picked
a lock.

Her head was pounding and she knew she needed food. She
hauled herself up and shut off the water. Luke had insisted
all expenses were covered for the three of them, rooms and
meals until they could return to the house. An insanely generous offer that she was in no position to turn down. She was
so diminished even her pride had evaporated. She had phoned
him early this morning, desperate to have a friend to lean on,
and he'd been almost frightening in his tightly controlled fury.
She'd told him not to come down, there was nothing he could
have done at that point, and he'd agreed to wait a few days.
So, for now, she'd order room service then sleep and stay in
her room until tomorrow. Josephine and Emerson were here
too, somewhere along the corridor, but she couldn't face them.
She wouldn't be able to hide her simmering distrust. Either of
them could be responsible. Had Remi thrown open her door
and invited a dangerous adversary into her home? She had no
idea why either of them would want to hurt her, but even an
old friend—someone she thought she knew—could lash out if
their bitterness and envy festered into something more brutal.

Brittney was evidence of that. These were women she barely knew and what they'd shared about themselves could be complete bullshit. Maybe they were in it together.

***

An hour later, after she'd eaten a plate of pasta methodically and with little enjoyment, Remi closed the curtains against the early darkness and climbed into bed.

She still hadn't paid Simon and she couldn't find the energy to care. In this moment, the thought of selling the house wasn't so terrible. She couldn't even care that Kayla would get what she wanted.

Was Simon a suspect? Was Kayla? Yes. They had a motive. They wanted her to sell—either willingly or through the terms of the agreement.

She could rule out Luke. Couldn't imagine any scenario in which he benefitted from messing up her life. In the eighteen years she'd known him, he had always, *always*, been there for her—her friend and her support.

The only other person not on her list was Brittney. She had form, as they say, but Brittney wasn't responsible for trying to burn down her house, hacking her computer or killing her dog. Brittney couldn't hurt anyone anymore.

CHAPTER SEVENTEEN

JOSEPHINE

Josephine dropped her backpack on the floor of the hotel room and stood, hands on hips, staring out the window into the wet, dormant garden. The light was fading and it would be dark soon, but she barely noticed, her mind busy with analysing the best course of action. Her hiking boots were still on her feet and while she'd removed her Gore-Tex rain jacket, she was still wearing her fleece and all-weather pants. The trip had been immensely satisfying, but all the calm and delight she'd experienced on her three-day walk had been obliterated the second she'd taken the call from Remi. Now she was filled with anger and a determination to find answers.

She knew she should've done something earlier. Emerson had convinced her to keep quiet about the emails and that had been a mistake. She could've—perhaps—prevented this disaster. She acknowledged the critical voice in her head, then shut it down. Self-recrimination could wait. Chastising herself wasn't going to achieve anything at this point. No, she needed to continue what she'd already started—using the resources she had at her disposal to work out what the hell was going on.

She pulled the curtains together and turned to consider the room.

So, this was Luke Darlby's Hobart hotel. Impressive, of course. The design features were bold and a long way from boring or bland. He had created an excellent product with a well-defined identity. It was also extremely generous of him to provide these rooms for the three of them. He seemed a little too good to be true and, in Josephine's experience, when something seemed too good to be true, it usually was. But that could be her cynicism talking.

Josephine sat on the edge of the bed, bending down to unlace her boots before hauling them off her feet. She wriggled her toes as she removed her thick socks and stood to stretch, only a little stiff. The hike hadn't been arduous and her walks on the mountain were beginning to pay off. Not bad for someone who had done none of this until she'd arrived in Tassie.

She was about to strip off for a shower when there was a quiet knock.

'You're here!' Emerson's face lit up the second Josephine pulled back the door. She unleashed a torrent of words. 'I'm so glad to see you. I've been freaking out. Have you been to the house? Did you see it? I can't believe this has happened to Remi, to her lovely home. It's so, so awful.' Emerson surprised Josephine by throwing her arms around her in a fierce hug.

'It's okay.' Josephine hugged her back. 'It could've been worse.'

Emerson released her grip and collapsed into one of the armchairs. 'I know, I know. If Remi hadn't shut that basement door, if the firies hadn't got there so quickly. It really, really could've been worse. So much worse. The whole house could've been destroyed. But it's still very bad.' Dismay was evident in her shaky voice and the tears in her eyes. 'All my work and my drawing tablet, and all my art supplies, are gone.'

'Oh, Emerson, that is terrible.' Josephine sat in the second chair and reached across to grip her hand. 'I'm so sorry to hear that.'

Emerson returned the squeeze. 'It's only stuff,' she said, struggling to maintain her usual upbeat energy. She let go of Josephine and slid a finger under her glasses to catch a tear. 'But poor Remi. The basement is damaged, the hall is a complete disaster. It's going to take time and money to get it all back the way it was. And it must've been so scary for her. I don't know what I would've done if I'd been there.' She stopped and took a deep breath as she looked down, her fingers busy picking at each other. 'Josie? Should we have told her about the emails? Would that have made a difference?'

Josephine took her time before answering. 'We made a decision to keep it to ourselves because we didn't want Remi to worry. She'd had so many unpleasant things happen, and we didn't want to add yet another incident to that list. But in hindsight, maybe telling her would've been a better choice. On the phone she said someone had been in the house right before the fire. She heard them, then saw them walking away, but couldn't make out who they were. Maybe someone did set the fire deliberately.' She shrugged. 'But even if she'd seen those emails, what would she have done? There was no suggestion that whoever wrote them was going to do this.'

'Do we say anything now?'

Josephine had asked herself the same question. 'I think we should.'

'It was candles,' Emerson said quietly. 'I had left candles down there, but I promise I never used them. I didn't leave anything burning. I just liked the smell of them.'

'Do you think someone set out to make it look like an accident?'

Emerson nodded. 'I think so. Maybe. Which could mean those horrid messages are connected. They really were a warning.'

They looked at each other, Emerson's face a more expressive representation of her own fears. 'Or it might not be. It could be that someone wanted us to leave for another reason.'

'What other reason?'

Josephine hesitated, unsure about putting her thoughts into words. 'Well, I get the impression Remi is relying on our rent at the moment.'

Emerson frowned. 'They want her to go broke?'

'It's a theory.'

Emerson swiped through her phone, then read what was on the screen. '"You shouldn't be in that house. Get out while you can."' She tapped to the next one. '"It's not safe to live with Remi Lucans. Find somewhere else to live."' She gave a dramatic shudder. 'So creepy. If you hadn't been so calm about it, I might have actually left. They do sound like someone wanted us out. How did they get our email addresses?'

'I don't know. But if someone got into the house to set a fire, they could have got in earlier to gather personal details like email addresses or phone numbers,' Josephine said.

'That really gives me chills. The thought that someone has been coming into the house and going through our stuff. Have you noticed anything missing or messed up?'

'No.'

'Me neither. I wonder if Remi has. I've tried messaging her, but she hasn't replied, and I don't want to knock on her door. She was completely shattered, so I'm guessing she's probably sleeping.'

'It can wait till tomorrow,' Josephine said. 'In fact, it would be better to have that conversation after she's had good news— like when she's given the okay to go back to the house.' She put her hands on her thighs and stood. 'Now, I'm dying for a shower. Can we talk again later?'

'Oh, of course. I haven't even asked how your trip was—did you enjoy yourself?' Emerson was trying to sound positive.

Josephine nodded. 'Loved it, so beautiful and an abundance of wombats.'

'Wombats! I love wombats, they're so funny and make me want to get down on the ground and cuddle them.' She went to the door. 'Do you want to do breakfast together? I'm going out for a few hours tonight. For dinner.' She hesitated, her smile now back, even if it wasn't as wide as usual. 'I've made a friend and he's taking me to a cool Japanese place in North Hobart.'

'A new friend? Aren't you doing well. You can tell me all about him in the morning.'

***

Later, wrapped in the hotel robe, dinner tray left outside the door, Josephine sat at the small round table and laid out a notebook and pens. She'd held back from getting involved in Remi's affairs—or trying to solve her problems—but enough was enough.

Josephine had been living in the house for only two weeks but had barely seen Remi smile. Her discomfort at sharing her home was obvious and she could be a bit prickly. Josephine didn't hold that against her. But what did concern her was how Remi had brushed aside the previous incidents, dismissing the reviews and the sabotage of her car as coincidence or inconsequential. Josephine hadn't dared raise the question of whether the death of Remi's dog could be added to the list of worrying events.

Denial was a place of comfort, but leaving so many questions unanswered didn't sit comfortably with Josephine. There were too many mysteries and unsettling events around Remi for her to ignore. She needed to know more about the ex-husband. Also, what of the girl who'd attacked Remi back in 2009? What had happened to her? Did she have a long-held grudge? Who would gain from Remi going broke?

It was none of Josephine's business, of course. She didn't really know Remi and her involvement wasn't necessary.

But she couldn't let it go.

She liked to be thorough. She'd built her business and her life around following up loose ends and being vigilant about potential threats—not only to herself, but to those around her. Like her son.

Sam would be landing in Bangkok in a few hours. The next leap in his own adventure, his girlfriend Holliday by his side. Sam had said Hollie was a sensible girl. That she wanted to see elephants at a sanctuary, not get high on a beach. That their plans included a trip to Koh Lanta, a low-key island where they would volunteer at a rescue centre for street dogs. He'd promised they wouldn't ride mopeds—at least not if they'd been drinking. Josephine had been relieved Sam was making an effort to assuage her fears and had forced herself to not lecture him on safety and security.

She'd always done everything to protect him. Had taught him to swim when he was still in nappies. Drilled him on traffic sense. Confirmed where he was and who he was with. Had always been ready to pick him and his friends up if they were out late. Had talked endlessly about the dangers of drinking, made him understand how the chance of risky behaviour increased with every glass. Made sure he could prepare a nutritious meal and knew not to eat leftover takeaway after it had been on the bench all night. Mostly he tolerated and understood her anxiety. But there had been times when he'd bristled under her protectiveness, fought against her need to protect him from unlikely scenarios. Towards the end, he'd become vague about what he was doing, where he was going. They'd argued too often.

Then she'd gone too far, and the consequences for their relationship had broken her heart. Her fears and interference had pushed him away, and her reaction to his leaving had been dramatic. She'd closed down her old life, sold almost everything—including her business—and packed a bag. She'd run away from her empty, quiet home. Now here she was, sharing a house at the other end of the country. She hadn't planned to move to this odd little city, crammed between waterfront and mountain, where burgeoning progress nipped at the heels of a shabby, shady history. This city, like her, was an ageing woman dealing with rampant change. Some of which was exciting. Some of which was fought against. Some of which brought tears. They were a good fit.

But being informed, making considered decisions and being aware of dangers were hardwired into her core. Remi needed her help—whether she knew it or not—and so far, minding her own business appeared to have benefitted no one.

CHAPTER EIGHTEEN

JOSEPHINE
Sunday, 30 July 2023

Josephine had already finished her breakfast by the time Emerson slipped into the seat opposite. 'How was your night?' she asked, noticing that Emerson looked tired but happier than she'd been the night before.

'Divine.' The glow in her eyes said it all. She waited till the waitress had brought her tea and taken her order for an omelette, then rested her chin on her hand and giggled. 'Kristof is quite, quite lovely. He wants to make films. Which, like any creative industry, is a bugger to break in to. He works here to pay the rent. It seems I'm destined to always be attracted to artistic types. Which means I will never, ever be swept away for shockingly expensive holidays. Sadly. And I must also give up pursuing gorgeous experiences I can't actually afford. But, on the bright side, my artist and I will make beautiful art together.' She flapped the back of a hand to her forehead, her face an exaggeration of despair. 'Oh, the woes of being an artiste. We will love greatly, inspire each other endlessly and always be broke.'

'Sounds wonderful. I'm glad you had a good time.'

'I did. And what about you? Did you see Remi at all? Any word on the house?'

'No and no,' Josephine said. 'No sign of Remi, which is understandable, and no further word on what's happening.'

'I hope we can go back today. There's going to be a bit of work cleaning up. Then I really, really need to get on with this project for Luke.' Her smile faded. 'I wish I hadn't left my tablet in the basement. I much prefer working digitally for jobs like this. I can't afford to replace it at the moment.'

'How much?'

'A lot.' Em fiddled with the teaspoon next to her cup. 'Over a grand. Plus, I'm going to have to replace all my Copic markers and pencils, drawing pads.' She threw up both hands. 'I've lost everything that I need to do the *job* that I need to do to get the *money* I need to live.' Her laugh was forced.

Josephine sat back in her chair, debating for a moment the wisdom of making an offer to assist. Was there really any reason not to? What did she have to lose?

'That's a difficult situation. Maybe I could help.'

'Aw, thank you, Josie, but you're retired and living in a share house. Your situation is probably no better than mine. It's time to suck up my pride and go to Centrelink.'

Josephine tamped down her amusement. 'What if I lend you the money to set yourself up again and you repay me in instalments when the work comes in?'

An anxious expression passed over Emerson's face. 'I'm not sure that's a good idea. I don't want to have more debt.

I already owe a few people. Like, you know, the bank. And a few others.'

'Have a think about it. I really am happy to help and we can stretch the loan out for a good length of time.'

'Okay. Thank you.' She was still hesitant. 'Can I let you know later today?'

'Of course. Now, on a different note, I've been thinking about what to tell Remi about the emails.'

'She won't be happy we didn't tell her sooner.'

'Which is why I thought we might hold off for a couple of days. I might be able to gather a bit more information by then, which would offset the impact.'

The waitress slid a perfectly prepared omelette in front of Emerson.

'Thank you, that looks amazing.' She picked up her cutlery and took a mouthful. 'Information about what?' she asked after a moment.

'Background and details on those who might be behind this campaign against her.'

'A campaign? Like, all of this is connected and deliberate? The reviews, the fuel, the emails, the fire? All of these things was coordinated or something?'

'Exactly.'

'How do you get this information? Who are you investigating? And how does a retired shop owner investigate anyone, anyway?' Emerson seemed genuinely perplexed.

Josephine gave her a soft smile. 'I have my ways and means. And I don't want to say too much until I know more.'

'Josephine, do you have a secret past you haven't shared with me? Who *are* you?'

Emerson was teasing, laughing at Josephine's clandestine approach, but it was better this way. Josephine didn't want to say too much yet. She'd certainly warmed to her vivacious young housemate, but she wasn't sure Emerson could keep things hushed.

'Let's agree not to mention the emails for a few days. Focus on getting Remi's house cleaned up and getting all of us back home, and then we can deal with the bigger picture.'

'Okay. I'm good with that.'

'Here she is now,' Josephine said quietly as Remi stepped into the restaurant, hesitating, as though loath to join them. Emerson stood quickly, crossed the room and hugged her before the other woman had a chance to leave. Josephine could see Remi's startled expression at the overt display of emotion. After which, Remi had no choice but to follow Emerson back to their table.

'We're both ready and eager to get stuck into the cleaning,' Emerson was saying. 'I think if we all go hard at it, we could get the hall sorted pretty quickly. Do you know when we can get started? Do we need to go and pick up some extra buckets and mops and things?'

'What say we let Remi have some breakfast or at least a coffee, first?' Josephine intervened.

'Oh, gosh, yes, sorry.'

The waitress appeared and Remi ordered a latte and a pastry before finally meeting Josephine's eye.

'How are you doing?' Josephine asked.

Remi looked away, her gaze drifting around the room, not focusing on anything. 'I'm okay.' She flicked the briefest glance at Josephine, her discomfort obvious. Her voice was dull, with a trace of anger at the edge. 'I thought bad things happened only in threes. Obviously, that's not true.'

'Isn't this number three?' Em said. 'The reviews. Your car. And the fire?' She counted them off on her fingers.

Remi stared out the window, not saying anything for a moment, before taking a deep breath. 'And Mavis, my dog, was poisoned. And someone hacked into my bank account to take all my money. That happened right before you arrived. Then there's Simon and Kayla being pushy and nasty and trying to force me to sell. Plus, taking in tenants, which I never wanted to do. And I'm missing some expensive jewellery. Honestly, everything is fucked up. I'm over it.'

Emerson's face fell at the suggestion that she was not wanted in the house, but Josephine wasn't perturbed. She could understand Remi's position; financial need had driven her to let out her rooms, not a desire for company.

'Simon is your ex-husband?' she asked.

A latte and a gooey Danish had been placed in front of Remi and she took a sip of the coffee before answering. 'Yes.'

'And Kayla?' Emerson had an odd look on her face.

'His second wife.'

'Um, is she by any chance blonde? Is she an influencer?'

Remi's distaste for this woman was obvious in her scowl. 'Yes, she's blonde. And, yes, she struts her stuff on social media.' She took a bite of the pastry and chewed methodically, still not making any real eye contact with either of them.

'Why do you ask?' Josephine directed the question to Emerson, who appeared to know something.

'Oh, no reason.' Emerson gave Josephine a look, her eyes wide, as though trying to convey a message. 'Just, you know,

I'd heard of someone called Kayla who's an influencer. She's married to some rich guy. That's all. I don't know her or anything like that. Is your ex rich? And why does he want you to sell? It's a bit mean to try and make you sell your house. You've worked so hard to make it beautiful.'

Josephine had noticed Emerson's speech sped up—even more than usual—when she was nervous. Right now, she was going double time.

'Em, let's not throw too much at Remi this morning.' Josephine smiled to let Emerson know she wasn't being chastised.

'Yes, right, absolutely. Of course. Sorry.' Emerson nodded vigorously and looked down at her plate before picking up her cutlery to finish her meal.

They sat in silence. Remi ate slowly with no sign of enjoyment, as she stared out the window. Finally she turned to look at Josephine. 'The fire was deliberate. Someone lit candles in the basement, then let a stack of paper catch alight. They moved everything closer together, so that the fire would spread more easily. The police are likely to get involved.'

Emerson had stopped eating and was staring, while Josephine held Remi's gaze and waited for her to continue.

'Someone came into my home, and not for the first time. I think someone has had access and has stolen expensive jewellery and tried to burn down my home.' Remi appeared calm, but Josephine could sense she was on the brink of fury. 'And they lit that fire the night I was there alone. The first time I'd been alone in over two weeks, as though they knew. Almost like they planned it that way. And they had turned off the mains power. At first the inspector presumed the fire service had switched it off when they arrived, but that wasn't the case. When I pointed out the power was off earlier, she suggested someone had tried to disable the hardwired smoke detectors. Except it didn't work. The detectors have backup battery power. Someone wasn't as smart as they thought.' Remi raised her eyebrows, as though asking a question or passing judgement, but her gaze didn't shift.

'Oh my god,' Emerson whispered with quiet horror.

'I saw the person who did this,' Remi continued. 'Something woke me, and I looked out the window. They were walking away. That person set the fire, waited for the flames to really take hold, left through the front door and calmly walked towards the city as though nothing had happened. Knowing I was inside. Can you believe that?' She gave the smallest shake of her head. 'Unfortunately, I couldn't see them clearly. And everyone in Tasmania has a black puffer jacket.' A long pause, before she said, 'You have one, don't you, Josephine?'

Josephine let out her breath slowly. 'Yes. I do.'

'What about you, Emerson?'

'Me?' Emerson looked ill. 'No. No, I don't. I don't have a puffer. I don't like the noise the nylon makes. That swish-swish when you move your arms. And they're ugly.'

Remi watched Josephine, scanning her face. 'Was it you?' The question was blunt, delivered without emotion. 'Did you do this?'

Emerson gasped but Josephine didn't flinch. 'No, it wasn't me. I was on Maria Island. With a walking group.' She wasn't offended by Remi's question; being suspicious was a natural response.

Remi remained taut, scrutinising Josephine for several seconds. 'And I suppose you can prove that?'

'Yes, I can. There were eight of us on the walk.' Josephine didn't elaborate any further.

'And you, Emerson? Were you really here all night?'

'Yes! Of course!' Emerson sounded on the brink of tears. 'Why would I set your house on fire?'

Remi's rigid posture held for a few long moments before she crumpled. 'I don't know.' She rubbed her face with both hands. 'I don't know anything. I don't know why someone would do this. I don't know why these things are happening. I don't know what's coming next!' Her shoulders fell and she looked away, her hands still on her cheeks. 'I don't know what I'm thinking. This is all so screwed up. I've had enough and I really am ready to walk away from everything.'

'Can I make a suggestion?' Josephine said.

'Sure.' Defeat hung heavy in Remi's voice.

'Let's focus on getting the house back in order, including changing the locks. Then in a few days, when you're settled back into your home, you can look ahead to what comes next.'

'You make it sound so easy.'

'Bite-sized pieces,' Josephine said.

'And we're here to help,' Emerson said eagerly. 'We're totally ready to get cleaning. Aren't we, Josephine?'

'Absolutely.' Josephine gave Remi a gentle smile.

Remi sighed. 'I think it's fine to go back and start cleaning today. And if I can get the basement windows boarded up or the glass replaced then we should be right to go home. So, one more night here, I guess.'

'Yay.' Emerson had pulled out her phone and was swiping the screen. 'I googled how to clean soot off the walls after a house fire and it's not difficult. I'm not too sure what trisodium phosphate is, but I'm sure we can find some. Bleach we can get no problem. And we'll need more buckets and sponges. Do you have a ladder? Of course you do! Gloves would be a good idea. I'm not too sure what we will be dealing with downstairs. Obviously, that's going to be a bigger job. But if we can get upstairs sorted, then we can go back to being cosy and comfortable. What if Josie and I go and get all the supplies, and we can meet you at the house ... What?' She looked up to find both of them watching her, the smallest hint of a smile finally twitching at Remi's mouth.

Josephine shook her head. 'You do love a project, don't you?'

'Absolutely.' Emerson's face lit up. 'Let's knock this over, then everything can go back to normal. And I can get on with what I need to do for Luke.'

'I'm sorry you've lost all your work and materials,' Remi said quietly. 'I might be able to claim your tablet under my contents insurance.'

'Oh, that would be good if you could. Thank you. I'm going to go to the art shop tomorrow and get the basics, good old-fashioned paper and pencils, so I can get going.'

They returned to their rooms, Remi to organise an emergency glazier and a locksmith and Emerson to write a shopping list for cleaning supplies. In an hour she and Josephine would go shopping before meeting Remi at the house.

Which gave Josephine time to continue with her own project. She now had two more names to consider: Simon and Kayla. Even without surnames she had enough to begin. She opened her email on her phone and sent two messages. It wouldn't take long to find out what she needed to know.

CHAPTER NINETEEN

EMERSON
Wednesday, 2 August 2023

Her phone rang as she was laying her new drawing equipment on the kitchen table. They'd made a good dent in the cleaning on Sunday afternoon and had been home since Monday. The hallway walls, floor and ceiling had been thoroughly cleaned, but the basement was still off limits. The windows had been replaced, but the damaged plasterboard walls and ceiling had been removed and taken away in a skip bin—Emerson delighting in the act of demolition—and the stone surfaces were dark and stained. The smell of smoke was still noticeable, so Josephine had set up an air purifier near the door to the basement. For now, though, Emerson was free to get on with her work.

She glanced at her phone screen as she opened her new drawing pad. Giselle. Again.

Shame immediately crushed the optimism she'd had moments before. She wanted to ignore the call. Wanted desperately to avoid this conversation. But she also wanted to be a good person.

'Giselle. Hi.' She spoke with more bounce than she felt.

There was a noticeable silence before her friend replied. 'Hi. I wasn't expecting you to answer.'

Which was a fair enough statement. Emerson had 'accidentally' missed quite a few calls in the last couple of weeks. She'd occasionally followed up with a perky message, asking how life was back there, giving hints about how great everything was going, making vague promises to send money. But she'd avoided a real conversation.

'Well, good timing, then. I was just packing up. I've finished the first part of a new commission,' she exaggerated as she walked to the window, staring out at the walled garden. 'You know the hotel project I mentioned? It's all going ahead. I'm working with the guy who owns the brand. He's great. It could end up being a big job. Moving here was so the right thing to do. Hobart is amazing, very cool—'

'Look, Em, that's great, but honestly I don't care.' Giselle cut her off. She was not interested in a catch-up. 'Have you been paid?'

'Um. Not really.' Emerson hesitated. 'There will be a small upfront confirmation fee, but the job keeps expanding and Luke—the owner—will settle on completion.' Which was sort of, but not entirely, the truth.

'Em.' Giselle was frustrated. More than that—she sounded desperate. 'You owe us so much. You left without warning and we need that money.'

'Didn't my bond cover a big chunk of the rent?'

'What bond?' Now Giselle was angry. 'You never paid any bond.'

'Yes, I did.' She was sure there had been a discussion when she moved in. 'Wasn't it two weeks' rent?'

'You never paid it. You kept putting it off, then we stopped asking. You were a friend. We never thought you'd do the wrong thing.'

The icky feeling intensified and Emerson rested her forehead on the glass. 'I'll get it sorted. I'm making things happen, right now.'

'You owe six weeks, Em. And your share of the power bill. You've left Erin and me in a really bad position.'

'I know,' Emerson mumbled.

'Please find some money. Please. You have to repay us.'

What could she do? Emerson ended the call with more promises. Giselle didn't sound convinced.

If only Emerson hadn't lived such a magnificent life. If only she hadn't been quite so addicted to showing off. Amazing bars, destination dining, glorious weekend escapes. Lush, enviable holidays with gorgeous, perfect-for-now lovers. Settings, scenes, Insta-worthy experiences.

She groaned. 'Fuckity, fuckity, fuck.'

The phone rang again. What now? Who else wanted to make her feel bad? She checked the screen.

'Hi Luke,' she answered, hiding her shame and misery. 'I'm working on your designs right now.'

'That's great. I know it's been a difficult time. How are things there?'

'They're good. The house is mostly back to gorgeous and comfortable.'

'And Remi? How is she doing?'

Emerson considered her answer for a moment. She was unsure how much to say, not wanting to gossip about her housemate, but wanting to be open and honest with the man who was offering her work. 'I think it's been really, really hard for her. The fire was a huge scare. It shook her up and I don't think she's recovered.'

'Yes, that's what I thought, too. With that in mind, I'd like to ask a small favour of you?'

Weird, but okay. 'Sure.'

'I want to take Remi away for a few nights, give her a break from all the stress and drama. Not only from the fire, but from that moron of an ex-husband and his demands. Give her a chance to re-energise. I've asked her, but she wasn't particularly enthusiastic, and hasn't said yes. Could you perhaps encourage her to come away? I really believe some time away will be the best thing for her.'

Remi's already high opinion of Luke climbed a few more notches. 'Of course I can!' She wanted to ask what he meant about Remi's ex but that might sound like she was talking about Remi behind her back. 'That's such a lovely and thoughtful thing to do. I'll say something today.'

'Don't let on I've asked you to, in fact, probably better you don't let on that you know about my offer.'

'Right, so a subtle suggestion that she should take a break, have a holiday, get out of Hobart. That we will look after the place for her. That sort of thing?'

'Exactly. I want to go this week.'

'I'll see what I can do.'

'And then when we get back, you can show me your ideas and we can discuss taking the project forward. Sound good?'

'Absolutely.'

Everything was going to work out for everyone.

***

A few hours later, Josephine and Remi returned from a walk. Josephine immediately began pulling things from the fridge to put together a cheese board while Emerson packed away her work and Remi finished up a call with her insurance company.

'I thought I'd get dinner delivered soon, but here's something to tide us over.' Josephine put the board on the table, then picked it up again. 'Why don't we sit in the living room? I could really do with a soft armchair.'

'Sure,' Remi said, as she took down wine glasses and collected a bottle of red. The walk had been Josephine's idea and Remi had reluctantly agreed. It seemed to have done her some good, there was definitely some colour in Remi's tired face. Talking with Josephine had probably helped, too. She was still a long way from happy, but she appeared to be a little less anxious. Fingers crossed she'd be open to the suggestion of time away.

In the front room, Emerson sank into the sofa while Remi settled on the floor by the coffee table, her back against one armchair. Josephine sat in the other. The heat panels had been turned on and the room was soon warm. The side lamps glowed with soft light and Josephine had drawn the curtains against the rapid onset of darkness. Slivers of light swept through the gaps as peak-hour traffic crawled past outside. They were in a plush, warm nest.

'I don't think I've ever had people in here like this,' Remi said, looking around. 'This is nice. Cosy.' She reached for a cracker and a wedge of King Island triple brie. 'I don't have friends to do this with.' She said it without angst.

'Have you not met people down here?' Josephine asked.

'No. Not really. I've been so focused on the renovation. And for a while there I often had the day-to-day company of the tradies. Plenty of banter and chat and sharing coffee and a biscuit. Now I don't tend to do anything where I'm going to meet people.'

Emerson couldn't imagine living so alone. 'What about friends from Sydney? Friends you had before you moved here? Old friends? Don't they come and visit?'

Remi sipped her wine. 'Those people who had been friends in Sydney were Simon's friends, and he kept them. Or they were people who wanted to be associated with him, not his ex-wife. In the end, I realised I had no one in our social circle who I cared enough about to want to maintain a connection.'

'And before that? You must've had heaps of friends when you were on TV. You would've been working with fun people, wouldn't you?'

'Yes. We had a great cast and crew.' She was pensive as she considered the question. 'After the attack, I couldn't face them. I didn't want to go back to the set. I didn't want anything to do with the world of acting and TV. I cut myself off from all of that. Then I married Simon and got swept into the life he wanted.' She ran a finger around the rim of her glass. 'I did have a friend from before that. Other than Luke, she was the last close friend I've had. Brittney and I used to share an apartment, back in Melbourne when we were both aspiring actors and worked in hospitality together.'

'What happened to her?' Emerson asked.

Remi gulped her wine. 'Well … we didn't see much of each other after I got the role and moved to Sydney. That was my fault. Then she moved there too, and at first everything was great. Then Simon and I got together, the show kept me busy and there were interviews and events. I didn't intend to cut her off, but it probably felt that way to her.'

Emerson chewed her thumbnail. Doing the wrong thing by a friend—even something done without malice—was a situation too close to her own actions. She was going to set things right as soon as she could. 'You stopped being friends?'

'Worse.'

The room was quiet, Emerson and Josephine waiting to hear what happened.

Remi looked uncomfortable, and Emerson was a little surprised when she kept talking. 'She attacked me. Physically. She read some rumours and believed them, then thought I needed to be taught a lesson. She wasn't in a good place mentally or emotionally.'

'You mean the person who attacked you, put you in hospital and ended your career was a friend?' Emerson gaped at Remi. 'But why? Why would she do that?'

'Because of lies and rumours that were spread about me. They were all complete bullshit. I didn't have a fling with that producer, Connor Mallick. I didn't sleep with him. I only met with him twice, once over lunch, once in the foyer of his hotel. He was in the early stages of preproduction for what would be the first series from his own company. He wanted to meet me to test the waters, I guess. That was all. There were photos taken that night that were supposed to be evidence of our affair. We had a brief hug at the end of the meeting, nothing more. Funny thing is, they didn't hit the magazines until weeks after the rumours that I was sleeping my way into a role first appeared. When the images were published, they appeared to provide proof.'

'How horrible.' Emerson accepted the cheese board from Josephine and assembled a couple of crackers. 'Do you think someone held onto them until they would have the biggest impact?'

'I presumed it was a twist of timing.'

'You've never wondered if someone orchestrated the whole thing?' Josephine sounded doubtful.

Remi frowned, her mouth pulling down. 'If I had thought that, I might have gone a wee bit mad. Because, well, because the attack wouldn't have happened if those stories hadn't been spread. If those photos hadn't been printed. It would be seriously awful if I was ...' She paused, trying to find the right word for what had been done to her. 'If I was hurt as a consequence of someone conducting a deliberate smear campaign. Anyway, what happened was horrible. Truly terrible. But I eventually recovered.'

'Do you miss it? The acting? Being famous?' Emerson asked.

'Yes and no. A big, fat no to being famous. I feel exposed and uncomfortable if anyone recognises me these days.'

'Does that still happen?' asked Josephine.

'Sometimes. There was a level of public interest in the first few years afterwards, around my marriage and those pieces they write about "whatever happened to that person we used to watch". But less and less as the years went on, much less after the divorce. Absolutely nothing recently.'

'I imagine having someone you cared about and trusted do something so terrible would've made you wary of getting close to people,' Josephine said with empathy.

Remi smiled a little. 'You could say that. I've become a bit of a recluse.'

'You do have Luke,' Emerson said.

'Yes, I do. The funny thing is we all used to work together— Luke, Simon, Brittney and me—we were all at the Worthington

Hotel in Melbourne, back when we were younger than you. It's strange how everything unfolded. Luke despised Simon even back then, and when Simon and I hooked up for a month or so that year, Luke tried to convince me I was making a mistake.' She dropped her head back against the armchair. 'Should've listened to him.'

'He seems really great. Very caring.' Emerson held back on mentioning the trip.. 'Have you ever considered being more than friends? I mean, he is rather lovely, not bad for an older guy. Not that I'm thinking of me. But he'd be perfect for you.'

Remi laughed. 'Em, you would have to be one of the most upfront, unfiltered people I've ever met.'

'Sorry. I don't always think before I speak.'

'It's fine. Yes, the possibility of being more than friends has come up on the odd occasion. But it's never been the right time and, honestly, I'm reluctant to change the dynamic. He's not perfect. A bit of a player, a bit of a rogue charmer. If we changed the nature of our relationship and it didn't work out, I'd lose my one true friend. I can't afford to do that. I mean, he's always supported me. After the incident I recuperated at his place, so he's seen me at my very worst. My parents were driving me insane and I wanted to stay in Sydney. He'd moved there by that stage and I stayed with him until I healed.'

'And then?' Josephine asked.

'And then Simon strolled back into my life, and I foolishly decided to marry him. Which seemed like a good idea at the time.' She hugged her knees to her chest. 'Then there was Kayla. I found out about her when I saw my husband with his hand down her dress at the opening of Strike Hobart. I left him the next day and was happier for being alone.'

'And now?' Emerson asked.

Remi shook her head. 'I've become a haggard middle-aged hermit. I'm not exactly relationship material.'

'Wow, if you're haggard, what does that make me?' Josephine asked with a huff of laughter.

'Conqueror of mountains,' said Emerson emphatically.

'A woman of wise counsel,' Remi added.

'A damn hot chick of unknown years.' Emerson laughed. 'And a very generous person.' She'd finally accepted Josephine's offer to lend her the money for a new tablet but was far from being comfortable with this new debt. 'For someone who had to take an early retirement, who had to sell everything you owned and is renting a room in a share house, you are extremely generous.'

'Well, it wasn't so much that I *had* to sell everything, it was more a case of my decluttering getting carried away. And I haven't retired. At least, I don't think I have. I like to say I'm between projects—I sold my business for a good sum.'

'What exactly was your business, Josephine?' Remi asked. 'Didn't you have a shop or something? I thought you'd said you were in retail.'

Josephine ducked her head for a moment then looked up with the smile of a proud mother. 'I was in retail. I did have a shop. I began with one shop and ended up with a few more.'

'Wow. What were you selling?' Emerson asked.

'I had a line of stationery. Journals, notebooks, pens. I had my own brand.'

'Like Naked Paper?' Emerson knew the brand well. There wasn't one in Hobart, but they were in most of the other cities and she was already missing having the store available. You could never have too many beautiful notebooks, and the Naked

Paper stuff was fun and gorgeous and clever. She'd always left their shops with things she hadn't known she needed.

'Um, yes. I was Naked Paper.'

'Holy shit,' gasped Emerson. 'Really? You're Naked Paper? That's crazy! I love, love, love Naked Paper. Why did you sell? I mean, obviously you must've made a few squillion dollars. In which case, what the hell are you doing here with us?'

Josephine laughed as she lifted her glass. 'I didn't have a plan. Sam left and I started stripping back my life and couldn't stop.' She took a sip, then added, 'Now I'm trying to rebuild myself. And to distract myself from worrying about Sam.'

'You're still worried?' asked Emerson. 'He sounds like a good guy. Why do you worry so much?'

Josephine let out a long sigh. 'Something happened, years ago, that really affected me.' She went to take a bite of her cracker, as though that were all she had to say, then stopped. Setting it down on the edge of the coffee table, she wiped her hands together, and kept talking. 'My sister Sarah and I were at a party. I would've been the same age Sam is now. There was a boy we were both interested in. I can't even remember his name. Anyway, when I saw him kissing Sarah, I got stroppy. She was a year younger than me. He was a year older. So, by my logic, he should've been with me.'

She picked up her wine and sipped. 'I drowned my sorrows with lots of Bundy and Coke. But when the party wrapped up, I went to find her—we were both still living at home—and I had called a cab. She was with a group, the boy's arm around her. They were getting into a car. A purple Ford Falcon, with actual fluffy dice hanging off the mirror. I remember that car so well.' Despair was evident in the softness of her voice and the sag of her face. Emerson could see how difficult this was for Josephine. 'There was no doubt they'd all been drinking, including the girl who had the keys. Sarah looked at me—she was hesitating.' Josephine turned her glass around in her hands. 'Looking back, I don't think she really wanted to leave with them. But, you know, the hot guy had her attention. I don't blame her for wanting to stay with him a bit longer. Parties were like that. If they were good, if good things happened, you never wanted them to end. Especially if it involved a romantic hook-up. But at the same time, I could see that she knew getting in that car wasn't the best idea. Convincing her to come home with me wouldn't have been hard.

'I didn't even try. I was so pissed off at seeing her with that handsome boy. I told her to go, said something snarky like, "You've made your choice." I remember how hurt she looked. But I turned my back. I left her.' She took a long breath.

Remi and Emerson waited, their drinks and snacks forgotten.

'The driver was speeding and lost control on a bend, wrapped around a power pole. There had been five of them in that car. The police said Sarah didn't have a seatbelt on. She'd probably been sitting on the boy's lap. She was in a critical condition for six days before she died from her injuries. She never regained consciousness. The driver was the only survivor.'

Emerson put a hand over her mouth, tears hovering in her eyes. 'Oh my god. No. I'm so, so sorry.'

'That was thirty-two years ago,' Josephine continued. 'A few years back, I asked an investigator to track down the driver. Turns out she had taken her own life two years after the accident.' Sadness creased Josephine's face. 'We were kids who made bad choices. Those choices had terrible, terrible consequences. And I can't seem to stop myself from worrying about my beautiful son and the choices he will make.'

'You've told him your story?' asked Remi, swiping a tear that slipped over her cheek.

Josephine gave a small smile. 'Oh, yes. It wasn't quite a bedtime story but we've had a few heart-to-hearts about it over the years. Probably why he's been such a damned sensible teenager. I've scared the hell out of him.'

'Then you've done everything you can. And by the sound of it, he is a responsible young man. A kid with his head screwed on. He'll be having a wonderful experience in Thailand.'

They sat in silence for a moment.

'Maybe he'll check himself into a Buddhist monastery while he's there,' Emerson said, the sombre mood making her anxious. She wanted to bring them back to easy chat and laughter. 'And the biggest thing you'll have to worry about is him shaving his head and giving away all his worldly possessions.'

'I could live with that,' Josephine said. 'For a few months. Then I'd be lecturing him about finishing his degree and getting a job.'

'Or he could announce he's getting married,' suggested Remi. 'No. He could tell you he *is* married. He and his girlfriend had a quickie ceremony on a Thai beach.'

'Or he's going to be a dad. Or he's going to open a sanctuary for injured monkeys.' Emerson was on a roll. 'Or he wants to teach English to Thai orphans. Or he's going to open a shack bar on a remote island and surf all day.'

'Okay, okay.' Josephine laughed, holding up a hand to make them shut up. 'Stop filling my head with ideas. Or I'll have to go and climb that bloody mountain again. Let's talk about something else.'

'Well, given the spirit of confession that has come over us, it must be my turn,' said Emerson. She took a gulp of wine and set the glass on the table. This was going to hurt, but it felt like the right moment. 'I have a huge credit card debt I can never pay back. And when I say huge, I mean thirty-thousand-dollars huge. I have nothing to show for all my spending, but I do have lots of cool shots and posts from all the amazing places I've been and things I've done. Because.' She looked at each of them in turn and held up a finger. 'It is not about acquiring stuff but having *experiences.*' She said 'experiences' with dramatic emphasis, as though talking about the most wondrous salvation of the modern day. 'And making sure your experiences get shared with everyone. Then they can crave experiences like yours. But better.' She picked up her glass again. 'Unfortunately, I didn't actually have the money for all those experiences, just credit—which is sadly all maxed out. But, hey, nobody can take away my glorious memories. Especially when your social media footprint is forever.' She waggled her eyebrows and laughed. That hadn't been so bad.

A half-choked laugh burst from Remi. 'We are such a sad, sorry bunch, aren't we?'

'Yes. But we're getting it together,' Josephine said, joining in the laughter.

'Are we, though?' Remi asked. 'I still have to pay Simon this month's repayment. And I can't seem to rekindle my passion for this.' She waved a hand to encompass the room and the rest of the house.

'You need to take a break. Go away for a few days and you might come back with fresh enthusiasm and energy,' Emerson said, grabbing the perfect opportunity to nudge Remi towards

Luke. 'Trust me, I'm an expert in the rejuvenating powers of an indulgent short break. I highly recommend it.'

'That's not a bad idea,' added Josephine. 'Em and I can look after the house.'

'Hmm. Luke has suggested the same thing. He has offered to take me away for a few days.'

'See! Perfect. It will be wonderful.' Emerson clapped her hands.

'But what if something else happens? If all this hasn't stopped?' Remi asked.

'Then we will deal with it.' Josephine said. 'You've changed the locks, which is a good start, and I'm not easily intimidated.'

'I don't know.' Remi didn't sound convinced.

'You can trust us.' Josephine said. 'We will look after your home. I do think, however, you should get up to date with your repayments first, that way you retain the ability to make decisions regarding the house and can control the process.'

'Okay. You're right.' Remi nodded. 'Stay in charge and then recharge. Decisions can be made later.'

'Here's to that.' Emerson raised her wine. 'And to getting it together.'

As their glasses clinked, Emerson was filled with a fizzy rush of optimism and excitement. Everything was going to work out—life was going to be fabulous again.

CHAPTER TWENTY

JOSEPHINE
Monday, 7 August 2023

Josephine climbed. Head down, grasping at boulders for balance, testing the loose rock before she shifted her weight from one foot to another. Hunters Track was proving to be one hell of a steep climb, taking her from the easily accessible Junction Cabin up to the chalet. From there, according to her map, another track looped back, leading down the mountain. Or, for the fit and brave, there was the Zig Zag Track towards the summit. Right now, she wanted the easier option. Her thighs were burning and her breath came in deep, sucking pants. This was bloody hard work and the track was poorly defined. A steep scramble over the rocks and scree, the path was marked by occasional reflective orange tags, which weren't always easy to find.

Only a few scruffy trees clung to this section of the mountain, leaving walkers exposed, and while the wind wasn't fierce, it was bitterly cold. The sky, at least, was clear. The views, when she turned to look out instead of down at her feet, were amazing. She'd checked the weather report thoroughly before setting out. Walking on the mountain in winter could be dangerous and while there was no snow today, she understood how quickly things could change. Her small backpack held everything Parks and Wildlife insisted a hiker should carry: sturdy rain jacket, first-aid kit, food, water. A whistle and a compass dangled from a loop. Her waterproof map was in one pocket. There was a space blanket tucked inside. Plus those fabulous pocket warmers, which she bought in bulk. Just open the packet, give them a shake and within a few minutes they were thawing her hands or warming her face.

A month ago, before she'd even set foot on the mountain, she'd spent days studying the advice in the hiking guide and had been diligent in ticking off her list as she bought supplies. Hobart had a cluster of outdoor supply shops and she'd become familiar with all of them. She'd asked questions, listening intently to the staff, their passion for adventuring evident in their enthusiasm for thermals and boots, packs and kit. If something went wrong, she was ready. She'd even invested in an EPIRB—an emergency position indicating radio beacon. It was always better to have things you might need but didn't use than to need something and not have it.

The rock-hopping finally gave way to a narrow track, but the incline remained punishing. She stopped, slipping her pack off her shoulders to retrieve her water bottle. Deciding a square of dark chocolate was well deserved, she snapped off two, her gloved fingers awkward, and popped them in her mouth.

Then she pulled her beanie low around her face, replaced her water bottle and hoisted the pack onto her back before continuing the slow trudge to where she would cross Pinnacle

Road and reach the chalet. The last few steps of the path were stone blocks cut for seven-foot giants. The muscles in Josephine's thighs quivered relentlessly as she pushed herself up, her legs threatening to give way and dump her on her arse.

Reaching the bitumen of Pinnacle Road was anticlimactic. Standing on level ground felt good, but the contrast between the exposed wilderness and the road was sharp. She waited as a slow flow of cars passed on their way to the summit. A few curious faces turned in her direction, perhaps wondering where she had emerged from.

The chalet was an old hiker's shelter set above the road. Built of heavy stone, it was open at the front and had two large wooden tables and a fireplace. Sadly, there was no fire. Josephine took a seat, spreading out an early lunch of a filled roll, dried fruit and one of Emerson's raspberry-chocolate brownies. God, that girl could bake. It was just as well she was hauling herself up and down this mountain. The cakes and slices and biscuits kept appearing and she kept scoffing them down.

As she ate, she tapped her phone.

The email from Shareena had come through, the investigator proving herself as efficient as always. Josephine scanned the information, her attention immediately snagging on a section of the report. Well, that was interesting. It unequivocally ruled one name off her list. Did Remi know about this? She hadn't said anything to suggest she did.

Josephine finished the brownie, dusted the crumbs from her fingers and tapped out a response to Shareena before repacking her backpack. She stood and considered where to go next: up or down. Her legs had settled, she was well prepared and the weather forecast remained promising. She followed a wide flat track that passed beneath the exposed face of the towering

Organ Pipes, then stopped again at the junction of two paths; the Zig Zag to the top, or the Pinnacle Track back to the Springs where she'd left Emerson's car.

Climbing to the top would be immensely satisfying. But today was not the day to head for the summit; she had work to do. Remi would be home from her holiday tomorrow and Josephine wanted to be able to give her as much information as she could. She'd made the decision to move into a share house so she would be forced to reconnect with the world and, if she were being honest, in the hope of rediscovering the enthusiasm, passion and energy she'd had when she'd been in her twenties and living with friends. As it had turned out, she appeared to be right where she needed to be.

***

Josephine ended the call, setting her phone on the cafe table while she wrote in her notebook. Nothing she'd learned this afternoon was much of a surprise. Vashti, as her long-term business advisor, had given her the inside rumours, some facts and her thoughts. She was a woman with contacts and friends throughout the business world and had been thorough and quick, taking only forty-eight hours to pull the information together.

Josephine put down her pen and picked up her mug, reading over what she had written while she finished her coffee.

'How's things today?' the waitress asked as she passed the table.

'Hi, Esme.' When exactly had the golden-oldie names started making a comeback? 'Excellent, as always.' There was a small delight in being recognised as a regular, in knowing the names of the staff. She was becoming a local. 'How are your studies going?'

They chatted for a moment, Esme giving a quick rundown of her pile of assignments, Josephine commiserating. When Esme tossed out the idea of taking a year off from uni, Josephine mentioned Sam and his travels.

'You must be a cool mum,' she said. 'My parents have a breakdown every time I even mention taking a gap year. They're terrified I'll run off and join a cult or a commune. Or worse, that I'll marry some guy and end up living on the other side of the world and they'll never see their grandkids.'

'They actually say that?'

'Yes.' Esme rolled her eyes and groaned. 'Or—tragedy—I'll never get a degree. But honestly, I don't see the point in accumulating a stupid huge study debt unless you really believe in what you're studying.'

Josephine didn't disagree. 'Having your kids go off into the world is hard.'

'But isn't that the point of raising children? To prepare them for their lives as adults? At some point, parents have to say, fly be free, don't crash.'

Out of the mouth of babes. 'You're right. Doesn't make it easy though. There's a lot of things to crash into out there.'

Esme collected Josephine's empty mug. 'Things can go wrong anywhere, though, can't they? What if everything went pear-shaped and you'd never even stepped outside your comfort zone? Now, that would be a tragedy. Isn't that what's so sad when someone young dies? "She had the whole world, her whole life, in front of her." That's what they always say.'

Josephine remained sitting after Esme had moved on.

The girl was right. That was exactly what everyone had said when Sarah died. She had been so young. Her whole life was in front of her. The world had been hers to take. Sarah never got to leave and fly. She hadn't been flitting about the globe. She hadn't been having adventures in way-off places. She'd been at a party two suburbs over from where she'd grown up. Where she'd lived her whole life. Josephine should have stopped her from getting in the car.

Sam, on the other hand, she'd done everything to protect. But her job had been to give him skills, then set him free. She had to let her son learn from his own experiences. To become an adult and live his own life.

And she had to learn to let go. Climbing the mountain seemed to help with clearing her head and giving her perspective. As did involving herself in the lives of other people. She had a purpose.

She flicked the notebook open, reread her notes, then picked up her phone. Before she did anything, she needed a second opinion.

***

Josephine had ordered and drunk half of her second coffee when Emerson strode through the door. Today's combo included lime green tights under a short forest green skirt, a tan jumper and a voluminous scarf in emerald. She had on her white-framed glasses.

'Hi Josie-Jo.' Emerson took the seat next to Josephine.

The nickname was a surprise. The only person who'd ever called her Josie-Jo had been Sarah. The memory flared, and with it came a stab of loss that quickly faded. Emerson using the name felt playful and affectionate. She liked it.

'That was quick.'

'I was already in town. And let's face it, this town ain't the biggest.' Emerson ordered a hot chocolate from Esme. 'What did you want to talk about?'

'I needed to get your opinion. I've found out something to do with Remi and I'm not too sure what to do next.'

'Gosh. Okay. Not about Luke, I hope.'

Josephine shook her head. Emerson was obviously a die-hard romantic. 'You really are hoping they'll get together, aren't you?' Of course, she had also requested the investigator do a quick dig into Luke, but there was nothing in Shareena's report to arouse her suspicions.

'Absolutely.' Her drink arrived and she poked the marshmallows into the foam with her teaspoon, bobbing them up and down. 'They're both so lovely. And I'm pretty sure Luke has been in love with her for a super long time. He's never given up. He would really look after Remi. They'd have a wonderful life together. She deserves that kind of happy ending. Don't you think?'

Josephine made a noncommittal noise. 'Not everyone wants to be looked after. I get the distinct impression Remi is determined to pull her life together on her own.'

'Oh, sure. I get what you're saying. What I mean is, they would look after each other. Obviously, she's probably a bit wary, especially after her ex turned out to be such a wanker. He sounds like a real piece of work. Have you seen some of the shit he posts? He's all about flashing the cash and strutting about with his plastic-fantastic, couture-clad new wife. All arse, no class.'

'That's sort of what I wanted to talk to you about.' Josephine couldn't help but lean forward, bringing their heads closer together over the table. 'Simon Hanland may appear to be cashed-up and successful, but it's all a front.'

'Really?' Emerson's eyes widened behind her glasses. 'Who told you that?'

'I asked my business advisor to do a little digging. She's a woman used to peeling away the veneer and getting to the truth of how a business is faring. What she had to say about Hanland Luxury wasn't good. He's in a world of financial difficulty.'

'But they've got, what, four stores now? And he's a Hanland. And I've found out that's one hell of a family to have. Serious coin. And that wedding. I mean you can't have an event like that without being mega-bucks wealthy.'

Emerson's nose had a small dollop of milky chocolate on the tip. Josephine's hand twitched, wanting to take a napkin and wipe it clean. She stopped herself, tapping the end of her own nose instead. 'Chocolate,' she said.

Emerson tried to peer down. 'Ha. Thanks.' She dabbed it clean.

'What I've been told is, Simon went out on his own when he started Hanland Luxury—did it without the backing of his father. In fact, it seems there's been a significant falling out between father and son. Simon opened those stores against his father's advice and is on his own. Apparently his business is already in massive debt, partly due to expanding too quickly. More store fronts may equal more turnover, but it also means more running costs, which come on top of the cost of setup and fit-out. He's also lost the sales contract for one of the top luxury watch brands. Which would hurt—apparently that brand alone contributed to a significant percentage of the annual turnover.'

'And personally? Doesn't he have a house with Sydney harbour views?'

'Views and a huge mortgage.'

'Wow. Might've been an idea to keep the wedding to a one-day affair. Not three.'

'Competitive ostentatiousness.'

Emerson laughed. 'I totally get that. My spend is bigger than your spend. My experience is more impressive that yours.'

'Exactly.' Josephine sat back. 'Knowing all this, it makes sense that Simon is so determined to sell Remi's house.'

'What would he get though? What's left of Remi's loan? I mean, to me, a few hundred thousand is a humongous pile of money. But to people like them, it wouldn't go far.'

'It could buy them time. Clear some space on their mortgage. Pay off a personal debt or two. Whatever the case, they seem to need it. The question is, how far have they gone to force Remi's hand?'

It took a second, then understanding had Emerson's mouth falling open. 'Whoa. No. You mean all the shit things that have happened?'

'Everything that has happened has affected Remi's finances. The sabotage of her car. The money out of her account. Possibly even the poisoning of her dog—that vet bill would have been a real financial hit. And remember she said some jewellery had gone missing? Completely different acts, but all targeting her bank balance. Which, I'm guessing, was the intent. Remember, Simon can force her to sell if she defaults. She's barely scraping the monthly repayments together. He wouldn't have expected her to bring in tenants, and if she hadn't, she'd have nothing.'

'And the fire? And those emails?'

'Yes, maybe all that too. Trying to frighten us into leaving so she wouldn't have the rental income. And the fire might have been a scare tactic.'

'But that's awful. It's criminal.' Emerson's voice rose. 'That bastard.'

'Do we tell her? I mean, the stuff about his financial situation is more than a guess. But we have no evidence he's behind the other things.'

Emerson pressed her palms to her cheeks. 'I don't know. Would it help? Or would hearing this stress her out, make things worse?'

'Information is knowledge and the more knowledge you have, the better decisions you make.'

They sat quietly, weighing up the question.

'She's home tomorrow,' Emerson said. 'She'll be happy and relaxed. Do we want to ruin that? I mean, I would be surprised if Luke and Remi don't return as more than friends.'

'My feeling is she will cope with knowing about Simon and she'll be ready if he tries anything else. She'll realise how serious he is about getting what he wants.'

'Okay. Yeah, that makes sense.' Emerson wriggled back in her seat, looked around the cafe then turned back to Josephine. 'What about that girl, the one who attacked her? There could be a chance she's still carrying a grudge. She did sound kind of messed up.'

'It can't have been her.'

'Why not?'

'I had a private investigator check for me. She died a few weeks after the attack.'

'Seriously? Okay, two things … first of all, you hired a PI?'

Josephine smiled at her reaction. 'Yes, I have an investigator I use from time to time. She really is useful and much more reliable than Google.'

'Really? That's kinda cool. Who else have you had investigated?'

Josephine pressed her lips together. 'I used Shareena to find the driver of the car Sarah died in.' She wasn't going to mention the background checks she'd done on Sam's friends. She wasn't proud of that, even if the reports had covered only the basics and she hadn't gone as far as having them followed—at least not for any length of time. 'And secondly?'

'Secondly—that's messed up. Not the PI bit, but the girl dying. What happened?'

'Hit and run. The driver of the vehicle was never found.' Brittney was never charged and had died before she could be questioned. Shareena had been unable to find any further details.

'Look, I know she did a horrible, unforgivable thing, but that's still a sad story, isn't it? To go from being Remi's friend and housemate to hurting her, to then dying on the side of the road. It's kind of tragic.'

'It is, I agree.'

'And Remi's story is pretty messed up, too.' Emerson looked forlorn. 'The attack by someone who'd been a friend, the loss of her career, a dick of a husband, living like a recluse because she's been burned and let down so much. Then all this crap, including her home being set on fire.'

'Which is why we're helping her,' said Josephine. 'She needs us.'

CHAPTER TWENTY-ONE

EMERSON

Emerson and Josephine walked back to the house. The day was clear but cold, and it felt like it might snow. Maybe. Not that Emerson had a clue about what imminent snow felt like, but it was definitely cold enough.

'You know, I was a bit wary about moving into a share house with older women,' she said as they neared home. 'But you know what? I think it's working out really well. We make a good team.'

'We do.' Josie sounded amused. 'What's so intimidating about "older women"?'

'I guess I didn't think there would be anything to talk about. No shared interests. No parties or even fun in the house. I thought it could be boring and, I don't know, weird.'

'Well, it certainly hasn't been boring.'

'You can say that again.'

'And at the end of the day, just because I'm over fifty doesn't mean I'm an ancient artefact. I even listen to Billy Eilish and Frank Ocean, and don't mind Harry Styles.'

'Ha! Look at you. See, you're super cool and hip.'

They were both laughing as they let themselves into the house.

'Oh, I've had a thought,' Emerson said suddenly. 'Before we say anything to Remi, could we do more investigation? Simon might not have even been down here when her car was sabotaged. We don't want to put the idea in her head if there was actually no way it could've been him.'

'We'd better consider his wife as well then.' In the kitchen, Josephine opened the wood heater and stoked the fire.

'Smart thinking.' From what Emerson had seen, Kayla was no fairy princess.

'And we know she was here the day after the car went kaput, because she cornered Remi in town. The question is, was Simon here as well?' Josephine asked.

'Well, wifey pours herself all over social media. There will probably be posts about her darling husband as well.'

'If you look over that, I could make a few calls. Check Hobart hotels, see where they stayed and for how long.'

'Isn't that information private?'

Josephine cleared her throat. Then she held up a hand with thumb and little finger extended and said in a clipped, efficient voice, 'Hello. Yes. This is Vanessa from Hanland Luxury, I'm Mr Simon Hanland's personal assistant. I'm trying to finalise the June expenses for him and Mrs Kayla Hanland, and the records are incomplete. Could I please confirm the dates he stayed with you?'

'Give the woman respect! Josie-Jo, you continue to amaze me.'

'What can I say? Sometimes I amaze myself.'

Emerson took a seat at the table as she swapped her shoes for a pair of purple Ugg slippers. 'As much as I'd like to watch you do that, I can probably save you the effort. I know for a fact Kayla has stayed at Strike.'

'At Strike? At Luke's hotel?'

Emerson nodded emphatically. 'I saw her there. I didn't know who she was at first. But I noticed her the day I had the first meeting with Luke. She was a bit hard to miss.' She didn't want to mention that Kayla and Luke had interacted. That detail wasn't relevant to this and Josephine—being the suspicious type—might begin thinking Luke was somehow involved. Which was absolutely not possible. 'I think that was the day after she confronted Remi down at the waterfront.'

Josephine checked some of her notes. 'And the day before *that* was when the thing happened to her car.'

'But there's more. I also saw her at the hotel the morning after the fire and she looked furious.'

Josephine was still standing with her back to the wood heater, warming herself. 'But no sign of Simon?'

'Nope.'

'He wouldn't be staying at Strike,' Josephine mused.

'I shouldn't think so, not if he and Luke despise each other.'

'So if Kayla was here, but Simon wasn't …'

'Then Kayla probably did all of it. Or maybe he did some and she did some. Whoa. That's scary.' Emerson tried to imagine the pristine Mrs Hanland sneaking in and lighting the fire. 'Is she really capable of dirty work like that? I mean, you should have a look through her Insta.'

Emerson had spent a good hour or so cyberstalking Kayla on the socials. She looked like any other pretty, wealthy young woman. Her hair could only be achieved with regular hours in a salon. She had a wardrobe of high-end clothes and in her photos, she was almost always staring wistfully into the middle distance or in a carefully posed facsimile of someone caught laughing and loving life.

Josephine took a seat and started scrolling while Emerson did another search, this time digging a bit deeper.

After twenty minutes she slipped her notebook out from under a pile of loose pages. 'Naked Paper 2021, burgundy and gold range,' she said, stroking the cover. 'One of my favourites.'

'One of mine too,' Josephine said, nodding approvingly.

'It's a pity you're not still the CEO, you would've been a fabulous contact to have. I might even have been able to wrangle a mate's rate discount.'

'But then I wouldn't be here.'

'This is true.'

They continued in silence for a few minutes, then Emerson put down her pen and pushed her glasses to the top of her head to rub her eyes. 'This is interesting,' she said. 'Kayla wasn't always so high end.' She turned a few pages. 'She has a less flashy history. Years ago, she was working in a bar in Sydney.'

'When?'

'Um … 2008. Wow. Must've been young. Her bio says she's only thirty-three. I think she might be fibbing a bit about her age. She would've only been …' She tried to do the maths.

'Eighteen,' Josephine said. 'Old enough to work in a bar, I guess. If you've got your RSA.'

'Sure, right. But the bar was at the Park Hyatt, which is kinda fancy.' She tapped back to the article she'd been reading. 'This article is an *I-knew-her-when* expose from someone who wasn't happy to see her flouncing about town and marrying a millionaire. Happens all the time. Some girl pulls herself up, gets money and fame, and all the girls she trod on to get there, or who just plain envy her, trot out their stories.'

'So much for the sisterhood,' Josephine said, sounding disappointed.

'Yep. Anyway, according to this ex-friend, Kayla was open about wanting to nab herself a wealthy man. Eighteen is kinda young to start on the gold-digger path, don't you think?'

'Probably. But not out of the question. What year did you say—2008?' Josephine asked and Emerson nodded. 'Remi would've been filming *Our Street* in Sydney that year. She was on the show from 2006 to 2009.'

Emerson shrugged. 'It's a big city. Remi says she didn't know Kayla even existed until she found out she was the woman screwing her husband, which was only a few years ago. The night before she ditched him.'

'Yes, it could be a weird coincidence. But still. Remi, Simon and Kayla would all have been in Sydney that year. Remi and Simon were living together.'

The whisper of several unfinished thoughts slipped through Emerson's head and she tried to grab at them. Luke would've been there too. He'd moved to Sydney not long after Remi. She pushed that idea aside, knowing it wasn't relevant. But there was something else. Remi may not have known Kayla, but had Simon? No. Now she really was forcing pieces to connect, determined to create a bigger picture. She scribbled a line on the page, then continued swiping, her fingers darting over her phone. There was something else she remembered.

'Okay. This is another teeny, probably irrelevant coincidence.'

'What is it?'

'Well, the other night, after Remi told us about those horrid rumours. I might have done a bit of reading up on how it all went down. You know, the old gossip and the stuff about what happened to her.'

'Okay.'

'Anyway, you know the story, right?'

Josephine nodded. 'Only what Remi mentioned.'

'The whole rumour and gossip thing about her and the producer Connor Mallick really got out of hand when photos came out of the two of them at the Park Hyatt. And there was a supposed eyewitness report from someone who worked at the hotel of them getting lovey-dovey in a dark corner of the bar and heading up to a room. Right? The photos showed them standing outside the front entrance, embracing. A day later Brittney went batshit crazy and bashed Remi up.' Emerson nibbled her thumbnail. 'This might be way off the mark. I mean, most the time, those stupid magazines make up their so-called sources. They're all lies.'

'But?'

'But the hotel where those photos were taken, where Remi was supposedly seen being cosy, was where Kayla worked. It's another weird coincidence, right?'

Josephine considered the information, seeming to turn the pieces around in her mind. 'Or it may not be a coincidence at all.'

'But what would that mean? That Kayla took photos and fabricated a story about Remi back in 2009? Then years later became involved with her husband? Married him. Then embarked on a nasty campaign to oust Remi from the home she adores?' Emerson counted the points off on her fingers. 'To do that, she'd have to be totally obsessed or have a long-held grudge.'

'That's presuming each step was planned. Even if Kayla is responsible for all these things happening, it doesn't mean coincidence didn't play a part. She might have seen an opportunity to make some quick cash when she saw Remi and Connor sitting together. Connecting with Simon years later could've been a separate event.'

Emerson flopped back in her chair. 'So, way back in 2009, Simon dumped Remi when the rumours started. Rumours about a film industry man she is supposed to have hooked up with at the Park Hyatt. Where Kayla was working, her eye on the rich men in the bar. After Brittney attacks Remi, Simon gets the guilts and draws Remi back into a relationship. Off again is on again, and they marry. Skip forward years later, Remi's marriage is shattered and Kayla turns out to be the other woman. Then, nasty shit happens to Remi, and Kayla is in town when Remi's car is sabotaged and then there's the fire. If Remi has no money and has to sell the house, Kayla benefits.' Emerson raised her eyes. 'There's a whole lot of Kayla in this story.'

Josephine sat back in her chair. 'That's one hell of a conspiracy theory. But just because lines can be drawn between events, doesn't mean they are connected. Correlation is one thing. Cause and effect are something completely different.'

Emerson had gone back to flicking through the glossy, styled photos on Kayla's Instagram feed. 'She's clearly a woman who likes money,' she said. 'I can't imagine she's happy with Simon stuffing up his business. That kind of downfall wouldn't fit her perfectly curated image or her cash-splash lifestyle.' She set the phone down as she remembered what she'd overheard Kayla saying at the hotel. 'You know I said I saw Kayla at Strike? I also heard her talking to someone on the phone.

Something about, "not my problem" and "no one died, get over it". That was the morning after the fire. Doesn't that sound a bit suspicious?'

Josephine nodded, her eyes wide. 'Who would she have been talking to?'

'I don't know.' But there was a niggle at the back of Emerson's mind. She pictured the first day she'd seen Kayla, the way she and Luke had interacted. It didn't mean anything, did it? No. It couldn't possibly be connected.

'Which brings us back to the question,' Josephine was saying. 'Do we tell Remi?'

'Not everything.' Emerson shook her head as she returned to searching her phone. 'Not the stuff we're guessing.'

CHAPTER TWENTY-TWO

REMI
Thursday, 3 August 2023

Remi reached for the rung of the steel ladder, the small boat shifting beneath her feet as she hauled herself up. Luckily, the trip from the deep-water mooring of the seaplane to the end of the long jetty had been quick. Any more time spent bobbing about and she would've been heaving over the side. The motion of the ocean did not agree with her stomach.

Luke reached down and took her hand, helping her up. When she was standing beside him, he rested a hand lightly on her shoulder. 'And here we are. Hadleigh Island. Home for the next four nights.'

Remi clutched her straw hat in one hand, the breeze coming off the water making it difficult to keep it on her head. 'Well, it's not a crowded high-end resort. I love it.'

He flashed the delighted smile of someone who knew they were delivering the perfect gift. 'You can head up to the beach if you like. I'll help with the bags and supplies.'

He reached down to where the young caretaker was passing up their luggage. They'd each brought only a small bag, but their haul also included several boxes and two large eskies. Supplies, Luke had said. Not wanting to be useless, Remi took a bag in each hand and turned to walk along the wooden pier towards the sand. She'd said yes to this trip forty-eight hours ago, and somehow Luke had made it happen. The island belonged to a friend, he'd said, and there was a brief window when the house was available, which he had wanted to take advantage of. Remi had spent yesterday in a mad flurry of waxing and grooming, and trying to find a decent swimsuit, a near-impossible task in Hobart in the middle of winter. Squishing herself into lycra had been a hideous moment, forcing her to confront the change-room mirror with a body that hadn't seen sunlight for months. She couldn't even remember the last time she'd been outside in anything skimpier than t-shirt and shorts. Years too since she'd bothered with the gym, or pilates, or watching what she ate. She'd given all that away as soon as she left Simon. His subtle little digs about her shape no longer mattered. No more commentary about her body, no more *I'm just being honest, babe* or *Have you thought about botox, darling?* or *Those jeans are looking a little too tight, thought you'd like to know sweetheart,* or her all-time favourite, *It's so unfair women get judged on their appearance, but it is what it is, so maybe you should skip the carbs for a week or two.*

The changes to her shape had been stealthy. There was more curve, more softness. Fewer flat bits or defined lines. Except her arms. They still had muscle. Apparently carrying boxes of tiles, swinging a sledgehammer and cleaning and stacking old bricks made for a great workout for the biceps.

The pier ended above the high-tide line. Remi loosened the laces on her cheap canvas sneakers, pulled her feet free and stepped into the warm sand. Utter bliss. She scrunched her feet down further. Giggled. Enjoyed the sun on her bare arms and legs and on her cheeks as she tilted her head back, her hair blowing around her face. Usually, the closest she got to barefoot was walking from her bed to her bathroom and back. It had been months and months since she'd felt a warm breeze on her skin. She filled her lungs. At home, the air was fresh. Invigorating. Here it was thicker, heavier. Scented sweet and salty. The cold of Tasmania a universe away. So too the ugliness of the last month.

Thank you, Luke, she thought. *Thank you for knowing what I needed. For doing this for me.* A laugh gathered in her chest. Magic. Pure magic. Tropical Queensland should be prescribed to everyone in need. Stress and worry were being drowned in the giddy endorphins of pure joy.

Remi crossed the sand to a path. Ahead of her sat a high-roofed timber building, the front dominated by a covered outdoor room. Set into the deck was a small pool. There were oversized rustic chairs and daybeds, made comfortable with jewel-toned cushions. She set the bags down, tossed her hat on the nearest low table. Even in the shade it was warm. If this were a resort she'd flop down and wait for a tall, cold drink to appear. But here there were no staff. No bar. No chef. She and Luke were to be self-sufficient. Just the two of them.

The house had wide bi-fold doors pushed completely aside, leaving barely any definition between the outside and the inside. Ceiling fans turned slowly, breeze buffeted gently up from the beach and through the rooms. The furnishings were simple but generous, the colour palette a blend of natural tones, white, and deep, tropical greens. An open-plan kitchen and dining space held the centre, with an ensuite and bedroom on each side, all of the rooms open to the outdoors. The huge beds were made up with taut white sheets, piles of pillows and a mosquito net hooked at each corner to a thick bed post.

Two separate rooms. Two separate beds. Luke wasn't making presumptions.

The question of would she, wouldn't she? hovered as she walked around. Was she ready to begin something between them? Did she want to? Was she taking advantage of him by accepting this holiday when she was still unclear about what she wanted? The last thought came with a thick layer of guilt. *No strings*, he'd said. *We're friends. I'm doing this for you. That's all*. He'd been emphatic.

But did she want more? She wasn't sure she didn't. Why else would she have put herself on the waxing table for the first time in three years?

***

'That was fabulous.' Remi set down her knife and fork. Leaning back in the chair, she stretched her legs out under the table. Fifteen metres from her feet the sea bumped the shore, each tiny wave making a gentle rush on the sand before being sucked back. Insects chirruped in the undergrowth. Jazz piano played so quietly through the small speaker it was almost lost under the soundtrack of nature. It was all sublime.

'How did I not know what a great cook you are?' she asked.

'I'd like to take the credit, but all I did was put the fish on the barbecue. It came ready wrapped and prepared. I couldn't even tell you what the added extras were. There might have been lemongrass? And ginger? It even came with a note about how long to cook it.'

'You made the salad.'

'I put it on the plate.'

'The entrée?'

'Assembled as per instructions.'

She laughed. 'Is there a dessert to unwrap?'

'Individual lime tarts. With fruit. I might have to cut the fruit.'

'You have shattered the illusion. The next time you tell me to leave you alone in the kitchen, I won't feel so guilty.'

'I tell you what, you can do tomorrow's dinner.'

'Deal.' She sipped her champagne. Luke had opened a bottle of Billecart-Salmon brut rosé before they ate, and she kept drinking it even after he offered a white wine. 'Did you remember this was a favourite?' She held up the glass, the flicker of the candles making the pink bubbles glitter.

'Of course.'

'Thank you.' She would never open a bottle on her own, even if she could afford the luxury. The last bottle she'd drunk would also have been shared with Luke. 'Your attention to detail is amazing. This whole setting is incredible.'

'You deserve this.'

'I don't. But I do truly, truly appreciate it. I've been scrubbed clean of all the angst and stress. And we haven't even been here a day.'

His face lit up with satisfaction. How did some men age so well, seeming to grow into their features, the lines only adding character?

'If you're relaxed, then I have achieved my mission,' he said. 'Imagine how you'll be in four days.'

'You might have trouble getting me back on that plane.'

'Would that be such a bad thing?'

She loved her house. But thinking about it also meant thinking about everything else. About the fire. About her finances. About Simon and Kayla. About his need to get her to comply, and what he may, or may not, have done to achieve that aim. It was hard to admit, but being away from Hobart was a relief. She was experiencing a lightness she hadn't experienced for a very long time. Was she hanging on too tight? How would life look if she stepped away?

'Not so long ago you would've scoffed at any suggestion you might not stay in Tasmania,' Luke said, when she didn't reply. He sounded curious. 'I'm surprised you're taking so long to contemplate the idea.'

She sipped her champagne. 'I tell you what,' she said, forcing an airiness into her voice. 'Ask me again before we leave. After a few days of unwinding, I might be full of vim and vigour and impatient to get back.'

'Or?'

'Or I might decide Simon is right. I might see the wisdom in selling the house. Of taking the money from the sale, paying him out and escaping to the mainland. I might decide to begin a new chapter.'

Luke looked out towards the dark water. He was relaxed, his mouth curving in a light smile. He too was under the influence of the island. He spoke without turning to her. 'What is vim? I've always wondered. We say "vim and vigour". But what is the vim?'

'Ha. I have absolutely no idea. I'd suggest we look it up, but I seem to be without a device.'

He laughed. 'Isn't it great? Disconnected from the world.' He looked at her, his eyes still creased with amusement.

She held his gaze. 'Yes. It is.'

***

Later they stood with their feet in the ocean. They'd opened a second bottle of the Billecart-Salmon and polished off the lime tarts. The dishes got plonked in the sink, neither of them able to face the mundane domesticity of washing up. They'd turned off all the lights and lit a few more candles. Stars flooded the sky. Tiny jewels of light marked the distant coastline.

Without thinking, Remi entwined her fingers with his. 'I'm so glad we're here,' she said.

'I'm so glad you agreed to come.' He squeezed her hand. The warm breeze gentle against them, the rush and retreat of the water around their ankles. 'I wasn't sure you would.'

'I nearly didn't. This is so amazing and special. This,' she swept her arm wide, 'this is not a casual lunch. This is so much more. It's romantic. And intentional. And seductive. I knew it would be. My first instinct was to say no.'

She was aware of him turning to watch her.

'What changed?'

'I guess I realised how much I needed to get away. I knew I was going to fall apart if I didn't get some distance from everything.'

'And you could only spend time with me because you were miserable? Because everything had got so bad, you had no choice.' There was a hint of irritation in his voice.

The champagne had flooded her body with warm, fuzzy ripples of unfamiliar joy and she was struggling to straighten her thoughts. 'Don't sound so offended. You know I don't want to risk our friendship by changing what we have. And it wasn't easy to admit I needed to get away. I don't want to be saved—I can save myself.'

'Isn't that what friends do?' He *was* annoyed. 'Help each other. Support each other. Be there to pick up the pieces. You've needed me in the past, had no trouble accepting my help then.'

'You're talking about after the assault?'

'Yes Before Simon reappeared.' Luke's dislike for Simon was obvious in his sneer.

'After I was released from hospital, I had no choice.'

'No choice? What? You only stayed with me because there was no one else?'

Why were they talking about this? 'Of course not. You were my friend. You were wonderful. It meant so much to have you, to have someone I could lean on.' She dug around trying to find the words that would return the easiness to their conversation. 'I wanted to be there with you.'

'Did you?'

'Yes!'

'Until Simon crooked his finger and enticed you back. As though I had been a convenient stopgap. Next thing, you're engaged.'

Laid out like that, the story didn't sound good. 'Engaged. Grand wedding. Years playing the good wife. Looking good, being good, achieving nothing. Put aside. Divorced.' She tried to make it sound like she saw the humour in her sad life. 'And you were never a stopgap. You were—are—the person I trust the most.'

'But you didn't trust me enough to be more than friends. You should never have gone back to him. You should've stayed with me.'

She dropped his hand and folded her arms tight across her chest, turning to face him. 'Why are we going over this now?

Yes. I went running back to Simon. Yes, I was a bloody stupid fool. Yes, I made a really bad decision. You were right. Simon was a lying, cheating, charming bastard. It took me years to face the truth and get out. Is that what you want me to say? I should've chosen you?'

Waves continued to rock against her ankles, her feet sucking down into the wet sand. Couldn't they go back to drinking champagne and soaking up their freedom?

'Why didn't you?' he asked after a minute. He glanced down at her, then back out at the water. 'Why didn't you choose me?' His irritation had eased a little. Now he might as well have been asking why she chose to live in Hobart or to decorate the downstairs loo with luxuriant wallpaper.

Remi breathed deeply and looked up to the sky.

'I've always presumed the allure of his family wealth had something to do with your choice,' Luke continued when she didn't immediately answer. 'I'm not suggesting you were a gold digger—'

'Thanks.'

'—but that you had an inherent understanding of his greater social worth. Family name. Financial security and comfort, and all the trappings that came with that charmed life. I don't blame you, really. You deserve the best and at that time, I couldn't offer you any of those things. Back then, if you weighed up Simon and me, he was obviously the more polished package. I knew I would one day surpass him, but at that moment in time, he shone brighter. I knew I couldn't win. Which was why I didn't fight harder for you. Of course, he was also an entitled, arrogant, useless piece of shit.'

'Oh, stop it, Luke.' This digging into their past was pointless. 'Play the martyr doesn't suit you.' Was he trying to make her feel bad? She glared at him. He remained impassive, focused on the far-off horizon. Men and their egos.

She dropped her arms by her side, curled and uncurled her toes in the sand. 'I loved him,' she said at last. 'He was fun and exciting. I felt special when I was with him. And maybe you're right, part of that came from the lifestyle he offered. Eating out, spontaneous trips, parties. But you must remember, those first few years in Sydney, we were living mostly on my money. Even afterwards, it was my savings that were gobbled up, until his dad put him in the company. I didn't marry Simon for money. I married him because I had been crushed and I thought being with him was the only way I'd ever feel good about myself again. I was so desperate to return to what I'd had—what I'd been—before the attack. He represented that. Now, can we please stop talking about him?'

'Sure.'

Remi stood in front of him. After a long moment, he finally met her gaze.

'And to answer your original question, it's not that I don't appreciate your support. I do. I really do. But I really thought I needed to be the one to sort myself out this time or my sense of self-worth would be forever trampled. As it is, being here with you, accepting all this'—she threw out her hands to take in everything about the island—'it's really hard. It's like admitting I can't look after myself. That I was struggling. That I need to be saved. Yet again.' She flinched, the words reminding her of Kayla's condescending attitude. 'I know this sounds cliched, but it has been as much about me, not just you.' Trite, but mostly true. 'Although your preference for short-term relationships with little depth or real commitment does encourage me to keep us as friends.'

A muscle in his cheek flexed beneath the bristles of his clipped beard. If she kissed him, would it be prickly? She watched him, waited for his response.

He gave a slow nod, a flicker of a smile. 'Harsh,' he said.

'It's true though, your relationships never last.'

'None of them have been you.' He lifted a hand and pushed a strand of hair from her cheek but moved no closer. The moment lingered.

Then he looked away, his hands sliding into the pockets of his shorts. Remi walked a few steps back to the dry sand and sat. Eventually he joined her there. The silence was heavy with history. Remi scooped a hand through the sand, watched the white grains trickle between her fingers. She glanced sideways, saw him watching her.

'Our timing has always been wonky.'

'And now? How's our timing right now?' he asked.

So much loaded into one question. He wanted to know if she wanted more. Could they be lovers? Partners? Was she prepared to take that risk? They were questions she'd been too afraid to fully consider. As she'd waxed and tidied and desperately rummaged through her paltry wardrobe, she'd been preparing herself for the possibility they'd cross this line. *Just in case*, she'd thought, as she'd stood in front of her mirror. *Something might happen.* Might, maybe, could. She'd skipped around her own intentions. Knowing, but not admitting, she was preparing for intimacy. But, apart from being open to sex with Luke, what did she want? Did she even know? Did she love this man?

She lifted her gaze to meet his. Unable to answer with any degree of certainty, she leaned towards him, their lips meeting, their eyes open. Their kiss was tentative and questioning, until sensation took over. He really did deliver the most magnificent kisses. The beard only scratched a little, not enough to slow the build-up of intensity. She reached for him and as he buried his hands into her hair, she felt more than heard the low vibration of his groan, a sound of such longing it imbued her with power. There was pleasure in being wanted. She stopped trying to work things out and let her body take over.

***

Over the next few days, they only needed one bed. The other went mostly, but not entirely, unused. Twice Remi had retreated to the clean sheets and quiet of the second bedroom. She'd grown accustomed to sleeping alone and a shared bed did sometimes leave her wanting space to stretch out. The first time she'd slipped away, Luke had come looking for her, confused and concerned. The second time he understood not to worry.

Days, too, were spent mostly side by side. They cooked together, often eating meals with feet or legs entwined. They walked the island, swam in both the pool and the ocean, lay on the daybeds reading books chosen from the well-stocked shelves. There were afternoon naps, usually after a languid, sweaty tumble in the sheets. Games of Scrabble, Monopoly and Connect Four. There was no television, and the phone reception came and went. Remi managed to ring home once, the girls reassuring her that everything was great, that there had been no more unwanted events. Emerson was working on the project for Luke and Josephine was again trudging on the mountain. Emerson had been giddy to get details of the holiday, and Remi had sighed happily and said, 'I'm in heaven and I may not come back.'

On the second or third evening, after a meditative outdoor shower, Remi had found Luke at the far end of the deck, hunched over a phone call. When she overheard his terse voice, she presumed he was on a work call, squeezed in during one of the rare windows when they had two-bar reception. He'd sounded angry, his tension an unwanted intruder in their bubble of bliss. She'd walked to him, laid a hand on his neck. He mustn't have heard her barefoot approach because he'd jerked around, startled by her sudden appearance. 'I have to go,' he'd snapped into the phone. 'Do as I've asked, there will be no more of this bullshit are you clear on that?' She realised she'd never heard his angry boss voice. She hoped the poor employee on the other end wasn't in too much trouble.

'Everything okay?' she asked, sitting down beside him. 'Was that work?'

'Hmm? Yes. Work. Nothing serious.' He'd sat up straighter, reached out to rest his hand on the back of her neck, pulling her in for a gentle kiss. 'How was the shower?'

'Heavenly. There is something delicious about being naked outside. Not that I'd be advocating outdoor showering at Macquarie Street. On one hand we might scare the neighbours, on the other there's the issue of hypothermia.'

He'd laughed, turned off his phone and got to his feet. 'Come on, I think there's one more bottle of the champagne.'

***

They didn't talk about their future together or bring up the past again, happy to simply be together. There were moments, though, when she couldn't ignore the force of Luke's emotions.

'You are worth waiting for,' he'd said, his eyes locked on hers, his body pressing hers down.

'How long have you been waiting?' she'd whispered, caught in the moment.

'Since before you even knew I existed.' It was a disgruntled snarl.

'What do you mean?'

'You didn't notice me. But I'd seen you. Saw you for the perfect thing you were.'

'When?'

He kissed her. 'At the Worthington.' He kissed her again. 'I knew you were precious before you even knew my name. You should've gone with your instincts.'

'My instincts?'

'That kiss. That game. You should've been honest. You felt it then, didn't you?'

She had. But how could she reply to such intense emotion? Then he'd eased into her, and she didn't bother with speaking, instead showing him that she was here now.

Other times the atmosphere was light and playful. She saw he was happy and was humbled to be the cause of his joy.

Monday night, he finally asked, 'What happens next?'

'I'm not sure.' They were leaving the next day.

'Do we make plans? Does anything change?' He lay on his side, pushed up on one elbow, his free hand trailing from her neck to her stomach and back again.

'Yes. Of course. Things have to change.' She watched his face. 'We've been friends for so long. But this has to be more than a friends-with-benefits arrangement.'

'More than friends now?' He raised his eyebrows in a smiling question.

'Yes. But I don't know how that looks or how we make it work.' She thought about the options. 'Is it possible to base yourself at the Hobart hotel? I mean, you travel so much any-way. It wouldn't make any difference.'

'It's possible.' He lay back, hands behind his head. 'Would you ever consider moving?'

'No,' she responded, then stopped. Her answer was auto-matic, driven by her fierce commitment to the house. But what if leaving had nothing to do with failing? What if this chapter was nearing a natural end? 'I don't know. I'd have to think about it. I'm not ready to leave. Not yet.' It was treason to even say such a thing. When she'd worked for so long, fought so hard, changing direction was terrifying. 'I've got Josephine and Emerson to think about.' She rolled over to him, wriggled closer till her leg was over his, her head on his chest. 'I don't want to leave here.'

'Aren't you keen to get back home, to check the house, warm your toes in front of the wood heater? Getting you to step away from Hobart has been nearly impossible, now you don't want to go back?'

'Being here has been like stopping and taking a deep breath after running flat out for far too long.'

He shifted his arm to hug her tight to his side. 'Doesn't that tell you something?' he murmured into her hair.

Maybe it did.

As she began to drift into sleep, Remi heard him speak: 'It's all been worth it.'

CHAPTER TWENTY-THREE

JOSEPHINE
Tuesday, 8 August 2023

Josephine and Emerson arrived back from a walk to find Remi home from her holiday and contemplating the contents of the fridge.

'I don't want everyone to think we have to keep doing the family dinner thing, but I'm feeling inspired. Thought I'd see if I can do a stir-fry. There'll be plenty to go around. Not that I can guarantee it'll be any good. It won't be up there with your cooking, Em.'

'Welcome back! Tell us everything. Was it amazing? Was it warm? Did you swim in the ocean? What's happening with Luke?' Emerson pulled out a stool, sitting with her elbows on the island bench.

'It was bliss.' Remi's face lit up in a way Josephine had never seen before. 'It was the most perfect escape, warm and relaxed, and totally indulgent.'

'It must have been one amazing holiday. You're radiant,' Josephine said, bemused by this change. 'What did that man do to you?'

Emerson hooted. 'I think Luke may well and truly have moved out of the friend zone.'

'What makes you think that? Isn't it possible that sun, sand and a warm ocean, not to mention a total disconnect from all the crap, would be enough to smooth out my frazzled edges?'

'Sure.' But Emerson obviously wasn't buying it. 'Let's go with that. I'm sure your bliss has nothing to do with having your socks rocked.'

Remi ducked her head back into the fridge, but not before they saw her flushed smile. 'There might have been some special moments,' she muttered as she rummaged in the vegetable crisper.

'I'm happy for you,' said Josephine. 'You've come back a new woman. It's so obvious he's good for you.'

'Luke definitely gets my vote.' Emerson said.

Josephine came around to peer over Remi's shoulder. 'I can help,' she said. 'Although, I'm not much of a cook, either. I swear, when it was Sam and me, I had the same five dishes on rotation.'

'Have you heard from him?' Remi asked, passing a bag of mushrooms, a zucchini and a punnet of cherry tomatoes to her co-chef. 'Has he joined that cult yet?'

'They've been walking rescued street dogs on the beach and taking Thai cooking classes.'

'Oh no. That sounds dangerous,' Remi teased.

'It is.' Josephine pretended to be anxious. 'They might try to bring a dog home. But I've already done the research, and they can't. Australian quarantine and customs say a firm no to dogs who've been in Thailand. But then I started fretting about the cooking. I mean, what if Sam doesn't cook his chicken well enough and he gets gastro? What then?'

Emerson and Remi laughed, realising she was poking fun at herself.

Over a half-reasonable meal, Josephine and Emerson reassured Remi that nothing untoward had happened in her absence, teasing and making her laugh as they attempted to elicit more details about the holiday and Luke. Then Emerson entertained them by demonstrating how to take the perfect candid photo, a process involving lighting, posing, the self-timer, her phone balanced on a pile of books and dozens of shots.

As Remi was clearing the plates, Emerson and Josephine shared a questioning glance. Was now the right time to open this conversation?

'What's going on?' Remi asked. 'Are you two keeping secrets?'

Emerson kept quiet, waiting for Josephine to take the lead.

'There is something,' Josephine said.

Remi returned to her seat. 'Yes?'

Josephine clasped her hands together and rested them on the table, her back straight. She collected her thoughts before speaking. 'A few things have been bothering me,' she said, her focus on Remi. 'On the one hand, you've had a series of unpleasant events which have affected you financially and emotionally. I think you agree it's likely to be more than a coincidence.'

Remi sat back in her chair. 'Yes. I'd wanted to believe this was all just a run of bad luck, but there's a possibility at least some of these things have been deliberate. I know what I saw the night of the fire.'

Josephine nodded. 'You also have an ex-husband deter-mined to force the sale of the house. And everything that has happened—from the hefty vet bills for your dog to the fire—has directly impacted your ability to meet your obligations. There is a real possibility they are connected.'

'Oh, that's ridiculous! Simon is many things but he's not an animal killer. Or an arsonist. None of this is his style.'

Josephine angled her head, her eyes still on Remi. 'I've been given information that Simon is not doing well financially. His father is not supporting his business endeavour in any form and Simon is significantly in debt. Both in his business and personally.'

'That doesn't sound right. He's expanded the business and there's considerable turnover. They make it look like they've got money to burn. Even if the business wasn't doing bril-liantly, Simon would have made sure he was cashed-up. He'd be drawing a hefty salary.'

'He probably is,' said Josephine. 'But even people on huge incomes can blow their budgets. If they even have a budget.'

'That wedding didn't have any limits,' Emerson added. 'And there was something in the social pages about the place they bought in Sydney. Worth tens of millions.'

'But he's a Hanland.'

'As I understand it, Daddy Hanland has removed all his financial safety nets and forced him out on his own. There was a falling out over Hanland Luxury—Hanland senior didn't see the numbers adding up. Plus, he had an expectation Simon would stay within the family company. Apparently, he was angry when Simon went out on his own.'

Remi frowned. 'Right, well, I guess that sounds plausible. Simon's father has a tough approach to business and to his son.'

She considered what Josephine was saying. 'And Simon stuffing up his business doesn't sound out of the question either. His confidence was always greater than his competence. We'd ended up in Hobart because his father had wanted him to lead the opening of the first Tasmanian branch of Perfect Home. The fact that the store only materialised well after Simon left says a lot. Okay, so I accept it's possible he could be financially stretched and that he might see calling in my loan as one way to fill a hole in his cashflow. But there is no way he would play that dirty. I know him,' she said. 'He isn't the sort to sneak around or to engage in nasty online trolling. He certainly wouldn't poison my dog and drag around a can of petrol to stuff up my car. He always kept his hands clean. He's a charmer, a man who got his way through persuasion and conviction, and sometimes manipulation. Even when he was assertive, it was usually presented with a wide smile. He was obvious, not underhand, and honestly, a wee bit of a coward. There is absolutely no way he would do something like set a fire.'

'What about his wife?' asked Emerson quietly.

'Kayla? You think Kayla would do those things?'

'We do know she was on her own in Hobart when someone tampered with your car,' Josephine said. 'Simon was in Sydney.'

'And she could've organised those reviews,' Emerson added. 'You can buy bulk fake ratings and reviews. Or even written them herself.'

Remi looked at her housemates. 'And Mavis?'

'It could well be that she didn't intend to kill her, only to bring big bills into your life,' Josephine said.

'That's a wild accusation. But you don't know if she was here—in town—when some of those other things happened?

I mean, yes, I did run into her the day after my car problem. But the fire? Was she here then? And even if she was, how would she have got in the house?'

'She definitely was here,' said Emerson. 'I saw her at Strike the morning after.'

'At Strike? At Luke's hotel? But there is no way Simon would want her staying there. His animosity towards Luke runs deep.'

'Maybe he doesn't know,' suggested Josephine.

'This is one hell of a conspiracy theory. I mean, maybe Simon is more desperate for the sale than I realised. And a loss in financial status would infuriate Kayla. But a deliberate strategy to ruin me, to force me to sell? To go to the extent of risking my life in a fire? Would they do that?'

'Desperate people do nasty, crazy things.'

'Don't worry, I know crazy,' Remi pressed the heel of her palms against her eyes. 'Brittney was crazy, at least for the time it took to hurt me.'

Josephine gave a small nod. 'Do you know what became of her?'

'Not the specifics.' Remi looked away.

'I asked my investigator to look into her,' Josephine continued, 'to determine if she could possibly be behind—'

'You what?' Remi interrupted. 'You had an *investigator* look into her?'

'I did. I have someone I use regularly who made some enquiries.'

Remi stared at her. She finished what was left of her wine, set the glass down carefully and folded her arms. 'I didn't need you to do that. I didn't ask you to get involved in this— whatever *this* is.'

Josephine looked at her hands where they still rested on the table. 'I like to gather information. To understand a situation fully and to assess threats.' She looked up and said quietly, 'I was concerned for you.'

Remi looked away. 'And this information on Simon and Kayla. How did you *gather* those details?

'Mostly through my business advisor.'

'And I was the one who saw Kayla here in Hobart, at the same time some of those things happened,' Emerson said.

Remi looked at each of them. 'Thank you for your concern, and I truly do appreciate the support you've given me since you've been here, but I don't need to be looked after or rescued, or to have people conducting *investigations* behind my back.'

An uncomfortable silence stretched between them. Emerson was fidgeting anxiously while Remi poured more wine into her glass. Josephine was calm.

'You believe we've overstepped the mark,' she said. 'But this affects us too. Emerson and I received threatening messages in the week before the fire. We didn't say anything because we didn't want to add to your worry. I believe the messages were a scare tactic to get us to move out and to again reduce your income thereby limiting your ability to repay your debt. And, honestly, it was only a quirk of timing that neither Em nor I were here the night of the fire. If someone has a vendetta against you, then we deserve to know. And I will not sit back and wait for something else to happen while I have the capacity to ask questions.'

'Someone threatened you? How?'

'We both received emails, sender unknown, telling us it wasn't safe to live here.'

'And you didn't think to tell me?'

'You were dealing with enough at that point. The emails were short and were, I believe, intended to make us leave. They did not give any indication of being a precursor to something more serious.'

'Fair enough.' Remi slumped back in her chair, then seemed to come to a decision. 'Brittney died,' she finally said, as though talking about this was difficult. 'She was hit by a car two weeks after the attack. She died on the side of the road. It's not something I like to think about.'

'And nobody was ever charged.' Josephine phrased it as a statement, not a question.

'No. At that point, I'd only just given her name to the police as being my attacker. The media hadn't picked up on her involvement, but Brittney was going to be questioned the following day. There were some people—including the police—who wondered if she hadn't deliberately stepped out into the road. It was sad and horrible and even after weeks of investigation the driver was never found. So, no, Brittney could not be involved with what's been happening.'

'And Simon and Kayla?'

'I don't know. Maybe.' Remi didn't look entirely convinced—or rather she didn't *want* to be convinced 'But it could be anyone. A completely random person.'

'I really can't see any of this being the actions of someone you don't know,' said Josephine. 'It's far too personal. Maybe it's time to go to the police?'

CHAPTER TWENTY-FOUR

REMI

Tropical air and salt water still lay on her skin. As did Luke's touch. The last five days were more vivid and real than the dramas here. Remi didn't want to be sucked back into the stress and anxiety now surrounding her home, but she had no choice. The conversation with Josephine and Emerson over dinner had brought everything back to the fore. Not that she'd forgotten. Just shoved it all to the back of her mind.

The chances were Simon and Kayla had been behind the horrid things that had happened. It seemed the most likely scenario, and it was almost a relief to know who wanted to disrupt her life. She could imagine Kayla writing the reviews and those emails to her tenants, and perhaps even hacking her bank account, but she still wasn't convinced that the death of Mavis, the demise of her car or the fire were Kayla's doing. Maybe Simon did in fact have a key. Which would explain the missing jewellery, too. That could be how this all began, Kayla rummaging through her things, recognising the value of the ring and taking it for herself.

Remi sat on her bed and dialled a number she never used.

When Simon answered, he sounded surprised. 'Remi?'

'Hello, Simon.'

'How are you?' He was stilted but polite.

'Great. I've just come back from five days in North Queensland.'

'What? Can you afford to be spending money on holidays right now?'

'Oh, Simon.' She almost laughed. 'You can't help yourself, can you? On the one hand you're hoping I'll end up flat broke so you can force me to sell. On the other, you can't stop telling me how to manage my money.'

There was a dark pause. 'I don't want you to end up broke,' he said tersely.

'No. Maybe not. Just temporarily without funds.'

'When the house sells you will pocket a sizeable amount.'

'And you will get your money back. Which I gather you are rather more desperate for than you've indicated. I believe you're in something of a financial hole yourself.'

His response was immediate and defiant. 'Who told you that? That's not true. The business is expanding. Turnover is exceptional and we're more than okay.'

'Then why do you need the money from this place? Recouping the outstanding mortgage, even with the interest you're charging, should be pocket money to you if you're going as well as you say. Given that your turnover was, what did you say, twenty-five million last year?'

His breathing quickened and she could imagine him pacing his harbour-view house. 'I would rather the cash than the debt, that's all. It's good financial management.'

'Hmm. I gather Kayla has strong opinions on the situation.'

He hesitated. 'Yes. She's got a good head for business.' The tone of his statement was less than convincing. 'She pointed out how much smarter it would be to put the profit in our pocket and to invest in something with a better return.'

'Profit I created, through hard work and investment of my settlement.'

His irritated snort said it all.

Whatever. No point arguing, he'd never admit her vision and work had given them an agreed value far exceeding what they'd originally paid.

'Kayla doesn't like our agreement,' Remi continued, stating an accepted fact.

'No, she doesn't. You understand how new wives feel about any connection with old wives.'

'I don't, actually. But I'll take your word for it. I guess that's why she's so determined to force my hand. Why she's pulled these tricks.'

'What the hell do you mean? Pulled what tricks?' He sounded confused, but then he was a well-practised liar.

'I mean, you work as a team, don't you?'

A slight hesitation. 'Yes.'

She continued as though discussing something he understood. 'The reviews were clever. And, I admit, ruthlessly effective. There hasn't been a single job since that little campaign.'

'What are you talking about? What reviews?'

'Sabotaging the car, though, that was nasty. But again, it hit the mark. My poor Subaru still isn't fixed. I can't afford to. Another hit to my finances. Another push towards defaulting on my repayment.'

'I have absolutely no idea what you're going on about. What are you insinuating?'

'Don't you?

'Can you backtrack please?' He was being officious, buying time as he either tried to process the accusations or manufacture denials and excuses. 'It's true I would prefer the house sold. Or, really, to get the loan fully repaid. But I've done nothing to force you into it. I don't need to; you'll dig yourself into a financial hole without my help. What the hell do you mean by "sabotaging the car"? And what fucking reviews? I have absolutely no idea what you are on about.'

'Petrol in my diesel tank. Could only have happened while the car was parked at the house, so must have been deliberate. And the reviews were clearly deliberate and, I might add, extremely effective.'

A few beats of silence passed before he spoke. 'You put the wrong fuel in your car and you're blaming me. That is ridiculous. I really don't appreciate what you're suggesting. If you make mistakes don't go looking for someone else to blame. When did this even happen? Have you forgotten we live in Sydney?'

'A bit over two weeks ago. You may have been in Sydney, but Kayla was here when it happened.'

He scoffed. 'You're wrong there. My wife hasn't been to Hobart without me. She's not comfortable down there. She dreads running into you, because of your continued antagonism towards her.'

This time she really laughed. 'She was here.'

'Bullshit. Two weeks ago, she was on a girls' trip to a wellness retreat in the Southern Highlands.'

'You might want to check that. Because she did run into me and she was delighted to give me a lecture about how I should give up and move on. And she was still down here a number of days later. Right up until the day my home nearly burned down.'

'What? Are you joking? I haven't heard about this. There was a fire? Fuck, why didn't you tell me? That's my asset too, I need to be kept informed.'

'I wasn't hurt, by the way. Thanks for asking.'

'Oh, park the sarcasm, Remi. Obviously you're fine or you wouldn't be ringing me with all this conspiracy bullshit. Is the house damaged?'

'Not significantly. But, if the aim was to further drain my funds or to make me want to give up or to scare my house-mates into leaving, then it was a bit of a failure.'

'You cannot seriously be suggesting Kayla was involved? That she's, what, an arsonist as well?'

'She was here. She hates me. She wants me to lose the house. Quite honestly, the idea that she's acted against me isn't so crazy.'

She could hear him moving around, the sound of fingers on a keyboard. He must be checking details. 'Like, I said, she wasn't there. You're mistaken.'

Had she lobbed a problem back to Kayla? Simon would not like his wife being anything less than honest with him.

'Oh, by the way, congratulations on the pregnancy. Or at least, I presume it's congratulations. You were always so sure you weren't suited to being a father.'

Another long stretch of silence, as he realised there was only one way she could know this detail. 'Things change,' he muttered. 'Kayla and I are delighted to be starting a family.' It was a cliched, insincere response, completely lacking genuine enthusiasm. 'And I do not accept a word of what you're saying.

I'm sorry to hear you've had some bad luck. But not even Kayla would do these things to you. She doesn't need to anymore.'

Wait. What? 'Anymore?'

'Oh, you know.' He was exasperated and distracted, still tapping on his computer. 'Long-held grudges and all that, from losing me to you. She might once have been a bit resentful. But that's long gone, we're together now and we're happy, so none of that matters.'

What the hell was he talking about? Kayla didn't lose Simon to Remi, it was the other way around. Unless ... 'Simon. When did you meet Kayla?'

'What do you mean?'

'You said she has a grudge because she lost *you* to *me*. Which doesn't make sense. So please tell me, how far back do you two go? When did you meet her?'

'You mean, the first time?' He was stalling.

'Yes.'

He cleared his throat, stopped clicking his keyboard. 'Right. Um. I thought you knew this.'

'Remind me.'

'Well, it was in Sydney. You were still on the show. But we'd broken up.'

'Wait. You mean in 2009, after the rumours started, in that sliver of time before the attack? When you dumped me?'

'Yes. I thought you were cheating on me.' He blew out a lungful of air. 'But I'd ended things with her more or less before we got back together. Way before we got married.'

'Well, that's good to know. There's a—what—ten year age difference between you? She must've been barely an adult back then.'

'Yeah, well, she was old enough. Nineteen, I think. And very mature and together.'

'Great, that makes things everything okay.' She didn't hide revulsion.

He ignored her and continued to speak. 'She was a bit upset back then. Resentful of our relationship—of you. She had the idea you faked the attack to get sympathy, to win me back. Of course, I told her you hadn't. She wanted me to choose and then she didn't like the choice I made.' Simon said this last bit as though he deserved to be rewarded. 'And, yes, when we met again, later—years later—she still seemed to be holding onto some negative opinions of you.'

Simon and Kayla. Together. A brief fling before he married Remi. Perhaps not so brief. Had Kayla been in the background during their marriage? Was her antagonism born of a long-burning jealousy? Had Simon soothed her with lies about his demanding, unbalanced wife? That would explain Kayla's bitterness.

'It would be safe to say she still hates me. You need to speak to her about that.'

'Yeah. Fine.'

She'd known the call would be unpleasant, had prepared herself to rise above and not react, but this felt like wading through filth. She didn't want more of this in her life.

'Remi? Can we sell the house? Please? I really would prefer the money in the bank.' He was pleading.

'Still paying off that wedding?' The little dig slipped out.

'That could be a small contributing factor.'

'You want me to sell the house that I love, that I've slaved over, put my heart and tears into for the last two years.

Renovations I paid for. To help you pay off your ridiculously over-the-top wedding to the woman who hates me.'

He sighed as though worn out, an old trick: acting the part of an endlessly patient man, harangued by an emotional, ranting woman. Unable to reason with her. His face would be a picture of distress and sorrow. A great way to avoid any discussion he found difficult.

'You would be free from debt. There'd be no connection left between us.' True to form, he ignored her succinct summary of the situation.

What a dick. 'I'll let you know.'

Keeping him hanging felt good.

CHAPTER TWENTY-FIVE

EMERSON
Wednesday, 9 August 2023

Hobart was capable of the most spectacular days. Emerson pulled up at the red light and reached for her sunglasses. Take today, for example. Blue skies and sunshine. Perfect day to act like a cat—find a sheltered sunny spot and doze in the warmth. No dozing for her, though. Absolutely not. She was seeing Kristof again.

He had worked the breakfast shift and she was picking him up so they could head out for lunch. They'd wander about till they found somewhere that looked good. Maybe head up to North Hobart. Maybe they could do a picnic. That wouldn't be a bad idea. Hunt and gather at Salamanca Fresh, then find a spot at that little park in Battery Point, the one with the fabulous views over the Derwent. She'd suggest it to him, see what he thought.

She swung into the carpark at Strike, finding a spot between two shiny SUVs. While she waited, she pulled out her phone. Kristof had sent a message to say he'd finished and would be there as soon as he'd changed out of his uniform. She flipped down the visor to check her face, ran a finger over her eyebrows, inspected her lipstick. She had her glasses off and was reapplying a light coat of mascara when she noticed movement behind her. Up close to the mirror and focused on not smearing, she didn't pay too much attention. Only when she sat back, fluttering her lashes to dry them then replacing her glasses, did she recognise Luke.

She reached for the handle, ready to leap out and say hello, tease him about the smooching good holiday he and Remi had enjoyed. But he wasn't alone. A woman faced him, her body language tense. She looked angry, her hands raised in sharp movements to emphasise what she was saying. Luke's hands were in the pockets of his jeans, arms locked. He was listening, his face calm but not relaxed.

'Shit,' Em breathed. What was Kayla doing back in Hobart? And what was she doing with Luke?

Emerson tried to remember if there was any connection between them. One degree of separation, of course. But in the history that she'd heard and read, there was no time where their paths crossed. Luke and Simon, sure. She'd heard the story about the kissing game and how Remi had chosen Simon, even though Luke's kiss had made her toes curl. They'd all shaken their heads at the twists of fate, talked about sliding door moments and how nobody recognised them when they were happening. Then last night, over hot chocolates and marshmallows, Remi had shared what she'd discovered: Simon and Kayla went way back, the two of them hooking up before Remi had married him. None of which explained why Kayla was arguing with Luke in the carpark of his hotel.

Damn, Emerson wished she could lip read; she could just hear their voices but couldn't make out what they were discussing. She grabbed her phone from the passenger seat, swiped the camera function into video selfie mode and held it at her shoulder. The footage wouldn't be great, she was filming out the back window of her car, but she would have something. Holding the phone in the best position possible, she watched what was happening in the rear-view mirror.

Kayla stopped talking and folded her arms tight across her chest, her chin jutted out. She was waiting for an answer. When Luke spoke, his stance was tight. Whatever he said was short and to the point and was followed by an abrupt nod from Kayla and a few words. She spun sharply and strode away. Luke watched her leave. Even watching him in the small mirror, Emerson could see a dark, angry expression on his face. Then he walked through the carpark and climbed into a car.

Something wasn't right about this. Her spidey senses were zipping on high alert. She played the video, trying to decipher what it all meant.

When the passenger door suddenly opened, Emerson gave a small yelp. Kristof ducked his head and gave her his lopsided, gorgeous smile. 'Sorry. Didn't mean to scare you.'

'I was off in la-la land.' She tucked her phone away as he climbed in.

There was a split second of awkwardness as they tried to determine whether they were at the point of kissing for greeting. Emerson made the decision for them. As she leaned towards him, he rushed to meet her in the middle, immediately distracting her from thoughts of intrigue.

'Sorry I made you wait,' he said when they broke apart. 'I had to hold back till Luke moved. I'm pretty sure staff aren't meant to be using the guest carpark for their meet-ups.'

Emerson turned the keys. 'Yeah. Bit inconvenient having him stand right behind the car.' Questions tickled the tip of her tongue, but there was no point throwing them at Kristof. It was unlikely he'd have any insight into the relationship between Luke and Kayla. She reversed carefully before heading onto the road. 'I was thinking, it's a lovely day, how do you feel about chips, dips, cheese and a picnic?'

***

Emerson had expected a fun day to blur into a glorious night. She'd pictured a picnic and strolling hand in hand, followed by Kristof's bed. Surfacing for takeaway before burrowing back into the warmth for more playtime. They only got as far as strolling.

'I have to make a quick call,' she'd said to him. That one call had dismantled her plans.

People were creatures of habit, especially when those habits involved having the best of the best. Phoning the hotel and requesting to be put through to Kayla Hanland's room had confirmed she was staying at Strike again.

Kristof had looked dejected when she'd told him something had come up. She'd kissed him long and hard to let him know this wasn't about him, that she really wanted to have the day together, to get naked, but she had something important to do.

She was nuts.

Now here she was, spending a perfect Saturday staking out the hotel on the off-chance Kayla would walk past. The whole thing was just a wee bit bonkers. She was sitting in the lounge area of the small bar, so she ordered a cocktail to blend in and doodled elf-like characters in retro eighties gear in her notebook while she waited.

Engrossed in what she was doing, she would've missed her prey if Kayla hadn't stepped into the lounge and taken a seat on the other side of the room. So much for being a secret agent— she'd nearly failed her first mission. Emerson scrambled to her feet, stuffed her book into her bag and walked around to sit next to the woman who was making trouble for her friend.

'Hello. Oh, gosh, sorry, I scared you.'

'Can I help you?' Kayla's voice held zero warmth but a tonne of disdain.

'Yes. Well, I hope so.' Emerson arranged a cushion so she was more comfortable. Then she crossed her legs and angled herself towards Kayla. Two friends chatting, that's the picture she was creating. Although, no one was ever going to believe they were. The differences really were too great. Gosh, Kayla really was stunning. 'I'm Emerson. We're sort of connected.'

'Really? I don't know you.' The appraising glance made it clear Kayla doubted very much that they had anything in common.

'Actually, a couple of connections. Although, they are loose connections, I must admit. Firstly, Luke is a client of mine. I've been doing some graphic work for him.'

'Luke?' A tiny, questioning lift of her brows.

'Yes. You know. Luke Darlby. Owner of this hotel and several others. I know you know him. And I live with Remi Lucans.'

At this, Kayla's expression shifted. Her careful, smooth veneer slipped to reveal something nasty and sour.

'Your husband's ex-wife. I think you've known her for many, many years. Although, let's face it, you really *don't* know her, do you? More like ...' Emerson tapped a finger against her mouth as she crafted the perfect phrase. 'More like, she's been your opponent in your quest to bag Simon. Right?'

Kayla stared at her as though she were vomit on a plate, revolting and incomprehensible. 'Why are you talking to me?'

'Okay. A few things. Firstly, can I say, I loved your wedding dress. Not the big gown you wore down the aisle, but the second one you changed into for the first part of the reception. Truly stunning. I can't even imagine how much that must've cost, let alone the whole three-day circus. I'm all for creating amazing experiences, but you blew the notion out of the water. Nobody will match that for a while. I guess you're still paying it off.'

'We can afford it.' Cold as dry ice.

'Can you, though? Because you seem to be mighty obsessed with getting your hands on Remi's house.'

Cool blue eyes assessed Emerson, giving her a look that sliced away her confidence. 'She owes us money.'

This woman was small but scary, but there was no point backing down now. 'And, like I say, I think you need that little package of cash at the moment. Enough that playing dirty seems justified.'

Kayla's eyes narrowed.

'The question is, does Simon know what you've been up to? He told Remi he doesn't. The reviews, the stunt with the car, the emails to her housemates? The fire?'

She watched Kayla's chin lift a fraction higher. Defiant. Calculating where this was heading, and not prepared to storm off in case there was something more. But neither was she denying anything. There wasn't even a glimmer of confusion.

'Look, I don't know Simon, but he seems like a bit of a dick. And not a very bright one. I'm guessing he doesn't realise you know Luke.'

Emerson had the video playing in seconds. Kayla watched only long enough to see herself in the shaky footage, then turned away.

'My husband is well aware I know Luke. It's not a secret.'

Interesting, if it was true. 'Simon has never got along with Luke, has he? A bit of rivalry by the sound of things. I can understand why. Luke is a successful self-made man. While Simon got a job in his father's company. Anyway, that's beside the point.' A swarm of frantic butterflies slammed into Emerson's ribs as she prepared to throw out the next hook—the idea she hadn't been able to put aside. Here goes nothing. 'I'm also guessing he doesn't know you were behind those rumours. The ones all those years ago about Remi and Connor Mallick. He might be confused, shall we say, if he learned what a manipulative woman he'd married.'

Kayla snapped her head round to glare at Emerson. 'I beg your pardon!'

'Oh, sorry. Do I have that wrong? Was it only a coincidence you were working at the Park Hyatt Hotel where Remi and Connor were photographed? It must've been another anonymous staff member who told the press about them going upstairs to a room. A complete lie, by the way. Or another person who took the photos. The ones that sent a deranged young woman over the edge and led to Remi's brutal assault. Three ribs, four fingers and her cheek, all broken. Gosh, that was truly horrific. Imagine what a field day the *Daily Mail* would have with those details. What a saga. Hell, even the mainstream press would salivate over the story. Sydney social pages would burn.'

Kayla's eyes had gone wide. Her nostrils flared, even as the rest of her face remained rigid. 'Who would believe you? There's no proof.'

Emerson let that slide. 'The thing is. I'm not too sure what your connection with Luke is. That's the bit I can't figure out. He loves and adores Remi. Do you just hate to see her happy? Is that it? Because if you're trying to wreck things for her— like, beyond the financial stuff—then that's not nice.'

Kayla gave a sharp huff, a blend of outrage and amusement. 'Oh, yes. Saintly, magnificent Remi. You think you know so much. Do you know she stole Simon from me? No? We were together, in love. Then that bitch milked her little incident for all it was worth. Made him feel sorry for her. Wouldn't let him alone. And, trust me, I am not the one obsessed with her.'

'Then why go to so much trouble to make a mess of things for her?'

'Because she's an obstacle.' She looked Emerson up and down, scorn on her face. 'Who exactly are you?'

'I'm Emerson. I'm Remi's friend.' She plastered on a huge smile. *See, I'm a harmless girl. No danger in talking to me.*

'Well, Emerson.' Kayla spat her name as she shifted position, crossing her legs and leaning forward. 'I don't give a shit about your precious Remi. I care about myself. And Simon. And my husband does not need to stay connected to his idiot ex-wife by some stupid debt agreement. He's being taken for a ride. I— we—want that money. Easy enough for you to understand?'

'Sure, sure. I get it.' Emerson mirrored Kayla's position, posing as though she were a confidante to this snooty cow. 'You're a woman who works for what she wants, like getting Simon. Kudos to you, you won him. Now you're running with the society girls. Gosh, what a life. I follow you on Insta—everything looks amazing. The clothes. The travel. Being invited to the Birdcage at Melbourne Cup. And your in-crowd, A-lister, glamorous friends who come from the big bucks. You were sitting sweet until your golden ticket husband went and got himself cut off from the family money. And the luxury business is a little stretched, right? It might not be much, but the money from Remi's house will let you keep up for a while longer. In the meantime, I'm sure Simon will get his act together and make proper money soon.'

'He will.' Strident defence of her husband, even if she didn't sound entirely convinced. Kayla snapped her mouth shut, realising she'd confirmed part of the narrative Emerson was spinning. 'And you've got no evidence of anything.' She shifted her focus and stared into the distance. 'Why is she even holding onto the place? She can't afford it. If you're her friend, do her a favour, tell her to sell, take the money and do something else.'

Emerson shrugged. 'That's Remi's decision. Personally, I enjoy living there.'

Kayla's chin went up again. She smoothed a strand of hair from her face and moved her hand to her throat to play with her rose-gold necklace. 'Are you finished?'

'I guess.'

Kayla stood, Emerson following.

'You said you're not the one obsessed with Remi.'

'I'm not.'

'Then who is? Who is obsessed with her?'

As Kayla turned her head to look at Emerson, a sneer curled her lips. 'Don't you know? He's always been there for her, waiting to pick up the pieces. She's so woeful, she takes him for granted. There's been a few times he's had to ... how would you say it?' She lifted a hand, flipped it over in an elegant gesture, as though waiting for the word she wanted to fall into her palm. 'He's had to *shape* things to his advantage. Despite our history, he didn't help me reconnect with Simon only out of the goodness of his heart. I may have had some persuasive leverage, but he's also driven by his own motives. He wanted them to separate.'

'Hold on, are you talking about Luke? What are you saying?'

An elegant shrug of one shoulder. 'Luke and I go way back. He can be extremely helpful when he wants to be.'

'Reconnect? Are you saying Luke was somehow involved in setting up your affair with Simon? In breaking up Remi's marriage?'

Kayla's belief in her superiority was obvious in the flick of her head and the cruel curl of her lips. 'He owed me a favour and he didn't object to setting her free, as he put it.'

'I don't believe you. Luke's a really decent person. He wouldn't do that. He wouldn't set out to hurt Remi.'

Kayla gave a tiny snigger of amusement. 'Luke Darlby is a strategist. Always has been.'

'What else has he done?' Emerson's mind reeled. Not Luke. He was the good guy in all of this.

'That's not for me to tell. Let's just say he does like to see himself as the protector of that stupid woman.' Kayla shook her head in exasperation. 'If you want to talk obsession, look at her fixation with that place. Seriously, can she take any longer with the renovation? She needs to learn to let go. Move on. Find something else to occupy her little mind.'

'But ...' Emerson trailed off, thoughts bouncing around in an incoherent mess.

'I have nothing else to say to you, now leave me the fuck alone.'

CHAPTER TWENTY-SIX

REMI

'Luke! What are you doing here?' Remi pulled the door wide and wrapped him in a hug. He pressed a firm kiss to her lips before softening to gentle passion.

'I missed you,' he said, pulling back to look at her. His hands came up to cup her face.

She laughed. 'We left the island yesterday morning. It hasn't even been two days.'

'It feels longer.'

She led him into the hall, closing the door behind them. 'It does, doesn't it?' She kissed him again. 'Aren't you meant to be running an empire? You can't keep gallivanting about the countryside.'

'Actually, I can. One of my many skills as a hotel owner is to hire only the best managers. They don't need to have their hands held. Besides, I like to visit all the properties regularly.'

'Especially Hobart?'

'Especially Hobart.'

They walked into the kitchen. The wood heater was burning. Remi's laptop was open on the table, a glass of red and a plate of crackers and cheese alongside. A small speaker played some folk-pop quietly in the background.

'You're on your own tonight?' he asked.

Remi poured him a glass of wine and set it next to hers as she took her seat. 'Em has been out most of the day. May not be back tonight—seems she's got a special friend. And Josephine went off to dance in the dark. And I don't mean in a club. It's some sort of fun exercise thing. No booze, just lights out, comfy clothes, loud party songs and let yourself go. I might have to try it.'

Luke didn't sit. Taking his glass, he moved through the kitchen to peer into the garden. 'Sounds fun.' He returned to sit beside her. 'You seem relaxed still.'

'I am, actually, despite nothing being truly resolved. Maybe my worries and fears were washed away in the ocean. Maybe being with you has given me a new perspective. A little more sunshine and positivity, and a whole lot less angst. Besides there have been no more incidents.' She kissed him lightly. 'And you've been good for me. Thank you. I think I've got my strength back. I'm more resilient.'

He stood, pulling her to her feet. His arms tightened around her and he put his mouth to her neck. 'What say we take that sunshine and positivity upstairs?' he whispered in her ear.

***

Remi lay on her back, her arms above her head on the pillow, eyes closed. Her mouth was tender, her body in a state of bliss.

Luke's leg rested over hers. He lay on his side, one hand propping up his head, the other drawing intricate patterns on her stomach and over her breasts. The doona was pushed aside, the room and their skin still warm from their exertions.

'You're more beautiful now than you were when I first met you.' He brushed a kiss over her lips.

'Not true. But thank you for boosting my confidence in my ageing body.'

'It is true. You were a pretty girl. You're now a beautiful woman.'

She opened her eyes. 'And you, Luke Darlby, are a very handsome man. Definitely worth the wait.' She tossed his words back at him.

He frowned then eased into a sad smile. 'It really shouldn't have been such a long wait. We should never have been apart. We could have built Strike together. Shared so much.'

There was no changing the past, she wanted to say. There's no point dwelling on what might have been. They'd made choices. Or, come to think of it, she'd made her choices. Mostly bad ones.

'There will be other things for us to do together,' she said.

'I've been thinking about that. I'm on the brink of securing a property in Perth, we'll be opening another hotel there. I'd like you to be part of that process. To work with me.'

She reached for the doona, pulling it up as she wriggled out from under him, turning to face him instead. 'Work with you? What do you mean?'

'I mean I'd really like you to be with me. I don't want to waste any more time. Come with me. Move to Melbourne, then travel with me. Be part of my team. You obviously have a good eye for design. You could be involved with the shaping of the next Strike.'

Excitement stirred within her. Working with Luke and, she presumed, a design consultant, to create a look, sourcing feature elements, coordinating colours and textures. 'I'm not qualified for that kind of work. The boss bringing his new girlfriend to meetings about the next hotel will just look ridiculous. No one would take me seriously. And I wouldn't blame them. I'd only be there because we're shagging. Everyone would know. They'd be nice to my face and roll their eyes at your foolishness the minute you walked away.'

'I think you're underestimating yourself. What you've done with this place is so impressive. You do have an eye for style. You've managed this project single-handedly, you have experience.'

She shook her head. 'I've seen it among the bored wives of Simon's wealthy mates. They'd do up their own house, sometimes twice. No money spared. Hooked on the process, they'd take themselves off to do a course then launch as an interior designer. They had the contacts, a love of spending money— even if it wasn't theirs—and the safety net of financial security. They'd get a few jobs through friends and social connections. Do a feature spread in a glossy magazine.'

'I'm not suggesting you become an interior designer. I'm not offering you a job.'

'Aren't you?'

'No.' He touched her face gently, his thumb brushing over her mouth. 'I want you with me. I don't want to do long distance. I don't want to wait any longer. Or put off a life together.'

She could hear his impatience. 'We've only just begun whatever it is we have.' She didn't know if she was ready for more. But then, he had a point. He wasn't someone new to her life.

'That's not true. What we have, what's between us, began eighteen years ago. Eighteen! We know each other. We have been through awful times together. And good times. If Simon hadn't got in the way, we would have been together. You know that.'

He was right. Wasn't he? Those months living with Luke after the attack, he had given everything. Remi had felt safe, protected by someone who would always put her first. There had been no intimacy during those days, not of the sexual kind. But emotionally, Luke had seen her stripped bare and vulnerable. He'd held her as she'd sobbed day after day. Had sat quietly with her when she needed peace, had listened when she needed to vent and rage and question her world. If Simon hadn't swaggered back into her life, would the relationship have evolved? Probably. Why on earth had she been so susceptible to Simon's charm? At that point, she'd wanted so desperately to reclaim the life she'd had before the attack. She'd wanted to rewind time. There was also a sense of vindication when Simon had come crawling back—well, strolling back, with vague apologies and persuasive entreaties about how much he loved her. He had finally accepted that she hadn't cheated.

'He wanted you back because you were with me,' Luke continued. 'He had a need to win. And you were the prize.'

'Oh, come on, that's not true.'

'Isn't it? I've never told you, but when you first moved to Sydney for the show, he made a point of getting in my face, of laughing at me for being left behind. Saying you would never have walked away from him, you would have begged him to go with you. That you were only hanging out with me in the first place because he'd broken your heart. He spoke to me again, two months later, before he moved there. Letting me know he'd be looking you up, that you'd be straight back in his bed. That he might make things serious this time. That you'd been sweet and cute before, but now you were a hottie actress you were good enough to be a girlfriend.'

Anger poured through her, despite Simon being out of her life. Despite knowing he was a manipulative, smug prick. Despite these things having happened so long ago.

'Why haven't you told me this before?'

'It's never been the right time.'

'You should have told me before I married him!'

'When? Before the Connor Mallick rumours, you were madly in love with him and living together. We saw each other three times in the three years you were acting. You were busy, your life full—you wouldn't have listened to me.'

He had a point. But. 'Simon told me not to see you.' He'd been emphatic. The first time Remi had seen Luke in Sydney, Simon had been furious, thrown quite a tantrum. The next couple of times she'd kept their meetings quiet. Hadn't mentioned the emails they shared either.

'After the attack, when you were at my apartment, there was no point. Simon had shown himself to be a tosser. He was no longer around and you were dealing with other issues.'

'And when Simon wanted me back? How about then? Wouldn't that have been a good time to let me know?'

'Would you have listened?

'Yes.' Would she? She had been thrilled when Simon rang her, when he took her out, gushed about how much he loved her, how he wanted to make it up to her. 'Maybe.'

'I tried, you know. Every time I started to speak about Simon you shut me down. Said you knew him better than me. That you wouldn't hear me speaking rubbish about him. You loved me as a friend, but Simon was your boyfriend.'

'Oh my god. I was so stupid. So, so blind and stupid.' She buried her face in the pillow.

'We can make up for those lost years. It's our time, now. Come with me. Come and live with me in Melbourne to start with, then we will go to Perth. Be part of my world. Make a life—a full life—together.'

She peeked up at him. 'I have to think about Josephine and Em.' Not that she was considering his proposal. Not seriously. But what if? What if this was her chance for real happiness?

'I understand, but this was always going to be temporary for them, wasn't it?'

'I'm not interested in doing the society thing.' Remi would never return to a life of pampered preening.

'Neither am I. Except for the grand opening of one of our hotels.'

'I could manage that.' Standing proud beside Luke.

'We might have to spend quite a few months in Perth.'

'I could handle that too.'

***

Remi left Luke taking a shower and made her way downstairs in an old sweatshirt and her pyjama pants. Emerson was in the kitchen. Remi had a flash of embarrassment, hoping she and Luke hadn't been too obvious or noisy.

'Hello,' she said. 'Didn't expect you back, thought you'd still be with Kristof.'

Emerson pulled a tray from the oven and slid three slabs of toasted sourdough onto her plate, each thick with bubbling cheese. 'Something came up,' she said. She kept her focus on her food, glancing only briefly at Remi. Her usual energy was missing.

'You okay?' Remi asked.

'Hmm? Yes. All good.' A quick smile that barely reached her eyes. 'Would you like one?' She nudged the plate towards Remi. 'Cheese and Vegemite on toast. Keeping it simple tonight.'

'Looks good, but I'll pass. Luke's here. He'll be down soon. We'll probably get something together.'

'Luke's here?'

Remi didn't miss the surprise in Emerson's voice. Surprise, and something else. Concern? Worry? Her reaction was unexpected. Emerson was Luke's second biggest fan. Was there a problem with her work? Or was it discomfort at unexpectedly having a man in the house, a man in Remi's bed? That weird blurring of lines between Emerson's home life and work life.

'Yeah. Just having a shower. He, ah, just flew in this afternoon. To surprise me.'

'Okay. That's nice.' She was cleaning the tray quickly. Cutting her toast in half. 'I might just take this to my room. Leave you two in peace.'

'You don't have to go.'

'No. It's fine. I'm a bit tired anyway.' Emerson made to leave but stopped as Luke walked into the room.

'Hi, Emerson.' In jeans and a white long-sleeved tee, his hair damp and skin flushed, he looked casual, gorgeous and at home. And like a man who had recently been tumbling Remi between the sheets.

'Hello. I'll get out of your way.'

'You're never in the way.' Luke spoke with the largesse of a contented man. 'And I haven't had a chance to say thank you in person, for the amazing work you've done.' He slid his arm around Remi, pressing her against his side. 'I'm pleased with the direction you're taking.'

Remi expected delight or even giggles but got neither. Emerson only looked at them with an indecipherable expression. There was something wrong. A falling out with Kristof? There was nothing worse than seeing others in their loved-up bubble when your own romance was crumbling.

'It was nothing,' Emerson mumbled.

An awkward silence fell between them until Emerson lifted her head, radiating a weird mix of guilt and restrained anger. Remi had only ever seen Emerson in two modes: full of easy-going humour and joy or intently focused on her art. This felt out of character. But then, what did she know? They hadn't been friends all that long.

Emerson looked at the plate in her clenched hands. 'I'll see you later,' she said.

As she walked away, Luke shot Remi a questioning look. She replied with a shrug.

CHAPTER TWENTY-SEVEN

EMERSON
Thursday, 10 August 2023

'Hey, are you here for breakfast?' Kristof greeted Emerson as she walked into the restaurant.

'Yeah, I'm meeting Luke.' She looked around.

'He's not here yet, but he's got a table reserved.'

She followed Kristof as he wove his way through the room. 'Look, I'm sorry about yesterday,' she said before she sat, knowing this wasn't really the right time for a chat. 'There was something I had to deal with. Someone I had to talk to. For a friend.'

'It's okay. Don't apologise.' He wedged his hands into the front pocket of his black apron and gave her a suggestive look. 'You can make it up to me tomorrow if you like. It's my day off.'

'I think I could do that.' The urge to kiss him was so strong she was on the verge of doing something hugely inappropriate. The connection and rush of desire helping to push aside her anxiety.

'I'd better go,' he said after a few long seconds. 'Oh, um, tea or coffee to start?'

'Tea, please.'

'Lemon scented?'

'Perfect.'

Luke arrived as Kristof returned with her pot, cup and saucer.

'What did you need to see me about?' he asked, after ordering a long black. He looked relaxed. Happy. She guessed Remi might have a lot to do with that.

Emerson fussed with swishing the pot, pouring her tea. She'd planned how this conversation would go, but now the words wouldn't come.

'Is this about your work? You know I'm very happy with what you've produced. I've got a meeting in Melbourne next week with the manager there and my marketing person. She's keen to look at creating hotel-specific design sets for the other hotels. There's a chance we could be keeping you busy for the next few months.'

A precipice opened beneath Emerson. Speak, and she would be hurling herself over the edge. Asking her only client if he had set out to destroy a marriage was not likely to end well. At best he might laugh her off, denounce Kayla as a liar. And what then? Would he decide he no longer needed her services? Luke managed his team with tight efficiency and high standards. If he saw Emerson as a gossip, as someone who liked to involve herself in his private life, then she doubted he would want to work with her.

Why was she here? She should have gone straight home yesterday and relayed Kayla's accusations to Remi. This wasn't Emerson's business.

Except Luke had been there and hadn't left till hours later. Even then she couldn't say anything: Remi had been all soft and glowing. Happier than Emerson had ever seen her. Taking note of how Josephine handled things, she'd decided to get clarity and explanation before she did anything.

'Did you have a good holiday?' she said at last.

'Yes. We did.' He watched her. 'It seems to have made a difference to Remi, don't you think? It was good for her to get away from all the problems she's had down here.'

Emerson nodded. 'Yes.' She cleared her throat before continuing. 'She had a conversation with Simon last night. He's not doing well financially and he was probably behind some of the things that have happened.'

'Extraordinary.' He accepted his coffee from Kristof with a generous smile. Took a small sip. 'I did wonder how his little enterprise was going. Can't say I feel sorry for him. The man is an over-indulged fool. Did he admit to anything?'

'I don't think so.' She fiddled with the teaspoon, flipping it over and over on the table. 'It seems highly likely Kayla was also involved. She was here when things happened, like the car and even the fire. You know her, don't you? Kayla?' She tried to sound nonchalant. Conversational.

'I've met her.' Luke's expression didn't change, no flinch of guilt or wariness. 'She was here the night of the Hobart grand opening, if I recall. Remi saw her with Simon that night.'

Emerson set the teaspoon back on the saucer. The video on her phone proved he was lying, but she hesitated. What would she achieve by showing him what she knew? It could wait. 'I had a conversation with Kayla yesterday.'

His brows raised a fraction. 'Really? Do you know her?'

'No. But I'd noticed her here, at the hotel. And I found her here again yesterday.'

'Found her? It sounds like you were hunting her down.' His gaze was teasing. Questioning. 'Were you?'

An irrational guilt crept over Emerson. How did he do that? Make her feel like she was the one at fault? She pulled herself up straight. 'No. Not hunting. Just talking.'

'And how did that go?'

'I wanted to ask her why she was targeting Remi. I thought if I asked her outright, we'd know for sure if it was her.' She took a breath. 'And I'd seen her talking with you. Here, in the carpark, yesterday afternoon. And another time, a few weeks ago. I was curious.'

Luke didn't move, yet his air of easy good humour dissipated. 'I see.' He rested his hands on the armrests of his seat. 'Like I said, I do know who she is, and have spoken to her, but I wouldn't consider that we had any connection beyond her being a guest at the hotel.' He paused, his gaze assessing her. 'And how was it? This conversation you had?'

Oh, shit. Shit. This was the point of no return. Her toes on the figurative edge. She could still back away. 'She said some things. About you.'

'Really? Such as?'

Oh, what the hell? If he'd done this, she didn't want to work with him anyway. 'That you have always wanted Remi.'

He gave a fleeting, tight-lipped smile. 'Yes. That's true. And it's hardly been a secret. I fell in love with Remi many, many years ago.'

'Before she landed the TV role?'

'Yes. Well before that.' He considered her intently before he continued. 'Remi was extraordinary even at twenty. I was training myself to be more, to be better. But she had such class. She was beautiful, obviously, but she had something more. She had this way of holding herself a little back from others. Not shy but cautious. Not someone who needed to demand attention, yet she got it anyway.'

Emerson knew what he meant. Remi was reserved, at least on the surface, and Emerson had often overcompensated, being even more exuberant than usual, because when Remi smiled and laughed and connected, it was like getting a shiny sparkly reward.

'I saw how wonderful she was,' he continued. 'And I saw what she needed. I came from nothing, but I knew I was going to succeed. Just as I knew then, and have never doubted, that Remi is the woman for me. Our connection has always been there. She needs me, she belongs with me and I love her. She should never have been with Simon.' The depth of his feelings was evident in his eyes. 'This is a very intense and personal conversation for a breakfast meeting.'

It sure was. Emerson sipped her tea, set it down, stared at the cup. But she needed clarity. Didn't people do outrageous things when they were so in love?

'Sorry. There's some things worrying me, things that don't make sense. Kayla said you helped her find a way back into Simon's life. That you wanted to break up their marriage.'

'She said that?' He regarded her as though she were an illogically irate guest, remaining polite but not buying her nonsense. 'So now you think I actively placed Kayla in Simon's path to tempt my friend's nefarious husband?'

His composure was sapping Emerson's confidence. 'That was what she suggested.'

'What else did she say?'

'That the two of you go way back. Which I took to mean you knew her when she was working at the Park Hyatt. Before Remi's attack.'

He shifted his gaze to look through the windows. 'I see. Interesting.'

'And that she has leverage over you.'

Tension seeped into the air between them. 'Dramatic.' His chuckle was small and tight. 'And do you also think I've been behind this campaign to ruin Remi's life, just so I can ride in and be the hero? Or so she'll leave Hobart and fall into my arms?' His mild amusement did little to hide a taut ferocity. This was not a man who took accusations lightly.

Emerson's stomach flipped. 'No, no, I think all those things were Kayla and maybe Simon.'

'Well, that's a relief. Good to know I'm off the hook for that, at least.' So far he hadn't denied any of her accusations, merely deflected them.

'And what about breaking up her marriage?'

'I think we can agree Simon did that all by himself. He cheated and lied. And he did not treat Remi well.'

'But Kayla said you were responsible for putting her back in his life.'

He didn't reply, his gaze now fierce. She'd done it. She'd well and truly screwed up her work with Strike. She'd never dealt with this side of Luke, but she knew instinctively he would not tolerate such disrespect. Their easy-going relationship was shattered. For what? None of this was any of her business.

He looked away. 'I hope you haven't discussed these theories with Remi.'

'I haven't.'

His eyes flashed to hers for a moment. 'Good.'

Did he think she'd leave it at that? Damn it. She needed something more concrete.

'Luke. Did you play a part in the end of Remi's marriage?'

'Have you met Simon?'

'No.'

'I met him before I met Remi.' He sounded chatty, like a man recounting a story from his youth. 'I knew him immediately for what he was: a spoiled, entitled, arrogant prick. Smoothed over with charm and fun and laughs. Good looks. Confident. Rich. He always got what he wanted. He, Remi and I, we all worked at the same hotel in Melbourne. He'd slept with half the girls before he got to Remi. Unfortunately, she fell for his facade. He kept her for a few months, then he dumped her, when the next hot thing wandered past. At least, until she landed the show, and then he deemed her worthy. Of course, he dumped her again eighteen months later when there were some stupid rumours about her cheating. Says a lot about the man, doesn't it? Unfortunately, after a few months—after she healed—he came back, convinced her to marry him. Do you see a pattern here?'

Emerson nodded.

'He gave her a life she didn't even want. Made her miserable. You've known Remi how long? A month?'

'A bit more.'

'Well you have no idea about her life before. How unhappy she was in her marriage. How Simon kept stringing her along, making her doubt herself while he played around. Too smart to leave irrefutable evidence, too convincing and manipulative for Remi to ever work out—or accept and believe—what was really going on.'

Emerson bit her tongue. This was not the time to interrupt.

He rested an arm on the table, shifted forward in his chair. 'If you saw someone you love, a friend you cherish, miserable and trapped, wouldn't you want to help?'

'Yes.' Of course. The word 'but' stuck in her throat. Was he confirming what Kayla had suggested?

'I'm going to be honest with you, Emerson, because I feel I can trust you. Can I trust you?'

How was she supposed to answer that? Was he asking her to keep his secrets? She had to respond, so she nodded. Despite everything, even now she wanted his approval. Wanted to be good enough. She held back on the urge to convince him, to tell him how trustworthy she was.

'Kayla approached me, made it clear she wanted Simon for herself. They'd been involved previously and she wanted him back. I agreed to help facilitate her plans. Given her hunger for the status and wealth Simon would provide, I knew she wouldn't settle for being the bit on the side. I believed—and I still do—that the short-term pain of discovering her husband's infidelity was worth it for Remi. She has found freedom and happiness.' He sounded so reasonable.

'What did you do exactly? To help her? To help Kayla?'

'Not much. Took her as a plus one to a charity ball I knew he'd be attending. An event Remi wasn't going to—she was here in Hobart and was reluctant to return to Sydney for a fancy dinner. I did that twice, actually, positioning Kayla right in Simon's path. The rest was up to her. She's a woman who has always known how to achieve her goals. Which would almost be admirable if she weren't so Machiavellian. And so limited in her pursuits. Anyway, that was the extent of my involvement, other than inviting Kayla to the opening party here. I left it to them and it didn't take much. Simon remembered her well.

And I had given him the impression she was with me, which he hated.' He sounded nonchalant, a little proud of his efforts.

'Okay.' Relieved, Emerson leaned back in her chair. His explanation didn't sound so bad. Almost understandable.

'Remi is happy,' Luke said. 'Please don't say or do anything to change that.'

She opened her mouth. Shut it. He was asking for her silence. She poked the idea, testing her reaction. Remi *was* happy. She didn't want to be responsible for undoing that, especially when she'd been such a shitshow. Luke was saying he trusted Emerson. He had confided. Okay—he'd spilled the beans after she'd thrown out a few whacky accusations. But had he done anything truly terrible? His love for Remi was real, he'd only wanted a better life for her. Sure, he may have interfered in a minimal way, but the outcome was positive. Keeping quiet about what she knew wouldn't be so bad. She was comfortable with keeping his secret. Wasn't she?

'You look conflicted,' he said.

'No. It's all good.' She made her face relax.

'Excellent.' He picked up his coffee, indicated a change of tone with a smile. 'Let's talk about your next project. Or projects, plural. It's time to start planning the designs for the other hotels. Organise your site visits.'

Really? 'I wasn't sure you'd want me to continue?'

'Why? Because you raised your concerns with me? No. That shows you care about Remi. And that you're comfortable talking with me directly. For that, I am appreciative. Going forward, I know you will do the right thing. I can trust you. Of course I want to keep working with you. In fact, I don't believe we are paying you enough. Your work is excellent.'

'Thank you.'

'If you can complete the designs by say, the end of September, then there should be a healthy bonus for you. How does that sound?'

Was he serious? She'd be able to clear some debt, even pay back Giselle and Erin. 'Wow, that's incredible. That schedule is definitely doable.'

'Right, are you free to do a tour of the hotels in the next week? I think you'll need a few days at each. Time to explore and get a sense of each location. You'll be away, at a guess, for ten days. Maybe two weeks.'

'Absolutely.' And just like that, she was back on his page.

He stood, his expression warm, and she got to her feet and shook his hand. 'I'll confirm as soon as my PA makes the arrangements. And Emerson?'

'Yes?'

'Thank you.'

Emerson watched him leave, waited till he had left the room, before sinking back into the chair. Two weeks' travel. Exciting, vibrant hotels. More money. An amazing project. A bonus!

She knew she was being bought.

***

An email arrived before the end of the day. If it suited her, she was to leave for Brisbane on Saturday. There was a twelve-day itinerary. An attachment with a new schedule of fees for her work. It was ridiculously generous.

Emerson dropped her phone off the side of the bed. Fuckity fuckity fuck. A dream job with amazing perks and travel and luxury experiences. A dream job with massive, morally suspect strings attached. Excitement kept trying to override her doubts.

The doubts kept trying to explode into a state of agitated guilt. Tricky thoughts stomped around her head.

She went over and over what he'd said, aligning his explanation alongside Kayla's comments. There was a blip. Something not right.

Kayla had said she and Luke had a shared history, described him as having *always* been a strategist. Luke considered Kayla to be a woman who *always* achieved her goals. Similar comments about similar attributes, with a strong suggestion of knowing each other, of knowing the other's characteristics and values. Surely that knowledge was based on experience?

According to Luke, Kayla had approached him, asked for his help in getting into Simon's line of sight. Why did she ask him? How did she know he was the man who could—and would— achieve her goal? That he would be prepared to help?

How far back did they go? How long had they known each other? He hadn't confirmed or denied that he'd known Kayla back when she worked in Sydney. And why had he done what she'd asked? What was her leverage?

PART THREE

DEFENCE

CHAPTER TWENTY-EIGHT

REMI
Wednesday, 23 August 2023

Remi set two glasses on the table and took her seat opposite Josephine. 'A local drop,' she said. 'Recommended by the barman.'

'Thank you.' Josephine raised her glass. 'Here's to the beginning of new chapters and closing the door on the dramas of the last.'

'Cheers to that.' There had been no ugly events since she'd confronted Simon and her life was again moving forward. She even had enough cash to pay him in a few days.

They sipped, Remi letting the ambiance of the intimate bar flow over her. Comfortable chairs, low-hanging copper light fittings. Lots of timber and texture. Bold splashes of colour toned down the rustic vibe, making the space sleeker and more dynamic. A juxtaposition that somehow worked. She would snap some pictures before they left, file them away for later reference—for when she and Luke began planning the Perth hotel. She'd only made the decision two days ago and was both nervous and excited about what lay ahead.

'I have news, too,' Josephine said. 'Not as big as yours, but pretty exciting.'

'Tell me.' Remi had spent so many hours talking to Josephine over the last week, working through her thoughts until she'd reached a verdict. Now it was decided: she was leaving. The house would go on the market—she would join Luke. Hearing Josephine's news would be a welcome distraction. 'What's happened?'

Josephine set down her glass and clasped her hands around a knee. 'Well. I had a call from Sam today. He and Hollie are heading to Vietnam.'

'Sounds like Hollie is very much a fixture then.'

'Yes. And travelling together doesn't seem to have been a problem. It must be serious.' Her face lit up. 'Sam has asked if I would like to join them.'

'Wow. That's fabulous. When do you head off?' She was thrilled for Josephine. Though her fears for her son had eased, Remi knew she still worried and missed him horribly.

'I was thinking I'd fly out in a week or so.' Her joy was obvious. 'They leave Thailand next week. I'll meet them in Hanoi. I'm going to see him! He wants me there.'

'How long will you be gone?'

Josephine took a mouthful of wine and pulled a sad face. 'This is the difficult part. I don't know, exactly. Sam and Holliday are a bit vague about their plans. They've got no end in sight at this stage. And as much as I want Sam to go back to uni, I'm not going to push him. And who knows how we will go, the three of us together? He may decide having his mum along for the ride isn't much fun after all.' She took a deep breath.

'You're thinking you might not be back before I sell the house?'

'I might not.'

Remi wasn't ready to say goodbye, Josephine had become a real friend. It didn't matter that Remi had already pencilled in a prospective finish to their living arrangements: her proposed end was ages away, not in a week. Suddenly change was rushing towards her.

'Remi?'

'Hmm.' She didn't trust herself to speak.

'Are you sure you want to sell?'

She swallowed, controlling the small blip of unease. 'Yes. No. I don't know. Yes.' Change was hard, she'd told herself. It was natural to be having doubts. The house meant so much. But she had an opportunity for a different life now. A life with Luke. He wanted them to be a team, for her to contribute to Strike and learn the business. Simon had never wanted to be a team. He had held the glory role and Remi had been a sidekick, trotted out for events and showings.

There was no comparison between the two men. Luke valued her, wanted her opinion. Didn't care that she had no interest in parading on the social circuit. He'd even suggested that, if she wasn't comfortable with integrating herself into his company, she should take on her own renovation project. He was right, it made complete sense to sell her house. She couldn't stay here, not if her life was to be with him. And there was little point in holding onto the property. It was time. But letting go was painful.

'It makes sense. It's just hard. Seems I don't do change very well.'

'Oh, I don't know. When you kicked Simon to the kerb you leaped into change.'

'That was different. It was a long time coming and I had a real passion to drive me forward. To fill my life.'

Josephine laughed gently. 'Doesn't Luke rate as a real passion? From what you say, he's ready to fill your life.'

'I know. I know. The future looks amazing.'

'But?'

'But.' What exactly was her problem? 'I don't want to say goodbye to you. Not yet.' And she didn't want to walk out her front door, knowing she'd never be back.

Josephine rested her hand on Remi's arm. There was so much comfort in the simple gesture.

'Remi. We'll still be friends. I'll probably head back to Brisbane eventually, or I could visit Perth. We could end up in the same city for a bit.'

Remi covered Josephine's hand with her own and squeezed. 'Emerson's back tomorrow. She's going to be handed a few surprises,' she said.

'She's got a lot of good things going on. She'll be fine.'

***

Emerson wiped at the tears racing down her face. It was not the reaction Remi had expected and she felt guilty for causing this distress. 'I'm sure it won't happen too fast,' she said. 'It could take ages to sell. Then there's the settlement period. It will be months before we have to move out.'

'But you love this house. You've worked so hard. It's not finished.' Emerson's voice rose into a wail.

'It's the right time. Luke's planning a new hotel in Perth. He's asked me to be part of the process.' It was becoming easier to say, easier to accept as the right decision. So long as she didn't think too long or too hard about leaving.

Emerson sniffed. She broke her biscuit into half. Then into quarters. None went into her mouth, though her plate was piling up with crumbs.

Remi glanced at Josephine, whose own face was downcast. 'The trip sounds like it was fun,' she said to shift Emerson's mood. 'I can't believe Luke flew you everywhere and put you up in his hotels. He must be your all-time favourite client.'

'Sure.' Emerson's response was a long way from enthusiastic. Odd, but then Remi guessed she was both tired and upset.

Remi had picked Emerson up from the airport, her car finally back on the road after Luke had insisted on paying for the repairs. He'd been adamant she needed a reliable vehicle, had suggested it was only her pride preventing her from accepting his offer. He might have been right, although Remi tended to think it was more a case of not wanting to become financially reliant on another man. Still, she figured she would pay him back after the house sold.

Emerson had been a little quieter than usual on the drive home, answering Remi's questions but sounding distracted. The three of them had gathered in the kitchen with tea and bakery-bought biscuits, Josephine telling Emerson how much they'd missed her and her baking. It had not been the same with Emerson away. The absence of her chatter and laughter, of her energy and presence, had left a tangible gap in the house.

Josephine had shared her news first, leaving out the small detail that she wouldn't be returning. Emerson perked up when she heard Josephine would be joining her son, instructing her to get active on Instagram so she could post pictures for them all to see. Then Remi had dropped her bombshell with a heart-shaking thud.

'Which hotel was your favourite?' Remi asked, desperate to shift the conversation.

Emerson sighed. 'I don't know. They're all great.' She met Remi's stare. 'Are you really sure you want to give away every-thing you've worked for? To follow Luke? Isn't it all happen-ing a bit quick? Three weeks ago, he was just a friend. He gave you a nice holiday and now you're selling the house? Have you really thought about this? You're giving Simon and Kayla what they want.' She said the names as though they stung her tongue. 'Doesn't that bother you?'

She was making Remi's new plan sound rushed and shallow. Making her sound flippant. She was wrong though, it wasn't like that. 'Em, Luke isn't just a friend. I've known him since I was twenty. There's nothing rushed about this.' Her laugh was breathy. 'He's been there through the toughest parts of my life. Stood by me. He knows me. I know him.'

'Do you, though? Do you really know him?'

'Absolutely.' Of course she did. Sure, there had been many years they'd barely seen each other or even talked. But when-ever they reunited it was like they'd never been apart. She was comfortable with him. Could tell him anything. Trusted him. Why was Emerson so anxious? 'I thought you liked Luke? You gave him a tick of approval when he took me away. I expected you to be excited for us.'

'I know. I did. Like him, I mean.'

'You did? You don't now?' Josephine asked, sounding worried. 'Has something gone wrong? Is there an issue over your work?'

'No. The work is good. It's nothing.' She looked from Josephine to Remi, and back. 'Sorry. I'm being a real downer. Sorry, sorry.' She rubbed her eyes. 'I like living here. I guess I didn't expect things to change so quickly. I'll be fine. It'll be fine.' She stood. 'Is it okay if I hog the bathroom? I might have a bath.'

She stepped towards the hall, then stopped and looked back. 'Josie, you are coming back from Vietnam, right?'

Josephine shook her head.

'Oh.' Emerson's small voice was full of hurt. 'Okay.'

Josephine waited till they heard the bath running. 'That was unexpected. I thought she'd be thrilled by the romance of it all.'

Remi had been so sure her announcement of a future with Luke would be greeted with shrieks of excitement that she'd chilled the champagne. She'd anticipated celebrating, not sitting around the table with dry, uneaten biscuits and cold tea.

'I can understand her being a bit sad about the house. But I honestly thought she'd be happy for me and Luke.'

'I think something else is going on. Shall I talk to her?'

Remi nodded. She hated seeing Emerson unhappy, but neither did she particularly like having her decision questioned. She'd considered Luke's suggestion for over a week. Sleep had been lost, hours spent sitting in the kitchen staring at nothing, her thoughts in a conflicted jumble. In the end she'd simplified the problem: where did she want her life to be, with Luke or with this house? Which did she love more? Looked at her choice like that, it made no sense to hold on to sandstone and wood while saying no to flesh and life. She chose to write an end to this season—to this storyline—and to begin afresh.

CHAPTER TWENTY-NINE

EMERSON

That night, Emerson tried to disappear into mindless sleep. Unfortunately, skipping dinner and hiding in bed meant she slept from five till eight, then lay awake for three hours, her guilt swirling in ever faster circles. Remi was selling the house. To be with Luke.

How would Remi react if she knew Luke's full story? Would she still go? God, poor Remi. Just when her life was looking so good and the worry had lifted from her. Emerson had to say something. Tell Remi what she knew. Her loyalty should be to her friend and not to her client. However he justified his involvement, Luke had done the wrong thing. He'd said he wanted to free Remi, but good guys didn't interfere in other people's marriages. Maybe what Luke had done wouldn't matter to Remi, but at least she'd know. Maybe she'd be grateful Luke had helped bring an end to a relationship that wasn't so great. Because all Luke had done, really, was put temptation in Simon's path. Simon didn't have to take the bait.

Except Luke and Kayla were still up to something. Right? Why else would they have been arguing in the carpark of his hotel? What's more, they'd met there several times. Luke despised Simon, there was a long-time feud, and yet Simon's wife continued to stay at Strike Hotels. That was strange. Kayla and Luke also had more than a little history: recent, a few years ago and way back. There were things they'd both said. Slipped words and references. Emerson didn't know the details, but there were clues.

It was driving her nuts. But she didn't have to keep his secret. Her silence hadn't been bought.

Except, it had. Luke hadn't needed to say it out loud, but it was obvious. *Hey, Emerson, don't say anything to Remi about me being an interfering manipulative bastard. And, by the way, here's your dream job with a motza of cash and a big juicy bonus. Be quiet. Take the money. Got it? Good girl.*

Yeah. Nah.

It had proved very hard to enjoy her reward. Guilt really interfered with lush experiences. Nearly two weeks of quality hotel living, sheesh, she should have been in ecstatic bliss, not taking notes diligently and spending her nights holed up and oblivious to the surrounding decadence. Bloody moral compass, ruining a perfectly fabulous trip.

And now Remi was selling the house. Leaving what she loved to go and be with him.

Things had got worse.

Emerson flipped over, then back. Tried to get comfortable, then gave up. She pulled on her new dressing gown, the heavy white towelling embellished with the Strike logo. *A gift from*

Strike management, the card had said. Along with the matching slippers, the fruit and chocolate basket, the bottle of wine at each hotel. Luke had held nothing back. There was no way a lowly graphic illustrator would normally be treated with such generosity.

If his collaboration with Kayla came from a place of care and concern for Remi, if his involvement was so small, why was he so intent on Emerson keeping quiet?

The kitchen was warm, the embers in the wood heater still glowing. She turned on the light in the rangehood, not wanting to sit in brightness, and opened the fridge. Cheese on toast would do the trick.

Josephine found her twenty minutes later, cross-legged in front of the fire, her second generous serve of cheesy toast on a plate in her lap.

'Did I wake you?' Emerson asked as Josephine dropped a cushion on the floor and sat next to her.

'No, no. Just suffering from middle-of-the-night active brain. You know, when you wake up and your brain switches into high gear and burns through plans and strategies. They say the best thing, if you can't sleep, is to get out of bed, read or something, then go back to bed when you're tired again.'

'Does it work?' Em asked.

'Sometimes.'

'Want some?' Emerson held out her plate.

Josephine hesitated before taking a slice. The two of them ate quietly, watching the glow of the fire.

Emerson broke the silence. 'It's too soon for everything to change.'

Josephine didn't answer straight away. She finished her toast, dusted the crumbs from her fingers. 'Is this about having to move out? Or do you think Remi is moving too fast with Luke? That she hasn't thought this through?'

'Yes.' Her answer was emphatic. 'It's like, she loves this house, has worked so hard on it for so long. Then that woman interfered, did all those horrible things and everything got all difficult and challenging and nasty. And her ex came stomping around, insisting on selling and Luke sweeps her away and what he offers is too tantalising. I mean, I get it, sort of. It's been hard. Here's a chance to let go and do something else. But, what if ...' She held her hands open to emphasise a bucketload of questions.

'What if, what?'

'Nothing.'

'Tell me. What if?' Josephine waited, then filled in the blank. 'What if she's making a mistake?'

Emerson pulled up her knees and wrapped her arms around them. 'What if Luke isn't the great guy she thinks he is?' She peeked to her left, found Josephine watching her intently. 'You know, what if there's stuff about him she doesn't know?'

'Like what?'

'I don't know. Like things he's done. Or things he's been involved with.'

'Em, has something happened?' Josephine's voice was quiet but firm.

Words fired like popping candy on Emerson's tongue, but she said nothing. Sleeping in those plush designer hotel beds and signing off on the new fee and work schedule had cast a spell of silence. Her mouth wouldn't open and her stupid thoughts tangled into a knot that wedged in her tightened throat.

'You were very quiet before you left for your trip,' Josephine said. 'You seemed to have something on your mind.'

Emerson gave the smallest of nods.

'Okay. Well, I'm guessing this has to do with Luke.' Josephine watched her for a response, then said, 'Because your opinion of him seems to have changed.' Another pause. 'My question is, was it something he did to you?'

Josephine's question held a whole lot of unpleasant suggestions. Emerson didn't want anyone to think that. 'No. I'm okay. I'm overreacting to something I found out. That's all. It's probably not even that bad.' She tucked her head down even further. 'I hate keeping secrets,' she mumbled into the bunched fabric of her robe.

A moment passed. 'Who are you keeping a secret from?'

Josephine's calm was soothing. The spell loosened a fraction, enough for one word to slip out: 'Remi.'

'And who are you keeping a secret for?'

She felt like a child being asked to explain some terrible deed. 'Luke.' The word was a whisper.

'Would it help to tell me? If I promise not to pass it on? I might be able to give you some perspective.'

That could work. Yes. She could trust Josephine. Emerson lifted her chin, kept her gaze on the red embers. Start with the simple stuff.

'Kayla. I cornered her. She didn't deny she was behind all of Remi's recent problems.'

'You spoke to Kayla?'

'Yes.' Another deep breath helped to dissolve the constriction in her throat. 'I saw her again at Strike, the day after Remi got home from the trip. She was arguing with Luke and I got curious so I waited for her and asked a few questions.'

'I didn't realise they knew each other.'

'I don't think Remi does either.'

'And did you ask her about the sabotage and reviews?' Josephine asked.

She nodded. 'And about the fire. I accused her more than asked. Nicely, though. I wasn't aggressive.'

'She admitted being involved?' Josephine was incredulous.

'She didn't deny anything.' Emerson hesitated. But this was Josephine. She would help her decide what to do. 'She also said Luke is the one obsessed with Remi. He helped Kayla win Simon back. Helped end Remi's marriage.'

Josephine put her hand on Emerson's arm. 'Hold on. What are you saying exactly?'

She turned her head to meet Josephine's gaze. Such intelligent eyes. Kind, too. She sighed, then started from the beginning. She told her about the conversation with Kayla and the meeting with Luke. About what he admitted, the part he played in the end of the marriage and how he saw his actions as helping Remi. How he asked Emerson to stay quiet. How he offered her more work, more money and a juicy bonus. How that money meant she could pay back the friends she'd hurt. She didn't rush, trying to keep the details in order.

'I also think he was aware of what Kayla had done—you know, the things to get Remi out of here. He might not have been involved directly, but I think he figured out what Kayla was up to, especially when he found her staying at Strike. That's why he was arguing with her. And there's this thing in the back of my head. This idea that Kayla and Luke have known each other for a long time and that she must have some leverage over him. She as much as said she did.' Her voice drifted into silence.

They both sat watching the fire, and eventually Josephine spoke. 'That is shocking, but plausible. I'm guessing you feel guilty for not telling Remi.'

Emerson could only nod.

Josephine scooted closer and put her arm around Emerson's shoulders. 'And now she's running off with Luke, and you think she should know before she sells the house. You're worried for her.'

'Remi said Luke is coming down tomorrow to spend a few days with her. Maybe if I talk to him?'

'And say what?'

She shrugged. 'I don't know. Let him know I can't keep this secret. Ask him to tell Remi himself. If he really believes it was the right thing to do, then he should be honest with her.' She half laughed. 'And then I'll tell him I really don't want to lose the job.'

'He should never have put you in this position.' Anger tightened Josephine's voice. 'It's an abuse of power. He knows you need the money.'

'He's wanted Remi for so long, he said. Now they're back together, I guess he doesn't want to jeopardise the relationship.'

'Well, then, he should have thought more before he did what he did. You, Emerson, are not responsible for saving him from the consequences of his own actions.'

No, she wasn't. But, damn it, she couldn't afford to lose this income. If she saw him, she could maybe make him understand. She would convince him to confess.

CHAPTER THIRTY

JOSEPHINE
Thursday, 24 August 2023

The next day Josephine watched Emerson hunch over her phone, ignoring her lunch. She was worried for her friend. How dare Luke put her in such a position. What sort of person thinks that sort of setup is okay? And what sort of self-centred creep works to destroy a friend's marriage? Or stands by while someone makes her miserable so he can play the bloody hero? If that man walked in here now, she'd have a few things to say, none of them polite. She lifted a forkful of pasta. Today was Thursday, her flight to Hanoi was booked for next Friday, over a week away. Maybe she should push back her flight? As desperate as she was to see Sam, she didn't want to leave Remi and Emerson if everything deteriorated into a horrendous mess. She *was not* going to leave with this hanging over her friends. There would be a resolution before she left the house, she would make sure of it.

'Tonight,' Emerson said suddenly, her eyes still on her screen. 'He said he'll meet me tonight.'

'Did you say why you wanted to see him?'

Emerson set the phone face down beside her plate, picked up her fork but didn't eat. She looked miserable. 'I said I wasn't comfortable keeping his secrets.'

'He probably thinks you want more money.' Josephine's opinion of Luke had fallen from respect to expecting the worst. Last night, when Emerson had relayed Kayla's accusations, words like 'obsession' and 'strategist' had appeared like red flags in Josephine's mind.

'Do you want me to come with you?' She would be more than happy to offer support. Her presence would force Luke to be reasonable. He couldn't threaten and bluff Josephine like he could Emerson. Although sitting quietly and keeping her opinion to herself would be a serious challenge.

Emerson stabbed a single gnocchi. Set her fork back down. 'I think I'd better go alone. He won't be impressed if he finds out I've told you.'

'Are you clear about what you want to say?'

'I guess.' She pushed her glasses back up her nose. 'Tell him I'm not comfortable keeping quiet. Stress how much I value the work I'm doing with Strike. Suggest it might be a good idea for him to be honest with Remi. Oh god, what if he doesn't like being told what to do? What if he thinks I'm giving him an ultimatum?'

'Don't think of it like that. You're giving him an opportunity to discuss what he did with Remi before you say anything. You're being considerate and respectful. Not that he deserves it.'

'He's going to cancel the project.'

'He might. There's nothing much you can do about that. But Em.' She ducked her head to catch Emerson's eye. 'Honey, you are a talented illustrator. You do exceptional work. Losing the Strike contract is not the end of your career.'

'But I owe so much money. I've been paying off some of the cards. I won't be able to keep doing that. It's been so good, not getting the phone calls. No one has chased me for two weeks. But it's not only the banks. I did the wrong thing to some friends.'

'Right. Well, let's look at getting a pause on your repayments. Give you some breathing space. Then work out what to do moving forward. Okay?'

'Okay.'

Josephine wanted to wrap Emerson in a huge hug. Seeing the effervescence drained from her was heartbreaking. 'Do not let your fear of what Luke might do stop you from doing what you think is right. He is just a client. And you will be fine without his business.'

Emerson ate a few more mouthfuls, the food seeming to do her some good. 'Are you really not coming back?'

'I'm not exactly sure how long I'll be travelling, so I can't keep my room. The house might be sold before I make it back.'

'It's going to be so weird without you here. I'm going to miss you.'

Josephine tried to find a smile. 'It's not forever. You can come visit me wherever I end up.'

'I might not stay either. I've got to find a new home anyway. You're leaving. Remi's leaving.'

'Come on,' Josephine said. 'Let's finish this and go for a drive. Have you been down through the Huon Valley yet?'

'No, I haven't gone anywhere much.'

'Well, there's no point sitting around the house worrying about all this. Let's be tourists.'

Emerson raised her head. 'Will there be ice cream?'

'Absolutely.'

'Can you drive?'

***

The mini road trip was exactly what they needed. Emerson pumped out an eighties playlist, both of them belting out the songs. Josephine was amazed that someone born in the late nineties would know the words.

'These are retro classics,' Emerson enthused. 'Golden oldies. I love them. Especially the electro-pop stuff. Spandau Ballet, Duran Duran. And this one, absolutely love this one.' Her fingers sped over the screen of her phone, releasing the catchy beat of A-ha into the car, the two of them screeching out the high notes. They stopped for ice cream in Huonville; hokey pokey for Josephine, chocolate choc-chip for Emerson. In Cygnet they got out and walked the main street. They stopped at an apple cider maker on the way home. And they avoided talking about Luke or keeping secrets or conspiracy theories involving Kayla.

They were back at the house by six. Luke had taken Remi out for dinner, so Emerson wasn't meeting him until after ten.

'Teach me to bake something,' Josephine suggested when she sensed Emerson beginning to fret. She took some convincing, but in the end, throwing together a sticky date pudding proved to be a good distraction. Even if Josephine managed to send half the mixture across the bench when she pulled the beaters out of the bowl without turning them off first. Laughter soothed and mellowed Emerson's mood. By the time she left, she was calm. Almost confident.

'I've imagined the worst,' she said. 'Now I want it over with. An hour from now I'll be free from the uncertainty. I'll be free from keeping his secret. And I can stop trying to second-guess what I'm doing.' She threw her arms around Josephine. 'Wish me luck. And thank you for today. You really are awesome.'

'I'll wait up for you.'

'Okay. I shouldn't be too long.' Emerson swung her bag over her shoulder and pulled on her pale pink pom-pom beanie.

'And call me,' Josephine said. 'No matter what the time. If you need anything, just call.'

***

Half an hour later, Remi arrived home, bursting with the details of the estate agent visit and her dinner with Luke.

'I still haven't told Simon,' she said, pouring wine for Josephine and herself. 'I can't stand the thought of giving him what he wants. I mean, he and Kayla are going to think their nasty little tricks worked. Or that he still has control over me. Which he doesn't. I'm doing this for me.'

There was something going on beneath Remi's enthusiasm. She was too animated. Too energetic. Sitting for a minute, then jumping back to her feet to flit around the kitchen. Her hands were making rapid grand gestures. Her first glass of wine disappeared in seconds, the glass refilled immediately. It was as though she was trying too hard to be excited. Forcing herself to be all things sunshine and sparkles and bottomless positivity. Like she was determined to drown out any discomfort with waves of exuberance.

'How do you feel? About selling?'

'About selling? Great! It was so much fun to show off the place to the agent. She was so impressed.' Remi dragged out the 'so' for extra emphasis, her eyes going wide. 'Oh my god, you should have heard the praise. I loved it. *Loved it!*'

She was channelling a hyped-up teenage girl and Josephine watched her with growing concern.

'Where's Emerson?' Remi asked, suddenly. 'Is she out with Kristof?'

So, Luke hadn't mentioned he was meeting her. 'There was someone she wanted to see.'

'Oh. Okay. Anyway, the agent said it would take a week to get the listing up. A photographer will come in the next day or so. Yikes. I might have to go berserk on the clean-up before then.'

'Will you stay here until it sells?'

'I don't know. Luke is keen for me to join him in Melbourne as soon as I can.'

Josephine looked at her watch. Emerson had said she was meeting Luke at ten—it was now after eleven thirty. She should be home soon. Josephine tapped out a quick message: *Everything OK?* And waited till the status changed from delivered to read. But there was no reply.

'Checking up on Sam?' Remi asked. She was filling her glass again. Her hand was a little unsteady and her body swayed slightly as she stood by the table.

'Emerson.' Josephine put her phone face up on the table. 'I thought she'd be home by now.'

Remi flopped into a chair, lifted her glass. 'Oh, she's fine. She's out there having fun.' She gave a dismissive wave of her hand.

But Emerson was not out on the town having fun, she was negotiating with a man who was close to achieving his goal and wouldn't appreciate the interference.

'How long has Luke been keen on you?' she asked.

Remi giggled into her glass. 'Apparently forever. He said ... what did he say?' She tried to remember. 'He said, "I have wanted you since before you knew I existed" or something like that. Isn't that romantic? He said he noticed me and was interested before I'd even met him. Way back when we were all working at the Worthington. I was so young and so oblivious. So smitten with stupid Simon. What is it about the cute, popular, fun boys? You want them because being chosen by someone like that is a ...' She waved her free hand around again, this time trying to find a word. 'Validation! It's a validation. You're worthy. But you know what? Luke was definitely the better kisser. Definitely.' She leaned closer, her expression serene. 'And he said I was magnificent. Way, way back then. I first broke his heart when I hooked up with Simon ... the first time. Then when I skipped off to Sydney. But you know, I was self-absorbed, I was going to be an actress. A TV star. The world was my oyster.' She sat up and threw her arms wide, sloshing her wine. Held the pose for a second before slumping back. 'Until Brittney ruined everything. My crazy, scary friend and those crazy, stupid lies. How different my life would've been if those stories hadn't been written.'

'And Luke was there to look after you? He was in Sydney, too?'

'Uh-huh.' Remi gulped more wine. 'Yep, in Sydney. You know what he confessed to me the other day? I hadn't realised this, but he said he chose Sydney for his first hotel because I was there. Isn't that incredible? He could've opened in Melbourne, but he went to Sydney because he wanted to be closer to me. He said he wanted to impress me. I had no idea. Honestly, I mean, who does that? Who makes major choices and business decisions based on where a friend is living?'

Someone with an unhealthy obsession.

'Do you think he opened a hotel in Hobart so he had an excuse to be down here?'

Remi pulled a look of surprise. 'I've never thought of that. I'll have to ask him. You know, he might have.' She laughed. 'Wow. Talk about making a girl feel special.'

'He's certainly been committed to you. And now you're finally going to be together?'

Remi nodded. 'Yup. He says he's been waiting a long time. That's why we're moving kinda fast. Because so many years have been wasted. All those years with Simon. Thank god that ended.' She giggled again. 'I might have to send Kayla a thank-you card. "Thank you, Kayla, for being a skanky ho and stealing my husband. My life is now so much better. But don't come anywhere near my new man."'

'They don't know each other?' Josephine probed, wanting to know if Remi had any knowledge of the connection or if Luke had kept it hidden.

'Nope. Thank goodness.' She gave a dramatic shiver, as though the thought was repugnant. 'Just think, as soon as this house is sold, I need never speak to Simon or his wife ever again. Ta-ta to those two tragics.'

Josephine checked her phone. Still no reply from Emerson. 'Are you comfortable with things moving so fast? A month or so ago, Luke was just a good friend and you were vowing to keep your house, whatever it took.'

Remi's face puckered, an expression of doubt wiping her glee. Then she shook her head and forced a wobbly smile back into place. 'Things change. *Need* to change. Luke is amazing. So caring and patient. Okay, I mean, he's been a bit of a player, a bit of a Casanova, but that's because he's been waiting. He's waited for me for so long. He's always believed in me. Do you know how that makes me feel? It makes me feel valued and special. And I've been so alone for the last couple of years. I was a hermit until you guys came to live here. And now I have someone who loves me. And that feels so bloody great. I *am* lovable, you know? And I can't keep him on hold for any longer. It's now or never.'

'Do you love him?'

'Yes.'

It was the most uncertain confirmation of love Josephine had ever heard.

'I mean, maybe not the way he says he loves me. But he's great. You've met him. He's great. Isn't he?'

What could she say?

The sooner Remi knew the truth, the better.

CHAPTER THIRTY-ONE

EMERSON

'Can I get you a drink?' Luke smiled as though they were two friends catching up.

Emerson didn't want to mess up her thinking, but one drink to calm her nerves, that wouldn't hurt. 'Gin and tonic, please?'

'Name your flavour. Hendricks? Poltergeist? That Tasmanian one made from sheep's whey? That's meant to be good.'

He'd suggested they meet away from the hotel, and this gin bar had been his choice. A glowing wall rose behind the bar, rows of bottles from the bench to the high ceiling. A sliding ladder at the ready if a customer wanted something out of reach. 'Sure. I'll try that.'

She'd arrived to find Luke already at a table, a drink in front of him. He'd looked relaxed, watching the darkened room from his position in the corner. Then he'd stood when she came down the stairs and greeted her with no sign of worry or displeasure.

None of which made her feel any better. She wanted this conversation over, consequences dealt with, no more dubious arrangements to worry about. Then she could get back to sorting out the messy jumble that was her life.

He set the drink down. 'It's good to get out of the hotel,' he said as he sat. 'Have you been here before?'

'No.' She took a sip, resisting the urge to slide into small talk. 'Thank you for meeting me.'

He gave her a serious look. Nodded once. 'I was a little surprised. But you said it was urgent.'

She lifted her glass again. Drank several gulps. What to say first? Was there a magic order to her words that would make it all work?

'I can't keep your secret.'

He didn't react, his fingers turning his glass where it sat on the table. Once. Twice. 'I see.'

'I haven't said anything to Remi.'

'Haven't you?'

'No. It's not my place.'

'But you want to?'

'Yes.' Her voice came out almost at a whisper. She took another sip.

'What do you want to tell her?'

'About you. And Kayla. About all of it. I think she should know about your involvement. About all that stuff.' She trailed off, waiting for Luke to reply.

He said nothing, but kept watching her. She squirmed, the silence stretching till she had to speak.

'But I don't want to tell her. Don't you think you should tell her? Please can't you explain to her? I mean, you're setting up a life together, so shouldn't you start from a place of honesty? Don't you think? Isn't that better?'

Luke lifted his glass. 'Did you enjoy your trip?'

'Yes, of course. The hotels are beautiful. But, Luke, I know it's tit for tat.'

'Tit for tat? Sometimes you say the strangest things, Emerson.'

'If I say something to Remi, will I still be working for you?'

Anger flashed across his face, vivid and fierce. Then he took several sips from his drink and returned the glass to the table with deliberate control.

'What do you think my relationship with Kayla is?'

It wasn't a question she'd expected. How to answer, with what she knew or what she suspected? What the hell, she was on a gangplank over deep water, might as well make every step count. 'I suspect you've known her since she worked at the Park Hyatt. Since before Remi's career was ruined by rumours. Rumours that were made worse because of a source at that hotel.'

'It's interesting that you reference that particular point in time.' His calm was unnerving. 'Are you suggesting Kayla was involved in that debacle?'

'Yes?'

'Hmm.' His gaze shifted away from her, travelled around the bar.

She followed. Every chair was taken, every table occupied by relaxed, happy people. There was a lovey-dovey couple with entwined fingers and intimate body language and a cluster of women sharing stories. Voices raised in an undulating wave of noise.

'You're right. Honesty is the best place to start.' Luke glanced at her, caught her watching. 'I'm going to get you another drink and I'm going to tell you a story. Then we can decide what to do next. Sound good?'

'Um, sure.' She wasn't here to drink, but if one more meant Luke would give her details, then it wouldn't hurt.

He took longer this time but finally returned with two glasses.

'Sorry. Needed to use the amenities.' He set the drinks down. 'Thought we could try a gin from one of the small local distilleries.'

'Sure. Okay.' She took a sip. Stronger than she liked, the flavours more complex and bitter than she was used to. She drank again, not wanting to admit her tastes were basic. 'Interesting.'

He nodded. 'Quite a pungent arrangement of the botanicals.' He mulled over his drink for a bit.

'Luke, I can't keep any more secrets. So please don't tell me anything you aren't prepared to share with Remi.'

He chuckled. 'But don't you want to know the truth? About what a dastardly villain I am?'

Was he serious? She drank, even though she wasn't enjoying the taste.

Luke leaned forward. 'I tell you what, Emerson. I'll give you the whole truth. And I promise, anything I tell you, I'll also tell Remi. How does that sound?'

While she weighed up her response, he spoke again. 'I've got a better idea. You tell me your theory and I'll tell you how close you are to figuring it all out. Because, quite honestly, it would be a relief to have someone to talk to about all this. You're right, keeping secrets is hard. What do you think, Emerson? What did I do?' He raised his eyebrows and smiled, challenging her, urging her to speak.

She drained her glass, leaving the ice cubes to clunk together. 'I think,' she said slowly, pulling together all her suspicions and all the flimsy connections. 'I think you wanted to break up Simon and Remi.'

'Old news.'

'I don't mean recently. You wanted to break them up back when Remi was on the show. You must've known Kayla back then, too, and you worked together to get those rumours out there. The ones about Remi and Connor Mallick. Kayla was the anonymous source, the worker at the hotel who was supposed to have seen them go up to a room. And you—or she—took the photos. Gave them to the press.'

He was sitting back in his chair, his legs crossed, a knowing, arrogant smile on his face. 'You've taken some imaginative leaps, wouldn't you say?'

'A little. Maybe. Just putting things together. *Did* you know Kayla then?'

'Yes, I did. She was an ambitious, beautiful girl, who was determined to climb the ladder. We had a short fling—I wouldn't call it a relationship; the age gap was too significant—and I could see what she wanted and how determined she was to achieve it. Needless to say, we were not a good match. I suggested Simon would be a far more suitable lover.'

'But he was with Remi.'

'Yes.'

'Which was why the two of you made up those rumours, took the photos.'

He made a speculative sound in his throat. 'What you're suggesting, that's a terrible thing for someone to do.'

'Yes.' She rubbed her forehead. Her phone chimed and she glanced at the message; Josephine checking up on her. She'd answer in a minute. Lovely Josephine. So caring and protective and capable. 'Yes, it was a terrible thing. And I think you're sorry. I hope you're sorry. Because those rumours had terrible, horrible consequences.' The words got a little stuck on her tongue.

'They did, didn't they? That girl, Brittney, messed up Remi badly. An unexpected outcome and one I could never have foreseen. But a reality I've had to live with all this time. And I'm sure you'll believe me when I say, one that nearly broke me.'

'You're admitting it?' She tried to sit up straighter. 'It was you.'

'And Kayla. You're right. I must applaud your puzzle-solving skills. Yes, Kayla was the anonymous source. Yes, I took the photos. I really did want Simon to let Remi go. I knew, with his ego, her infidelity would kill the relationship.'

'But she didn't—'

'Didn't matter. I knew he'd believe what he read. Pitiful, really. That he would believe gossip over the word of the woman he was supposed to love.' He drank more of his gin. 'What you must understand, Emerson, is that I have loved Remi more fully than anyone. I have always seen the magnificence within her. She is special. Simon wasn't worthy, he did not deserve to have her, but she was blinded. I forgave her foolishness, but I wasn't prepared to stand aside forever. Do you even know true, unmeasurable love? Do you? Do you, Emerson?'

'No.'

'Well, that's all I've ever been. A man prepared to do anything to gain the love of the woman he wants. The woman he knows will be happiest, will be most fulfilled, will reach her potential, when they are *together*. This—all of this—is for Remi. I've always, always been there for her. She needs me.

And I must reiterate, while I have worked with Kayla in the past, in no way do I condone her recent actions.'

'Did you know what she was doing? Was that why you were arguing?' The gin was going to Emerson's head and her thoughts were a bit fuzzy. 'And why does she stay at Strike? That seems a bit weird, you know?'

He laughed. 'Kayla and I have an arrangement. She is free to stay at Strike whenever she wants to. No charge, I might add. And yes, I very quickly made the connection between Kayla being in town and some of the things that happened at Remi's house.' His face became serious. 'But the fire was not okay. I was furious with her. Putting Remi in danger like that was unacceptable. No matter how much I tolerate or accept Kayla's behaviour, that was a step too far.' He was observing Emerson intently, a thin, chilling smile on his lips.

'What does she have over you? Is it just the, um, rumour stuff?'

'Well, Emerson, I'm going to tell you this because I'm confident you won't share my darkest secrets.' He leaned across the table towards her again. 'I avenged Remi. It wasn't planned, but everything aligned. I saw an opportunity and I took it. Kayla was with me, it was her car, but I was the one who turned the wheel and accelerated.'

Emerson didn't understand what he was saying. She rubbed her forehead. It was becoming hard to line up her thoughts.

She looked into his eyes as his mouth stretched into a contemptuous smile. 'You didn't guess that bit, did you, Emerson? I killed Brittney Moore and I don't for a second regret it.' He tilted his head a fraction as though conceding a point. 'Unfortunately Kayla does like to hold it over me.'

'Whoa.' Huge. This was huge. She'd only been guessing about the other stuff. But this ... whoa ... this was fricken huge. And bad, very bad. Definitely bad. Luke had been the driver who'd hit Brittney. And Brittney had hurt Remi because of what Luke and Kayla had done. Luke wanted Remi for himself. He was obsessed. Scary obsessed. He was not a good person. 'Luke?'

'Yes, Emerson?'

'I think I should go.' She bent to pick up her bag from the floor, her head whooshing dangerously.

'Here, let me get that for you.' Luke was by her side, collecting her stuff. 'Do you want to go home?'

'Yes, please.' She was standing and he put his arm around her waist, offering support. He was helping her, which was nice. Nice Luke.

No. Luke was not the good guy.

'Come on, then, I think you've had a big night.' His voice was cheery, almost bantering. 'But I don't think you're right to drive. Let's get you out of here.'

CHAPTER THIRTY-TWO

REMI
Friday, 25 August 2023

It was the middle of the night. She'd drunk too much. Her head was thick and she was aware of her stomach squelching unpleasantly.

'Remi.'

A hand on her shoulder, shaking her. Remi didn't want to wake up. She uncurled, rolled to her back. Josephine was beside her bed, dressed for the outdoors. Why was she dressed like that?

'What time is it?'

'Two.'

'In the morning?'

'Sorry to wake you, but I need you to get up.'

Remi hauled herself into a sitting position. She had drunk too much. Not enough to throw up, but close. 'What's going on?'

'Emerson hasn't come home.'

'Oh, Josephine. She's a grown woman. She's got a boyfriend. She's probably in bed having a great time. And you're not her mum. Stop worrying.'

Josephine didn't leave. She stood there, hands on her hips, waiting.

Remi moved to lie down. 'I know you've got issues because of what happened to your sister, but seriously, you can't spend your life worrying and fretting and expecting the worst for people around you. If shit happens, it happens. Trust me. I know all about shit happening.'

The bedside light snapped on. Remi groaned and flung an arm over her eyes, blocking the glare. This was too much.

'Leave me alone.'

'What's going on involves you. So, no, I'm not going to leave you alone. If you don't get up, then I'll stay here. But we need to have a discussion. Right now.'

See, this was what happened when you shared your house. Other people's dramas, interruptions, a shattering of the peace. 'What the hell are you talking about? Why can't whatever this is wait? I'm not getting up.'

Josephine crossed her arms. 'I haven't got time to wait for you to get it together. Emerson did not go out to meet up with Kristof or any other friend. She went to meet Luke.'

'No, she didn't.' Remi squinted against the light as she looked up at Josephine. 'Luke had to go to the hotel to deal with an issue there. Something about an emergency in the kitchen. God, I don't remember. A dishwasher that flooded. He was not having a meeting with Emerson.'

Josephine sat on the edge of her bed. 'Before she went away, two weeks ago, Emerson found out something. When she asked Luke about it, he confirmed what she'd learned. He asked her to keep it a secret—to keep it secret from you. But she didn't want to keep his secret any longer. She arranged to meet him to ask him he tell you himself.'

Remi squinted at Josephine as she spoke, trying to grasp what she was saying. Nothing made sense. 'Luke wanted Em to keep a secret from me?'

'Yes.'

She sat up again and leaned against the bedhead. Pushed her hair off her face. 'What secret? I don't follow.'

Josephine looked around the room before she met Remi's gaze. 'This was not for me to say. But I have to.'

'So, say it. What secret?'

'Luke worked with Kayla to undermine your marriage to Simon.'

'That's bullshit. Luke doesn't even know Kayla.'

'He does know her. And when she wanted to worm her way back into Simon's life, she asked Luke to help. Which he did. He took her to places where Simon would be. A dinner in Sydney, an event you didn't want to attend. He also brought her down here for his opening, the night you saw them together. He justified his actions by saying he was freeing you from a bad marriage. That he was helping you.'

'What the fuck?' Remi clutched at the doona. 'That's not true.'

'It is.'

'You don't know that. This is second-hand information. A story. Something has got confused in the retelling.'

'No.'

'Really? You're telling me Emerson is supposed to have found this out two weeks ago and she didn't come and tell me? Why not? I'm sorry, but that doesn't add up.'

'She didn't tell you because Luke asked her not to and in the same breath offered her more money and that interstate trip. She feared he would cancel her project and she needed the income.'

'Luke wouldn't do that.' Luke was generous and he was fair. He didn't go around buying the silence of people who depended on him. He *didn't*. And he didn't help Kayla. 'This is bullshit. I don't know where the hell this is coming from, but you can stop now.'

'He has been obsessed with you for many years. For—what? Eighteen years?—you have been his goal. And tonight, Emerson will have told him his little secret is about to come out. That you will know about some of his less attractive actions. He won't have liked that. If he was prepared to bribe her to keep quiet, then he obviously doesn't want to be exposed. She met him at ten, that's four hours ago, and her phone is off. Luke is a man with an unhealthy obsession, Emerson has threatened to disrupt his plans, and I'm worried.'

What the hell? Seriously, what the fucking hell? This was too much. Remi pressed her hands against her aching head. 'You're trying to suggest Emerson might be at *risk* because Luke's worried this *secret* will get back to me?'

'Yes. And I'm sorry to be so blunt with you, but this is not the time for a gentle reveal. Also, you should know, Kayla worked at the Park Hyatt in Sydney. She was working there when those photos were taken of you with Connor Mallick.'

Remi stared at Josephine, then gave a sarcastic laugh. 'You are crazy. You are out of control. Obviously, you see danger everywhere. But Emerson does not need saving. This is not like your sister getting in that car.'

Josephine's eyes were fierce but steady. She sat straight, fully controlled. A woman delivering hard news with a minimum of fuss. 'I need you to understand my concern. To understand I am not overdramatising or imagining risks that don't exist. You're right, I have all sorts of issues because of my sister's death. One of them is that I swore to myself if I ever have a gut feeling of danger around a situation, then I will act. And right now, every instinct in my body is saying something is very wrong.'

The first whisper of fear unfurled through Remi. Josephine's composure was stopping all her denials and arguments. 'I need to think. Shit, I'm still drunk.' She struggled to the side of her bed, untangled her legs and got her feet on her floor. 'I have to pee,' she said as she stumbled to her bathroom.

She sat on the loo longer than needed, head in her hands. This was not happening. Her life was going great and Luke was wonderful. She was ready for things to change. Next chapter and all that. Luke loved her and had always loved her. Always, always, always.

She flushed, went to the basin and splashed her face. Dried off, muttering a burst of profanity under her breath.

Josephine was standing in the middle of the room.

'On the island, he said something.' Remi tried to remember the exact words. 'We were talking about how it had never been the right time for us. He said something like, all his plans and efforts fell through because of bad timing.'

'What plans?'

'I don't know.'

'Luke is a smart, goal-orientated man. He works hard to achieve those goals. He has wanted you for a long time, may or may not have tried different strategies in the past to make things happen the way he wanted. And he may have seen Emerson as threatening a success that was finally within reach. Kayla apparently described him as obsessed. And obsessed people don't react well to being continuously denied what they want.'

'Stop. Please stop.' It was frightening how easy it was to imagine Luke the way Josephine was describing him. He was driven. He was honest about his long-held desire for her. He hated Simon. He was very enthusiastic about her selling and moving in with him. 'What about all the horrible things that have happened over the last couple of months? You're not suggesting Luke was involved with that, are you?'

'No I'm not. But he might have known what Kayla was doing. He knew she was here at the time. I don't know. Look, we're not going to work everything out by sitting here. I need to find Em. Could I please borrow your car?'

'Sure.' Remi felt defeated, a sparkly, helium-filled party balloon shrinking and sinking to the floor. 'Wait. How are you going to find her?'

Josephine was pulling her hair into a low ponytail. 'I don't know exactly. Hobart is not that big. I'll look for her car. Keep trying to call her.'

'Not a great plan.'

'It's the best I've got.'

'Let's try something simpler.'

Remi reached for her phone on the bedside table. She wasn't sober and her head hurt. And her roller-coaster life was creeping to the top of another massive drop.

Luke's number rang out. She tapped again. This time he answered.

'Hi, darling, what are you doing up?' He sounded quiet but not asleep. More like someone who didn't want to be heard. Someone who'd been interrupted.

'Hi, sorry, I couldn't sleep. Aren't I awful, inflicting my insomnia on you? Sorry to wake you.'

'That's okay. I don't mind being woken by my beautiful girl.'

'Did you fix the flooding problem?'

'Yeah, yeah, all sorted. Did you get to bed early?'

'No.' She groaned in pretend playfulness. 'Josephine and I had some wine, sat up and chatted. I drank way too much.'

'Probably why you can't sleep.' He yawned. It wasn't real.

'Yeah, you're right. Hey, you didn't by any chance see Emerson tonight? She said she'd be here. We were going to watch a movie together.'

'Emerson? No. But I wouldn't worry, she's a young woman with a boyfriend and a social life. Darling, I hate not giving you my undivided attention, but I've got an early start tomorrow.'

'Of course, I just needed to hear your voice. Sleep well.'

'Goodnight. I love you.'

Remi put her phone down and met Josephine's questioning look. 'He was not in bed. Not unless they're letting plovers wander around the rooms of the hotel.'

'Plovers?'

'The bird. You know those ones that nest on the ground and screech even in the middle of the night.' She went to the chair and pulled a pair of jeans from the pile of clothes. 'Fuck,' she muttered. What the hell was happening? Why was Luke lying? 'Give me five. I'm coming with you.'

CHAPTER THIRTY-THREE

REMI

This was crazy.

Luke did not help Kayla seduce Simon. He'd said he didn't even know her. He certainly hadn't told Emerson to keep quiet while handing her money. That was bullshit.

And he hadn't just lied about being asleep at the hotel.

Except he had.

He wasn't in bed. She knew that much. But it didn't mean all the other stuff was true. It didn't mean Emerson was with him. Why would she be?

Remi pressed her hands against her face. Hard. Fingertips in the sockets of her aching eyes.

'You okay?' Josephine asked. She was driving, slowly working her way through the empty streets.

Remi raised her head, looked out the window. The streetlights gave off a faded glow, filtered by the damp blanket of thin cloud that had settled on the city.

'No. Definitely not okay.' Remi let her hands flop into her lap, pulling the sleeves of her jumper over her fingers. Even with the heater blasting, it was cold. Her toes were numb, the thin socks in her runners doing nothing to keep out the chill. 'Why is everything going to shit again? And why did I drink so much?'

'Good question.' It wasn't said with judgement. 'I haven't seen you drink like that before. You were throwing down that wine like it was pink lemonade at a kid's birthday party.'

'Celebrating?'

'Were you?'

Josephine would make a great counsellor. Some people had a way of asking what seemed like a simple question, when they were actually hitting the emotional truth. Did she know Remi had been drowning her doubts with booze and fake-it-till-it's-true enthusiasm? It was her fear of change, Remi had told herself. A reluctance to let go of her dream, even if she was replacing it with a new vision—one that included Luke, a new project and working as a team. There'd be no more loneliness. No more isolation. All she had to do was let go of this house. And a life that was improving every day.

Now this, the ultimate *What the fuck?*

In the last couple of weeks, she'd realised her feelings towards Luke had changed. She was ready to love him. Then—*pow*—she was being slapped around the head with the suggestion he wasn't the man she wanted him to be. In all the time she'd known Luke, he'd always been decent, kind, generous. A charmer who avoided commitment, and was a little intense and fearsome in his work, but that wasn't a bad thing. How could he be something else, something uglier?

Except she did, in fact, know him, and maybe it was time to be honest with herself. He had a dark side.

'Did you like Luke?' she asked.

'Hmm.' Josephine didn't immediately answer. 'I think I respected him for what he has achieved,' she said at last. 'And I had thought he was very decent to Emerson, giving her the project. Although, obviously, he wouldn't give her the work if she didn't have the skills and ability.'

'But?' She could hear a silent qualification dangling from the end of Josephine's words.

'I really didn't interact with him.'

'Oh, come on. I know you have an opinion.'

Josephine considered the question for a minute. 'When I saw him speak at the conference a few years ago, it was obvious he was an extremely driven man. Competitive. Someone who would remember anyone who had wronged him, anyone who scoffed at his ambitions or doubted him. That he would get immense satisfaction in trumping them or proving them wrong or beating them at the game. He made a point of saying that holding onto those moments when someone considered him less gave him fuel and motivation to succeed. That having the focus and unwavering determination to achieve long-held goals, despite obstacles, required patience and commitment and creative thinking.'

'Right. He has the attributes and beliefs of most self-made men.'

'Perhaps. But do you think holding onto past grievances, striving for success so you can get revenge is healthy?'

Remi sighed, hunching further down in her seat. 'No. Probably not.' Bitterness was a dangerous mindset, it warped every other emotion and emphasised the sense of being a victim. Bitterness thickened over time, hardening till it became more and more difficult to shake off. But Luke didn't see himself as a victim. He was simply ambitious. He wasn't bitter, he was fuelled by self-belief.

'He said,' Josephine continued, 'most people were weak. They let go of their dreams when they aren't obtained easily and quickly. Those who do succeed own their obsessions. Honour them, strive always to attain them. Obsession, he said, was a maligned term. He considered it a virtue.'

Worded like that, Luke's declaration of long-held love sounded less romantic and more grotesque. Weren't obsessed people capable of justifying all sorts of terrible behaviour?

Remi shivered. 'And you think I was one of those obsessions?'

'You know you are.'

She couldn't have this conversation yet. First, they had to find Emerson. And Luke.

'Do you know where she was meeting him?' she asked.

'A bar near Salamanca. I can't remember the name. Typical Em—despite the circumstances, she said something like, "good choice, cool venue".'

'Everything will be closed now.'

'We might see her car.'

They drove in silence, looking for a red hatchback. A few cars remained in the parking bays lining Salamanca Place, the popular strip eerily quiet. The odd person walked the street, shapeless in coat and hat, hunched against the cold. Bakers going to work. Cleaners. Hospitality workers heading home. A police car passed them, moving slowly. Twice Josephine braked when they spotted red. Neither was Emerson's car. Before the road headed up into Battery Point they turned around and retraced their path.

'Luke wouldn't hurt her,' Remi said.

Josephine didn't answer straight away.

'He wouldn't,' Remi repeated. 'Why would he do that? She'll be fine.'

'We don't know that for sure.' Josephine turned the car into Montpelier, heading up towards Sandy Bay Road. 'But someone who has waited so long, who has gone to such lengths to get what he wants, is not going to like having his success threatened right before he achieves his goal.'

'You make it sound so cold. You make me sound like a prize.' Which is exactly what she had been that night all those years ago, when Simon had won the kissing game. She'd seen the animosity between the two of them and hadn't cared about being fought over. In fact, had been quite flattered. Was this even about her—or was it about Luke beating Simon at every game?

Josephine suddenly pulled the car into the kerb and pointed out the window. 'The Gin Den. That rings a bell. I'm sure Em said she was meeting him at a gin bar. But is this the place? It doesn't look like a bar?' The sign gave little away and the entrance was shuttered with a grey roller-door set in the corner of a bland building. A wall of pale brick rose above, a small line of narrow windows at pedestrian level. It looked vaguely industrial. A printer's perhaps, or somewhere that sold gadgets and widgets or hospitality supplies.

Remi checked on her phone. 'Yep. It's a bar. Must be downstairs. Looks to be quite nice.'

'There's a parking place next door.' Josephine twisted to look behind them.

'It closes at eight, so she wouldn't have used that.' Remi looked across the road and pointed to an open-air parking lot. 'But there's all those spaces over there.'

Josephine swung the car across the road and drove around the dozen or so cars. They found Emerson's car at the furthest end, hidden beside a huge dual-cab ute. They got out to check, but it was locked, with no sign of Emerson. Her coat lay on the back seat, pink beanie on top.

'Now what?' Remi asked. The cold had instantly soaked through her jumper and into her flesh and she was shivering from the inside, every muscle tightening.

'She must've left with someone. If she'd walked, she would've taken her coat.'

They climbed back into the car, Remi pumping up the heat. Dread slid through her, making her stomach heave.

'If her phone was on, we could find her. We've got each other on Find My Friends.' Josephine tapped her phone. 'Nope. Still says location not available.'

Remi peered at the app when Josephine angled the screen towards her. 'Sam can see your location,' she read. 'He doesn't mind you stalking him?'

Josephine looked at her screen for a few seconds.

'I can't see him—he hasn't accepted the connection. And he won't.'

'Fair enough. Young men don't want their mum watching over their shoulder.'

Josephine gave a short, harsh laugh. 'Right. Mothers should trust their children, respect their right to privacy and not stalk them.' She sounded angry.

Remi held her hands in front of the air vents. 'Was that an issue for you and Sam?'

'You could say that.' Josephine staring out the window. 'He wasn't happy to find tracking software on his phone.'

'You mean that app?'

'No. Something else. Something I installed without his permission. Or knowledge.'

'Um, wow.'

'Yes. Wow.' Josephine was silent, staring out the window. 'And I went too far. One night, he hadn't come home, he wasn't answering his phone. I panicked.' Regret was in every word. 'I turned up where he was. A friend's house. It wasn't a raging party or a drug den or a back alley. It was five friends drinking good bourbon, talking, sharing a joint. Not driving or being stupid. Just chilling. And Sam's mummy turns up.'

The poor kid. Remi could imagine his reaction. 'Was he embarrassed?'

'Mortified. He told me to leave.' She leaned her head back, closed her eyes. 'Then he figured out how I'd found him and he never came home.'

'What do you mean?'

'He stayed with friends, spent a few weeks planning his escape from me, then left for London. He never forgave me.'

'Until now.' Remi rested a hand on her friend's arm. 'He wants you to travel with him. And his girlfriend. I can see why you're so excited.'

'Yes.' Josephine grimaced. 'I've learned my lesson though. No more stalking my loved ones. And before you ask, Emerson connected with me first, said it might help if I ever got lost on the mountain.'

'What about me? I might need to find you one day.' She was trying to make Josephine feel better. 'Do I have that app?' She opened her phone.

'I think it's automatically installed.'

Remi slid through her pages of disorganised icons. 'Here it is. I've never even noticed it.' A map of Hobart opened with a blue pulsating dot, which she guessed was her. Further away, another marker, a grey circle with the letters LD. One name listed below.

'I don't understand. I've never used this. I don't know how to use it.' Remi stared at the screen. 'Why is Luke on here?'

Josephine took the phone from her hand. 'I think we can safely presume he wanted to keep tabs on you. It would only take a few minutes to connect the two of you.'

'So, if he's on here, then I'm on his?'

'Yes.'

'He can see where I am, at any time. The absolute bastard. What a sly, controlling thing to do.' Remi suddenly had a great deal of empathy for Josephine's son.

Josephine was still watching the screen. 'His location hasn't updated since two-ten. Forty minutes ago.'

'Right after I spoke to him. Where was he?'

'Up on Queens Domain. Near the athletic centre.'

'Why the hell would he be up there? Why hasn't it updated?'

Josephine started the car. 'He probably turned it off after your call. Or his last location would have been the hotel.'

'Where are we going?'

'Up to the Domain, we don't have anything else to go on.' Josephine handed Remi her own phone. 'Can you please keep an eye on that, see if Em comes back online.'

'Sure. But why don't we check at home first,' suggested Remi. It would mean doubling back, but the roads were empty, the detour short. And she was desperate to *not* find Emerson with Luke.

'Let's make it fast.' Josephine hooked the car through the intersection on a red light.

'Shit, Josephine. It's not going to help if we have an accident.'

'And it's not going to help if we sit there waiting while god knows what is happening to Em,' Josephine snapped.

'Nothing is happening to Em.'

'You don't know that. Em is missing.' Tension radiated from Josephine's body. 'Luke is a manipulative bastard. It's almost three in the morning and he's up to something. You tell me, which part of this picture is pretty?'

They drove in silence after that.

'Do you really think Em is with him?' Remi said eventually.

'I don't know. Maybe. It is very possible. But I'm not going to sit around waiting for her to wander home.'

Remi looked out the window, then glanced at the temperature readout on the dashboard. Two degrees. Near freezing. She thought of the thick coat in the back of Emerson's car.

CHAPTER THIRTY-FOUR

REMI

Josephine pulled up in front of the house, the light still on in Remi's upstairs room, the rest of the windows dark. 'You look,' she said. 'Make it quick. And grab a proper coat.'

It took Remi less than five minutes to check every room. She even looked in the basement. No sign of Emerson.

'Quick! Em's phone came back on!' Josephine said as soon as she was back in the car, handing her phone back to Remi.

'Really? Where is she?' Remi stared at the unfamiliar arrangement of streets on the map. 'South Hobart? But that's so close. What the hell is she doing there? This makes it look like she's on the rivulet track.'

'I don't know,' Josephine snapped. 'But something isn't right about any of this.'

Remi was quiet, clutching her parka in her lap. What were they going to find? What if Luke *had* done something? The remnants of alcohol in her body had become a sour puddle in her stomach. 'It could just be her phone, right? Maybe some-one stole it and tossed it away down there.'

'I hope so,' said Josephine quietly as she sped along the empty street.

The cottages of South Hobart were dark. There was no one moving, no lights or signs of life. The wind had picked up and while she couldn't see it, she could sense the mountain looming.

'Down here,' she said, checking the map. 'Turn right.'

The street was short and a dead end, finishing at the Hobart Rivulet where a bridge crossed the water. Cute wooden houses sat tightly together for the first hundred metres then the build-ings and facilities of two separate primary schools flanked the narrow road, one private, one government. It would be a traffic nightmare during school hours, Remi thought. But tonight, there was only one car parked to the side of the turn-ing circle.

Josephine stopped opposite. 'It's got a hire car sticker,' she said. 'Is that the car Luke had today?'

'I don't know. Yes? I think so?' She hadn't taken a lot of notice. But she vaguely remembered a dark SUV. Much like this one.

'Is he here?' Josephine looked up and down the street, her hands gripping the steering wheel.

Remi checked her phone. 'It's still only giving me his last location. Is this thing accurate?'

'Mostly. And this is showing Emerson down there.' She pointed to the trees at the end of the road. 'The rivulet runs through there.'

They looked at each other, the reality of wandering around in the frigid darkness making them reluctant to leave the car.

Nothing about this felt good. Josephine pulled her beanie low and, with fierce determination, stepped out of the car.

Remi braced herself, then opened her door, fumbling her arms into her coat as she stood. Christ, it was cold. The wind wasn't slamming, but it sliced with mean intent. Every muscle contracted in defence, her body like stone as she followed Josephine. They stopped at the hire car, putting their faces to the glass to peer inside. Nothing. 'There's a chance they're both here,' said Josephine.

'Okay. What do we do? There are two paths,' whispered Remi. 'One this side that runs between the school oval and the creek. Or we go over the bridge and along the other bank.'

'I can't tell from this which side she's on.' For the first time that night, Josephine sounded unsure. 'Do we split up?'

'I think we have to,' Remi said with zero confidence. 'Let's just find her.'

'Okay. I'll take this side.'

They both switched on the torch function on their phones, the white lights small and pitiful against the heaviness of the night. Remi walked to the end of the road, crossed the bridge and turned right. The path was wide and clear, a slope of bush rising to her left, grass and small trees leading down to the creek on the right. She couldn't see much, but she could hear the water. The rivulet track led all the way into the city and in summer she sometimes walked here. On those days, the creek was quiet. Tonight, it was loud, full of rushing energy, the winter rains adding to the flow. The ground crunched under her numb feet, the torchlight jerking as her hand and arm vibrated with cold. Her heart was racing.

Once, when her adventures had been more glamorous, she'd dived into the dark ocean from the back of a yacht. It had

been midnight and she'd been naked, the sounds of jazz drifting out into the darkness. Walking this path, she had the same
sensation. Not of hedonistic exhilaration, but of being small
and vulnerable, floating in an environment where she didn't
belong. She was blind to anything or anyone out there circling
her as she abandoned safety. That night in the ocean her pulse
had raced as she imagined the vastness of the depths below her,
yet she'd also been able to sense the beauty of the night sky and
the caress of the warm water. Tonight, she was aware only of
danger and menace.

Who or what was watching her? She was alone, isolated.
A target.

All those years ago, on the city street, she'd heard the footsteps of someone coming, had heard her name called and the
rapid breathing and muttering of her attacker—of Brittney. She
had turned, surprised but pleased to see her friend. The shove
had been a surprise. A hand in the centre of her chest, driving
her back. Then back again. She'd instinctively tried to move
away but had been driven into an alley. Crazy talk lashed her,
then the first blow. She'd crumpled forward, then fallen when
the steel smashed into the side of her thigh. Curled up as a foot
connected. Tried to get away. Then pain. So much pain. And
utter helplessness. It had taken months and months of counsel-
ling to move past what had happened. Now slivers of familiar
fear were working their way into her mind and body.

Why was she on this path? What the hell was she doing? She
sucked in deep breaths. Too fast. Her head was spinning.
She was going to be sick. Or faint. She bent over, hands on knees,
then sank to a crouch. She dropped her arse to the ground with
her head between her knees. Trying to find control.

Oh, come on. She thought she was past this. It had been years since she'd had to battle this level of anxiety.

A ripple of anger pushed against the suffocating fear. She was not going to give in. She was not going to sit here, a cowering victim in the mud.

'Remi? Remi! What the hell?'

There were hands on her. Big, gentle hands. No. Not gentle. Firm. Too firm. He was gripping her way too tight.

'Let go.' She tried to shake him off. 'Luke. Stop.'

'It's okay. Come on. I've got you. Let's get out of here.' He lifted her to her feet, his hands still wrapped around her upper arms. 'I don't know what you're doing here, but we need to get you warm.'

'I'm fine.'

'You are having a panic attack. It was lucky I found you. Come on.' He began to walk her back along the track.

'I said I'm fine.' She yanked free of his grip and stopped. 'What are you doing here? What *exactly* are you doing?'

'I'd say I'm rescuing you.' He shone his torch over her. 'You're a mess. I've no idea why you're here, but you can explain later.' He reached for her again.

She stepped back. 'For the last fucking time, I do not need to be rescued.' Her anger had gone from a ripple to a heaving wave. 'And where the hell is Emerson?'

His shock was evident in the short silence before he answered. 'Why are you asking me? I don't know where she is.' He was furious. Defiant. *Lying.* 'Now, walk, sweetheart. Or I'll carry you. It's freezing.' He took her arm and pulled her towards the road. 'And for the record, you don't think you need rescuing because you know damn well you've got me—have always had me—right there as your permanent safety net. Which has suited you just fine.'

He might be right, or he might have delusions about his role in her life. Either way, now was not the time to unpack that accusation. Her jaw was jittering and she was still struggling to slow her breathing. Adrenaline and cold were having an effect. 'She had a meeting with you tonight, after I left you.'

He kept them moving. 'Who? Emerson? Why the hell would we be meeting at night? And how did you know I was here?'

'I didn't. I'm looking for Emerson.'

Their feet hit the bitumen and they crossed the bridge. When they reached his car, Luke opened the passenger door, trying to manoeuvre her inside.

'Get in, Remi, let's at least get warm. You're shaking.'

She relented. She needed answers but standing in the cold wasn't going to help.

As soon as he was in the driver's seat he turned the key, cranking up the heat before reaching over to take her hands and rubbing them vigorously. 'You shouldn't have been out there. You're so cold.'

She pulled her hands away from his and tucked them under her thighs. 'So you didn't meet Emerson?'

'Tonight? No.'

Liar. 'And I guess you haven't met up with Kayla either, right?' She wanted to see what else he would lie about.

He hesitated. 'Simon's wife? I don't know her.'

'Bullshit!'

'I don't know what's got into you.' He put the car into drive and released the brake. 'But we're going to go somewhere warmer.'

'No, wait! We've got to find—'

'No! Enough. That girl can look after herself. If she's gone and got drunk and wandered off, that's her problem.' He accelerated away from the kerb. 'My job is to look after you. End of story.'

'Luke. Please. Stop.' He was scaring her. Josephine was still at the creek and they hadn't found Emerson.

'Oh, Remi. Why don't you sit quietly, be a good girl, and let me take care of you, okay?'

He had never spoken to her with such controlled rage. Never made her retreat as she was now. The energy coming from him was dangerous and ugly and she could see him struggling to maintain control.

What the hell had he done?

CHAPTER THIRTY-FIVE

JOSEPHINE

Josephine followed the path. To her right, a chain-link fence ran the length of the school oval, high enough to keep adventurous kids from wandering off school grounds and into the rivulet. On a warm day this would be a pretty place with willows draping over green banks and a gentle trickle of water. Tonight, it was a place of deep black shadows under groaning trees, the quiet trickle of the rivulet now a torrent furiously rushing down from the mountain.

She walked slowly, her phone torch casting a tiny light at her feet. She swung her hand wider, trying to see down the bank towards the water. Emerson was here, somewhere. Or, at least, her phone was.

On the other side of the water she caught a flicker. Remi moving in parallel, the spot of white light appearing then disappearing as she, too, searched. What the hell would they do if they came across Luke? She hadn't planned this very well,

343

hadn't thought that far ahead. The urgent need to find Emerson had pushed her into a frantic chase around town, but she had no strategy. Gut instinct alone was driving her forward. Emerson was in danger. Josephine was absolutely sure of that, without any evidence and nothing to support her conclusion, only unfounded fear. She could be wrong. All of this could be a stupid pursuit. There would be an innocent explanation that would have them all laughing tomorrow. The others would look at her like she was a crazy, paranoid old woman. She wouldn't care. Better to be wrong and to have done something than to be right and have done nothing.

The wind had picked up, trees thrashing back and forth. Even with jumper, coat, gloves and beanie the damp and intrusive cold was seeping through to her skin. Emerson didn't have her coat. If she was here, she was in danger, if not from a man's hand, then from the elements.

Josephine wove along the dirt path, determined to be thorough, checking along the edge of the water and behind trees. She expected to be confronted by Luke at any minute. He would have some rational—bullshit—explanation for being out here at this time. Or to find Emerson huddled on the hard ground. Or to find them both. What was a man like Luke capable of? What would he do if his goal was threatened?

She reached the bitumen of another cul-de-sac and the end of this section of path. A wooden bridge cut back across the rivulet, taking her to the path on the other side. There was no sign of anyone. Josephine crossed over, debating whether to turn right and to continue further along or to go left and meet up with Remi. She must be moving slowly, Josephine thought. Or she had found something.

Or someone had found her.

Josephine turned left, moving quickly, swinging her phone, scanning the darkness. She listened intently, desperate to hear something over the roar in the trees. How could she have been so idiotic? They should've stayed together. They'd made a bad decision. The wrong choice. Dammit. Stupid, stupid, stupid. She had to find them.

She nearly missed the muted colours near the water, had passed before her mind registered the incongruous shape, the maroon and grey stripes. She spun back, stepped off the path, her light jerking over the ground.

There. Shit. It was Emerson. She wasn't paranoid, this was real. An instinctive calm settled on Josephine. It was time for action not histrionics.

'Emerson!'

The girl was on her side, curled around herself, legs pulled in towards her chest, her back to Josephine.

Her knees hit the mud. She dropped her phone, grabbed Emerson's shoulder.

'Em! Emerson! Can you hear me?'

There was no reply. Beneath her hands, Emerson's body shook with bursts of violent shivering. The skin of her face was ice, her eyes shut, her mouth open.

'Em!'

Josephine pulled off her own puffer jacket, swearing in frustration when one arm got temporarily tangled. Ripping it free, she tried to pull Emerson to a sitting position, knowing it wasn't enough to throw the jacket over her. She needed to get Emerson's frozen body off the damp, cold ground. Heat loss by conduction increased the risk of hypothermia. Her wet clothes were an even greater danger. She was soaking, had she been in the creek? Josephine couldn't carry her out of here and an ambulance could take too long. She had to get her warm—or less cold—and she had to do it now.

Josephine knelt behind Emerson, somehow managing to haul her upright. The girl slumped forward, head hanging low, arms flopped in her lap like a ragged, sodden stuffed toy. Josephine yanked down the zip at the back of the dress, then wrestled Emerson free of her clothing. Nothing about it was easy. The dress caught, Emerson's arms were heavy and her body continuously tried to slide back to the ground. As soon as the dress came free, Josephine ripped off her own jumper and pulled it over Emerson's head, dragging her arms through the sleeves one at a time. She shoved her beanie over Emerson's wet hair and wrapped her jacket around her body. Then she shuffled to the side, laying Emerson down as she fought to do up the zipper. She hadn't bothered with arms in sleeves. The puffer was a couple of sizes too big for Emerson and, done up, it was like a short sleeping bag. Emerson's legs were still in the saturated tights, but Josephine was sure they were wool, and didn't wool stay warm even when it was wet? She didn't want to leave her legs exposed. With one hand, Josephine rubbed Emerson's face, while she groped for her phone with the other.

'Ambulance,' she said when the triple-0 operator answered. Where was she? She had no idea what street they'd come down. In the end, she gave details of her surrounds. The Hobart Rivulet, South Hobart, behind the primary school—the state school, not the private, between two side streets, the far side of the creek.

The operator stayed on the phone with her. 'How is she doing, now? Has she gained consciousness?'

'No. No response. Still shivering. Shaking hard.'

'Are the pauses when she's not shivering, are they getting longer?'

'No. It's stop. Start. Stop. Start. No wait, I think it's getting more spaced out.'

'Okay, monitor the rate of shivering. If the pauses get longer it means her core temperature is dropping. You're doing a great job.'

Was she? Had she done everything she could? Was it enough? A sob stuck at the back of her throat.

Then red and blue lights pulsated in the distance, washing through the darkness at the end of the track. Strong torchlight moving. She tried yelling, knew her voice wouldn't carry on the wind. Waved her phone, hoping they'd see her light, too terrified to step away from her friend.

'Is that the ambulance there with you now?'

'Yes. Yes. They're here.'

'Okay, I'll leave you with them. You've done well.'

Josephine hung up as two bulky figures came into sight. 'Here!' she called. 'We're here!'

CHAPTER THIRTY-SIX

REMI

The car sped through the deathly empty city, Remi clutching the seatbelt where it cut across her chest. She patted her pockets, searching out the reassurance of her phone. Nothing. Leaning forward, she fumbled around her feet, hoping it had slipped to the floor.

'What are you doing?'

'My phone. I can't find it.'

'You must've dropped it,' he said. 'Back there when you were having your little attack.' The tone in his voice was dipping closer to normal, his grip on the wheel easing a little as though his self-control was sliding back into place. 'You scared the hell out of me, seeing you huddled in the path like that. I mean, what the hell? You shouldn't have been there. You seriously freaked me out.' They slowed to a stop at a red light and he turned, openly scrutinising her face. 'I thought you'd been attacked. I could not go through that again. I mean, of course,

I could. For you. But I wouldn't want to. I hate seeing you suffer.'

This was a man she knew, right? Someone who loved her. Someone she cared for deeply. He would never hurt her and she had no reason to be afraid. It was all okay. She could talk to him and he would tell her the truth. Wouldn't he?

'Like when I was unhappy in my marriage. I know you tried to get me to leave him.'

A look of calculation passed over Luke's face before he spoke.

'I hated seeing the way Simon treated you.' He reached across with one hand, grasped her fingers with an affectionate squeeze. 'I know finding out about his cheating truly hurt you, but to be honest, I'm glad Kayla came on the scene.'

'I would probably still be with him if I hadn't seen them together. I guess I should be thankful. I've often wondered how she ended up at that party.'

The light changed and he pulled away, glancing at her while he drove. 'Alright, I admit she was an invited guest; I knew her from my early days in Sydney. But I didn't know she was going to take your husband.' He paused. 'I've never told you because I didn't want you to think badly of me.'

'When did you meet Kayla?'

'When I first arrived in Sydney. She was working at a hotel bar and asked me about a job at Strike.'

'Okay. So you're saying you do know her.' How could she be sitting here, having this little chat? Listening to him reveal these secrets while Josephine was out in the cold and Emerson was god knows where? Did any of this really matter right now?

'It's not like we're friends. But back then we clicked. I recognised her ambition for a better life and I encouraged her. We *were* friends.' He glanced at Remi. 'Although, in the spirit of honesty, we did sleep together a few times. But it was a long time ago, and we knew it wasn't going anywhere.'

What the actual fuck? 'You too! You and Simon both screwing this eighteen-year-old girl. And you would've been, what, twenty-eight?'

'Twenty-seven—it was in late 2008.' He didn't seem the slightest bit concerned about the inappropriate age difference, or the abuse of his position.

She pulled back towards the door, instinctively needing space.

'To be fair,' he continued, 'she was a very confident young lady.'

Hearing the same justification Simon had given, her perception of Luke lurched even further away from respect and affection. What could she say? Thanks for the honesty but this is creepy and wrong?

'Sorry, darling.' He gave her a quick, apologetic look. 'I know this is a bit of a shock. But none of it is relevant, is it? I know you're happier for being out of that marriage. I mean, you knew it was bad, but you needed the evidence. Needed the confidence to leap clear. Don't you agree?'

No. But yes. Yes, it hadn't been great. Yes, she'd needed irrefutable proof in order to push back against Simon's excuses and bullshit. But the idea that Luke had interfered? No. That was not okay. 'Yes.'

'Yes?'

'Yes. It was a bad marriage.'

'And you're happier being free of him.' He was telling her, not asking.

'Yes. I'm happier being free of him.' It was not the time for a lengthy exploration of ethics. Remi shut her eyes, tried to find composure and control. When she opened them, they were pulling into Luke's reserved space at Strike.

'Anyway, that's all well in the past. Ancient history. Irrelevant. Now you and I are creating our own magnificent future. Come on, let's get inside.'

'Actually, I'm feeling better now. Would you mind if I just went home?'

'Don't be ridiculous. It's late. You're cold. And we're here now.' He came around to her door, his hand on her arm as she got out of the car. He walked her through the staff entrance and up the service stairs, passing no one. They emerged in the corridor of the top floor and he opened the door to his suite.

'I'm going to run you a bath,' he said, passing her a robe. 'You need to warm up.'

A bath? Seriously? She watched as he went into the bathroom, heard the taps come on, the clunk of a plug dropping into place. The seductive scent of gardenia body wash being added to the water.

She looked at the robe she was holding, then at the door. She should leave. Get back to Josephine and help her find Emerson. She couldn't seem to judge the right course of action. Restrained panic fluttered in her like a moth at a window. Everything about this situation was off balance. Out of focus. Like when you took off your 3D glasses and the crisp, vivid images on the screen became blurred and indistinct. And she badly needed to see the picture clearly. She needed more answers, not least what had happened to Emerson. She was convinced Luke knew.

He shut the bathroom door, probably to use the toilet, and Remi hurriedly stripped off her clothes and shoes and wrapped herself in the robe. In the mini-bar fridge she found two chocolate bars. She tore one open and scoffed it down, hoping a sugar hit would spark her sluggish brain.

When Luke came back into the room she was sitting on the end of the bed. He sat beside her, putting his arm across her back, pulling her close and placing a kiss on her temple.

'Come on,' he said. 'The water's almost ready, let's get you in.'

She met his gaze. 'You're good at looking after me. Thank you.' Passive, thankful, trusting. She had to play him if she wanted to know what had happened, not only tonight, but in the past.

'It is, and always will be, my pleasure.' He traced a finger down her cheek.

'And thank you for telling me about Kayla. I totally understand why you did what you did. It was the right thing to do. I am so much happier out of that marriage.' She could make herself believe it, at least for the length of this performance.

'What I did?'

'Letting Kayla reel Simon in. Not stopping her, not stopping them. And not telling me. It worked out for the best.'

He searched her face, trying to read what she did or didn't know. She kept her smile small and grateful.

'We're going to have a great life together,' he said.

'I know.' When he cupped his hand against her face, she pressed into his palm. 'Can I ask, was Kayla responsible for those stories about me and Connor? Was she the Park Hyatt staff member who lied about seeing me go up to his room? Emerson seemed to think Kayla worked there around that time, and you just said she worked in a hotel bar.'

She felt his fingers stiffen on her cheek before they pulled away. He stood, his edgy impatience tangible. 'Emerson said that? How would she know where Kayla worked back then?'

'I don't know, I'm guessing something she found online.'

'It sounds to me like Emerson likes to stir up trouble.'

'You said Kayla worked at a hotel, was it the Park Hyatt?' Was she pushing too hard? She needed to find Emerson, but she needed to find the truth, too.

'Yes. But that means nothing.'

'She could've been the anonymous source. The girl who made up that story, who said I went up to Connor's room.'

'Maybe she did. I don't know. Why does it matter? Let it go.'

'But you think she might have?'

His hands went to his hips and he looked at the floor. His chest raising and falling as he struggled to stay calm. 'Do you really want to dig into this right now? It's late. You've been drinking. Been out stumbling about in the cold. It's not the time.'

'I need to know.'

'Fine. Yes, she might have.' Irritation made him spit the words.

'But why?'

'Why?' Luke visibly weighed up his possible answers. He could deny outright, claim Kayla to be innocent, or he could throw her under the bus. 'Because she had met Simon. He'd fucked her a few times, told her he felt something, even though he was still with you. Why did she do it? Because, to her, you were the obstacle to them having a proper relationship.' He held up a hand. 'I'm not excusing her—she is quite mercenary. For her, Simon was a good catch. A way up in the world.' He looked at Remi, read the distress in her face. 'Oh, come on, you know what a liar and cheat he was.'

So that much was true. And if that was true ...

'When did you know about her and Simon? And when did you know—sorry—suspect she was responsible for the story about Connor?'

He ran a hand through his hair, gave an exaggerated huff of air. 'Sleeping with Simon? I knew back then. The other stuff, I don't know, it was a thought I've had over the years. I did consider telling you, but what would have been achieved? I didn't want to dredge up those dark days.' There was wariness in his eyes, as though trying to gauge her reaction.

She gave a tiny nod, let pain then resolve pass through her eyes as she looked up at him. 'What she did—'

'If she did it.'

'—was so horrible. Had such terrible consequences for me.'

'I know.' A flash of anguish in his eyes. He held out a hand. 'Come on, bath then sleep. There's no need to talk about this now.'

She put her hand in his, let him lift her to her feet. 'But, Luke, if you thought she was capable of something so underhand, so nasty ... why would you want to bring her anywhere near me? Why have her at your party here?'

He looked over her head, then shut his eyes for a second. A man whose patience had worn so thin it was about to rip apart.

'It's okay,' she said. She slid her arms around his waist, pressing her face to his chest. Then tilted her head and gave a sad smile. 'I know you, Luke. Whatever was done was done for me. You probably thought she'd help herself to Simon, and I would be free of him.' She stepped back. 'Will you join me? Keep me awake in there.' She knew from experience Luke liked to share the bath and she wanted him to keep talking.

His laugh was one of relief. 'Is now really the time?'

'It's always the right time. And you were out in the cold too. Warm up together, then snuggle into bed for a Sunday sleep-in.' She pulled back, untying the sash of her robe and letting it fall. She walked towards the bathroom.

Luke followed, dropping his clothes as he went.

In the blissfully wide bath, she settled between his legs, leaning back against his chest. Her hands traced up and down his thighs. 'What a night.' She let her body yield to the warmth, let herself go soft. 'Did you see Emerson? Earlier?' She pretended the question was unimportant, had popped unbidden into her thoughts.

'Hmm?'

'Only, she said she was meeting you.'

He took a moment to respond. 'I did. It really is a night for confessions, isn't it?' He massaged her shoulders. 'We had a brief meeting.'

'What about?'

His hands stilled, then squeezed tight before continuing with a gentle knead. 'I won't be going ahead with her project. At least, not with her. I've had a few reasons to be concerned with her work standards. But she's your friend and I was hoping to reach an amicable agreement.'

'And you weren't comfortable telling me?'

'No.' He tilted her head to one side, smoothed the wet hair from her neck and kissed her skin. 'It's an awkward situation.'

She was a sleepy, contented woman, she told herself, believing every word of his lies. She wove the illusion by sighing deeply. Happily.

'I wonder where she went?' she mused.

'No idea. She wasn't happy. I left her at the bar.'

'Probably sleeping it off somewhere.'

'Probably.'

'Why were you out there?' she asked after a bit.

'You woke me when you rang,' he said. 'I couldn't get back to sleep. I decided to go for a drive. I came to your place, saw the lights were off and presumed you'd gone back to sleep. I kept driving and ended up in South Hobart, thought I'd walk along the rivulet.'

He scooped bath foam into his hands, used it to wash her arms. Tending to her, gentle and caring. Remi made a throaty noise of contentment, let her eyes close.

'In the middle of a freezing cold night?'

'Crazy, I know.'

'Crazy.' Her laugh was soft, but her inner voice screamed, *Crazy, lying fucker.* Her light had been on when she rang him, and still on when she returned to the house to check for Emerson.

Claustrophobia squeezed her, an urge to get away from his touch. This was too much. She tried not to tense, instead forcing a giggle.

'You know what we need?' She pulled herself forward and stood. 'We need chocolate.'

'We do?'

'Well, I do. I'll be right back.' She climbed out of the bath and wrapped a towel around her, closing the bathroom door behind her. On the way across the room, she dropped the towel and pulled on the robe, knowing it would take too long to get dressed. She picked up her runners and carefully and quietly took the keys for the car from the coffee table. She had to leave. Had to get away from the man who'd always been there for her. Always. When things went bad, he was there. Ready. Prepared. Her rescuer. The constant in her life. The man who, until tonight, she had always trusted.

He was lying to her, hiding what he'd done—tonight and in the past. It was as though all the filters and touch-ups and photoshopping had been stripped from an image to reveal a flawed truth. She was seeing him and his generous, dependable presence through a new lens.

She gripped the door handle, turned it gently and pulled. It was locked. She twisted the knob, heard the hollow metal thunk of the bolt shooting free.

'No.'

The command was one of fierce, furious authority, thrown at her a second before his hand closed around the thick towelling sleeve of her robe. He yanked her backwards.

'You do not walk away. Not from me. Not ever again.'

CHAPTER THIRTY-SEVEN

REMI

'Where did you think you were going?' Luke walked Remi back into the room and pushed her down into one of the armchairs. At his open suitcase he found a pair of navy trackpants and pulled them on. 'Answer me, Remi. Where were you going?'

'Home. I wanted to go home.' She didn't know how to handle Luke like this. Had never seen him fed by such ferocity.

'Bullshit.' Fine drops of spit spun from his mouth. 'Christ, you can be so ungrateful. I'm always there for you, and you lap up the attention, then scurry away to someone else. You take me for granted.' His eyes went wide, a thought hitting him hard. 'Is that it? Do you have someone else? Have you, once again, screwed me over for another guy? Is that where you were running off to? Is it?'

'No. No!' She tried to make him hear. 'Of course there isn't anyone. That's insane. I just want to go home.'

'Why? Is this not good enough for you?' He swung an arm wide. 'What I've created? What I've built for you? This? *Me?* Am I still not good enough for you? Did life with Simon give you unattainable expectations? Is a self-made man not good enough? Is what I've achieved not enough?'

'Luke, you're being ridiculous—'

'Am I? Really? Because when I find my girlfriend creeping out of my room, not even bothering to say goodnight, it sure as hell looks like she's found me lacking.'

He was irrational. Dredging up what must be long-held fears and completely ignoring the more immediate situation. It was as though something had snapped within him, his focus veering towards old doubts and grievances. This unpredictable volatility scared Remi more than the idea he had interfered in her life. Or the idea that he had hurt Emerson.

'It's not that. I'm scared for Emerson. You don't think I should be, but I'm really worried about her.'

'Move on, Remi. Move on. That stupid girl doesn't deserve your concerns.'

'What about Josephine? I need to get back to her. I can't sit in the bath here while she's still at the rivulet, she can't—'

His head reared back. 'What? She's there? No. She's not. I didn't see her. You're lying.'

'Why would I lie? We went together and she'll be worried about me. I disappeared.'

He turned away, dragging a hand over his mouth then back and forth across the bristle on his cheek. He walked to the window, twitched open the curtain and stared blindly into the darkness outside. Then his shoulders slumped, as though absorbing an unwanted inevitability.

He straightened and returned. 'Why is she there? Why were *you* there? Really? What did you think you would find?' His anger was threaded with something else. Despair? Or fear?

'I told you, we were looking for Emerson. Josephine is connected to her location, and her phone came back on.' She sat back in the chair as he came close, leaning over her where she huddled. His breathing was rapid, his face flushed. 'It had been off, then she must've turned it on again, and we could see she was there. Or at least her phone is.'

'Jesus. You were out there scouring this shithole city for her. Why, Remi? Why so worried about your little friend?'

She shook her head, trying to put together an explanation. 'Josephine said that Emerson told her some things ...' She couldn't bring herself to say it.

'About?'

'About you.'

'About me? What does that have to do with Emerson having a big night out? What were these women saying about me? What lies were they making up? What stories did they tell you? Come on, I'd really like to know. Because, obviously, you've bought into whatever poison they're selling. You're looking at me like I'm the problem. Is that what you think now?'

'Stop it, Luke.' Desperate for space, Remi put her hands up, pushing on his stomach. He resisted while she struggled to her feet. 'Back up. Please. You're scaring me.'

He relented and took a step away from her. 'You don't understand. Goddammit, you've never really understood.'

She managed to stand and to get behind the chair as Luke paced across the room, fists buried in his pockets, before doubling back.

'Then tell me,' she begged. 'Explain what has been going on. Make me understand. Stop hiding stuff from me. I deserve to know. Please, be honest. If you truly believe in what we have, then have some faith in me.'

He stood watching her, his gaze scouring her face for what felt like minutes. When he spoke, his voice had calmed. 'I always had ambition, Remi. Always had a vision of what I could be. When you came into my life, I knew you were a part of that vision. I had a purpose. I have been following that purpose ever since.'

'But—'

His raised hand silenced her. 'Listen! You want to know? Fine. I'll tell you.'

'Okay.'

He lowered himself into the second chair, facing her. Still and calm, his intense energy contained. Remi sensed he was on the brink, that he was going to take her into his truth, and she wanted to run.

'You, Remi. You have given my life meaning beyond mere acquisition and achievement. I love you. I fell in love with you immediately. It's the type of love that means something. That means *more*. It is not fickle or transient. It is forever. But you didn't see that. You were blinded by the sheen of Simon. He fooled you. It has been your one failing, your one flaw, to succumb to that man's pathetic charm and status. Don't you agree?'

'Yes.' Agreeing felt safer.

'I helped Kayla when she asked to reunite with Simon. I have no guilt about doing so, other than knowing it caused you temporary pain. Freeing you of him meant we could eventually be together. And you are happier for it.'

'Okay.' She swallowed. 'Why did you not want me to know? Why did you insist Emerson keep quiet?'

He sighed, bringing his hands together and entwining his fingers. 'I predicted you would resent my actions, at least initially. We are about to start a life together and frankly, our happiness wasn't something I wanted to jeopardise.'

'And Kayla. She did those things to make me sell the house. Did you know about that?'

For a moment his eyes slid away from hers. Then he lifted his chin and looked at her again. 'I knew she had intentions. Yes.'

She gasped, gripping the back of the chair. 'You knew. About those horrible, horrible reviews. My car. Threatening my housemates. Hacking my bank account? Even stealing my jewellery? Was that all her?'

'I guessed she wrote the reviews and tampered with your car. I knew she'd accessed your house.'

'How?'

'What do you mean?'

'How did she get access to my home?'

He stood, his hands going to his hips as he took a few steps across the room. He turned back to look at her. 'Kayla took my key.'

'Took it? How on earth did she do that? Sneak in and steal it from you? Or did she ask nicely and you handed it over?'

He didn't answer, her last accusation confirmed by his silence.

'I don't believe it! You helped her! Well, fuck you, Luke.'

'I was extremely reluctant, I didn't do it willingly,' he said as though that made a difference.

'Oh, well that's good to hear. Let me guess, she coerced you into handing over my key. Blackmailed you into being her accomplice. What does she have on you, Luke?'

He remained quiet while he intently scrutinised her face.

'What about Mavis? Was Kayla responsible for killing my dog?'

'I would never have allowed her to do anything truly danger-ous,' he said without any evidence of contrition, avoiding that question, too.

'She set my house on fire, Luke, with me in it. You don't think that's truly dangerous?' Fury spilled out of her.

A flash of something akin to remorse crossed his face. 'I agree she went too far. We have spoken and there won't be any more trouble. There haven't been any further problems, have there?'

'Well, thank you, Luke, for saving the day,' Remi said with disgust. This betrayal had ripped apart the one fragment of trust and connection in her life.

'You'll feel differently when you've had time to think this through. And while I wouldn't say the end *always* justifies the means, we have come through this to a better place. You don't need the house anymore. Letting go has been good for you.'

She stared at him, unable to connect this person with the friend he had been. 'Unbelievable. You actually think there's a future for us. You are delusional.'

'This is why I asked Emerson to keep quiet. Why I asked her to be considerate, to think about you. I knew you'd overreact.'

'Overreact?' Too many times Simon had told her she was being too dramatic, irrational, upset over nothing—she was not going to be silenced again.

Luke continued speaking. 'But wasn't the end result always an improvement? I gave you an opportunity to recognise Simon for what he was. And now you can see beyond the narrow con-fines of your little renovation project. Can see it's time for us. I helped you, Remi.'

'Helped me? *Helped me?*' Her voice rose, higher and louder. 'I didn't need your help.'

'Of course you did. Your marriage had dragged on long enough. I was everything you needed and wanted. But you needed to be set free.'

'Stop telling me what I needed. Do you really think letting Kayla terrorise me and my housemates was *helping* me! My god, you and Simon, manipulative. Both of you. Treating me like a commodity.' She felt reckless in her rage. How dare these men lie and scheme and arrange her to their whims.

Luke lunged across the room. 'Don't ever say that. I am nothing like him. Nothing. I am ten times the man he will ever be.' He pulled her from behind the chair, gripping her arms, holding her tight. 'He is weak and stupid. He would be nothing without his family's money and prestige. He is an arrogant, lying, piece of trash. You fell for it, over and over, when you should have been with *me*. You kept repeating the same mistake. The things I have done are your fault.' He shut his eyes but didn't release his hold.

When he opened them, Remi saw tears and pain. One hand came up to stroke her face.

'I have done things I regret, Remi, that had consequences.' He said the words quietly. 'What that girl did to you. That killed me. To see you broken and shattered. I was not to blame. I couldn't have foreseen what she did.'

That girl? He was talking about Brittney. About the attack. She could only stare at him, her mouth open.

'I watched over you. I moved to Sydney to be closer to you. I made sure you were not alone. Sometimes I took photographs. I wanted to document your life.'

Instinctively she tried to pull back, but Luke's hands tightened again to keep her steady. 'You took the photos. The ones outside the hotel. Of me and Connor.'

'Yes, and later I recognised they could serve a purpose. If it had been any other hotel, maybe things would've happened differently. But Kayla was there. Simon was already screwing her behind your back, and she was more than happy to help end your relationship. I knew he would kick you out if he thought you were cheating on him.'

The lies. The story and gossip about an affair that had never happened. Luke had created them for his own purpose, he had set in motion the event that had ripped apart her life. The fear and physical pain, the destruction of her career, the shattering of her joy and trust, the hours and hours of recuperation and sessions with psychologists. The trauma in her life had happened because this man had been scuttling around in the shadows trying to twist and turn and control her life.

She wrenched herself back, but he didn't let go.

'Don't fight me,' he said softly. 'You need time to think this through. But when you stop and see the whole picture, you'll understand.'

'Understand?' She had her hands braced on his bare chest. 'You fucked up my life.'

'No. I didn't. I have only ever done what was necessary. I have always done what was needed. I've taken the necessary actions to achieve success. I just wish I'd done more and done it sooner. We've wasted so much time.'

She went still. In her mind there was a click of connection between two moments. 'I know what it is,' she whispered.

'What are you talking about?' His hold eased and she took a step away from him.

'You did something terrible and she knows. You might have a hundred ways of justifying the interference and manipulation in my life, but you've also done something with a far more serious consequence, haven't you?'

His face went blank. 'I don't know what you're talking about.'

'That day the police came to your place, two weeks after the attack, the day I finally gave them her name. You were there with me.'

'What are you getting at?'

'You went to work at the hotel, then later that night, you came home. I was all dosed up on painkillers and a sleeping tablet, but I heard you. You made yourself a drink, then you were on the phone arguing.'

'I have no idea what you're going on about.'

'I heard you,' she repeated. 'Not all of it, but enough. I didn't know who you were talking to, and it didn't mean anything at the time. You were telling someone to "shut up" and "keep your mouth shut" and then making a deal, something about "it being in our mutual best interest" and that "you were there".' At the time she'd registered the unfamiliar aggression in his voice. Then he'd become quieter, persuasive. That side of him she'd recognised.

His expression shifted. 'What is it you think I did? Say it, Remi.'

'You sat with me while I talked to the police, you heard me give them Brittney's name. You knew who she was—you would've remembered her from the Worthington.'

'Go on. Say it.' His words held a cold ferocity, but she was reckless with the need for answers.

'Was it planned, Luke? Did you lure Brittney out or did you just see her there and decide to do it? Was it an accident or did you deliberately run her down? Did you set out to take revenge, Luke? For me? Was that it? Did you justify your actions by thinking she deserved to be punished? What evidence does Kayla hold over you?'

He closed his eyes for a moment, breathed deeply. 'That's irrelevant at this point.'

Oh, fuck. It was all true. 'You killed her. You killed Brittney.' Why the hell hadn't she put the pieces together years ago? Had she deliberately avoided making the connection? Had she consciously chosen to remain oblivious? No. She wouldn't have kept Luke in her life if she suspected he was so ruthless. That he was capable of such violence.

'What that girl did was inexcusable, and I know you wanted her to pay for it. You said as much.' He was throwing this back at her, once again rationalising his deeds.

'I didn't want you to kill her!' She had never wanted that. 'This is too much. What you've done ... it's horrendous. And now Emerson. Did she figure this out, too? Have you done something to *her* to keep her quiet?'

His reaction was immediate, reaching out to grab her by the wrist, yanking her close. 'Enough!'

They jumped as the trill of the hotel phone cut across the room. Luke looked at the desk where it sat, as though trying to fathom what it meant. He didn't move, waiting as it rang out. When his eyes meet hers, they were dark but devoid of emotion, the blankness worse than his anger. His focus shifted to where his hand was tightly gripping and twisting her wrist. His fingers released.

The phone rang again. Before she could react, he cupped her face and bent to press his lips to hers, then walked to the desk and picked up the handset.

'Yes.'

She watched as he responded with clipped answers. *Yes. It's fine. No, she's not. I'll be down in thirty minutes, please ask them to wait in the bar. No, they don't need coffee.*

There was a moment when Remi could have left. If she'd moved quickly, she could've reached the door. But her urgent need to flee had dissipated. She felt like she'd been tumbled by an enormous churning wave. She was bruised and exhausted, and needed time to breathe, to process what Luke had done. Her life had veered from its newly mapped path, and she had no idea what any of it meant. She had too many questions, dread tightening around her as she considered what his words might mean.

The call finished and Luke dressed, swapping trackpants for jeans, t-shirt and a lightweight jumper. At no time did he look at her. When he sat to put on his shoes, she went to him.

'What's happening?' she asked. 'Luke?'

He didn't answer immediately, waiting till he had tied his laces. Then he stood. Reached a hand to her shoulder, he slid his fingers beneath the robe to caress the skin of her neck. 'Our lives together would've been incredible. It seems it's now too late.'

'What do you mean? Who was on the phone?'

'On the phone? Reception. I'm needed.' His thumb brushed hypnotically backwards and forwards across her collarbone, soothing her rough, raw emotions. He gave a sad chuckle. 'My hotels are so beautiful, don't you think?'

'They are.'

'I built them to impress you. To create something worthy of you.' He kissed her softly, his lips lingering. 'I did so much for you.'

Remi tensed but didn't pull away, not wooed by such over-the-top declarations. Being cast as his one and only in this tale of long-held fixation was not romantic, it was suffocating. His longing to acquire her was less about Remi and more about his obsessive need to reach any goal he set. She would not be cast as his justification for the despicable things he had done.

'If I went too far, if I made a mistake, it was for us. To protect what we have, what we could have been.' He had both hands on her shoulders now. Then his arms wrapped tight around her. 'The police are here.'

'The police?' She stilled. If the police were here, they must have a reason. 'Emerson.' She breathed her friend's name.

'I imagine so. It seems I have failed. I needed her to be quiet, to protect you from the truth, which—' He stopped, gave a short, humourless laugh. 'Which I have since felt compelled to share with you anyway, as it turns out. Ironically, Emerson was right: it was better you hear our true story from me rather than her or, say, Kayla. But it's too late to change that course of action.'

Awareness and a nauseating horror rushed through Remi. He'd silenced Emerson. She'd been so blind to who he really was, had let herself be flattered and bolstered by his desire and need. Had enjoyed knowing he was always going to be there for her. She'd allowed his obsession to simmer, had relented and let herself be convinced of their bright and shiny future.

Pushing against him, she tried to break his embrace. He resisted.

'I want you to know.' His breathing was becoming more ragged. 'I didn't hurt her. She drank too much. Was not dressed for the cold. She got wet. Fell asleep. It was painless.'

Oh, god. No.

'And Brittney ... well, she got what she deserved.' He walked her backwards a few steps till the edge of the bed hit the back of her legs. 'And us? Sadly our story ends here. I will not be paraded about and labelled a failure and I will not lose you. There is time for me to leave, but you must remain behind.'

He released her with a push so she fell back. Her feet were on the floor and he set his legs either side of hers, clamping her in place. Put one knee on the bed so his hands could reach for her neck. Closing tight. Squeezing.

'I love you, Remi.' His face was over hers, tears in his beautiful eyes. 'I'm sorry. I'm so very sorry. There is no choice.'

Panic became a clawing beast within her. Pulling at his hands, his arms. Pushing and hitting his face, his chest. She couldn't breathe. The pressure of blood trapped in her head. The fierce crush of his fingers on her windpipe as they gripped even tighter. Fear as sharp and real as the pain.

No. No.

No! He would not do this to her. He would not end her life. Would not play out his fucked-up, poisonous story to the great tragic ending he wanted. This bastard would not win.

She braced her hands on his unyielding shoulders and poured her rage into her legs, exploded her thigh upwards. Her knee missed on the first blow, she struck again before he could adjust his legs, connecting with the softness of his balls.

His lungs emptied in a long moan as his grip slipped. He crumpled a little, his head dropping. It wasn't enough. She struggled to bring her forearms inside his then exploded her arms wide, using what was left of her strength. His hold weakened, arms buckling, his chest fell on her, pinning her with his weight. He was saying her name, groaning and cursing, his head resting on her shoulder.

She shoved and fought, using her legs and hands, her elbow connecting solidly with the side of his head. writhing till she had nearly pulled herself up the bed and out from under him. He reached for her, trying to hold her, drag her back.

'Fuck you!' she yelled as she lifted her foot and drove it with all her strength into his face. Felt the soft crunch of his nose, saw the blood flow as she rolled away and fell to the floor. She crawled, struggled to her feet and lurched forward, not stopping to see what damage she had done, throwing open the door.

She screamed when she came face to face with a man. Then slid to the floor when she registered the police uniform.

In the chaos that followed, she heard her name.

Josephine rushed towards her, gathering her in her arms and pulling the open robe closed around Remi's nakedness.

'Emerson?' Remi whispered, her throat aching and raw.

'I found her. She's been taken to hospital. She's alive.'

'Is she … okay?' The words were ill-formed and raspy.

'I hope so.'

'I want to go home.' Remi realised she was crying.

Josephine stood, had a murmured conversation with one of the officers, then helped Remi to her feet. 'We can't leave yet, but we can go to another room.'

'You'll stay?'

Josephine hugged her hard. 'Honey, I'm not going anywhere. You are not alone.'

CHAPTER THIRTY-EIGHT

JOSEPHINE
Saturday, 26 August 2023

Josephine was doing the dishes by hand, the warm water and the mindless, rhythmic action of washing the stack of plates, cups and glasses a soothing meditation after the fear and havoc of the last forty-eight hours. When Remi walked into the kitchen, she dried her hands. 'Can I get you something?' she asked. 'Coffee? Tea? Something much stronger?'

'Is it too early for a wine?'

'Not at all. Four thirty is a perfectly acceptable time for a drink.' She retrieved a bottle of red and two glasses and joined Remi at the table. 'Did you have a nap?'

'Not really.' Remi accepted the glass, waited for Josephine to pour, then took a sip. 'I can't stop thinking about it all. About him and what he's responsible for—not just *this*, the here and now,' she said. 'But all the interference and manipulation, and his justification for what he did. I feel so stupid. But I'm so angry too. I want to yell and scream at him. I want to hurt him. I want him to admit how fucked up it all is—how fucked up *he* is.'

'You might never get that chance.' Josephine recognised that feeling, the churning of an intense, consuming anger that could never be hurled at the person who deserved it most.

'I know.' Remi pulled a face. 'Anyway, the detective said he will be held in custody for a bit longer. The magistrate will hear an application for bail on Monday. The police think it's unlikely it will be granted. There's a long list of charges.'

'Did they give you any idea what is happening with Kayla?'

Remi nodded. 'She was interviewed in Sydney yesterday afternoon. I would love to have seen her face when she opened her door to the police.'

'It will be interesting to see how quickly they turn on each other.'

'I got the impression she already has. The detective asked me if I knew anything about the hit-and-run of Brittney Moore. I presume Kayla gave them the details of Luke's involvement.'

'Probably in the hope of a plea bargain or some such,' suggested Josephine.

'Probably.' Remi ducked her head and sniffed. 'There's something I need to say. I have to tell someone—I want to tell you.'

Josephine watched her intently. 'Okay. What is it?'

Tears slid over Remi's cheeks. 'It was my fault.' Another loud sniff as she pressed the palm of her hand against a wet cheek.

'What was?'

'Luke going after Brittney. It was my fault.'

'How do you mean?'

'He did it because of things I'd said. At first—after the attack—I pretended I couldn't remember who had hurt me. She'd been my friend. There was a part of me that wanted to protect her. There was also a big part that wanted Brittney to come to me filled with remorse and guilt. I wanted her to explain. To beg for forgiveness. But she never did and my fury grew. I wanted her to feel pain, too. To be as broken as I was. I was angry and physically damaged. I wanted her to suffer, too. I said all this to Luke. I said I wanted the person who had done this to be left in the gutter on the side of the road. He was there when I finally gave the police her name. And after that Luke did what he did—he delivered my retribution.' Quiet sobs shuddered through Remi's slumped body.

Josephine grasped her hand. 'Did you get in that car? Did you aim that car at Brittney? Did you choose to accelerate and hit her? Did you leave her on the side of the road?'

'But he did it *for* me. He took what I'd said and twisted it, made it into action he could justify.'

'You didn't ask him to. He made his own choices. He made the decision to do that. He is responsible, not you. Brittney's death was not your fault.' Josephine stood and grabbed the box of tissues from the sideboard, sliding it gently in front of Remi, who grabbed a handful. 'If you had known he was going to do that, would you have stopped him?'

'Yes, of course!'

'Exactly.'

'The practical part of my brain agrees with you, but the emotional side is just a mess of shame and culpability.' Remi blew her nose. 'And then there's Emerson. She was trying to look out for me. Isn't that why she met with him? Because she'd figured out what an obsessed psycho he was, and wanted him to stop?'

Remi finished her wine, then refilled the glass before continuing. 'Plus, I keep thinking that if I'd put the pieces together about what I had heard and what had happened, if I had spoken to the police back when Brittney died, they would have investigated him. He might have been charged. Then Emerson would have been safe. None of this would've happened.'

'You can't think like that. There are so many things that could've altered the trajectory. I mean, if I'd just been a bit more thorough in checking out Luke and Kayla, if I'd done it sooner, if I hadn't let Emerson go off to meet Luke—hell, if I'd been sensible and gone with her! I'm so angry at myself for not doing more.' These thoughts had begun circling her mind about an hour after Emerson had been walked out the door that night. It was all very well to tell Remi not to blame herself, but stopping her own self-recrimination was impossible. She should've known better. Done better.

'If you hadn't listened to your instincts, she would've died out there,' Remi insisted. 'You did so much.'

'Not enough,' muttered Josephine. She went to the fire, stoking it and adding a log before returning to her seat.

They sat quietly for a few minutes, Remi drying her eyes and wiping her nose, until she was able to take a deep breath. 'Have you spoken to the hospital again?'

'Yes. She's doing well. Stable, awake. A bit sluggish, so they're going to keep her there for tonight then maybe another night after that.'

'She could be home tomorrow?'

'I'd say the day after tomorrow.'

'Did they think she'd been sedated?'

'Yes. They tested and it came back positive for traces of benzodiazepine.'

Remi wiped her eyes again. 'How could he be so cruel? So calculating? He nearly killed her.'

'Soaking wet, on the ground, in the cold—yes, she could've died from hypothermia. It was one hell of a way to get rid of someone.'

'Why do you think he turned her phone back on?'

'I have a theory. I think he realised that if she was found without her bag and phone it might look less like an accidental death and more like she'd been dumped. I also think when you rang him, he realised he had to turn off his own phone, that he'd overlooked that detail. That he'd realised if there was ever any suspicion about what happened to Emerson, that his movements could have been tracked. He would probably have been on CCTV at the bar, so he might have been questioned or investigated.'

'Maybe he had planned to dump her up at Queens Domain, and then, when he realised his phone put him there, he moved her to the rivulet.'

'Quite possibly, it would account for the timing.' She didn't need to add that he could also have decided that getting Emerson wet would speed up her deterioration.

'The police said they would be accessing the data on Em's smartwatch too. What do you think they'd be looking for?'

'At a guess, probably heart rate variations over that night. A low rate would be expected if she were sedated, being driven around and then being cold and hypothermic. If she did in fact go walking, as Luke was claiming, it would be elevated for that period. Which all contributes to the evidence.'

They were both quiet for a long time, as night fell and the room darkened. Eventually Josephine made them toast, which they ate in front of the fire.

The ringing of Remi's phone made them both jump. Remi looked at the screen. 'Nope,' she said, before declining the call.

'Simon keeps trying to contact me. I do not want to speak to that idiot.'

'You might be able to find out what's happening with Kayla,' Josephine suggested.

'You know what, I don't really care right now. I hope they arrest her and charge her with arson at the very least. Although, they may not yet have enough proof. But I'm too exhausted to have any sort of discussion with my ex. There's so much that's going to need to be investigated, corroborated, proven. There are going to be more questions for me, the process is going to be long and horrible, and right now I can't give any more.'

Josephine put her arm around Remi's shoulders and squeezed. 'I'll be here for as long as you and Emerson need me. You don't have to go through this alone.'

Vietnam and Sam could wait. He was doing just fine. This was where she was needed.

CHAPTER THIRTY-NINE

Eighteen months later

R emi sat, leaning her back against the stone wall. She closed her eyes and stretched out her bare legs. Sunshine on skin, the vibration of bees, the warm, sweet scent of star jasmine. Summer was bliss.

'Hey, sleepyhead, Josephine just called. She's left the airport. They'll be here in twenty minutes.'

Remi shielded her eyes from the sun and looked up at Emerson. 'Are you ready for a full house and crazy chaos?'

Emerson laughed. 'Absolutely. Are you?'

'No. But I can adapt. Bring it on.' She stood and followed Emerson into the kitchen. 'Is Kristof joining us for dinner?'

'Yep. He's on set until about five but should get here in time. They're filming at Kingston Beach this afternoon, so not too far away, and there's nothing scheduled for tonight.'

Watching Emerson's relationship flourish had been a joy. Kristof had been a frequent presence in the house from the day

Emerson left hospital and had been exquisitely attentive and caring.

A freshly iced banana cake sat on the bench next to a glorious bunch of cottage flowers. The windowsills were crowded with pot plants, and several more trailed down from hanging pots. The fridge door was covered with pictures. Some were of Josephine, Sam and his girlfriend Holliday in Vietnam. Some were cheek-to-cheek selfies of the three women—on the mountain, at a winery, or taken on their road trip around Tassie. On the wall behind the kitchen table hung one of Emerson's illustrations: three wild-looking creatures with twigs and leaves and flowers adorning them, their hands clasped, 'We've Got This' in a curling ribbon font at their feet.

Emerson ducked into her room, came out with a roll of paper. She unfurled the poster. 'Where do you think we should put this?'

'"Welcome to our crazy home",' Remi read aloud. 'Is that meant to be me?' She pointed at the figure in overalls. 'My hair isn't that wild.'

'Yeah, it is. And that's Josie, of course. And that's me.' Josephine looked powerful, wearing a vivid pink frock and hiking boots. The Emerson figure was unmistakable with a mass of curls, huge red glasses and a cake held high above her head.

'Why not on the wall over there, then poor Sam and Hollie can see us glaring at them every time they walk in here.' Remi wasn't too sure how long Josephine's son and his girlfriend would be staying. She didn't care if it was months, and not just because Josephine had her name on the house title alongside hers. It wasn't sharing ownership that had changed her, it was discovering the joy of family. Okay, so these people weren't her actual family—they were more. They were the people she chose. Bonds formed through friendship and care and compromise. And surviving adversity.

Because they had been through hell together.

Emerson had made a full recovery, but the doctors had made it clear it had been close. Luke had denied sedating Emerson and tried to claim he'd driven her home, suggesting that she must have wandered away from the house after he left. He was adamant he didn't know she was lying wet and freezing on the banks of the Hobart Rivulet. It was a coincidence he had been there, a terrible twist of fate. The evidence was circumstantial. If he had seen her, he would have been the one to save Emerson. Instead, he'd been too busy rescuing Remi.

No one believed him. Especially when the details of his obsession were laid bare. Even Kayla testified against him. Although not by choice: it was the price she paid for a reduced sentence. All of them had taken the stand several times, firstly against Kayla for her various efforts against Remi, then against Luke for the attempted murder of Emerson. Remi had also attended court in Sydney for the most recent trial—Luke's involvement in the death of Brittney.

Luke was already serving a ten-year sentence after being found guilty of attempted murder and, having been transferred to a New South Wales prison for his second trial, would serve his time there. The sentence for the vehicular manslaughter of Brittney would be handed down in a few weeks and would be added to his time. Kayla, too, had been transferred to a jail near Sydney where she'd given birth. Placed in a special mum-and-baby facility, she'd been permitted to keep her child with her. Now she was almost due to be released on parole.

There had been some interesting revelations during the trials. Kayla had insisted Luke had been behind the death of

Mavis. She'd asked him to remove the dog to make it easier for her to access the house without being noticed. She also claimed he had taken the money from Remi's account. Both of which he denied and couldn't be proven.

In the end, Kayla was found guilty of the theft of the jewellery—after a pawnbroker came forward with CCTV of her in his store—and of unlawfully setting fire to a building.

Emerson danced back into the kitchen. 'Hey, I meant to ask. Did you see the gossip?'

'You know I don't read gossip.'

'Yeah. But I thought you might have got this titbit direct. Simon and Kayla are divorcing.'

'How tragic,' Remi said with a heavy dose of sarcasm and absolutely no surprise.

'Terrible. His business goes belly-up, and he ditches his wife—or she ditches him, it's hard to tell—right before she gets to go home.'

'I wonder what he'll do now?' Remi mused. 'I wonder if he'll return to the family business?'

'Shall we send him a card?'

'A card?'

'A "You Deserve It" card. I could design a new one. Instead of flowers and butterflies and stars, it could be a loser standing on a pile of shit and burning money.'

Remi laughed. 'Let's not be mean.'

'Hmm. You're right. Let's not drop our standards. I can think of better additions to our collection.'

Emerson and Josephine were working together to design a stationery range—including cards—which would be produced locally. Which was only one of the new enterprises the women were developing. Over a late night of brainstorming, bubbles and pizza, they'd each talked about what they could contribute and what they could build together. The result was a plan for a coworking space in the city. Josephine and Remi had found a suitable shabby building that needed an overhaul. Remi was project managing the conversion. As well as hot desks and flexible drop-in working arrangements for other freelancers, digital nomads, programmers and writers, Josephine was going to provide a mentoring service for start-ups. The unjustified negative reviews for Remi's narration had been cleared after a few months of hardball from Remi and Josephine, and Remi was once again getting audiobook work. Plus Emerson had picked up a few freelance jobs and, thanks to word of mouth, was getting busier every week.

'They're here,' Emerson yelled as the Subaru pulled around the back of the house.

Remi watched from the kitchen as a tall young man with unruly hair climbed out of the car, followed by a pretty girl with two long braids and wearing a bandana as a headband. Josephine's smile was wide, a look of pure adoration as her gaze followed her son. Emerson was hugging them all.

Yes. The house was going to be a little crazy for a while, but the old building would be better for it. As would she.

This was no longer just a home to hide within. It was a home for living.

ACKNOWLEDGEMENTS

Writing acknowledgements for this, my second book, feels different but no easier. Now I have a very real fear of forgetting someone vital, or of remembering nearly all my writing buddies (but missing one or two and having them never forgive me).

I will start with the easiest. An enormous, heartfelt thank you to everyone who read, shared, borrowed, and talked about my first book, *The House of Now and Then*. Your support and response absolutely blew me away. Thank you to all those who reached out, sending messages to let me know how much they enjoyed the story, the characters, the surprises, and the setting. If you've ever wondered whether contacting an author to share your delight in their work is a good idea, let me assure you it is very much appreciated.

An enormous thank you to the bookstagrammer and review community. The work that you all put in to discussing and highlighting books is astonishing. Word of mouth is so important to the success of a book, and the unexpected wave of

Jo Dixon

endorsement you gave *The House of Now and Then* often left me in happy tears. I won't name individuals because I don't want to look like I'm schmoozing for positive reviews—I know you all put a high value on integrity and transparency.

Thank you to all the booksellers who gave my debut book a chance, kept it on the shelf, and recommended it to your readers. I am so very grateful for the support.

Thank you to the amazing team at HQ, some of the loveliest people I know. Firstly Rachael Donovan, my publisher. She puts up with my many questions, my insecurities, and my tendency to talk too fast. Rachael, with you I'm in excellent hands. I love working with you. Then there's the other Jos: Jo Mackay, head of publishing at HQ, who makes me laugh, impresses me with her energy and enthusiasm, and is a wonderful advocate for her authors. And Jo Munroe, head of marketing, who is so welcoming and makes me feel like anything is possible. Thank you also to Natika Palka for her publicity support and her persistence in chasing down opportunities, and to Eloise Plant who is queen of digital marketing (and says kind things about my social media, even though I think she's just being super nice).

Once again, I owe a huge thanks to the art department. The cover for this book evokes all the eerie, suspenseful vibes I love. Plus, it looks perfect sitting alongside the first book. Never underestimate the power of a great cover—there's magic in all those subtle messages that set up the reader's expectations.

Thank you, thank you, thank you to the sales team. You're the people who build the relationships and promote our books to the booksellers and get us that all-important shelf space. Plus, you take authors by the hand and drive us around for book signings, which I appreciate so much.

I want to give a special thank you to my editors, Julia Knapman, Kylie Mason and Sarah J. Fletcher. Julia, you always guide me, keep me to schedule and make the process as easy as it can be. Kylie, the structure of this book works so much better because of you, and I've continued to learn and grow as a writer under your editorial gaze. And Sarah, I don't know how you do it … your attention to detail is fantastic. To those who may pick up any teeny-tiny typos or errors in this book (if there are any), know that mine were the last pair of eyes to rove these pages and the buck stops with me.

I would also like to thank Rebecca Millar, a freelance editor, who was the first to assess and critique this manuscript way back in 2019. Her comments and notes made all the difference to this story, clearly identifying that the original version needed to up the level of suspense. Thank you for all your help, Rebecca.

Thank you to the amazing writing friends I've made in the last few years: to my fabulous friends Fiona Taylor and Jacq Ellem—we're an excellent team, and you'd better put me in your acknowledgements when your books are published; the lovely ladies of my frequently infrequent writing group lunches; the wonderful Rae Cairns, Pamela Cook, Claudine Tinellis and Penelope Janu who have helped demystify the publishing biz, plus the many others who keep me going back year after year to the RWA conference; Kylie Orr who inspires me with both her approach and her attitude; Kate Mildenhall and Katherine Collette for their enthusiasm and encouragement.

I have two special readers I want to thank: Kazza Lockley, who I met at the Rachael Johns Readers' Retreat. As I am local to her area, Kazza kindly offered to sell my book in her store, and has gone on to do a brilliant job, which is especially impressive because it's a chainsaw shop. No really, she keeps selling my book and promoting it to everyone who wants an edge-trimmer or a log-splitter. You're amazing, Kazza.

And Courtney Orr, a reader I met at a book signing. We continue to share book recommendations, and she was one of the first people to read this story. It is wonderful having someone so passionate about books, but who is not a part of the industry. Thank you!

Finally, all my love and thanks to my family. Damien, I could not have done any of this without you. I know you've always got my back and that you will continue to put up with the demands of this strange thing I do. Thank you isn't enough! To Ben and Jack who've flown the nest—could you come back now, I miss you and need help with the chores. Also, I'm ridiculously proud of you. Now how about you read one of my books? To Rebecca, thank you for being the person for Ben. You're every part a member of this family, and you *did* read my first book and said nice things (which makes you my favourite).

Finally, a very small author note: This book was written way back in 2018. When I was getting it ready for publication, I changed the year of the story to 2023 to make it more current. Which is fine, except the winter of 2023 has been nothing like I've portrayed in these pages. There's been barely any snow on the mountain, and the weather has been relatively mild. We'll just have to pretend it was very cold and that Hobart had an abundance of wet and truly miserable days.

You should leave the past in the past ...
or should you?

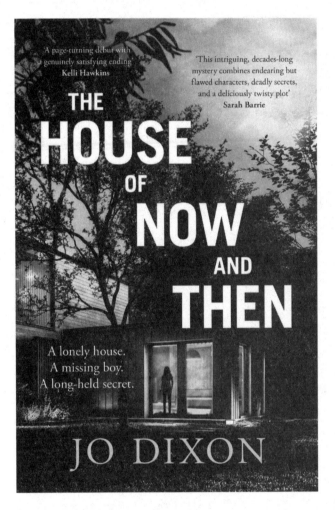

A jaw-dropping debut from
Australian author Jo Dixon.
Available now.

talk about it

Let's talk about books.

Join the conversation:

[f] @harlequinaustralia

[♪] @hqanz

[◉] @harlequinaus

harpercollins.com.au/hq

If you love reading and want to know about our
authors and titles, then let's talk about it.